A WIZARD'S SACRIFICE

BOOK TWO OF THE WOERN SAGA

BY

A. M. JUSTICE

ISBN 13: 978-1-63489-359-6
eISBN: 978-1-63489-368-8

Library of Congress Catalog Number: 2020913587
Printed in the United States of America
First Printing: 2020
24   23   22   21   20   5   4   3   2   1

Cover and interior design by Steven Meyer-Rassow

Wise Ink Creative Publishing
807 Broadway St. NE, Suite 46
Minneapolis, MN 55413
wiseink.com

For Eric

CONTENTS

PROLOGUE

Wizardry was outlawed for good reason. This simple truth nagged Victoria of Ourtown as another body crumpled. Another skull crunched; another torso smacked the sodden turf. *Nobody*, she thought, *should have this power.*

A trio roared toward her, two men and a woman, teeth bared, blades high. Tingling thrilled through Vic's nerves as her mind swept air molecules into a solid mass around the attackers. Her hand clenched, the mass contracted, and three more Relmans fell. Bliss suffused her blood, sizzled across her skin, turning the freezing rain to mist. She imagined she looked like a wraith, a passing haze that left a trail of corpses in its wake.

Around her, soldiers brawled, slipping in the icy mud. Grunts and shouts peppered the rain. Stoneknives scraped. Crystal daggers squelched. Screams melted into groans, into sobs. A Relman wept over a gaping belly wound. Imploring eyes found Vic's, and the soldier flopped back, her face clear of pain as red stained the grass beneath her skull. An officer rushed forward, a rare length of steel aimed at Vic's heart. She hardened the air. His sword snapped. His body crumpled. Killing was all too easy with a wizard's power, but she had a job to do: win the field for Latha and end a twenty-year war.

Her death toll mounted through the gray morning and long into the afternoon. At last a horn blared, and a small party

1

emerged from a rubble-strewn breach, white flag held aloft. At dawn, the Lathans had made a show of setting sulfa charges at the base of the wall surrounding Relm's capital, but it was wizardry, not ordinance, that had blown open that hole. At least the Relman surrender meant they were finally on the path to peace.

She released her power, and an ache bloomed behind her eye. Cresting a hill, she walked slowly back to the Lathan command pavilion, picking her way through a mile of sprawling dead before she left the battlefield and climbed a grassy slope to the royal banners. Her temple throbbed. Nausea clawed at her throat. The bleak, gray sunlight, weak as it was, hurt her eyes, and she wanted nothing more than to find a dark corner where she could curl around her pain.

"We won!" Princess Bethniel, Heir to Latha's throne, ducked out of the pavilion and threw her arms around Vic. "The fieldmarshal went down to meet the Relman command. We'll sleep in real beds in the city tonight."

"We owe it all to you." Prince Ashel's smile eased the pounding behind Vic's eyes. Black spiraling curls and midnight-dark eyes made him the masculine image of the princess, with a breath-stopping beauty that quickened her pulse. She forced her gaze toward the bandaged stump hidden in the folds of his cloak. She didn't deserve his gratitude. Six weeks before, she'd abandoned him to the Relmlord's depravities, and he'd lost half his hand.

In the field below, the Lathan fieldmarshal's banner rippled as it approached the white flag of the Relman command. The last battle in a twenty-year war was finished. In this single day, she'd slain more people than she had in the five years she'd gone by Vic the Blade, when she used to sneak into Relman camps and kill their officers. When her blood, hot for revenge, had entered the icy chambers of her heart, and remorse had steamed away like the rain. When she'd killed with her hands and a dagger. Drawing her blade, she held the cut-crystal weapon to her chest and felt her heartbeat reverberate through the hilt. Regret, not vengeance, ran through her veins now. No matter how many Relmans she'd killed today, it wouldn't make up for her failure to save the man standing in front of her.

PART ONE

Personal Log, Captain Franklin T. J. Wong, United Mineral Mining Vessel, Registry LSNDR2237, June 23, 2153

> There's sapient life down on the planet. Second team reported the arthropod colony they found on the central peninsula of the pancontinent isn't a colony, it's a city. A city inhabited by big, giant bugs. Heinlein big. Triangular heads, hundreds of legs and horns on their tails, standing five and six meters tall, with brains and language. Like something out of an old twentieth century movie. The Alien Invaders. Except we're the Aliens. Wonder if they've ever imagined anything like us.
>
> Their tech's all organic. Advanced stuff. Architecture, infrastructure, lights—all manufactured. Craig and his team are down there now, negotiating permission to land. We're stuck here, and I don't need any land wars with the indigenous. No manifest destiny here, just survival.

HOMECOMING

Wizardry was outlawed for good reason. This simple point of law nagged at Bethniel as her foster sister huddled on the opposite bench, knees curled to her forehead. Four months ago, Victoria of Ourtown had drunk the Waters of the Dead and become a wizard. Since then, she had won a decades-long war almost single-handedly, but the Lathan people would brand her an outlaw and banish her for life if they discovered how Vic had crushed their enemies. She had literally crushed them. And burned them to ash. Nose twitching, Bethniel pressed a scented handkerchief to her face, hoping to mask the stink of roasted flesh that festered in her pores. Vic had done many terrible things with her powers in the past four months, but the worst of those horrors, she'd done on Bethniel's orders.

The carriage jolted out of a rut, and Vic groaned. "I thought sea voyages were bad."

Bethniel moved across the cab and pillowed her sister's head on her lap. "Can I do anything for you?"

"Move, so I don't ruin that dress if I throw up."

She massaged Vic's temples. "I have dozens more at home." Snow-draped branches scrolled between velvet curtains, the scenery like any stretch of road in Kiareinoll Fembrosh, the vast forest that covered most of Latha, but Bethniel recognized the twining limbs. An old geilmor leaned out across the road, its spiraling needles a familiar landmark. "We're almost to Narath."

Lips pressed together, Vic cringed into a tighter ball. Wizardry

6

was outlawed not only for what wizards could do with their power but for what the power did to the wizard. The Waters of the Dead bore that name because most who drank them died. Vic had been lucky; she'd only been sick as a cat since the day she'd choked the Waters down. Sick as a cat but strong enough to blow apart a city wall and, before that, destroy a mountain.

The carriage stopped. Horses snorted, and Ashel poked his head inside the carriage. "We're in view of the city. Come look." Eyes falling on Vic, he sprang through the door and cupped her cheek. "She's worse?"

"No," Vic moaned.

"Yes," Bethniel said. "She's having a very bad day."

"Vic," he said, making that single syllable as rich and complex as the finest Eldanion red wine. He was called the Crystal Voice of Latha, his gifts so great that the son of a king had become a musician rather than a statesman. "There are banners everywhere, all hung in your honor."

Vic grasped his wrist, and he bent toward her, their gazes locked. Bethniel's heart skipped, hoping to see five years' worth of hints and nudges come to fruition.

"All right." Vic tugged herself up. "Maybe I can plunge this pounding skull into a snowdrift."

Ashel's smile melted as she slipped outside. Disappointment a cold knot in her belly, Bethniel squeezed his arm. "Be patient. She blames herself."

He grimaced at the glove covering his right hand. "She shouldn't." Fur-lined leather hid a stump and a lone thumb. Fixing his lips in a cheery mask, he urged her out of the carriage. "Come see, sis."

Greetings traced their passage through the royal retinue to the top of a rise. At the head of the column, Vic stood alone, feet apart and arms out, as if she fought for balance. Bethniel and Ashel each took an elbow, and their long, steady shadows sandwiched a small trembling one, all three pointing toward Latha's capital. Banners draped the palisade, bearing the image of a crystal dagger, symbol of Vic the Blade. Pennants stirred, and the sinking sun painted sky and snow a fiery golden red, like the hair breezing round Vic's face. The crystal atop the Senate building caught the sunset, refracting amber over rooftops. On the city walls, lanterns bloomed like glowbugs.

"It is beautiful." Vic's lips curved and froze. Her eyes rolled upward, her arms stiffened and back arched. Gagging escaped clenched jaws. Bethniel shouted for help. Ashel whipped off his cloak and laid Vic atop it. A Healer hurried through the retinue and wedged a knot of cloth between Vic's teeth until the fit passed and she slumped insensate in Ashel's arms.

"We must take her to the hospice," the Healer said.

Cradling Vic, Ashel climbed to his feet. "We'll take her to the Manor."

"Your Highness, she should be properly examined—"

"Ashel's right," Bethniel said. Fear stuffed her lungs, leaving no room for breath. Wizardry was outlawed. Vic would be exiled if anyone traced this illness to her encounter with the Kragnashians. "The Ruler's Healer will tend her. Get me a horse."

Surrounded by soldiers, they tore across open fields, around the city toward the Manor. Held tight to Ashel's chest, Vic slumped forward, head lolling with each bump and turn. On Manor Road, dense forest swallowed the last light of the sun. Hindquarters bunched and surged as their mounts rounded switchbacks, and every steaming huff crushed Bethniel's chest a little more. The Waters of the Dead bore that name for a reason. Her foster sister had survived slavery and war—she could not die now in sight of home!

At the gate, the guards shouted questions as they sped past. Hooves skidded on slick cobbles before the Manor's entrance, and Ashel leapt down and charged inside with Vic. Shouting orders at servants, Bethniel followed him up three flights and down a gallery to Vic's room, where they pulled off her shoes and cloak and tucked her into bed. Panting, Bethniel sank onto the mattress.

"What's wrong with her?"

Princess and prince jumped as if they were children caught at mischief. Queen Elekia of Reinoll Parish—their mother—stood in the doorway.

"She had a seizure," Bethniel said.

"Just now?"

"Just as we arrived in sight of Narath. We rode here as fast as we could."

Their mother crossed the threshold, and the door shut behind her, pushed by an invisible hand. "How long since she's used wizardry?"

"At least six weeks."

"All the way from Re, then."

"Since the peace treaty was signed."

Beaded braids clicked as the queen bent over Vic. Her scowl softened as she smoothed red hair from a pale forehead, but severity returned as she faced her natural-born children. "Did neither of you feel an urge to help her?"

"What kind of question is that?" Ashel snapped.

"The kind that needs to be asked, if your foster sister is having fits in sight of soldiers and courtiers."

"Of course we helped her," Bethniel cut in as Ashel's chest puffed. "But she's been ill since the Kragnashians made her drink the Waters of the Dead."

"Which is exactly why I sent you with her."

Bethniel winced at the sharp rebuke, though she had no idea what failure warranted a scolding. Latha's Ruler had sent the Heir to be her Emissary. A mission of statecraft—one meant to assure the Senate Bethniel was fit to rule—it had been a triumph. Vic may have defeated their enemies, but Bethniel had secured a peace treaty that would be hailed for generations. Mother's glower made her feel as if the signed parchment she carried in her satchel was privy paper.

"You had no desire to . . . share anything with her? Either of you?"

"Stop being so bloody cryptic, Mother," Ashel said.

"Cryptic? Watch and learn." Unsheathing her pocketknife, Mother sliced her thumb, dribbled blood onto Vic's lips, and slipped the digit inside her mouth.

Ashel's eyes snagged Bethniel's, his twisted lips mirroring her own revulsion as Vic's throat bobbed, swallowing their mother's blood.

"That should help her." Mother withdrew her thumb and graced them with a rare smile. "I am glad—very, very glad—to see you all safe. Welcome home."

Tenderness from their mother was so rare a treasure that Bethniel's shock melted and she flew into the queen's open arms. They held each other, tears wetting collars, a long time.

Fingers combed through Bethniel's shorn tresses. "You cut your hair?"

"The Kragnashians wanted it for trade. They wanted Vic's too, but she gave them only a single lock."

A crease marred their mother's forehead as she turned to Ashel. "I prayed Elesendar would see you home safe, son."

Glowering, he pulled off his right glove and showed her the stump. "When he took the first finger, Lornk Korng said, 'This is a gift for your mother.'"

"I heard you stopped Vic from killing him." She caressed his cheek.

"I thought you should do your own dirty work."

Eyebrows flattening, Mother stepped away from him. "Go rest, both of you. Tomorrow you can explain why you sent me the Relmlord alive, when I asked for his corpse."

"Because Lornk Korng's crimes were committed against an entire people," Vic said, elbowing out from under the blankets.

Bethniel bit back a cry of joy—neither Vic nor her mother cared for girlish squealing at any time, much less when it interrupted a discussion of their enemy's depravities.

"I didn't kill him," Vic continued, "because Ashel, with his butchered fingers on the floor, soaked in his own blood, made me see that Lornk didn't harm just him, or me, or you. Ashel spoke for every Lathan soldier taken in battle and sold into slavery, and for every Lathan farmer whose family was murdered by Relman raiders. He made me see that Lornk deserves to be tried and convicted and to starve and rot under the Shrine at Mirkeldirk. That's what you do with the worst criminals, isn't it?"

"It isn't so simple when the accused was a sovereign of a rival nation. I do not have legal standing to prosecute him."

"It's in the peace treaty," Bethniel said. "We made sure of it."

"And how did you get the Relmans to agree to that?"

Cheeks hot, Bethniel exchanged a shamefaced look with Vic. The worst horrors Vic had committed had been done on Bethniel's orders.

An invisible force yanks the Relman's arm out straight, and an iron gauntlet flies across the room and snaps round her hand. The metal begins to glow red. As the color brightens, shrieks rend the air. The Councilors' cries tumble after. The woman's keens squeeze into ragged breaths, billow again into an ear-shattering howl. Burning flesh jabs Bethniel's nose. A Councilor bends over, and a vile, stinking mess hits the polished marble floor, splattering boots and slippers and garment hems.

"This will end when one of you signs the treaty," Bethniel announces. Her voice is as icy as her mother's glare, but inside she's gibbering in horror.

"I showed them what their defiance would cost," Vic said.

"And carried out retribution against Lornk's chief interrogator," Ashel added, his eyes as hard as they'd been that day, when Vic had tortured a woman with wizardry and cowed the Relman Council into acceding to all their demands. Kindness had once been the keystone of her brother's character, but his ordeal had stripped away mercy. *That woman deserved none*, Bethniel reminded herself, summoning the cold, bitter rage she'd felt upon learning how badly Ashel had suffered while Lornk's prisoner. In Lordhome's dungeons, the guards had burned his hands with the same iron gauntlets Vic had used for retribution—and justice—in the Council chamber.

"We needed to secure peace," Bethniel said, "and the surest, quickest way to do it was a direct and undeniable demonstration of Vic's power."

"You used your power openly?" Mother asked.

"I had to," Vic replied.

"The Council was sworn to secrecy as part of the treaty," Bethniel said, drawing the document out of her satchel and handing it over.

"An impossible provision to enforce," Mother grumbled. Her eyes darted over the page. "What is this about a Penance?"

"There was a village—" Vic began.

"There were unavoidable casualties," Bethniel interjected. "We needed to maintain secrecy."

"This says three hundred and twelve Lathans shall serve Penance in the Badlands?"

"It was the one concession I gave the Relmans, and it was an easy one to grant. They didn't insist that anyone actually involved serve this Penance, only that any Lathan found in the Badlands do it until the number of Lathans matched the number of dead. There's no reason in the world any of our people would ever go into the nomads' territory, so I saw no harm in agreeing."

"You battled three hundred nomad warriors?" Mother asked Vic.

"Not just warriors. Elders, nursing mothers, children . . . I killed them." Vic finished with a whisper, speaking aloud with reverence and regret, in the manner Lathans always spoke of the dead.

"Elesendar," Mother swore aloud.

"It was necessary," Bethniel asserted, reverting to mindspeech. Lathans only used their voices for formal occasions or when passions reigned. Everyone needed to remain rational, so she spoke silently as one did about ordinary things. "I take full responsibility for it." She had steeled herself to accept the nomad massacre as a terrible judgment, but one that was inevitable and unchangeable. Her father had always said a ruler should learn from mistakes but never be crippled by regrets.

"What else did you do?"

Vic expelled a long breath. "Three hundred and thirty-seven people, most of them civilians, were crushed when I brought down the mountain palace at Olmlablaire. I blew a breach in the walls around the Relman capital, and of the three thousand Relman soldiers dead in that battle, a lot of those were mine. A lot."

"Just how powerful are you?"

Vic shrugged. "I tore apart a mountain."

"The official story is, we used sulfa bombs to blow up Olmlablaire and the wall at Re," Bethniel said in mindspeech, again trying to restore reason before Vic's regrets and Mother's fury dominated the conversation. "And the Relmans lost the Battle of Re because their command collapsed without Lornk Korng to lead them. Fortunately, it was raining that day, with a heavy fog and—"

"I thought the rumors were gross exaggerations," Mother said. "Vic, if your powers are undeniably revealed, I will have to exile you. I'll have no choice."

"You sit the throne with the very same power," Ashel growled aloud. Bethniel's hands itched to strangle him.

"I use my power only for small acts of convenience, and never in public. Vic has used hers as a weapon, and the Opposition can seize on that to stir up discord and undermine my government."

"You're never sick," Vic said. "I've been sick since the day I drank the Waters of the Dead, but you never are. Will I get used to it?"

"I told you when I sent you to save my son, that I was giving you the heaviest burden."

"You knew what the Kragnashians would do to me?"

Mother's lips curled into a sad smile. "You have the misfortune to be the second woman of renown to bear the name Victoria of Ourtown. The Kragnashians revere that name, and yes, I believed if they met you, they would give you the Waters of the Dead in remembrance of the One who killed Meylnara the Oppressor." She pressed her lips to Vic's forehead. "How do you feel? Any sickness or headache?"

Vic's fingers grazed a temple. "Better than I've felt in months."

"The Waters contain a parasite called the Woern, which kills most who consume it. Most of those who survive become wizards, like you and me."

"But you're not sick."

"No. My mother traces her family line back to Saelbeneth, leader of the very Council for whom your namesake fought in the war against Meylnara. Saelbeneth was said to be immune to the ill effects of the power. So am I, and I gave you some of my healthy Woern." She showed Vic the bandaged thumb. "Saelbeneth would do the same to heal her allies of Woernsickness. The Woern can be passed from one wizard to another through sweat, blood, tears, saliva—any fluid of the body. They are also passed from mother to infant in the womb. That was why I sent Bethniel with you—to help you survive."

"I'm not a wizard!" Bethniel cried.

"Your Woern remained dormant," Mother replied, "which has been a blessing."

Bethniel stumbled to the window seat, her skin oozing sweat and pebbled with cold. Outside, stars winked in a deep purple sky. A servant moved along the lane, igniting gas lamps, and snow drifts glittered in pools of yellow light. Vic or Mother could light those lamps with a thought. Bethniel could not fathom doing so. In Kragnash, she had offered to drink the Waters of the Dead in Vic's stead, but the Center, the leader of all Kragnashians, had refused and told her if she took the Waters, she would die. What could that mean, if she carried these . . . worms . . . already? "Why didn't you tell me about this before we left? How was I supposed to know I could help Vic if she got sick?"

"She didn't want you to know she'd sold you to the Kragnashians," Ashel spat.

"Ashel, you were in my womb when I drank the Waters of

the Dead, and since semen is, according to legend, a particularly effective means of transmission, you can pass your Woern to Vic rather easier than your sister or I."

Ashel's glare shredded into a flush while Vic looked at the floor, her cheeks almost as red as her hair.

Mother sighed at the blazing faces. "According to legend, only a very, very few wizards are compatible hosts for the Woern, in which case the relationship is symbiotic rather than parasitic. In every other case, Woern and wizard grow increasingly ill together. The only thing that can save either is an infusion of healthy Woern. Also according to legend, the Woern drive their host to seek out such reservoirs. Vic, I believed if you became a wizard, and then became ill, instinct would guide you to obtain what you needed from my children—especially Ashel. Glad as I am to have my foster-daughter home, I had hoped to welcome a marriage-daughter today. Sadly, I was wrong, or you wouldn't have had a fit within sight of Narath and dozens of witnesses."

"What's one more disappointment on your list?" Ashel asked.

"You're too old for petulance," Mother snapped. "Vic, when the Healer arrives, you should mention that incident of catatonia from last year, after your accidental encounter with the Relmlord. It will distract him from other possible causes of the seizure. And all of you should rest. We have a full day of victory celebrations tomorrow."

She left, and silence pressed like stone. Ashel rocked from foot to foot, his single fist clenched, while Vic hid behind a fall of hair. Bethniel climbed out of her own paralyzing consternation, took their hands, and pressed them together. "You two belong together. Mother's revelation doesn't change that; it makes it all the more true."

Their fingers slipped apart, and Bethniel couldn't tell which drew away first. Ashel's eyes lingered on Vic for a moment, then he mumbled a good night and left.

Vic rested a tear-stained chin on her knees. "The Center said you'd die if you drank the Waters."

"I know." Bethniel sat, trembling. It didn't feel like fear—she'd become all too familiar with that sensation over the last half year. Now she felt something more akin to anticipation, like a cat quivering before it pounced. "When it said I'd die, I thought it meant I'd be like most of the people who drink the Waters, where it kills them."

"But you already have these . . . Woern. So what did the Center mean?"

Drawing a deep breath, she pushed the past into a box and closed the lid. As her father said, don't be paralyzed by regrets. "We'll never know. Let's just be glad it's over."

Her sister squeezed her hand. "I am. And it's good to be home."

THE QUEEN'S SECRET

This deep underground, the earth itself rotted. Slipping on a mildewed step, Elekia grabbed her housemarshal's arm as an oath escaped clenched teeth. Olivet held her elbow until they reached the final landing, where a guard drew back a bolt and passed them into the prison's most secure corridor. Lamps guttered, the air dank and smoky. Another guard led them past three pairs of doors studded with hard crystal, each with a fist-sized window. At the end of the hall, they stopped.

"Wait by the stairs," Olivet ordered.

The guard retreated, and Olivet drew back the bolt. Frowning his disapproval, he went inside first. Elekia crossed the threshold and signaled him out. "He cannot harm me," she reminded the housemarshal. Snorting dubiously, he shut the door. The bolt clanged home.

Eyes watering, she peered into the fetid gloom. A silhouette rose from a cot. "What a pleasant surprise, to receive a visit from my wife." She tightened her belly, steeling herself, and spun dust and soot into a bouncing orb that cast cold, white light throughout the cell. Lornk Korng, former Lord of Relm, eyed the orb, then rested glacial eyes on her. "You finally have more than yourself to bring to our marriage, Your Majesty."

"And you have nothing," she said coolly. Her most closely guarded secret stood before her, hair lank and garments reeking, yet beneath the filth beckoned a scent that had once drawn her smiling into a bed of soft grass and wildflowers. Among Lathans, a first bedding was a wedding, but Lornk was from a land where marriages were made to grow fortunes, not love. Elekia had never expected him to follow Lathan custom, not for a horsebreeder's daughter. She, not he, had refused to declare and acknowledge their wedding. Not so soon, she'd said. She'd wanted to earn a status that made her worthy to become First Councilor to the Lord of Relm and matriarch of one of the Knownearth's wealthiest families. All she'd asked for was time, and a quarter century of betrayal, vengeance, and war had followed his refusal to simply wait. "Are your accommodations suitable? I ordered you be given the same comforts you gave my son."

He lunged at her. She stepped back and thickened the air around him, freezing his limbs mid-stride.

As he teetered on heel and toe, his lips twitched. "I only wanted to properly greet you, darling."

"With a kiss or a killing blow? How it must rankle to be defeated by the power you coveted." She stepped forward, pressing her cheek into an outstretched hand. His fingers softened, and she moved closer, holding him still as a statue. The memory of wildflowers tickled her nose, and she reached up and stroked his ragged beard. "Four months you held Ashel prisoner." Her hand dove beneath his waistband and began stroking. He glared, jaw bunching. "Three months you kept Vic, when she was hardly more than a child." Vic was not hers by blood, but Elekia loved her as fiercely as the two children she had borne. Lornk trembled as his cock swelled, short gasps exploding from his lips, but his eyes grew icier. She touched her lips to his, used wizardry to pry his mouth open. The girl in the wildflowers rejoiced to taste him again; the queen in the dungeon gloated over his sour flavor. Elekia was no longer a maiden; she was a queen and a widow, capable of arousing even a man who despised her. Lornk's tongue entwined with hers, his lips returning pressure as she squeezed and stroked. His trembling intensified, and the short gasps twisted into staccato moans. He reached the verge, and she released him, snapping his smallest finger with wizardry. "You broke them both," she spat.

Hunched over the fractured digit, he growled, "Do you think you can break me?"

She wiped her mouth and fingers with a handkerchief. "I don't know, and I don't care, since your life will end within the year. I do want you to suffer as long as you're alive. Here, a keepsake." She dropped the soiled linen.

Lornk wound it round his injured hand. "Victoria belongs to the Kragnashians now. They'll come for her sooner rather than later, and Elesendar help us if she fails to do what history has prescribed."

Knocking for Olivet, she said over her shoulder, "You are a sad, pathetic madman."

"My firstborn said the same thing."

On the other side, the bolt drew back, but Elekia held the door shut, her skin pebbling. "Ashel is not yours."

Devilish lips split, revealing perfect teeth. "Isn't he? I told him, Elekia. About you, and me, and your dear, departed Sashal, and how the pair of you betrayed me. From that seed will grow an ugly hedge between mother and son." A sinister laugh raised the hairs on her neck. "I planted other seeds as well, which will sprout in places you least expect. I'll reap what I've sown, and you'll weep—but the world will rejoice."

Bile churned in her belly, yet she raised a serene eyebrow. "The wisest decision I ever made was to refuse you." Olivet opened the door; she extinguished the light globe and sailed down the corridor. Grief wailed in her gut, but Lornk's threats left no time for tears.

THE COST OF FAILURE

Snow sifted from a gray sky, piling into fluted garlands on roofs and fences. Vic's boots sank in fresh powder, toes clenched against the cold. A blizzard in Latha was like a spring squall on the distant northern tundra where she'd been born, but after six winters here in the south, this gentle snow shower had her hunched into fur, wishing for summer.

You always want what you don't have, she thought, stopping in front of a modest peaked cottage. Not the sort of dwelling you'd expect a prince to favor, but Ashel was proud of the little house he'd bought on his minstrel's salary. In Latha, even royals worked for their bread, and the fact he adored his work was one of the things she loved about him.

"But you don't love *him,*" she muttered. It had been a litany she'd repeated ever since she refused to wed him half a year ago. His proposal had ambushed her, left her reeling in a vortex of hope and shame and fear that had churned for months until it spun out of control in Olmlablaire, leaving three hundred and thirty-seven people crushed under a mountain. And Ashel with half a hand. If she loved him, she would have rescued him before Lornk could butcher his fingers. She could have. She should have. She would have, except she'd been a bloody coward. Shame burning her cheeks, she remembered the root of that terror.

She sits with knees drawn up, watching the door open. Lornk's hand on the doorjamb is a hint of the dawn at midnight.

20

Wet heat blossoms in her loins, the blood rising to her skin, the hairs on her arms and thighs and nape standing to attention. Her awareness opens toward him. She smells him, herbs and musk; she feels him, warmth like the sun. The door fully open, he stands against the darkness of the tower stairwell, golden and terrible with eyes darkest blue, his hands large enough to encircle her throat. She rises to her knees, eyes on the floor, eager to meet his demands.

She'd been only fifteen when Caleisbahn slavers had taken her from her homeland and sold her to Lornk Korng. He had stripped away everything she cared about, had almost succeeded in bending her will entirely to his, but she escaped and found refuge here in Latha. Half a dozen years in the Lathan army had made her hard; the Waters of the Dead had made her powerful, but all that strength had evaporated when she confronted Lornk in his mountain fortress at Olmlablaire. Only Ashel's willingness to sacrifice his own flesh had saved her. Freed from the worst man in the world, she'd failed the best.

"Coward." She forced her hand to lift the gate latch, though her feet itched to turn and flee. "You will go in there, and you will say goodbye."

The gate banged shut. Snow crunched, porch boards squeaked, and her heart's pounding drowned out every step. The door creaked open. Ashel stood there, beaming, and her limbs quivered with the desire to run. To him or away, she wasn't sure.

"You're in town! Come in. How are you feeling?"

"Fine—much better, thanks." It had been a week since Elekia had fed Vic her blood—her throat closed on the memory of iron on her tongue when she woke up that evening. The headaches had returned within a day, but they were nothing to what she'd suffered after the Battle of Re. She squeezed between Ashel and a set of traveling cases piled near the door. "I was just down at the Cobblestone, talking with Helara about apprenticing with the Innkeepers."

"Vic the Blade—from soldier to chef, is it?"

"Not that. I'd prefer to avoid killing people from now on, but anybody who survived my cookery might wish they were dead." She grinned at his chuckle, then went on, "Helara's going to let me start as a maid and teach me how to manage the books and brewing. Bethniel said you're leaving."

His grin melted. "The Guild's sending me to Mora."

"You've chosen the Loremaster's path after all."

"*Chosen* isn't how I'd put it." He dropped onto the sofa, and a pang hollowed her lungs as he rubbed the stubble peppering brown cheeks and chin. Dark and beautiful, like stars on a quiet bay, he outshone even his sister. "Melody Reyendal said I'd be jeopardizing the dignity of the Guild if I performed now. People would be distracted by the stump, he said."

"That's ridiculous!" Her cry reverberated through the house.

"I'm not a master yet," he replied in mindspeech. She wished he'd spoken aloud, if only so she could hear the deep timbre of his voice. Six years she'd lived among Lathans, and while she'd come to think their winters cold, she'd never grown accustomed to their silent way of speaking. "But even if I were a master, I couldn't perform without the Guild's approval, which means Reyendal's permission, since he's leader of the Minstrels. The Loremaster's path is the only one left to me now." His lips sagged. "The Mora Guildschool is a worthy post, or so the Harmony took pains to remind me. Most Loremasters have taught there for a time, and it is an honor for a journeyman to have a residency there."

"You always said, if you were a Loremaster, you could leave a greater legacy than you could as a Minstrel."

"I believe what I said was, 'Stagecraft is ephemeral; scholarship eternal.' What a load of pompous rubbish! I suppose I thought in the end, they'd make an exception for me—or rather, for His Highness Prince Ashel of Narath, the Crystal Voice of Latha—and let me become a Master Minstrel *and* a Loremaster." Head down, he massaged the raw, pink patches mottling his maimed hand. In the hearth, crackling logs spat sparks up the flue, and beautiful dark eyes met hers. "The library in Mora is almost as big as the one here at the Academy. You'd love it."

Desire and terror grappled with each other, her gut caught in the middle. "I'm sure I would." Before she'd been a soldier or a slave, she'd been a Logkeeper, a scholar dedicated to preserving the ship's logs of the United Mineral mining ship LSNDR2237, aka the *Elesendar*. For three thousand years, the empty spacecraft had orbited the planet, appearing as a bright star that crossed the sky two or three times a night. For almost two hundred generations, her people, the Oreseekers, had memorized and passed down the text of every log in their possession. Lathan Loremasters revered the same documents but treated them as religious parables. To them, Elesendar was not a ship but a god. She cleared her throat. "I'm sure I would, but I'm a heretic."

He clasped her hand. "I don't care about that. Come with me."

Every cell in her body strained toward him, an instinctive need that splashed and roiled against her will like a river against a dam. *It's just the damn Woern—you do* not *love him.* Yet her hand rose and stroked his cheek. His lips parted hers, tongues twined, and warmth and energy flowed into her, wiping away the ever-present ache behind her eyes. He pulled her to his chest; one hand caressing her neck, sliding into her hair, a single thumb massaging the nape of her neck. Just a thumb.

Coughing, she pulled away. "I'm sorry." Eyes brimming, she stood and hugged her shoulders, struggling for breath. "I can't accept succor from you."

"Succor? That's not—"

"I can't. It isn't fair, not to you."

His mouth flattened, leeching the kindness from his face. A year ago she could not have imagined those beautiful eyes smoldering with rage, but now the heat rarely left them. "I do *not* blame you for this," he said, his thumb folded over his palm, severed knuckles bent into half a fist.

"How can you not? I could have saved you, but I saved myself instead. Some things are unforgivable, Ashel. You deserve better.

That's what I came to tell you—you deserve better. I hope things go well in Mora. Goodbye."

Porch boards banged and snow groaned under running feet. Ducking into an alley, she checked for witnesses, then shot through sifting white into the cold gray clouds blanketing the city. Her nerves sang with the rush of power, and bliss washed from her loins to her eyes. Her body hungered for more, and she breathed deeply, hurtling faster through swirling ice crystals, across the city and out over the forest. She had not used the Woern in nearly two months, not since the day she'd fried a woman's hand down to the bone. She would have gladly made the interrogator suffer for what she'd done to Ashel, but Vic would have done it with a dagger. Bethniel insisted she use her power, and the Relman Council hastily agreed to all their demands, to Bethniel's triumph and Vic's shame.

It had been so easy. Wizardry was outlawed for good reason.

Throat tight, she dropped into the forest. A mile or so from the Manor, she slipped down a familiar wooded slope into a glade dominated by an ancient cerrenil. Leafless branches drooped in the snowy gloom, a twig-laden veil. The trunk rose from drifted snow like the bodice of a fancy gown. In bright sunlight, the branches would reach for the sky, solid and strong, but at night they became as flexible as vines and hung like an old crone's ratted hair. Lathans revered these white-barked trees, called them old mothers and believed their god Elesendar came down and mated with them to beget humanity. A ridiculous story no one should credit, except everyone in Latha—in most of Knownearth, in fact—believed it a likelier explanation for human origins than spacefaring ancestors.

Vic settled beside the tree, one hand on the trunk. "How could everything go so wrong in half a year?" A twig brushed her cheek, and her lips curved despite the anguish gripping her heart. She had never *seen* the cerrenils do anything unusual beyond lift and lower their branches according to variations in sunlight, but she *knew* they had guided her steps and hidden her from enemies during the war. They had also somehow tapped into her memories, giving her strange visions and helping her find her path after she escaped from Lornk Korng. "Is that like the Woern?" she asked, scientific curiosity nudging aside her cares. As a soldier she'd suppressed her scholarly impulses, but it felt good to let her mind escape into observations and hypotheses, even if only for a moment. "Everyone in Latha having mindspeech—is that also due to an infection that opens the mind to strange powers?" There were people outside Latha who had mindspeech, but the Kiareinoll was the only place where telepathy was universal. She hadn't been born with the ability, but she'd gained it after she had come to Latha and lived several months in the Manor.

Tears brimming once more, she pressed her palm on the snow drift. "Thank you for taking me in." Beneath the folds of the cerrenil's roots lay the late King Sashal, Ashel and Bethniel's father. Lathans buried their dead in unmarked graves beside old mothers, returning the life the trees gave them, or so they believed. A kindhearted, generous man, the king had treated Vic as a daughter from the moment she arrived in his throne room as a terrified refugee. He was the polar opposite of Lornk Korng, the tyrannical madman whom he'd fought for twenty years. "Would you have wanted me to kill him?" she asked. In their youth, Sashal and Lornk had been friends, although she couldn't fathom how. "I think you would have approved of what Ashel did, overcoming his own pain to call for justice rather than revenge." She sucked in a sob. "I'm sorry I failed to save you." An assassin's blade had struck down the king and driven Ashel's ill-fated quest for revenge. "I'm sorry I failed to save your son. You both deserved more, and better from me."

Snow drifted through bare twigs, settling on her cloak and hair. Curled against the tree, she wept over her foster father's grave until the southern winter froze her tears.

LABOR OF LOVE

Ragged screams battered Vic's ears; sweat and blood stabbed her nose. And fear. The air reeked of it, sharp and raw. She tasted its foul dry flavor, and it bled from her lungs into her bones. She'd fought some losing battles, but none like this.

"Shrine's bitch, this is hard," Silla panted.

"You'll make it," Vic said. It was an order, crisp and cold, delivered in the same tone she used with worn-out troopers shrinking from combat. She hoisted Silla's arm over her shoulder, ignoring the ache in her own back. Her army comrade slumped against her, exhausted after hours of battle. "You'll live through this," Vic promised, a commander's vow to a beleaguered soldier.

"You're almost there." Maynon mopped Silla's forehead. His fear more than anyone's tainted the room, and tears raced the sweat trickling through his beard. All those times they'd hunkered in hollows or charged a line of foes, Vic had never seen Maynon scared, but now a prayer bubbled from his lips.

"No Shrine-jumping prayers, Maynon, or I'll—" A shriek drowned out the rest of Silla's warning.

"There's the foot," the midwife cried. "Husband, get down here."

Silla squeezed her eyes shut and mewled. Wild-eyed, Maynon stared between her and the midwife crouched beside the birthing chair.

"She's nearly done with her duty, now get down here and do yours," the midwife commanded.

"I've got her," Vic said. Maynon hesitated another moment, then knelt beside the midwife, his hands cupped and trembling under the chair. "Sisters in arms, Silla. Just like old times." Her cheek pressed against the laboring woman's, Vic tasted the salt of her sweat, smelled the iron of her blood. *Elesendar, please see her safely through this,* she prayed. She didn't believe in the Lathan god—or any god—but on the battlefield or the laboring room, it couldn't hurt to call out to a deity, or fate, or pure dumb luck. *Not her too, please no.* Silla's muscles tensed, then rippled downward, a scream pouring out as the midwife tugged the breached baby into Maynon's hands.

The afterbirth smacked the floor, and Maynon hallooed over the infant's cries. "It's a girl!"

Blood splattered and Silla's head lolled back, her weight sinking into Vic. The midwife cursed and grabbed her legs. "Get her on the bed."

Maynon lurched up with the screaming baby, the placenta dangling. "Take care of your daughter," Vic ordered, lifting Silla by the shoulders and hoisting her to the bed. Blood crept through the sheets. At the midwife's order, Vic fetched towels and water and sutures, held a lantern while the healer sewed. Silla's skin paled; her breathing eased, then died to a whisper. At the foot of the bed, Maynon sobbed and clutched the bundled infant. Clasping Silla's hand over her own pounding heart, Vic felt the stuttering echo of her friend's. *Elesendar, please see her safely through this.* She imagined traveling through Silla's veins, down to the place where her life drained out. The midwife whipped sutures through torn flesh, blood weeping over her fingers. Vic's skin tingled, and in her mind she saw damaged vessels pinching closed. Gasping sharply, the healer glanced up. Silla's chest rose and fell. With a puzzled frown, the woman finished the stitches and slathered the wound with slotaen, Knownearth's most prized healing ointment.

"She'll need regular salving for at least a week to heal and for the pain." Packing her things, the midwife cast a dubious look round the narrow room with its cold stove and ice-laced windowpanes. "And buy some coal, for Elesendar's sake."

Maynon nodded, lips curved downward. Vic tugged Silla's limp body onto clean sheets. "Thank you, Healer. If you can bring us the slotaen, I'll cover the cost."

The woman's demeanor softened, and she put down her bag to help Vic change the linens. "I am grateful for your service, all of you. War heroes . . . sometimes I wish the Guild rules weren't so strict on payment."

Vic shrugged. "Everybody's got to eat."

The coal pail banged Vic's shins on the way up the tenement stairs, rattled as she pushed into the tiny attic room.

"Thank you," her former second said. Propped against the headboard, Maynon cradled Silla and the baby as they slept.

Vic flashed a smile as she dumped the coal in the stone brazier. "I'll stay over the next few nights, until she's better."

"Vic," he said aloud. Eyes intent on her face, he kissed Silla's forehead. "Thank you. You did . . . something."

Vic lit the tinder, watched it flare blue and yellow while the screams of Relman children echoed in her mind. Her throat constricting, she retreated to the bureau where her friends kept their liquor. Pouring two glasses, she handed Maynon a drink and sat on the bed. "How did you know?"

He took a sip and grimaced. Harlolinde was as hard as the truth when you drank it straight. "Gossip's all over town. Every trooper, active or discharged, knows it wasn't sulfa that brought that mountain down."

Tears spilled, the first she'd shed all day. How many people had died because of the bad bargain that had made her a wizard? How many Sillas would she have to save to pay that butcher's bill? If she even could save them—she wasn't sure how she'd stopped the bleeding, if she had. "Imagine if I'd had that power when we were slitting Relman throats."

"Woulda made my job easier," he guffawed, then scrubbed a

sleeve over his cheeks. "Shrine's bitch, I can't stop bawling."

Wiping a damp chin, Vic huffed a laugh. "I'll keep your secret if you keep mine."

"Which secret?" He grinned. "That the Blade's an outlaw wizard, or that she turned to mush when she held my kid?"

A corner of Vic's mouth tilted up. "I haven't held her yet."

He patted the swaddled infant. "Her mother won't mind."

Heart skipping, Vic scooped up the bundle. A visceral longing punched her gut as the baby yawned and mouthed the blankets. Her skin was brown, her head covered with downy black. A few months ago, before she'd destroyed any chance of a future with Ashel, Vic had imagined her children would bear the same traits. Swallowing bitter regret, she handed Maynon his daughter. "There. I'm mush."

"You could have one of these."

"Ashel's gone."

"You went halfway round the world to bring him home. He's only the other side of Latha now. Maybe you should go there, make a new home." A wry grin tugged Maynon's lips sideways. "Wizardry's not outlawed in Semeneminieu."

"Who names their country something no one can pronounce?" she grumbled and sipped the harlolinde, letting it scald away grief.

"Listen, I know you were steeped to the eyeballs in shit since the king took it in the throat, but today you gave life instead of death. Seems to me that's your path forward, and though I can't see why you pine for that singing dandy, I'll grant he might be your best guide through the woods."

"Shrine, husband, I pine for that singing dandy too," Silla teased sleepily. "And you two started drinking without me."

The baby hiccupped into a squall. Maynon helped get her settled and nursing while Vic fetched a cup of watered wine for Silla. "What're you naming her?" she asked.

The couple exchanged grins. "Victory."

CALL OF DUTY

Papers thumped onto her desk. Dust billowed, momentarily obscuring Fensin's leer. "Three copies each," the Senator said. "Did you distribute the news?"

Bethniel pasted on a pleasant smile. "First thing this morning." Fensin sent every Heralds' pamphlet critical of the monarchy to the entire Senate. Delivering the copies was a near-daily task for Bethniel.

With a satisfied chuckle, the Opposition returned to his office, and she dipped her quill and began copying a speech decrying tariffs on Caleisbahn goods. "Not here to spy," she muttered. *"I didn't send you to work for the Opposition so you could spy on him,"* her father would say whenever she complained about Fensin giving her nothing to do but run errands and make copies. *"I sent you there to learn from him. He's the wiliest, most ruthless politician you'll ever face."*

Knuckling her back, she set aside the final copy and rolled her head and shoulders. Neck tendons ground and popped, and she longed for a hot bath. A cleared throat stilled her exertions, and her eyes blinked open to find a tall Caleisbahnin. Two silver rings adorned one ear. A red sash fixed a sword to his waist. The steel was worth a ruler's ransom.

"Can I help you?" she asked.

"I have an appointment."

She glanced at the Senator's schedule. "I don't see anything in the book. The Senator has some time next week—"

"Commander, welcome." Fensin appeared in his doorway. "Forgive my junior clerk's impertinence. My dear, you can go home for the rest of the day."

"Your Highness." The Caleisbahnin bowed, a mocking grin revealing a gap between his front teeth.

After leaving the Senate, she wandered in and out of shops, perusing laces and gloves, hats and jeweled brooches. Nothing caught her fancy, and the anxious smiles of the shopkeepers set her teeth on edge. It was a bright, fine day on the cusp of spring, yet few shoppers browsed alongside her, and even fewer carried purchases.

The shortest way home from the market took her through squalid streets where the guildless crowded into ramshackle tenements. In alcoves, figures huddled under threadbare blankets, and refuse slimed the walkway, forcing one to step carefully or risk a slip into muck. Dirty faces melted into shadows. Cats growled in reeking alleys. Passersby glared at her fur-lined cloak, and one, then two blocks passed without sight or sign of a constable. The neighborhood had always been poor, but the nervous quiver quickening her steps was a new sensation.

As she passed a tavern, shouts erupted and glass shattered. Someone screamed, and a tangle of fists and boots boiled out of the doorway. Bethniel scurried clear of the brawlers as more tumbled out.

A hand locked round her elbow, and the cold, hard edge of a crystal blade pressed into her chin. A hiss demanded her pouch. Her eyes slid along a greasy sleeve to a filthy young woman wearing a tattered army uniform. "I'll take that cloak," a second footpad growled.

She had been to war, but she was no warrior and didn't trust her skills against desperate discharged soldiers. "All right, just let me unhook it." Nervous fingers fumbled with the clasp. Why were there no constables about?

A rod rapped the first robber's head, and the woman dropped.

"Geram!" Bethniel cried as the lieutenant swung his staff at the other assailant. The man hit the cobbles. Geram grabbed her hand, and they ran, turning this way and that down side streets until they reached a lane bustling with shoppers and wagons.

"Thank you, Lieutenant, and thank Elesendar you were nearby!" She studied the milky clouds covering his eyes. "How did you do that?"

He stumbled, catching himself on the staff. "Would you mind keeping your gaze on the street, Highness? It helps me see."

She noticed a pressure behind her eyes, an urge to scan the cobbles ahead and the path through the bustle. It was an intrusion, but she didn't mind, not from Geram. She trusted him, even though he was a Listener—one able to Hear the thoughts Lathans chose not to express. He'd been captured and imprisoned in Lordhome with Ashel, where he'd lost his sight and somehow had become psychically linked to her brother. "The vision-stealing—is that how you beat them off?"

"It's borrowing, Highness, not stealing. We use what tools we have. May I escort you home? The streets aren't as safe as they were."

She took his arm, and they paced toward the gate. "I suppose it was foolish of me to take that shortcut home, but I'm awfully grateful Elesendar put you in the same neighborhood."

"I was visiting some old comrades from the Dagger."

"Vic's friends, the ones who had a baby?"

"The same. I'm afraid they're having a rough time. Neither has found work, though Maynon hopes the Potters will take him back. He was apprenticed with them before he became a soldier."

"So many of the guilds are culling ranks. I'll put a word in with the Kiln. It isn't right that two decorated heroes and their child should go hungry."

"It isn't right that anyone should go hungry, Highness."

"True. How is Ashel? I hope he's in Mora by now."

Geram grinned, his teeth bright in a dark brown face. "He says to try wearing plainer clothing next time you go slumming." After a moment, he added, "He also wants you to know there are rumors of squatters in the eastern Kiareinoll."

"Squatters?"

"He heard about it at several way stations in the east, and the cavalry outpost on the Mora road was going to investigate."

"Who are these people?"

"Culled from guilds, he's heard. Whoever they are, they're cutting trees for homesteads."

"What? You can't just farm the Kiareinoll willy-nilly! There are rituals, sacrifices, rules to follow, or they'll get themselves killed!"

"I'm from Alna, Highness. The way of trees is a mystery to me."

"It's a mystery to all of us, Lieutenant, which is why the forest must be treated with respect and reverence. Those people are putting themselves in danger, and if too much land is cleared, Fembrosh's retribution will strike more than the squatters. I must speak with the Ruler."

He stopped, a hand on her arm, concern etched deeply over milky eyes that fixed on her face, as if he could see her. "Ashel doesn't want the queen to know about our connection."

"Honestly, Ashel—forgive me, Lieutenant, but this is directed at my brother—I don't understand this sudden animosity you have for Mother! She's never been very, well, motherly, but that never used to bother you any more than . . . than it ever did. I wonder sometimes if you left town just so you could get away from her. In any case, it's silly to hide this ability from her."

Geram's face hardened. "It's not an ability, it's a curse."

"Is that from him or from you?"

"Both of us. And both of us ask you to keep this secret."

"Selcher probably knows already."

"I can hold my own against her."

She laughed, and Geram winced in a way that made her think Ashel's shoulders were jerking toward his ears too. "Selcher has been our family's Listener since my grandfather reigned, and there's no one she can't Hear. Ashel, you're a fool if you think she doesn't already know about you two, and you know that what she knows, Mother knows."

"Please, Highness. Do not be the one to tell the queen about us. Ashel says, tell her you heard about the squatters in a tavern or saw it in a report to Fensin—anything, but do not admit how you learned it."

"If I lie, Selcher will Hear it." She calculated the distance to Mora. "I'll say I learned it from Ashel, but imply it was in a letter. A fast courier could have come from the eastern Kiareinoll. Mother won't be surprised he wrote to me instead of her."

As they passed the city's east gate and trudged along Manor Road, the seed of an idea took root. Bethniel had climbed this hill to and from the city since she was seven years old. She knew the roads and countryside around Narath as well as she knew the city itself. She had traveled the verdant lands west of the Lathalorns and frolicked in the surf of the Yuslobna Kein, but she had never trekked into the vast wilds of the eastern Kiareinoll. She had visited the Eldanion court, traversed the Kragnashian deserts, and climbed the Lorn oc Re, yet she'd never seen the ancient, massive groves where Elesendar joined with the old mothers, or heard the lupears howl, or felt the thunder of a steed herd's approach. If she were going to rule all of Latha and rule it well, she should know the greater half of it.

Determination and certainty settled her mind. "If there are squatters in Fembrosh, they must be dealt with. I'm going east, Lieutenant."

GUILDLESS

Aldevaer's Arpeggio in D minor, twenty-fifth measure. Wineyll's tongue skipped through the sixteenth notes, dipping and climbing the registers. Her flute, hollowed from mine crystal, turned the melody into a symphony as each note resonated through the flaws. When her father had given her the instrument, he'd said no Trainer silversmith could make an instrument to match it. As proof of his words, when they'd performed together, audiences had listened, jaws slack with awe.

Alone in a practice chamber, Wineyll cloaked herself in the flute's harmonies. The Arpeggio was the most difficult piece she knew. She'd spent months mastering the variable dynamics and the triple tongued measures so she could fly through without a flub or slur for her senior levels. At the examination, even Master Grumblin had given her a standing ovation, and forgiven her for the moth hatchlings she'd left in his desk as a prank.

Her tongue, tired from hours of practice, slipped, and an accidental glissando marred the passage. It had been two years since she'd played the piece. Sighing, Wineyll set down the flute and flexed her fingers and jaw. Silence settled over the practice room, and screams and cajoling whispers echoed between her ears.

A rap sliced through the memories, and the practice room door opened on an apprentice.

"Reyendal wants to see you," he said. "You're to meet him in the Music's office."

A fist squeezed her chest. "Where?"

"The Music's office. The Harmony's there too." The boy's frown, serious and sympathetic, launched her heart into a faster rhythm. Hands shaking, she wiped down her flute, tucked it into its case, and made her way to the Music's chambers. Pockets of apprentices and students loitered in the hallways, the groups falling silent as she passed. Two years ago, they would have greeted her with jests and plaudits. Head bowed, her hair shielding her from their stares, she hurried onward.

The trio that led the Minstrels Guild sat in chairs on one side of a table, an empty space on the other side—their exact positions the day they'd expelled her father. Dread clogging her throat, she stood in the same spot he had and Listened to their judgment.

It wouldn't come from the Music. His thoughts were as confused as ever—for years, Wineyll had Heard the masters' private complaints that he ought to step down, but Harmony Silnauer had managed to keep the senile old man in place at the top. Melody Reyendal, as always, would follow Silnauer, and Wineyll knew the outcome before anyone spoke a word. Beneath her pitying smile, the Harmony's thoughts seethed with scorn.

"Thank you for coming so promptly," said Reyendal. "Do you know why we've called you here?"

Her heart drumming, she replied, "No, sir." She'd make them say it.

He cleared his throat and spoke aloud. "I'm afraid we must suspend—"

"Expel," interjected Silnauer.

"We are forced to expel you from the Guild," Reyendal said.

"Why, sir?"

He flipped through a ledger. "You were journeyed nearly a year ago, and yet you have not earned back your salary, much less your room and board. This organization is not a charity."

Anger struck the timpani in her chest. "You granted me a leave of absence when the throne asked me to help rescue Prince Ashel. I've only been back a month."

Reyendal glanced at Silnauer. "Yet since your return, you haven't earned a single crystal."

"I haven't been assigned any gigs. Did the Guild rules change while I was gone? I thought journeyed minstrels weren't allowed to manage our own bookings until we'd gained two years in the field."

"That's the problem. It seems no one wants to book a suspected traitor."

"I'm no traitor!"

"Yet rumors abound that you collaborated with Lornk Korng in the maiming of Prince Ashel—your own brother in the Guild."

Cold rippled over Wineyll's skin. "If Ashel were here, he'd tell you I did everything I could to save him."

"He is not here, and I find it unlikely he would vouch for you," Silnauer said. "Whatever his flaws, Prince Ashel recognizes that this Guild's primary mission is to spread Elesendar's word and live according to His prescribed virtues. You, like your father, seem to have forgotten our purpose. Your father indulged in pleasures of the flesh outside the sanctity of marriage, one of Elesendar's most sacred commands. You permitted yourself to be seduced by Lornk Korng, then you did his bidding during the battle of Olmlablaire. As a result, the prince lost his hand and any ability to serve Elesendar as a minstrel."

The Harmony's vile accusations were accurate, but none were *true*. Or supposed to be known. Geram, Ashel, Vic—they'd all promised no one would *know*. Fury roiling, Wineyll tore through their minds to find out who'd betrayed the secret. Silnauer swayed, her lips a rictus as she tried to block Wineyll's rifling, while Reyendal sat as dumbly as the Music, his memories as easily shuffled as a deck of cards. There she found a letter, scribbled on a scrap of dirty parchment, delivered by a shamefaced prison guard. "You believe the Relmlord?" The question came out as a scream.

"Your impertinence seals your fate," snapped Silnauer.

Reyendal cleared his throat again. "Wineyll, I hope you can appreciate the difficulty of this decision. We have known you from infancy. You were one of the brightest stars in our ranks. It is with the deepest regret and disappointment that we must rescind your Guild membership, but you force our hands."

Her body trembled with disbelief they would do this, even as Reyendal's words echoed the hollow regrets he'd pronounced to her father.

"We are not unmerciful," Reyendal continued. "We know very well that a young person such as yourself, who has known no home but this Guild, will need time to arrange employment elsewhere. You may keep your bed in the dormitory for another month, but by the spring equinox, you must leave." His chair squeaked against the floor, and he came round the table. "The case, please."

He may as well have kicked her in the gut. Unable to breathe, she hugged the flute to her chest. "My father gave this to me."

"All instruments are Guild property."

"But he said it was mine."

"As long as you earned it. You cannot work as a minstrel any longer, Wineyll. You'll have to find another path." The Melody pulled the flute from her grasp, and she felt as if he'd yanked out her heart.

"You should consider Alna," Silnauer said. "I believe the Courtesans there might welcome a pretty young woman with experience, particularly from so adroit a mentor."

Wineyll's gaze locked on the Harmony as a wave of memory struck her.

Silnauer's lips tilt in scorn. "How quickly did you learn your craft in Traine? You had a master of some renown, or so I hear."

Cheeks burning, Vic stares at Silnauer. "What have you heard?"

"Enough to know what sort of person you are. I see no place for heretics within an institution designed to revere Elesendar. Yet the Courtesans in Alna might admit you."

Dismissed, Wineyll stumbled into the hallway, still enveloped by Vic's memory from an encounter she'd had with the Harmony years ago, soon after she arrived in Latha. During the battle of Olmlablaire, Wineyll had dug into Vic's mind in order to subdue her because the Relmlord said if she succeeded, he wouldn't take any more of Ashel's fingers. Yet one by one the severed digits had dropped to the floor while Ashel begged her to leave Vic free, so Lornk Korng could be *stopped*. Ashel would have sacrificed his tongue to keep Vic out of Lornk's hands, and she would have drained Vic's mind entirely to spare her Guild-brother more agony. In the end, Ashel lost his fingers and his favored place in the Guild, and Wineyll was left with another woman's memories that would swamp her own now and then, flushing out her other failures.

Like all those massacred nomads. She, more than any other Lathan, should undertake the Penance the Relmans demanded. Vic had taken her on the secret mission to rescue Ashel because she could weave illusions and place them in others' minds. She'd sworn she could hide a raiding party, so the company could steal the horses they needed. Because she'd failed, they'd been forced to kill the nomads down to the last baby.

She trudged to her room as if hauling water in the Badlands. The Guild's paneled chambers, filled with music and chatter, were the only home she'd ever known, but maybe this wasn't the home she deserved. She ought to undertake the Penance, but did she have the courage to face the relatives of the massacred? A hero would, but Wineyll was no hero. She'd proven that at every turn.

TRUE GIFT

Quills scratched and tapped, each rap on an inkwell a counterpoint to the gentle squeak of nibs and slither of papers. Once Ashel's songs had held theatergoers enraptured. Now his lectures entranced students. Their gazes danced from desk to board, lectern to pointer, and he rewarded their attentiveness with a smile. Color rose in young women's cheeks. The young men copied the tilt of his lips. The admiration warmed him like the sun, and he launched the next topic as confidently as he'd begin a new verse.

Then, one pair of eyes dropped to the thumb hooked round his belt. He'd begun hanging the fingerless stump there—not in the swagger people took it for, but because he didn't know what else to do with it. Another gaze descended to the lone digit, and his gut clenched, toes curling in his boots. Like a flock of birds coming to roost, all eyes in the room wheeled from his face and landed on the maimed hand. Heat rising up his neck, Ashel rapped the pointer against the board again.

"'What can we know of the way of trees?' What does that line of scripture mean?"

A student raised her fingers. "It's the reason Lieutenant Grossmont gave for choosing to make a treaty for Landing with the erin instead of the cerrenils. He figured humans couldn't begin to understand the way a plant thinks, but the erin were at least sapient animals."

Ashel chuckled. "That's a heretic's answer. I'm looking for the scriptural meaning."

"But why do we have to view it through that lens?" she persisted. "Maybe he was just being practical. How can we communicate with *trees*?"

Ashel's amusement died as he remembered Vic making the same argument over ale, amid raucous laughter and chatter in the Cobblestone's tavern.

"We don't," he replied as Master Jahant came in and took a seat. "Not in the way you and I exchange ideas. But troopers who served in the war will tell you the cerrenils listen and will help, if it suits them. And when they choose not to help—what can we know of the way of trees? That line refers to the Kia, to the *mystery* of the old mothers. We know nothing of the cerrenils' thoughts or motivations. But can we ever completely comprehend why our friends love us and our enemies hate us? Even Listeners can't completely know those answers. Yet we have faith in our loved ones, and a kind of faith in our enemies too. 'What can we know of the way of trees?' The answer is: nothing. It's not knowledge but faith that's important."

"But," the girl said, "how do we know Elesendar told Lieutenant Grossmont to found the Erin Alliance?"

"There's that word 'know' again. Heretics will say they *know* the *Elesendar* is a spacecraft. They'll point to the Logs and say, 'These are historical records of the United Mineral mining ship LSNDR2237, which was sabotaged, leaving the crew marooned here almost three thousand years ago.' Adherents to the Faith of Elesendar will say, 'He is the Father of humanity, the cerrenils are our Mothers, and the Logs are allegorical and metaphorical, not factual.' What heretics think is merely a ship in orbit around this planet, adherents believe is a god watching over our world. The truth is, neither heretics nor adherents really *know*, and both groups must rely on faith, because we lack evidence either way."

"What do you believe?"

Master Jahant's eyebrows rose, but Ashel smiled. "The Logs make sense only when read as allegory, but ultimately, nobody but Grossmont ever knew his true state of mind. What's important isn't whether Elesendar truly spoke to him but that Grossmont believed He did—he had *faith*—and after he met with the erin, they came out of the highlands every spring and allowed themselves to be shorn. You can choose to believe Grossmont was a pragmatist—or a lunatic for that matter. But I guarantee the Weavers bless him for a saint."

The class laughed, and Ashel dismissed them.

Expression cheery, Jahant forded the outward flow of students. "Wonderful to see a history lesson garner such rapt attention, though our colleagues in Narath might be unhappy to hear you discussing heresies."

Biting his tongue, Ashel flipped open his satchel and stuffed his lecture notes inside. "Only a weak faith is threatened by debate, sir."

Jahant laid an arm across his shoulder. "And I encourage questions in my own classroom, but you're not yet a Loremaster, and journeymen are supposed to stick to approved doctrine." The master's smile broadened. "But you have such a gift for lecturing— I'm honored the Harmony sent you to me."

Mouth dry and sour, he ducked out of Jahant's embrace. "Thank you, Master. I'll see you tomorrow."

"Of course." The Guildschoolmaster closed his satchel and handed it to him, his eyes shrewd, regretful.

Outside the Guildschool, he passed yellow brick walls draped with ivy and crowned with potted trees. Mora straddled the Semena border, three hundred miles of dry grass between the city gate and the edge of Kiareinoll Fembrosh. Crossbows idle on their backs, guards on the parapets raised watering cans to greet passersby, yet all the greenery the city planted couldn't conjure the deep shade of Fembrosh. Not in this yellow place. Yellow plain, yellow bricks and cobbles, even yellowed wallpaper in the parlor of his boarding house. In his room, the grimy walls and frayed carpet did little to ease his eyes. Splashing wine into a cup, he settled into a creaky chair, a boot on the windowsill. The day he moved in, a month ago as winter unfolded into spring, the river

outside had reflected a sky brown with dust. The landlady had said
it was from the vast steed herds, migrating north. Wait till we have
a clear day, she'd promised. Today the sky was blue and endless.
The water remained brown.

I like your view, Geram said.

Ashel swallowed a draught. *One of the finest in the city, the
landlady said, when she still talked to me. Now she thinks I'm mad,
always talking to myself.*

Everybody talks to themselves, Geram replied.

Not like us.

No.

Geram, Ashel said firmly, as if shutting a door.

Ashel, the other man conceded.

The Archives at the Academy held an Ancient fable about
a wizard who was haunted by his own shadow, defeated it by
naming it. The wizard had sought to rejoin a split self, but Ashel
and Geram named each other to try to separate, as they had ever
since that terrible day in the Relmlord's dungeons. Ashel gulped
his wine, trying to drown the strident howls and sizzling meat
assaulting his memory. His screams, his cooking skin and muscle,
and Vendrael's shrieks and burning flesh too. Elesendar forgive
him, he'd felt nothing but satisfaction watching his torturer's
flesh burn, but since then, her screams had mingled with his
own. Both memories became the chorus to Lornk Korng's
insidious whispers, which had slid into his ear, revealing the lie of
his parents' marriage. Ashel couldn't say which agony had been
worse, the burning flesh or the searing truth that Lornk Korng
might be his father.

Geram had tried to block his pain during the burning, and
something had gone wrong. Now, regardless of distance and
time, they always knew each other's mind. They whispered their
names again, aloud. Sometimes, it worked. Not today—Ashel
felt Geram push his eyes after a piece of trash floating on the
river, his gaze lunging after it like a beggar diving for moldy
bread.

I enjoyed your lecture today, Geram said after the detritus disappeared beneath the bridge. *When I was a boy, the heretics used to gather in Aunt Celina's tavern. I don't remember anybody saying that belief by anybody but the believer isn't important.*

A memory slipped by, not Ashel's, of a table full of youths and oldsters, teasing him as he passed drinks to them.

A tentative rap broke the reverie, and the landlady cringed past his threshold. "You have visitors, Highness."

"Just Ashel, please," he said.

"Of course, High—of course. They're waiting in the parlor." The landlady scuttled away.

His boots echoed on the stairs. *She probably thinks Mother shipped me off here to get her lunatic son out of sight.* Instead his Guild had pasted the shipping label on his head.

Your mother is meeting with the Eldanion ambassador shortly, and I'm supposed to be there.

Anger stirred. *Why couldn't you just go home to Alna?*

Your mother sends my aunt and uncle a pension. I can do more for my family Listening to patricians prevaricate, than hearing fishers' fibs.

Ashel began a retort, but his ire melted as he crossed the parlor threshold. "Melba!"

His Guild-sister, and oldest friend, flung her arms around him. "Master Jahant told me where you were lodged."

"What are you doing here?" He looked between her and her companions. An older man wore his wiry hair dressed with clay and sculpted into a fan upon his head. On the woman, well-defined arms were crossed over a nearly bare torso. Only narrow leather strips covered small breasts set in a muscular chest.

She looks cold, Geram quipped.

An elbow jabbed Ashel's ribs. "This is Joslyrn and Kelmair," said Melba. "They're Herders."

Awe pushed out his right hand before he remembered the missing fingers. Awkwardly, he switched to his left. "Of steeds? My grandparents are horse breeders. I know it's a sorry comparison, but . . . Shrine, it must be glorious to ride a steed."

Joslyrn gripped the offered hand. "Do you think you could stay astride one, Highness?" He used his voice rather than mindspeech, as was common east of the Kiareinoll.

"I'd like to try," Ashel replied aloud. People from the Semena plains considered mindspeech rude. "And please, Ashel is fine."

"Might as well ride an ox as a horse," Kelmair said silently. She kept her arms crossed, lips taut beneath narrow eyes. Angry weals circled her neck, and her head was shaven except for a glossy black topknot.

She's Caleisbahnin, Geram said.

Anxiety squeezed Ashel's gut. "I'm pleased to meet you, but why are you here?"

Melba drew him to the sofa. "They have a proposition for you, to get you out of your debt."

His debt. It seemed a small thing next to all he'd lost in Olmlablaire, but he owed Caleisbahn gamers a huge sum after one stupid, drunken night, a year and a half ago—a carefree time. "And how do they know about that?"

"Welsher," Kelmair sneered.

"Kelmair, we're here with honey, not salt," Joslyrn said. "She has her own problems with the Archipelago, Highness, and my crew has its troubles, but there's a way we could all help each other."

What's a Caleisbahn woman doing with Herders? Geram wondered.

Ashel voiced another question: "How did you find Melba, and me?"

"We met in Narath," Melba said. "Joslyrn was there petitioning the Senate, and he caught my act at the Wind. We ended up chatting, and then I needed to get out here fast, so he offered me passage in exchange for introducing you."

Ashel blinked. "Why did you need to get out here fast? And I still don't understand how a Herder knows about my gambling debts."

"The Guild expelled Wineyll."

"What? Why?"

"They said she wasn't meeting her quotas, but they haven't given her any gigs, and she can't bring in revenue if she can't perform. There are some vile rumors circulating—it's like the situation with her father all over again, and the Harmony doesn't want any scandal."

"They expelled her? She's barely seventeen." His anger stirred, amplified by Geram's, over what Lornk had done to Wineyll in Olmlablaire. "Whatever those rumors say, the Guild should be sheltering her, not tossing her to the lupears."

Joslyrn shook his head. "All the guilds are purging ranks, Highness, Herders included. Our guild demanded all Lathan members pay double the grazing fees or turn our herds over to Semena crews."

"The Miners have culled too, and between the guildless and the discharged soldiers, Narath is full of trouble these days," Melba said.

"You should be talking to my mother about all this."

"I tried," Joslyrn said, "but I couldn't get an audience."

"Melba, you could have connected him with Bethniel—you didn't have to come all the way out here."

"I would have, and Wineyll would have asked Bethniel for help too, but she'd already left town on some mission for the throne."

"We have a different plan, Shemen," Kelmair said.

Melba gasped, and Ashel stared at the Caleisbahnin, a cold knot lodged in his stomach. *Shemen.* In the Archipelago, shemen were men deemed unfit for the sea. Geram knew the insult from the Alnan docks, where boys would sneer it at the weak or cowardly.

Melba cleared her throat. "While they were in Narath, Kelmair saw the Caleisbahn ambassador, and he told her the First will pay your debt if you spend a year at his court in Signon."

"He wants to hire me as a minstrel?" he asked, trepidation snarled like wire in his throat as he glanced at Kelmair. Elite Caleisbahn commanders kept comely shemen in their harems.

Joslyrn nodded. "Yes."

"The First likes music," the Caleisbahn woman added, her lip curled.

"What's your interest in this?"

"There's a bounty," Kelmair snapped.

Joslyrn's eyes snapped heavenward. "Shrine, woman! Honey, not salt! Forgive us, Highness. The Caleisbahn ambassador offered to pay us if we brought you back to Narath. Until we pay the grazing fees, we're outlaws. The money would clear our names and let us keep the herd."

He frowned, torn between a desire to visit the legendary Archipelago and suspicion that something nefarious was afoot. These people wouldn't be here if he hadn't succumbed to temptation—but then a lot of trouble could have been avoided if he'd had better control over his impulses.

"You want me to go to the Guild and ask permission to take this job?" he asked Melba.

"I do. The Guild cannot expel you, *Prince* Ashel. If you came back, it would force them to stop using flimsy excuses to purge everyone who isn't one of the Harmony's sycophants. Losing those fingers doesn't prevent you from singing. You should be headlining in Knownearth's capitals, not stuck out here *teaching*! If you were a Master, you could take any gig you wanted, including this one in Signon. Come back to Narath and demand the Minstrel performance exam, or the Loremaster composition section if you like. You could still lecture when you want, but *music* is your true gift."

True gift. He flexed the maimed hand, and Melba's nostrils flared. "Maybe I don't want to be a minstrel," he growled.

"Ashel, it's not what you want—it's what you are."

Vic had said something similar last summer when she rejected his offer of marriage. A few hours later, his father had been murdered in front of all of them. Sashal's blood, hot and sticky, had soaked Ashel's garments and filled his heart with a white-hot rage. He still carried that anger, banked but smoldering. Fury sparked embers, each with a glowing face: Lornk and all the guards and torturers under his command. Mother, for wedding someone so vile—even if they'd never declared, she had let herself be wooed and won. And Vic. *Some things are unforgivable.* Shrine, Vic's face floated out of that pit of rage too. All those times he insisted he didn't blame her for his lost fingers—those were more wishes than truth.

Scowling, he stood. "Joslyrn, I'll think about your offer. Melba, I'll see you tomorrow."

A nervous smile rippled the old man's mouth as he stood. "Would you at least like to come and see the steeds? We're staying at the steed paddock outside the city."

His ire faded, replaced by longing. "Is it true you can cover a hundred miles in a day?"

"Half a day, if need be," Kelmair sneered.

"Steeds like to run," Joslyrn said. "We could let you try riding one. A grandchild of horse breeders should make the leap easily."

They agreed to meet the next day after his classes, and he returned to his room, where he marked essays until the landlady brought supper. The fowl dry, the grains undercooked, he washed the food down with the rest of the open bottle, finished another while sitting in the dark, watching the river run black under dim stars. Stretched out on a too-short mattress, he welcomed Geram's dreams of crashing surf and seabirds, salty skin and gritty sand, then yelped out of nightmares teeming with dungeon noise and stink. Heart racing, he rubbed throbbing temples as dawn burnished the carpet a bright coppery bronze, like Vic's hair. Mornings like this, he'd wake wishing to find her beside him, that bright hair tickling his chest. But half his bed was cold, same as half his hand was missing.

THE DEADLIEST ONE

Dispossessed miners thronged the street, brandishing clubs and dirty faces, sending pedestrians scurrying onto jammed boardwalks. An elbow jabbed Vic's ribs; her nose bumped someone's shoulder. Arms aching, she hefted a tuber-filled basket, boosting it with just a touch of wizardry. Euphoria steeped at the back of her throat, and she longed to shoot skyward, out of the crowd. Swallowing the urge, she released the power, and pain bloomed behind her temple.

"I don't have time for this crap." Muttering more oaths, she plowed through the onlookers and into the tide of marchers, fording the street with a glare so fierce they lowered their cudgels and wove around her. Each step was a hammer blow against her skull, and nausea twisted her belly. Hurrying down a series of alleys, she emerged onto a street adorned with flower boxes wafting with spring. The Cobblestone beckoned from the block's end, its half-timbered, ivy-draped walls promising respite. Pain squeezing her temples, Vic gritted her teeth and slipped through the side gate.

Bed linens billowed, wafting scents of garden herbs and brewing ale. Eyes closed, she pulled the aromas into her lungs, willing the sweet air to ease her ills. Another wave of sickness bubbled up, and she groaned. She'd have to visit Elekia soon, or hole up sick in her room until the queen sent guards to fetch her. It had already happened once since Bethniel had left.

You've fought battles feeling worse, she reminded herself, shouldering open the kitchen door. She could at least bring in the laundry. Leaving the tubers with the cook, she took an empty basket outside. Clean sheets, clean rooms, clean reputation, Helara always said. Vic unclipped a pillowcase from the line, cracked it smartly, snapped it into a neat square, and pulled down a sheet. Birdsong trilled over the wall, and in the deeper tones of a nearby creek, she heard Ashel's baritone. A shadow crossed the edge of her vision—her heart in her throat, she peered through the billowing linens. But it was only the water, a passing cloud, and wishful thinking.

You don't love him, she repeated her litany.

"Vic," Helara called sharply from the kitchen door.

Swallowing pain, Vic creased the sheet. "Almost done."

The innkeeper came and put strong hands on Vic's shoulders, her narrow eyes and stark cheekbones set in a fierce scowl. "Shrine, you're green as a ghost. Come inside, now." She marched Vic into her office and slammed the door. "I won't have any trouble, you hear me?"

Vic's cheeks tingled as if she'd been slapped. "What is wrong?"

"This is a respectable place."

"I know. Why do you think I'm working here?"

"I will not have rumors going round about my employees." She swiped up a crumpled Heralds' pamphlet and flung it at Vic.

Smoothing the parchment against the desk, Vic laughed. The Heralds framed the facts of Olmlablaire's destruction—that Vic the Blade had used wizardry to blast a hole in the Relmlord's mountain palace—with an elaborate plot in which Kragnashians, the Caleisbahnin, rogue steed herders, and the Heralds' favorite villain—Queen Elekia—sought to undermine the guilds and dismantle them. "Steed rustlers? This is preposterous!"

"You're saying it isn't true?" Helara demanded.

Guffaws fading, Vic wiped her cheeks. "When did the Heralds ever print anything but fabrications ginned up to sell their papers?"

"I asked for the truth, not sass."

"This pamphlet is full of lies." Even if it wrapped the truth with them. "Why would you even think—"

"They say wizardry kills the wizard, Vic, and since you came back from the war, you haven't been yourself. You always look hungover, and you jump whenever I walk into a room where you're alone. I know you're not drinking my stocks. You're not smoking bliss, are you?"

"There are no bliss dens in Narath."

The innkeeper raised a shrewd eyebrow. "Don't be so sure of that, with all the miserable vagrants lurking about. I'll bring in the linens; clean up the common room and get yourself ready for the evening rush."

When she finished tidying, she climbed to the third-floor garret she shared with Helara's daughter. A journeyed Tailor, Lora had gone to purchase fabrics in Erin, and Helara had allowed Wineyll to take Lora's bed while she was away. Vic found the minstrel curled there, facing the wall, a position she occupied most of the time.

"Helara's booked a trio for the common room tonight," Vic said. "They said you're welcome to play with them."

"I'm not allowed."

"You're not allowed if Helara pays you. No one can stop you just joining in. Craftfolk sing along all the time."

"I don't sing. I played."

Vic sighed. Pulling Wineyll out of her funk was hopeless, and as each day wore on, Vic struggled against a desire to kick the girl rather than comfort her. She wished Bethniel was here—the princess would know exactly what to say and do. "I heard you don't have to be in a guild to perform as a minstrel in Eldanion. I'll ask Elekia to speak to their ambassador and get you a place as a court minstrel."

"You have to supply your own instruments, and I don't have any money to buy them."

Lips pressed together, Vic rubbed her temples. "You are a war hero, Wineyll. I'm sure Elekia would grant you a boon, or something."

The girl flopped over. Her glare pierced Vic's skull, cranking up the ache there. "I'm not a hero. As you well know."

"Wineyll, nobody knows better than me how Lornk can wind you up and spin you into doing the last thing you'd ever want to. I know sometimes we just want to wallow in our sorrows, but eventually you have to get up and move along with your life."

The minstrel stared at her, and Vic wondered what she Heard. She supposed some would hate the girl for what she'd done, but Vic *did* know all too well what had driven Wineyll that night, and the fact Wineyll had been there in the first place was Vic's fault. Another failure. "You should come down tonight," she said.

The girl turned back to the wall. Biting back a sigh, Vic washed and changed into the dress and apron Helara required for tavern duty.

As evening came on, craftfolk and shopkeepers arrived for ale and fish stew. Minstrels fringed the silent chatter with a fiddle and a drum. Maynon and Silla tramped in with some Potters and took a corner table. Vic cooed over Victory, snoozing in a sling round Silla's shoulders, and asked about their cheery smiles. "What are we celebrating?"

Maynon grinned. "The Potters took me back as a journeyman and apprenticed Silla."

"Well then," Vic grinned, "first round's on me."

"I'll get it," Geram called as his cousin Drak guided him through the door.

"You made it!" Maynon shook Geram's hand. Vic raised an eyebrow—the men had always butted heads when they were under her command.

"Ow!" Geram jumped, flapping his hand as if he'd touched a hot coal.

"My grip that strong, Fishlicker?" Maynon asked.

"It's always a shock to see you," Geram quipped and hugged Vic while Maynon's friends roared.

"You're not the only one who helped us keep the stove warm through the winter," Silla confided to Vic as the men traded insults. "And one of you must have put in a word with the Kiln, since the guilds are dropping people, not taking them on."

"That was Bethniel's doing." Geram's milky eyes crinkled as he kissed Victory's tiny forehead.

"Captain!" Vic opened her arms for Drak. His smile forced, the big man hesitated, then stepped back after a quick pat. She didn't blame his reluctance—he'd seen her do many terrible things with the Woern—but she regretted it all the same. She used to count on Drak's sense and sense of humor to keep her head straight.

She fetched the party's drinks while other craftspeople filtered in. The windows grew dark and tables filled. Servers slid through the crowd, taking orders, depositing dishes, sweeping debris. Helara poured and polished, lending half an ear and snippets of advice with every mug. Vic's headache faded, and she found it easy to jest with the patrons while bringing their ale and stew.

"I don't think anybody expected Vic the Blade to become Vic the Maid." Geram leaned an elbow on the bar while she stacked clean glasses on the shelves.

"I like it," she said. "Nobody gets killed." Years ago, she would have disdained this life of soiled laundry and drunken patrons. An odyssey of captivity and warfare could do a lot to change a woman's goals. There was only thing missing, she thought with a wistful frown at Victory, spitting smiles from Maynon's arms.

"Could have one of those, if you'd stop being stubborn."

"And you're not my shrink anymore."

He stiffened, his head cocked, and stumbled against the railing.

"Are you all right?" Her breath stopped. "Is it Ashel?"

"He's in trouble."

"What's happening?"

"Marshal Victoria of Ourtown!" There was a scuffle, and the crowd pressed back from a swaggering figure. Two silver earrings glinted from an ear. A tuft of seabird feathers, four long ones tipped with white, clustered around the hilt of his sword. Below narrow, tilting eyes, a gap between his front teeth turned his grin ghoulish. "Victoria of Ourtown?"

Vic's blood ran cold. If it weren't for the Caleisbahnin taking her off a beach in the distant north, she'd still be a Logkeeper, just now preparing to leave her father's lodge, ready with the spring to make her rounds among the Oreseeker villages. The peaceful path of a teacher and scholar, not a violent journey through slavery and war.

"My name is Gustave of Sect Dameron," the pirate answered her silence. "I represent interests who would benefit from your skills in unique situations."

"Order something or leave," Helara said.

"I'll pay for the marshal's time." Gustave laid a gold coin on the counter. Gasps fluttered around the bar. Silver the only metal more common than gold, both were still rare enough that few Lathans had seen either. He held up the Herald's pamphlet. "This says you destroyed Mount Olm."

"We used a lot of sulfa, pirate." Drak muscled through the crowd, Maynon behind him.

"And three thousand Relmans fell at the Battle of Re, yet hardly any Lathans," Gustave continued. "That's an unprecedented victory, Marshal."

"You need to go," Vic said.

Pink poked through the gap in his teeth. "We pay well, Marshal, especially for someone with your tactical abilities."

"You were told to leave." Drak shoved him, and the pirate grasped his sword hilt. Stone, porcelain, and crystal daggers whispered out of sheaths. The pirate was tall for a Caleisbahnin, but Drak loomed over him. "Go now."

Gustave's eyes flicked over the weapons, and he stepped back, hands raised, his gaze landing on Vic. "The marshal stands unarmed, yet we all know she is the deadliest one in this room. We'll meet again, Victoria of Ourtown." His ghoulish grin widened. "The rest of you should follow me out, while you still can."

Murmurs rippled as the door banged shut. Vic dug her fingers into Geram's arm. "What's happening to Ashel?"

A boom shook the inn. Glasses tipped off shelves and smashed on the floor. Shrieks and black smoke billowed from the kitchen. Helara bellowed orders while screaming patrons jammed the door.

The Potters surrounded Silla and plowed through the crowd. Victory squalled, her mother's hand cupped around her head. "Help Vic," Silla cried to Maynon.

"Clear the guests!" Helara cried, rushing upstairs.

"Maynon, help her," Vic ordered. "Drak, Wineyll's up in the garret. Geram, go with Silla."

Maynon pushed Geram toward the Potters, then charged up the stairs after the captain and Innkeeper.

"The cook is hurt," Geram yelled as the Potters dragged him outside.

Fire ballooned through the kitchen door. Vic threw up a shield of solid air, but the blaze shredded through it, flames scurling across the plank floor and paneled walls. The cook's screams choked off, and scores of voices, dying in a nighttime conflagration, echoed in memory. *Three hundred and twelve dead nomads.* Elesendar, not here.

Shutting her eyes, she spread her awareness through the air molecules vibrating near the blaze and willed them to slow. In the kitchen, white heat roared, blasting out of the bricks. She restrained the vibrating air, and the room chilled to an icehouse. The fire shrank as she bound the air together, smothering the flames with the thing that fed them. The cook lay near the back stairs, an enormous heap. Vic could spare nothing for him. It took all her concentration to hold back the fire.

Helara burst through the door with a sodden broom. Wet straw slapped against an invisible wall. Mouth open, she stared at Vic.

"Save the cook. I'll put out the fire." Sweat froze in ribbons on Vic's cheeks and neck, her head throbbing as if a balloon were expanding behind her eyes. A puff of smoke, then a gout of flame seared toward the ceiling. "Get out," she ordered. "Now, Helara."

"The pamphlet—"

"Get out!" Vic screamed, shivering with the cold and the effort. Smoke and flame sparked out of a dozen cracks. Air seeped through them, feeding the fiery monster that stretched once more toward the walls. "Let me do what I can do," she pleaded as Helara stumbled backward, her eyes wild.

"Help me with him," Geram slipped through the door and hoisted the cook's shoulders, groaning as he tugged. "Help me, Helara."

"Is the house clear?" Vic asked.

"Upstairs is empty. Drak and Maynon got everyone out." Geram grunted, and the cook's bulk edged toward the door. "Shrine, he's big. Help me with him, Helara."

"My inn?"

"Vic's taking care of it. We have to go now or your cook won't make it."

Together, they dragged the man out. The fire melted. Embers dimmed. Smoke clambered along the solid air mass, hissing out of cracks. Outside, the fire brigade whistled toward the house. Charcoal billows fogged, and a cough racked Vic's throat. Her head rolled loose on her shoulders.

A trooper did what she had to. Keep fighting. Fold the sheets. Birth a baby. Smother a fire. *Keep it up,* she gritted at herself. Keep it up. Soot clouds twisted across the ceiling. Her concentration faltered, but the flames were only embers now. Sinking to the floor, the strength gone from her knees, Vic coughed out thanks to Elesendar, same as she did in battle. She was a heretic, but Helara wasn't. And the inn was safe, thank Elesendar.

THE RUSE

The paddock was half a mile from the city gates, the closest steeds would come to the noise and stinks of Mora, Joslyrn explained. "You can coax a steed into a forest, even an abattoir, but not a city." Ahead on the chalk road, a merchant train trundled west. In its wake, leatherwings squawked and dove after spilled grain, an undulating tail to a very long worm.

Ashel breathed in the scents of dust and grass, felt the sun warm upon his head, the breeze brush cool across his skin. He shared an eager smile with Melba as they approached the twelve-foot paddock wall.

"You look like a boy on Winterfest morning," she said.

"I really have wanted to see one all my life."

She grimaced. "They're just ugly giant bugs if you ask me, although I'll admit they're fast, and I'm grateful to Joslyrn and his crew."

"Oh, Minstrel Melba," the herder said, "beauty's in the eye of the beholder. There's nothing prettier than a steed, except your crooning."

She laughed. "You haven't heard Ashel yet."

Joslyrn stopped at the gate. "They like a tune, Highness. It makes them sweet on the singer." His eyes slid to Melba, who grinned and knocked elbows with Ashel. He bounced on his heels, a thrill in his blood like he hadn't felt in ages.

"Better open that gate before the prince ruins his pants."

Ignoring the ribbing, Ashel followed Joslyrn into the paddock.

Necks entwined, tentacled manes wound together, a pair of steeds wheeled to face him. Breath gushed from his lungs. Chest burning, he had to remember to suck the air back in. Multifaceted eyes glittered like jewels. Chitin segments gleamed a rich brown, like an alloy of iron and copper. He stepped closer, and narrow bodies glided back, feet drumming like piano hammers on muted strings. He'd read each steed had seven pairs of hooves, though the animals moved too fast to be sure.

"It's a smoother ride than a horse, if you don't slide off," said Joslyrn. "Saddle or no, if a steed doesn't want you on its back, you won't stay there."

"They're so lithe."

"Yep. Those are mares. Don't like to bring the stallions into town—they could bust out of this paddock, and we need them to protect the herd from lupears, especially now in foaling season. These ladies are too old for foaling, but they're still strong enough to bear two. You want to go for a ride?"

"I do." Melba was right; he was as giddy as a boy at Winterfest.

Joslyrn disappeared into a stable and emerged carrying a saddle with dangling hooks instead of a girth. The seat looked long enough to sit two comfortably. Kelmair followed with a second saddle.

Ashel gulped and averted his eyes from puckered brown aureoles crowning her small breasts.

"Shrine, that woman's a strange bird," Melba muttered. "And she's sulkier than a Weaver's apprentice. What are you so embarrassed about? You've been to Traine."

Drawing in a breath, he wiped the shock off his face. He'd spent a summer in Betheljin's capital and had become accustomed to seeing nude slaves paraded around like prize horses. That most mistresses appeared proud of their thralldom only made it more abhorrent. Yet he'd been callow enough to approach one young, red-haired mistress, standing alone during a festival, and ask her to dance. Thank Elesendar Vic had had the good sense to refuse him. He was still ashamed of himself for succumbing to selfish curiosity, when his temerity could so easily have gotten her killed.

Joslyrn had fastened saddle hooks to the carapace on one steed, but the other creature danced away from Kelmair's saddle. Clucking, she hoisted it toward the steed, but the mare slipped away, her eyes fixed on Ashel and Melba.

"They're making her nervous," Kelmair grumbled.

Joslyrn studied the steed, then tilted his head toward Ashel. "Try a bit of song, Highness."

He glanced at Melba. "Is that true, singing calms them?"

She shrugged. "Coming out here, we sang a lot, but I thought it was just to pass the time."

As if he were stepping onto a stage, he embraced the tickle in his belly and began a herder's ballad.

> *The lupear's howl fills the night,*
>
> *But not my heart.*
>
> *Its mournful cry echoes through*
>
> *This plain so empty without you.*

The mare snorted and stepped toward him. He paced closer, singing a herder's lament for his lost love, drawn into the steed's glittering gaze. She glided forward and pressed a chitinous snout to his forehead. A purr rumbled a rough echo of his song. Love poured through Ashel, a sensation as deep as it was sudden. Tears running, he caressed her thorax.

Pain jabbed, and he jumped back, sucking breath into cramped lungs while a vicious sting shot up his arm. Trilling, the steed lowered her head and butted his shoulder. Iron gray tentacles writhed, each bearing a knuckle-length lancet.

Shrine, that hurts, said Geram. Ringed with tavern noises and scents, he shook the phantom pain from his hand.

Ashel winced, recognizing the sounds and aromas—Geram was at the Cobblestone. The other man hugged Vic in greeting, and Ashel stroked the mare's snout. "It's all right, girl." His hand throbbed, but the fire had already faded from his arm. The steed purred again. He swiped at damp cheeks as love swamped him.

Joslyrn gripped his shoulder. "I felt the same—both the gush and the sting—the first time I touched a steed. This one's name is Meager, and you'll want to wear these when astride her." The old herder handed him a pair of leather gloves. The fit was snug and the fingers too short, but the hide was supple. A tug of the laces stretched them so they almost reached his wrists.

"If we're going, we should go. You're with me, Highness," Kelmair said.

Joslyrn leapt astride the other steed. "They're strong, but we shouldn't overburden them with two men when we don't have to. Melba, up behind me, if you will."

Ashel stared at the saddle. "There are no stirrups."

Lip curled, Kelmair clucked, and Meager hunkered low enough for Ashel to swing a leg over her. "You can take the front," she said. "I'll let you guide her, so long as you follow Joslyrn."

He settled into the saddle, Kelmair's torso a hot pressure on his back, her arms locked around his waist as the mare rippled to her full height.

"We don't use bridles; you let her know where you want to go with the pressure of your knees," Joslyrn said. "You sit her pretty well, I'd say."

Copying the Herder, he gripped Meager's tentacles. Spines struck but did not penetrate the gloves. Joslyrn's mount flowed out of the paddock, and Meager's segments pulsed as she glided after.

It's like riding surf, Geram said, delighted.

"Her gait truly is smoother than a horse's."

"Wait 'til you feel her run." Joslyrn hallooed, and the steeds hurtled over the flat dry plain beside the road. The wind tore Ashel's whoop away, and his laugh was left behind as the grass rolled beneath their feet. In moments the stable had shrunk to a speck. In minutes, the city was only a smudge on the horizon. They sped west, faster than a champion racehorse and far past the point where a horse would have collapsed. Ashel reveled in the way the mare wove smoothly round rocks and scrub, turning swiftly and easily according to the pressure of his knees. They rode on and on as the sun sank slowly behind them, and their shadows lengthened across the dry grass.

"How long can they keep this up?" he asked.

"A long time, and they'll run faster if need be," Kelmair said. "They're anxious to reach the herd before the lupears catch our scent."

"Then shouldn't we head back to the paddock?"

He felt her chuckle. "We're not going back, Shemen."

"What?"

"We're taking you to meet your father."

Adrenaline surging, he hauled on the tentacles. Meager squealed, and she became a bucking, writhing, sinuous snake. The hooks shook free of their moorings, and the saddle slid off. Kelmair's muffled cry thrummed through Ashel as he landed atop her on the dry grass. They tumbled apart, and the mare's drumming hoofbeats faded.

Mouth and eyes fierce slits, Kelmair rolled to her feet. "You never, ever pull on tentacles like that!"

"My father is dead!"

Her sneer returned, and she tilted her head at Joslyrn's steed, hurtling after Meager. "Once they get back here, you're going to Traine."

Wrath seized him, firing nerves and muscles into a blow that knocked her sprawling.

Dust plumed as Kelmair sprang up, dagger in hand. "Easy, Shemen, or you'll get hurt."

He charged, eyes on the blade. She ducked inside his grip, threw her arms around his in a clinch. She was small but strong, her skin slick with sweat, stretched taut over muscles hard as iron. The dagger hilt dug into his back, and he knew she might hurt him but wouldn't kill him. He was too valuable to her. To Lornk Korng. Hatred flared, and he broke free, grabbed her knife arm, and wrenched her wrist. His ears twitched as the dagger thudded in the dirt and his elbow slammed into her jaw. She staggered back, and he pursued, grabbed the back of her neck, slammed her head into his knee. She hit the grass and lay still.

Chest heaving, he retrieved her blade and stood over her. He had never fought so fiercely in his life. *That was you, wasn't it?* he asked Geram. The other man had grown up on the docks in Alna, where street scraps were as common as trees in Fembrosh.

My instincts, my skills, maybe, but it was you that used them. You should kill her.

No. Once before, Geram's instincts and his own hatred had driven Ashel to fight and kill. *What good would that do?* Mora was gone from the horizon. A lupear howled, the cry pealing across the plain beneath rosy clouds. The two steeds ran toward him, their carapaces golden in the sunset. He'd have to kill Joslyrn too, without Melba getting harmed, and hope he could control the mounts well enough to reach the paddock before night fell. A lupear whistled, and another answered. Fear roiled in his belly. Only a fool traveled the Semena plains alone in the dark. Only a dead fool. *We're safer with the Herders than on our own. Is Lornk still in prison?*

Yes—

A boom, wreathed in screams, cut off Geram's reply. Through him, Ashel Heard Vic shouting orders into chaos.

"You try that again, and I'll kill you." Kelmair sat up, her head swaying in a woozy circle.

"You can try." The howls came again, closer. Whatever was happening in Narath, he needed his attention here. "How far is it to your herd?"

She staggered to her feet. "Closer than Mora. Meager won't take you to the paddock, no matter how sweetly you croon at her." Her lips twisted into a bitter grin. "You'll come with us if you want to live."

Joslyrn's steed skidded to a halt, Meager huffing beside it. "Don't ever yank on a steed's tentacles, Highness."

Hooks clinked as Kelmair picked up the saddle. Lupears

chorused, and the steeds whickered and danced. "Give her a song and calm her down, or they'll be on us."

"Ashel," Melba asked aloud, voice quavering, "what is going on?"

"I'm sorry, Mel." Humming, he stroked Meager's thorax while Kelmair fastened the saddle. When she was done, he mounted, Kelmair's dagger still tight in his fist. "Looks like we're going to have to spend some time on the range."

Schemes in the Dark

Vic's head lolled in Geram's lap as the carriage lurched through the switchbacks up Manor Hill. Her skin felt as hot as the fire she'd smothered, her mind as silent as a dead woman's, though her breath wheezed faintly. She had disappeared into the morass of her own thoughts before, but this was different. Now, she wasn't ensnared in dark and bitter memories; she was simply gone, absent from her own body.

I left my body once too, Ashel said. He sat in the Herders' camp, a bowl of stew growing cold in his lap. His captors hadn't bothered to bind him or Melba, relying on lupears and distance to hold their prisoners.

This isn't like that either. We know too well where you went. Trying to shield Ashel from the agonies wrought by those damn gauntlets, Geram had accidentally pulled the prince's mind into his own, and now half a year later and a thousand miles apart, they shared memories, thoughts, actions.

"Can you do anything?" Maynon braced himself on the other bench as the carriage swung through a turn.

"Maybe." He focused his attention on Vic. As he had once before when she was lost to herself, he held his breath and dove into the darkness.

Sickness ripped up his throat; dizzying pain filled the cavities in his skull. His knees smacked the floorboards, and Vic tumbled into a heap beside him. He fought a surging dinner while Maynon cursed and wrestled Vic onto the other bench. On the plains,

Ashel's groans echoed his own. Geram climbed into his seat, his head throbbing like an old smuggler's.

The carriage jolted to a stop. Voices swirled outside, orders were issued, and they lurched through the Manor's gate.

"Seems you did nothing but harm yourself, Fishlicker," Maynon muttered, Vic still slack in his arms. "I owe her—" He wiped wet cheeks. "Silla almost died at the birthing. Vic did something. I dunno what, but she saved her. She better not die now."

The carriage halted again, and Drak flung open the door. As his cousin carried Vic inside, Geram used Maynon's sight to see his way through the entry hall and up the stairs. A Listener's trick, it eased life as a blind man, though it didn't assuage the bitterness of being blind. At the second landing, he stumbled and banged his shin. Grunting, Maynon grabbed his elbow, and they hustled onward to Vic's room.

Elekia swept in as Drak laid Vic on the bed. "What happened?"

"A fire, Majesty," Drak said. "She breathed in a lot of smoke."

"She's feverish," Elekia snapped. "Smoke didn't cause that."

"She put it out, Majesty," Geram said, his mindvoice faltering as the queen shot him a piercing glare. Dropping Maynon's sight, he struggled against the desire to shrink into his boots.

"Selcher," the queen said, "she's in some sort of trance."

"I tried to revive her in the carriage," Geram said, chagrined he hadn't noticed the other Listener.

"And failed," said Selcher. "Like as not used a bludgeon where a needle is required. Tell me, Lieutenant, did you hurt yourself?"

Maynon snorted, and Elekia ordered them all to wait outside. "When the Healer arrives, send him in."

In the hallway, Maynon slapped Geram's shoulder. "You've got some competition up here, eh, Fishlicker?"

"He holds his own," Drak rumbled.

Maynon's lips drew down. "Don't leave Vic alone tonight, not while she can't defend herself."

"I won't."

"I'll see you out, Maynon," Drak said as the Healer arrived and went into the bedroom. "Geram, debrief the queen. I'll talk to the housemarshal."

Geram grasped his cousin's arm. "Tell Olivet Lornk Korng is planning to escape."

"You Heard that tonight?"

"From the pirate," he said. Kelmair was a Caleisbahnin and an outlaw. Close enough to pirate, and what she'd told Ashel made it clear her people would attempt a prison break soon.

"Right. I'll tell him."

Alone, Geram paced the hallway, heart pounding.

Do not tell Mother, Ashel said, swallowing cold stew. *There's nothing she could do anyway.*

How are you getting out of this?

I'll find a way. These people aren't soldiers. They're not even proper bandits.

They caught you easily enough.

The prince gazed at the massive herd of steeds milling nearby. *They had a good lure. Do not say anything to Mother, but make sure Lornk Korng stays in prison.*

I'm telling Vic—she'll come for you, and she'll need me to find you.

Mixed desire, chagrin, and apprehension were Ashel's only response.

Elekia emerged, issuing instructions to Selcher and the Healer as she shut the door. "So, Lieutenant, I see the other chickens have fled and left you to face the fox."

"The fox, Majesty?"

She chuckled. "A predator from Ancient folklore, one particularly fond of chickens."

He bowed his head, feeling uncouth as well as chagrined that kernel of knowledge hadn't popped out of Ashel's memories. "How is Vic?"

"She'll recover. You were there?"

"I was. So was a Caleisbahnin. I believe his associates set off an explosion. It was no ordinary kitchen fire."

Silence met the news, the queen keeping her thoughts well-muffled. "Was anyone else hurt?" she asked.

"The cook, Your Majesty. He was taken to the hospice. We brought Vic here—"

"You were correct to do so. Thank you, Lieutenant."

"There's something else, Majesty. I Heard the pirate think about a plan to break Lornk Korng from prison. Drak went to inform the housemarshal."

Another long moment passed before she asked, "Did anything else happen this evening?"

He remembered Selcher just on the other side of the door, hoped she was occupied with Vic. "No, Your Majesty."

"Truly? Come." She strode down the hall. Feeling as nervous as a schoolboy, he followed, using her sight to enter a small parlor without stumbling. She settled herself in a chair, fiddled with her skirt while he waited, fists locked behind his back. When her eyes rose, her vision focused on the line of his jaw and the breadth of his shoulders. Most people's sight slid off him as easily as the kitchen table. But she *looked* at him, the tight crop of black, wiry hair, the deep brown of his skin, the bulk of his shoulders—discomfited, he let go of her vision.

"Does it feel like you're looking in a mirror when you do that?" she asked.

"No," he replied curtly, trying to hide his surprise she could tell.

"What did this Caleisbahnin want?"

"He said his sect had a job for her, and he alluded to her power in front of dozens of witnesses."

"Shrine," she muttered. "Would my son welcome her company in Mora?"

"How would I know that, Majesty?" *If Selcher knows, Mother knows*, Bethniel had said. Shrine's bitch. So much for hiding his connection to Ashel.

"You shared a prison cell with him. You must have come to know each other well."

Sorrow tinged her mindvoice, and his fingers twitched with a mad urge to clasp her hand. He cleared his throat. "Majesty, it's no secret Prince Ashel loved Vic."

"Loved? Has he changed his mind?"

"I couldn't say, Your Majesty, as I haven't seen him in several months."

"Lieutenant, you have a comfortable position on my staff. Your duties are light, your salary generous. All I ask in return is your honesty."

He knotted his fingers together. "And you've received an honest answer."

"By the letter, perhaps, but not the spirit. I'm disappointed."

As always, Ashel said, settling onto a blanket Joslyrn gave him.

"If I'm not fulfilling your expectations, Majesty, perhaps it's because I don't know my purpose here. You have a Listener already. You have guards. You have aides. What can a blind Alnan fisherman do that they can't?"

Silk rustled as Elekia stood. Her perfume coiled around Geram's throat, filling his head with freakish longing. Her breath fell warm upon his face, smelling of herbs and dark wine. Heat prickled his skin, and he thought of the mudpit in Olivet's training yard, of stinking fish in the rubbish bin, anything to purge the wild and unbidden desire running through his blood.

"Will you answer my question honestly?" she asked.

"I resign my commission," he blurted.

"You would rob your family of that generous pension I send them, in these difficult times?"

"They'll forgive the loss, Majesty. Good night." He marched to Vic's room, settling himself on the sofa. Tomorrow, he and Vic would go together to find Ashel. Tonight, he'd sit beside her and give her what protection a blind man could from schemes woven in the dark.

† † †

Sleep shattered. Like the sea under a storm, shouts and screams clashed in the hall. Springing off the sofa, Geram felt his way to the fireplace and seized the ceramic poker—the closest thing in the room to a weapon. Deeply drugged, Vic slept, insensible to the commotion.

The mayhem rolled closer, crashes and shrieks, floorboard-rattling booms. He tried to Listen, to snag someone's sight, but his perception shrank from chaos, and he stood, knees bent, fist around the poker, head cocked.

The door banged open. Geram rushed forward, reaching for his opponent's sight, but he caught nothing, as if he'd tried to capture dust motes from the air. Doubly blind, he tripped on the rug.

"It's a Kragnashian!" Drak shouted.

Sprawled in front of Vic's bed, he heard an awful clicking, loud and regular, bearing down on him. Crouching, he snagged his cousin's vision. A trooper sat astride the Kragnashian's thorax, stabbing between whipping antennae, but the dagger only skittered over the creature's armor. Massive wing covers snapped, flesh crunched, and the soldier's scream died to a gurgle as her body thumped to the floor. A mandible caught Drak's head, and Geram's sight went black.

The Kragnashian shuffled forward, its clicking steady as a clock, a thousand tendrilled legs whisking over the carpet. Geram positioned himself in the path of the noise, nose twitching round the pungent, clean scent of its blood, like mown grass or slotaen, the curative ointment the Kragnashians distilled and sold from their deceased kin. The clicking stopped, and dread echoed.

Air hissed out of trachea, and he pulled the poker back along his arm like a javelin. Screeching, the Kragnashian leapt forward, air luffing beneath its wing covers. Geram dove into the swishing legs and thrust upward. Razor-sharp spines raked his skin. The makeshift spear pierced chitin as mandibles snapped, slicing flesh to the bone. Pain seared his senses. Bright white blazed through the charcoal murk of his sight. A scream ripped his throat as a choking cloud, cloying and thick, burst forth. The Kragnashian collapsed.

"Get a Healer!" Olivet shouted, dragging him from the entangling mass of legs and chitin. There was a whipping crack, and a leather strap was cinched round Geram's thigh. "A Healer!"

A bone-deep cold enveloped him, as if he stood naked in a sea of ice. Fatigue weighed upon his limbs and chest. His eyes fell shut, and shouts, cries, and orders shrank to incoherence as he sank below the frost. A tendril of Elekia's scent infused the cold, faded, returned, and faded again.

Geram! Ashel shouted. *The prison!*

His eyes jerked open, but it was dark. A hand clasped his, and he clung to it as lethargy sucked him back under. "Korng," he murmured as torpor took him.

IRREDEEMABLE

Smoke twined from beneath the door, rolling into black fingers that knuckled the ceiling and clawed slowly down toward Wineyll. She lay still on a damp pillow, breathing slowly and deeply as the sooty clouds descended, caught in her father's last moments.

> *He lies on the bed, lips sealed, nostrils flaring and sweat beading. A moan escapes; his knees fold toward his chest, his body clenched. The spasm subsides and he collapses, panting, tears running into his ears.*
>
> *She mops his face. "Let me ask for more." More slotaen. It can't heal the illness eating his insides, but it dulls the agony.*
>
> *"No," he groans. "No. Do not abase yourself to them." Them—the Guild, the Melody and Harmony, who have twice refused to pay the apothecary.*
>
> *With great effort, he pulls the pillow out from beneath his head, handing it to her. "Another way, my love. Only you can end my pain."*

Winder had dedicated his life to the Guild he loved, and they'd paid him back by making him die in pain and disgrace. As black clouds and panicked screams curled through the crack beneath the door, she offered thanks to Elesendar. She'd be with her father soon.

She wanted to take those prayers back when Drak burst into the garret and hustled her down the stairs. Feeling robbed and thwarted, she watched with the inn's patrons as Helara and Geram dragged the cook outside, as the fire brigade arrived to find their work done for them, as Vic's friends rushed her into a hired carriage and sped away. Helara began to usher guests back to their rooms, but Wineyll drifted down the street, all sorrow and anger drained away, leaving her a husk, just a shell enclosing a dark void.

As she passed an alley, someone darted out, clapped a hand over her mouth, and yanked her into the shadows. Her pulse thumped against a blade at her throat, filling her head with a thrill that was halfway between fear and excitement. All she had to do was struggle, and this footpad would do for her what she'd done for her father.

"Don't scream, neither aloud nor silent, young miss." Beneath the command, she Heard his purpose. He was Caleisbahnin, and his orders were to bring her to the prison. Relief flowed down her spine, surprise, shame, and anticipation tumbling with it.

"Lornk Korng is going to escape tonight."

The man's sharp eyes narrowed. Silver glinted at an ear. "Keep your mind to yourself, and no tricks, or there'll be more bloodshed than need be this night."

"You don't need the dagger. I'll come quietly."

He peered at her, suspicion twisting his mouth. "No tricks."

She pushed the blade down. "Take me to him."

They stole down quiet, dark streets. The man's fingers remained clamped around her arm until they turned down a blind alley and arrived at the city's north wall, where he shoved aside an old crate. A rope ladder, hooked to the timbered wall, descended into black.

"Down you go, and quietly," he whispered.

Wineyll's freed muscles throbbed, the skin tender over blooming bruises. Now was her chance to vanish from the pirate's perception, escape down the alley and warn the city guard the Caleisbahnin planned to free Lornk Korng tonight. She *could* escape and prove herself loyal to Latha, show herself a hero. But she wasn't one. Ashel had lost his fingers because she'd failed to bring Vic to heel, and at the nexus of her dark void was the part of Vic that had once been Lornk's slave. Wineyll had used that submissive girl when she tried to capture Vic's mind and restrain it to Lornk's will, and now she carried the thrall's mad desire to yield to the hunger in his eyes again.

"Go on now," the pirate pushed her toward the opening.

Cheeks hot with the shameful desire to see the Relmlord again, she climbed down the ladder.

Narrow and short, the tunnel must have been dug in a hurry. Clods cascaded, smacking her head and shoulders as she wormed beneath the city wall and emerged in a hedge of hoarsgrout. The pirate climbed out after her, kicked dirt and leaves over the opening. His fingers locked round her arm again, they clambered over roots and rocks through the woods, turning onto the prison road once they were out of sight of the wall.

Elesendar's meager flicker guided their footsteps. Was that tiny sparkling orb, which crossed the sky twice or thrice a night, a god or a spacecraft? Wineyll believed it—He—was a god. But the Father wasn't a doting one, not to her. She felt His judgment press upon her neck, a finger of dim light digging into her spine. His light was supposed to shepherd you on your path through life, but around her, forest shadows yawned like graves.

The trees ended, but the road continued across a field to a pair of gates set in fortified walls. Her captor stopped beside the last curtain of cerrenil limbs. "We wait here."

Branches limp as hair knocked softly together. Wineyll crept into the folds of the old mother's trunk and peered through her leafy hair at the meandering star—god or spacecraft, He was indifferent. She pressed her check against white bark and prayed for comfort and calm. Why, when she thought of the former Relmlord, did she remember his caresses more than his cruelties? Whatever he wanted now, she should refuse. A hero would refuse, just as Ashel had in Olmlablaire. But she was no hero.

The pirate's shoulders snapped straight, and men flooded out of the forest. Forming ranks, they trotted across the clearing, feet silent on the grass, swords hissing out of scabbards.

Shouting, banging, creaking drifted from the prison walls.

"Captain." Her captor saluted a new arrival and joined the men advancing on the prison.

The newcomer hoisted Wineyll to her feet. "The view will be better if you stand."

Arrows rained from ramparts. Caleisbahnin fell one after another until bodies littered the clearing, but other pirates hunkered under shields and flooded right up to the stone. Grappling hooks whistled in rapid circles, whooshed as they flew toward ramparts, clinked and grated as they caught stone. Men scurried up as nimbly as insects, but the defenders tossed down hooks and ropes faster than anyone could scale the wall.

"Looks doomed to fail, doesn't it?" the captain asked. "But just you watch, miss."

Staccato clicks snapped, and a Kragnashian charged out of the woods. Arrows flew, bounced off chitin. The warrior barreled up to the gate and flowed over it, disappearing inside. Moments later it appeared atop the wall, and guards flailed off the ramparts. Lines flew once more, hooked over crenellations, and the pirates swarmed up the edifice. Shouts and screams echoed. The portcullis groaned upward, and the rest of the attackers rushed inside.

Shrieks wove a bloody tapestry, and many long minutes passed before the last scream died. A man waved from the open gate. Surrounded by seamen, Wineyll followed the officer as they picked their way through the bodies. A few pirates roamed the field, checking their fallen brethren. Whenever they found a man alive but unable to rise, they kissed his forehead and sliced his throat.

In the prison, bodies were scattered across the yard, limbs torn off, heads smashed like crockery, packed dirt muddied with red. The Kragnashian slurped loudly at a bundle of its legs, its blood scenting the air with a pungent spring that covered the human stinks like lye over the charnel pit. Horror welling, Wineyll choked and swallowed, remembering carnage worse than this. In the nomad village, the stench of children's burnt flesh had been worse.

A gap-toothed officer approached and pressed a fist to his shoulder. "All clear, Captain."

"Thank you, Commander. Have you found him?"

"There, sir."

Men emerged from the prison building. Lornk's hair was a smudged beacon over the dark heads around him. Wincing, Wineyll shrunk back. A matted beard beneath bruised and swollen eyes, his shoulders and knees bent, he scraped weary feet across the ground. The captain spat and shook his head, but he knelt as Lornk halted. "I am at your service, Citizen."

Swaying, Lornk scanned the yard. His eyes passed over Wineyll, moved across the pirates surrounding him, then met her own again. "Well done, Captain."

"Done we're not, not yet, Citizen. The guards knew we were coming; we must be away."

Standing straighter, the former Relmlord resumed the air of nonchalance and mastery Wineyll remembered. A hand on the back of her neck, he tugged her close. He stank of the dungeon, but beneath the filth was a scent she could get drunk on. "Are you glad to see me, Songbird?" he whispered.

Cursing the warmth of his fingers, she nodded.

REPETITIONS

Light pried at Vic's eyelids, and she rolled over, away from the dawn, snuggling down under warm blankets and the soft pillow cupping her face. Fine linen—the weave silky smooth—caressed her cheek, urging her back to sleep yet pricking her awareness that she wasn't in her bed at the Cobblestone. The sheets were not so soft there. Bleary eyes blinked open, took in a lamp shaded with glass flowers. She was at the Manor.

A temple free of ache, a stomach devoid of nausea meant Elekia had shared her Woern again, but heavy muscles told of soporific medicines. Groggy, she swung her legs out of bed and stumbled against the bedside table, rocking the lamp. "Shrine, don't break it." She settled the lamp, looked up, and snapped awake. What medicines *had* the healers given her, that she'd slept through this? Red-brown gore splattered the walls. Gooey green and brown smeared the carpet, obscuring the weave depicting a battle between humans and Kragnashians in the jungles of old Direiellene. She knew that land as a desert wasteland, but a thousand years ago it had been a thick rainforest where the Wizards Council had fought a sorceress named Meylnara and her Kragnashian minions. With all the blood, it looked as if the figures had sprung out of the rug's warp and weft to savage each other.

An attack here inside the Manor, and the Cobblestone set ablaze. Heart thudding, she rushed to a window—and sighed in relief. No smoke or other signs of strife marred the pale sky.

Undisturbed, Kiareinoll Fembrosh flowed down Manor Hill, a leafy channel between Manor and city. The sun broke over the Lathalorns, and the giant crystal atop the Senate flared to life, refracting light into a rainbow. In the garden, a cerrenil shivered with dawn's first touch. Leaves unfurled in sunbeams, and one by one, the old mother's limbs rose to meet the light.

There was a knock, and Elekia barged in. "I'm glad you're up." She shut the door. "The Relmlord escaped last night."

"What?"

"At least one Kragnashian and several hundred Caleisbahnin assaulted the prison and broke him out. They killed everyone, guards and prisoners."

Vic sank to her knees and pressed her palms into the bloodied carpet. Within her, a girl hardly grown gibbered in fear as if Lornk would spring out of the closet and drag her off. But the wizard and the warrior took a deep breath and looked at the queen. "They went west?"

"Olivet has teams in pursuit. I need you to find Ashel." A sound cracked out of the queen, laugh or cry Vic couldn't tell. Her foster mother slid to the floor. Dried blood rimmed Elekia's nails, dark circles her eyes. "I need you to find Ashel *again*."

"Why?" Vic asked, dread seizing her breath. Geram had said he was in trouble last night, right before the commotion began.

Elekia's eyes and mouth pinched, then collapsed into a composed mask. "You may stop pretending you don't know Ashel and Lieutenant Geram are . . . connected. Selcher has Heard them speaking to each other, and last night she Heard them talking about some sort of jeopardy Ashel had found himself in, but she couldn't discern the details."

Vic's eyes darted between the blood staining Elekia's fingers to the rust-splattered walls. Her heart quailed. "And there's a reason you can't ask Geram?"

The queen's mask twisted into anguish, her palm muffling a sob. She blew her nose and hid her face in a handkerchief. Vic patted her shoulder, feeling helpless and baffled. Elekia's haughty serenity almost never broke, and Vic had no idea what to do or say. Awkwardly, trying to copy what Beth would do, she put an arm around the queen.

"I'm sorry." Elekia shrugged out of the embrace. "I'm not myself." She pinched the bridge of her nose, breathing deeply, and composed herself. "We know this much: your inn was set on fire, probably to force you to come here for the night. At least two Kragnashians came through the Device. One or more assaulted the prison, with support from the Caleisbahnin, freeing Lornk Korng and killing everyone else. The other came to this room, to kill you or take you, we do not know. Geram was severely wounded defending you. Which brings us to the last piece of the puzzle: something happened to Ashel, but we don't know what, and the lieutenant won't be able to tell us for some time, if at all. I need you to go to Mora and find out what happened."

Heat prickled Vic's skin, a mixture of dread and longing. Rising, she found some trousers and tugged them on. "I should go after Lornk."

"No."

"Majesty, I can find him and bring him back in a day's time."

Elekia's fists balled. "Four guards died and three were wounded last night, keeping you safe from a Kragnashian. I will not have you waltz into the clutches of another."

"And how many troopers will die recapturing Lornk?"

"The answer would be none if you'd killed him in Olmlablaire!"

Blood pounding up her throat, Vic glared at the queen. "He deserves to rot at Mirkeldirk. Killing him was too quick a death."

Elekia's glower softened. "Vic, the Kragnashians' purpose in freeing Lornk may have been to lure you into a trap. A backup plan, in case their attack here failed."

"Why would they do that?"

"I don't know, except they have an uncanny interest in you. I made a bargain with them long ago, and part of the price I paid was to give them news of anyone I met named Victoria of Ourtown."

Fury sparked. "So you did sell me to them?"

"No! It was your idea to go through Kragnash to reach Olmlablaire. But I thought they might make you take the Elixir if you went there."

The Elixir, another name for the Waters of the Dead. "And why didn't you warn me?"

Elekia sighed. "Because the Center assured me they'd leave you alone. I hoped it would keep that promise, even as I expected it wouldn't, and it didn't, because here you are, a wizard, just like your namesake." She waved at a pair of blood-soaked figures in the carpet, flinging woolen lightning at each other. "The Kragnashians first asked me about you when Ashel was in my womb, years before you were born. They asked me again and again over the years, as if they expected another Victoria of Ourtown to appear. When you did turn up in our throne room, alone and desperate for asylum, Sashal and I were terrified for ourselves and for you. We vowed, the two of us, to keep you close because we didn't know what your arrival meant." Tears streamed again, and Elekia let them run. "I'd never say so publicly, but like you, I am a heretic. Elesendar is nothing more than a vacant hulk of a spacecraft. I do not believe in prophesy or portents—yet here you are, Victoria of Ourtown, also known as the One. And here I remain terrified for you, for myself, and for this nation. I do not know why the Kragnashians are obsessed with an orphan Oreseeker, so I want you as far away from Kragnash and their infernal Devices as I can send you."

She took Vic's face between her hands. "Ashel was in my womb when I took the Elixir. Bethniel or I, we can help you survive. With Ashel, you can *live*. Go to Mora. Find my son. Help him out of whatever mess he's in, and this time, don't let him go." A smile caught one corner of her mouth. "Wizardry isn't outlawed in Semeneminieu."

A sob clogged Vic's throat. "I abandoned him! I found him the day before Lornk butchered his hand. I could have saved him then, but I panicked and fled because Lornk was there and—" she gasped for breath. The mingled hatred and desire she once felt for Lornk Korng had been subsumed by shame for that moment of cowardice, but the feeling was just as intense. "Ashel lost his fingers because I failed him. I cannot have either his forgiveness or his love, not after that."

She expected to see wrath and hatred written on Elekia's face, but she saw only inscrutable dark eyes above smooth, dry cheeks.

"Isn't that for Ashel to decide?" her foster mother asked.

"No."

Elekia grasped Vic's chin, and she fought the urge to shrink away.

"Consider your commission reactivated, Marshal. Now go find my son."

† † †

Geram lay in a room near the kitchen, drugged senseless by Healers. Drak looked up from clasped hands and saluted when he saw Vic's uniform. "Marshal. You going after Korng?"

She frowned at the red-stained bandage wrapping the captain's head. "The queen's sending me on a different mission. How is Geram?"

"That monster nearly cut his leg off. They said the bone's not broken, but it's cracked, and the flesh around it . . . It took the Healers a long time to stitch it all back together. The Ruler helped." His shoulders hunched. "They said she kept his heart beating. Didn't know you could do that."

She shrugged and slipped her hand into Geram's. His breath wheezed, his features pained even as he slept. "I'm glad she could. Thank you both for saving me. Again."

"Spears," he muttered. "Spears, Vic. Pikes with great long blades and thicker hafts. That's what we need to fight those things. Our daggers couldn't penetrate the shell, and it snapped our regular pikes like kindling. Geram got underneath it—that's how he killed it, and how it almost killed him."

"How did they get through the Device? Wasn't it locked?"

"Olivet said there's a master Device in Direiellene."

Her breath gushed. "That means—"

"They could waltz into the throne room any time they please. The Ruler has tripled the guards and ordered the doors barred from the outside."

"Shrine, even during the war there were never more than two guards in that room, unless the Ruler was holding Audience."

"No Kragnashian had ever come through. When something's never happened before, people think it never will."

Geram mumbled something.

Vic squeezed his hand as garbled whispers slipped past his lips. It was odd that he spoke aloud, as if it were important. "What did he say?"

Drak's frown deepened. "He keeps saying 'surf' and 'herder.' In Alna, for a lark we'd paddle planks into the surf and ride the waves back to shore. Geram was pretty good at it. And there's a sort of fish we call a herder, which drives other fish into shoals. Some fishermen keep and train them. Maybe Uncle Arnan had some."

Vic kissed Geram's forehead, hoping he drifted through happy memories. "My dear friend," she whispered, her lips at his ear. "When you wake, tell Ashel I'll find him."

KIAREINOLL FEMBROSH

A strange giddiness skipped alongside Vic as the road wound east through the Kiareinoll. Worry for Ashel shadowed her steps, but each footfall took her closer to a second chance. Despite all the ways she'd failed him, her heart thudded in anticipation of his dark eyes and the smile that would light them up. Whatever his trouble, they'd settle it, and then they could start over. She had the means now. When she had stopped by the Cobblestone to say goodbye, Helara had surprised her with a Guildbond.

> *"That should buy you a good-sized house."*
> Her eyes widen. *"I've only been your apprentice for a few months!"*
> Helara winks. *"Innkeeping isn't magic. Keep the sheets clean, the tankards filled, and the books straight, and you'll do fine."*

With the bond, she could buy an inn and a life. With Ashel. Anxious to reach Mora and find him, she searched the road for travelers. It was empty. Her feet left the ground. Warmth spread through her blood. Eyelids fluttered; her tongue kissed the edges of her teeth. The sweet decay of humus, the sharp tang of cerrenil flowers filled her lungs. The hues of the sky deepened, like a summer ocean overhead, and she rose above the canopy. A blue-green sea spread before her. Butterflies flitted among leaves and blossoms. The wind whispered a music of leaves, drummers, and gizzards. She felt alive, and she wanted a *life*. She shot forward, skimming treetops. Roosting birds squawked out of hidden nests, and her laughter whirled among the leaves in her wake.

The miles fell swiftly behind. She flew until a temple throbbed, walked until the pain eased, then flew again, straight across the expanse of Fembrosh, reveling in the unhindered use of her power and the speed it gave her. On the third day, a fiery dawn revealed the distant edge of the Kiareinoll and the yellow grasslands beyond. At this pace, she'd arrive in Mora in another day, two at most. A bank of storm clouds rolled toward her from the plains, but the Woern thrilled through her nerves, and she flew straight into the iron-colored mist. Thunder boomed, and lightning branded white shadows into her vision. Wind bailed rain. Clothing clammed to her shoulders, but the hairs on her arms stood straight and her cells brimmed with elation.

That the source of her power was an infection, not some mystical empowerment, reinforced everything she'd learned as a child. Humans had not emerged from an absurd union between a god and his harem of *trees*, but from the spacecraft *Elesendar*, the name nothing more than shorthand for the ship's registry. Their arrival here the result of sabotage, the marooned Ancients had regarded their future with despair. Over time, the machines they brought from the spacecraft broke down and couldn't be repaired. The technology disappeared. But the words—*quantum mechanics, micromolecular manipulation*—remained. In her youth as a Logkeeper, Vic had memorized them in hundreds of documents— her purpose to preserve them, not to understand them. As she rose now through the cold, blinding mist, electricity crackled around her. *Quantum mechanics, micromolecular manipulation.* Now she understood the words' magic, if not their meaning.

Bursting into the sunlight, she sailed through a shifting maze of charcoal-colored hulks. It was cold as death, and each silver claw that jagged out of a thunderhead jolted pleasure through her flesh. Thunder shattered her eardrums, but the sizzle down her spine numbed the pain. She flew all day, fed by the storm, delighting in the electric thrill. Only when the sun slipped below the easternmost clouds did she descend to the forest floor. Suffused with bliss, she curled beneath a cerrenil and sank into oblivion.

A sledgehammer inside her skull woke her, and an evil brew bubbled out of her belly and spewed onto the moss. Wan daylight dribbled through the canopy; rain cascaded through sagging cerrenil limbs. She needed a dry place to rest until the pounding faded from her temple. Shivering in sodden garments, she stumbled through the trees, gathering fallen limbs and hoin fronds. A heaving stomach doubled her over; firewood tumbled across roots and grass. Panting, shaking, she erected her tent and piled branches over soggy kindling. Sparks from her tinder box fizzled in the soaked moss. Steeling herself, she drew upon the Woern. Pain seared her temples, and she fell back onto a cold, wet blanket.

The hammer blows to her temple held her stranded, and for a week, every drip through the waterlogged shelter saturated her heart with dread. Ashel was in trouble, possibly in danger. She needed to *go* to him. But all she could do was shiver and moan while the long, dull, lonely hours stoked her longing. She didn't love him, but she loved his world of learned people who stayed up until dawn, banging fists on tables, pointing fingers, raising voices while they argued over minutia. Those debates were ridiculous and wonderful, and she loved how every evening ended with fond farewells, no matter how heated the arguments. She loved how he could make her giggle like a nitwit and how with him, she never felt foolish, even when acting the fool. She loved that he easily trounced her when they played chess or stones. She loved the tingle that raced to her heart when his fingers laced through hers, and when their lips met in a kiss . . .

That's just the Woern. Shrinejumping parasites! An infection of the nervous system—the source of her power and her desire for a man she'd betrayed and abandoned.

You don't love him, dammit. But she wanted him, and he needed her, and she was stuck in the mud because she'd thoughtlessly indulged in the transient pleasure conferred by the same parasite that drove her desire for him, and which would kill her sooner than later. The *Elesendar* was just an old abandoned spacecraft, but she prayed to it or fate or sheer damn luck that Ashel's trouble wouldn't bring him to harm before she could find him. For a week, in the rain, that was all she could do.

At last the throbbing in her temples receded, and she climbed a nearby promontory to get her bearings. Greens and blues carpeted the land in every direction. Dundlehead! She'd lost herself in the bloody storm and let it push her west, back into the middle of the Kiareinoll. She'd been almost to the edge of Fembrosh, and now she was hundreds of miles deep in its wilds. On foot, it would take a month to reach the forest edge. "A month!" she screamed aloud. A flock of warblers burst from a nearby tree, squawking and scolding, but that was the only answer to her frustration.

Trek east. That was all she could do. She slogged through soaked humus, clawed up slippery hillsides, slid down gullies into swollen streams. Her longing for dry feet rivaled her desire to find Ashel safe and sound, but the empty hulk circling the planet did absolutely nothing to stop the rain. Or fill her belly as one day flooded into another. Her provisions gone, she scrounged roots and sour green berries, hunted lizards and birds with her sling. Every attempt to use wizardry—for flight, fire, or forage—knocked her into the bush, retching up what little there was in her belly, so she relied on woodcraft as the weeks wore on.

And a little thievery. Wild cats prowled the forest, leaving well-stocked prey caches in sheltered hollows. The harrier she snagged was well worth a few red, angry scratches from wet, angry cats. After securing her prize and throwing off her spitting rivals, she climbed a tree to escape the muck, settled into the crook of a branch, and cracked the arthropod's shell. Her fingers dug into sweet, buttery flesh, and she sighed with pleasure as the first mouthful slid down her throat. Harriers were damn good eating. Hard to hunt, though. A clutch of the buggers could strip your flesh from your skeleton faster than you could scream—Vic had to admire the cats for finding a way to catch and kill even one.

A nearby patch of hoarsgrout stirred, and the bugs streamed across the rocks and shot into another hedge, squeals echoing over scrabbling claws. A whole pride of wild cats couldn't stampede that many harriers. Ears sharp for lupears, Vic pulled herself onto a higher branch, putting a screen of leaves between herself and the ground. Knownearth's deadliest predator mostly ranged the Semena plains, but a few packs hunted in Fembrosh. She'd never encountered a lupear and certainly didn't wish to meet one alone. Not without wizardry.

The brush rustled. Her pulse quickened. A Kragnashian's triangular head pushed out of the hedge, and her breath stopped. Tattooed mandibles clacked together; a harrier-stuffed net hung over a gleaming carapace. The creature cocked its head, antennae pinwheeling as it stopped beneath her tree. Raindrops splashed between bulbous, multifaceted eyes. She blanked her mind, just as she would in an enemy's camp. Her lungs burned as she held her breath for a minute, then two.

A squeal pierced the air; the Kragnashian's antennae snapped toward a scrabble of claws, and it dove into the woods. There was a clipped scream and then only the pattering rain.

Drawing in a deep, shuddering breath, Vic waited several dozen heartbeats before she climbed cautiously down. A Kragnashian in eastern Latha. A Kragnashian crossing *her* path in all the thousands of square miles of the Kiareinoll. A hint of spice and tease of citrus flared her nostrils, drawing her toward a cerrenil's flower-laden branches. During the war, she'd become so used to the Kia that she often forgot the forest sometimes altered the terrain, bringing parties together or separating them. The changes were usually too subtle to be noticed, but she'd found enough impassible hedges suddenly blocking familiar paths to know the Kia was real. The heretical question wasn't whether the Kia existed, but why and how it came to be.

And why it always helped her. Crouching, she found a harrier's wing cover and two of its spindly legs snagged in tangled roots. A lure for the Kragnashian, to reveal it to her, then draw it away.

"Thank you, Mother," she breathed, hand firm on the white trunk.

But was the Kragnashian hunting more than a meal? Was it hunting her or merely escorting Lornk and the Caleisbahnin into the east? What ploy could have brought his party out here instead of west toward an escape by sea?

Ashel's in trouble.

Elesendar.

"That wasn't for you, my dear," Lornk had said when she found them in Olmblablaire, with Ashel's severed fingers on the floor. Insight knocked her to her knees. Lornk's obsessions extended beyond her to Ashel's family. Sashal and Lornk had been friends, good friends, before a falling out had led to a decades-long war and Lornk's vengeance, painted in Ashel's blood, at the end of it.

Pressing her palm onto the cerrenil's cold, white bark, she called to the Kia for help. "I cannot let him hurt Ashel again. Please, Mother, show me the way to save him."

Leaves shivered, shaking water into her face. She swiped the drops out of her eyes, and there was a path, sandy and free of roots and leaves, arrowing away into Fembrosh.

STEEDFAST

Hooves struck the earth like hammers, and the rumbling seemed to shake the sky. Up ahead, two stallions broke from the tight-packed herd, one chasing the other, heads to the ground, snaky manes standing on end, mandibles clacking. Segmented carapaces rippled as the combatants surged over the grass, drumming a martial cadence. Gray swept from charcoal to sienna as the stallions rounded on each other, and the mares and foals ebbed away.

Amid the herd, a youth named Febbin whooped and leapt from steed to steed. He sprang onto his hands, feet kicking for balance, his face inches from writhing tentacles, laughing and hooting while the steeds hurtled across the grass.

Wincing at his own welt-riddled wrists, Ashel patted Meager's thorax. The mare tossed her head and crooned, segments rippling smoothly as they ran in a smaller pack comprised of the outlaws' mounts. They had roamed the plains for weeks, time Ashel had spent honing his riding skills. Escape wasn't yet a possibility. Meager responded eagerly to his commands when they were running with the band, but she refused to stray out of sight of her sisters.

In the main herd, Febbin flipped onto a stallion and cantered across the grass to join his fellows. "Minstrel Melba! Did you see?"

Hands locked around Ashel's waist, Melba faced away from the boy and pressed a cheek into Ashel's shoulder.

"She's worried you'll break your neck," Ashel teased.

"Aw, I've never fallen once."

Melba refused to answer. Squeezing Meager's thorax with his knees, Ashel tugged gently on her mane, and she slowed to a walk. The herd cantered on, leaving a wake of shaking ground and trampled grass. As their thunder faded, he said, "I thought we agreed we'd stay friendly."

"We've been out here for weeks, acting as if we're on a lark instead of waiting for some sort of . . . of slavers or pirates or worse to come for you, and when they do, it'll be on my head."

"It's not your fault, Mel."

"It is. If I hadn't met Joslyrn and asked him to bring me out here . . . and poor Wineyll. Elesendar only knows what's become of her. I could have stayed in Narath and helped her out, but no, I had to try to start a revolution within the bloody Guild."

"It's not your fault." Meager lowered her head to graze, tentacles calming as her mandibles swung through a patch of orange wildflowers. She kept an eye on the herd, though, and she'd bolt if they passed out of sight. They didn't have long to talk. Ashel bent his thumb into his empty palm. "This isn't your doing, Mel. It's Lornk Korng's."

"How? He's in prison."

"I believe he's escaped." In Narath, Geram sat in the throne room, bandaged leg throbbing and itching, Listening while a prison guard confessed before a jury to carrying letters for Lornk. Two other guards implicated in the escape were being tried posthumously, since they'd died during the Caleisbahn assault.

"What makes you think that?"

"Kelmair said they were taking me to him."

"Why?"

He expelled a breath. "He told me he was my father."

Her arms dropped from his waist. "Lornk Korng is your father?"

"He claims to be."

She smacked him on the shoulder. "Why didn't you tell me?"

"What?"

Smacking him again, Melba slid off the steed's abdomen, tripped, and plopped backward into a nettle patch. "We've been stuck out here for weeks, and you didn't tell me?"

Stunned, he watched her climb to her feet and yank stickers from the seat of her trousers. Her scowl could light a fire. "I'm telling you now. What are you so angry about? I'm the one with a maniacal tyrant after me."

"I gave up everything to come out here and bring you back to Narath, and you let me think this whole awful situation was my fault!"

"What do you mean, you gave up everything?"

Throwing back her head, Melba howled aloud. "Typical! You have no idea of anything beyond your own damn nose. I left the Guild because of you, dammit."

"What do you mean, left it?"

"I told off Reyendal before I left, and I've probably been expelled by now. Silnauer is getting rid of anyone who won't support her. You were the only person she couldn't dismiss, the only one who could stand up to her."

"I'm sorry, Melba. I have bigger problems."

"Which I would have known if you'd bloody told me! Did you tell that heretic assassin whore?"

Ire crackled through his blood. "Do not call her that."

"Is that why she turned you down, Ashel? Because she cared more about him than you?"

Hoofbeats rolled behind them. Joslyrn's steed whickered, kicking up dust as it stopped. The outlaw raised his eyebrows and angled his head back toward the herd.

"She wants to ride with you," Ashel said, kicking Meager's flanks. As the mare flew back to her sisters, he wrestled with doubt and disappointment and deep desire—everything he felt for Vic, and all of it wrapped up in resentment. The missing fingers ached, and he cursed himself. He hated this bitterness and hated himself for feeling it, and yet he couldn't help but wonder if her latest refusal—to come with him to Mora—was motivated by disinterest rather than guilt. *"You deserve better."* Shrine, that's what people said to end things gently.

More than a month had passed since the attack on the Manor, and Geram figured Vic should be in Mora by now. Ashel had been mad with worry until Geram regained lucidity and apprised him of Lornk's escape and Vic's mission. If by some miracle she found him and Melba and rescued them, what would happen afterward? What did he want to happen? He didn't know—all those times he'd offered himself only to be refused. How much humiliation could a man take? The ache in his missing fingers should be answer enough, but those same ghostly digits clung to a hope that haunted him more than all his regrets put together.

That evening, Elesendar came up in lavender fringed in amber clouds. A stew steamed around the cookspoon, and as the sun sank slowly into the grass, scents of herbs and charcoal sweet as summer curled through the camp. Men and women lounged on the grass, diced over a board, tossed stones at a stake. Erik, the crew chief, sucked from a flask of harlolinde and conferred over a map with Joslyrn and Kelmair.

Melba sat apart, plucking at a borrowed guitar. Tamping down the vestiges of his ire, Ashel brought her a dish of stew. "A peace offering." He settled beside her. "We should be in the Kiareinoll tomorrow or the next day, by my guess."

"Do you think Lornk Korng truly managed to escape?"

Ashel ground severed knuckles into his thigh, massaging a shadow of Geram's wound. Their connection was another secret he'd kept from Melba. With her mundane worries over Guild politics, she'd shrink away if he revealed the festering wounds still inside him. "If anyone could escape from the prison outside Narath, it would be him."

They swallowed a few spoonfuls of stew. Laughter drifted across the campfire. "We should do something together tonight," he said. Most nights, he and Melba had performed for the outlaws as part of their campaign to build sympathy and trust.

"Like what?"

"'Forge on the Council.'" Melba's favorite lay had everything the bandits loved—adventure, romance, fighting, treachery. Too many voices for two minstrels alone, but they'd once done a comedic production with just the pair of them, where Ashel had taken the women's parts, she the men's.

A corner of her mouth tilted upward. "It's been years, Ashel. We haven't rehearsed."

"When did that ever stop us? We'll muddle through well enough for this audience."

Her eyes glinted dangerously. "You're completely aggravating when you're trying to apologize. Let me warm them up first."

When everyone had settled round the fire, Melba took the guitar and stepped into the wavering light. The shadows rolled across her face, making her young, old, angry, sad. Her lips tilted mischievously, and she raised an eyebrow. Guffaws echoed through the outlaws, and Ashel leaned on an elbow. Melba's contralto seeped into the bones like a warm spring as she roamed the circle, speaking about Fembrosh, its hidden groves, its secret powers, the legends of how the trees birthed humanity, and in the wizards' time, humanity repaid their mothers by endowing the forest with *knowing*.

Kelmair settled onto folded legs beside Ashel. One finger pointed at his maimed hand, her eyes mere slits. "A harsh thing, Shemen."

> *Whither she wanders the Relmans will know,*
> *She laughs in their noses and offers them crow.*

"The Exploits of the Blade"—a raunchy tribute to Vic. Melba tossed him a wink, her lips wicked.

The Dagger is tricky, sneaky, and sly
And the Blade is as sharp as a harrier's cry.

The outlaws whooped. Blood throbbed through Ashel's neck, flooding in the same fury he'd fought for months. His stump butted his forehead. Vic could have saved him from the disgrace and the bitterness and the mockery in this song, and she hadn't. Melba caught his glare and missed a chord.

"A harsh thing, Shemen," Kelmair repeated, unfolding her legs.

Rising, he poured his rage at Vic, at Melba, at the damn plain and the outlaws and bloody Lornk Korng onto the pirate. Her gaze fell to their boots.

As Melba's last note faded, the bandits leapt up, hollering their approval.

Ashel stepped into the circle. "That hurt," he whispered.

Melba's shoulders tightened, but she held her stage smile, crying, "The sorcerer Meylnara would not obey the laws of the Council, and so to compel her, the Council brought a great army to Meylnara's lands, in Direiellene."

Ashel shook a tambourine, trying to expunge his anger. Melba walked around the circle, telling of the exodus of wizards and troops to the southern rainforests, bending low to portray the toil of the journey, standing on tiptoe to show the height of the trees. Ashel banged the heel of his maimed hand against the skin, rattling the drerwood disks around the rim. They could not take this from him, he reminded himself. Not Melba, not the Guild, not these outlaws, not Vic. He had his voice and would always have music, if nothing else.

Shoulders bent into the shape of a crone, he ambled around the fire while Melba plucked out an arpeggio. He took breath to sing, and at the first falsetto note, the outlaws roared with laughter.

I'll not abide,
I'll not abide,

Their laws are not for me.

To abide, I would lose myself.

I'll not abide.

Simple enough lyrics, but the coloratura melody rose and fell rapidly round a highly ornamented musical line. Even as a child, he could never hit all the high notes; now he deliberately strained for them, and more gales erupted round the circle. Strumming the guitar, Melba answered him, her voice a hoarse, false bass.

Meylnara, you are condemned by the Council

For crimes beyond measure.

You still refuse to abide?

His fists on his hips, with a toss of his head he sang his refusal, and Melba gave the reply:

Then the Council orders you submit to our judgment.

Justice calls for your death!

On cue, the outlaws mocked a gasp. He and Melba took turns introducing themselves as this and that wizard, then sang the narrative chorus together. Meylnara lived in a fortified castle built by her Kragnashian slaves. Beating the tambourine, he marched with Melba toward the siege, then sang of their first attack, the speedy defeat. Six measures into the soldier's dirge, Melba grabbed her chest and fell into the dust, gasped a death rattle, then popped up to choke out another verse. Ashel kneeled beside her, singing a widow's grief; Melba elbowed him out of the way so she could repeat the chorus. The rustlers roared as Ashel thrust her back and held her squirming on the ground until the widow's song was over.

When he let her up, she pinched the back of his hand, her

eyes piercing. He gave her a tight grin, belted out his next solo, the first of six weaving melodies in which the Council wizards dueled, plotted, formed and broke liaisons. Halfway through the system, Melba took up Saelbeneth's part. Written for a contralto of Melba's range, it was the only operatic role she'd ever played. Why she switched to the women's roles he couldn't guess, but the only response was to sing Thabean's part of the duet.

Dropping out of falsetto into baritone was like coming home. Thabean wanted to attack Meylnara directly, the twelve Council wizards alone against her, no troops or Kragnashians. Wrapping his counterpoint around Melba's melody, Ashel tied the herders up in rapture. He knew very well the power of his voice, relished the chortles dying into silence, the cultivated boredom falling from Kelmair's face. Thabean's argument swelled with contrition, contracted with spite, broadened again with his commitment to the Council's cause. Filled with asides, throbbing bass lines, grand melodrama, the descant rolled out of him, broad, complex currents like a river, the joy of the stage suffusing his blood, pushing everything aside. Here, under the stars before a flaring campfire, his stomach taut with sustained breath, Ashel longed for the lamps and spots of the stage. His parents, his sister, Vic, Lornk—all their ambitions for him drowned in the flood of music.

Taking his hands, Melba slid out of "Forge On" and into the final verse of "Wizard's Last Embrace."

In the sun, the flowers unbend,
Their light opening toward the dawn.
So my life has opened up to you,
But the sun must set, or the flowers die;
Too much of life leads to death.

This song was about the doomed love between Thabean and Victoria, his protégé. But it was also about forgiveness. While he stared at her, she repeated the last line, her fingers pressing into his hands an urgent message, her eyes shimmering with fought tears. His anger melted, and he offered the reply.

> *Forgiveness is the dream of those who love,*
> *And so I forgive you and the man you loved before me.*
> *But fate remains unforgiven*
> *For bringing you to me, too late for either life.*

With a squeeze, Melba released him and delivered the story of Thabean's death, chanting the stanza from Elberon's epic about the Council. Outlaws brushed their cheeks, laughter forgotten but not one of them lost. In unity solid as a practiced duo, he and Melba rolled into the finale of "Forge," and the final battle that destroyed Direiellene's rainforest and left a desert in its place. The herders gave them a standing ovation, and they took their bows, Ashel's face and hands warm, alive.

As the applause tailed off, he followed Melba outside the circle. They settled onto prickly grass and watched Elesendar paint plains and steeds an iron gray. Far off, a lupear howled, mournful and hungry. A cloud sailed across the sky, a blot on the glittering carpet of stars.

"Hasn't she hurt you enough?" Melba asked.

His missing fingers ached. "Not having her hurts more."

Lips sour, she yanked out a tuft of grass and tossed the blades into the wind. "I know, Ashel. Too well."

A herder sawed on a squeezebox, and the others belted out a raucous song. Ashel leaned close. "Once we're in Fembrosh, we'll make a break for the outpost on the Mora road. They can't take the whole herd into the forest, so I expect it will be Kelmair, Febbin, and just a few others. It'll be our best chance."

"Febbin? He's just a boy."

"He's just a boy who can make a steed do anything he wants it to. Steeds don't like wooded areas where predators can sneak up on them. Febbin commands the trust of these animals more than Joslyrn or any of the others. He was with Joslyrn and Kelmair in Narath, wasn't he?"

"He was. But if the others can't bring steeds into Fembrosh, what makes you think you can make Meager go where you want her to?"

"I probably can't, but I'm going to try. And once we're in the Kiareinoll, we'll have the Kia to hide us."

"Will it? What can we know of the way of trees, Ashel?"

His smile was bitter. "Nothing. That's what faith is for."

A Task for an Alnan

Ears intent, Geram thwacked the post with his spear. The whistling haft gauged his speed. Each knock and clack spoke the truth or falsity of his aim. Gravel ground beneath soles as his weight shifted, crunched as the spear butt slammed the dirt and pain webbed out of mangled muscle, down into his knee and up into his hip. Panting, he clung to the haft. Sweat dripped off his nose and chin, pattered on the ground. Rivulets trickled down his spine and seeped into damp trousers. His arms and shoulders quivered with fatigue.

Trees whispered, and the predawn breeze caressed slick skin, gentle and cooling. Hefting the spear, he attacked the post, pushing tired limbs to thrust and swing, jabbing stone blade into wood, wondering if steel would be easier to drive into thick, chitin shells. It surely would, but not even fieldmarshals carried swords. Iron and steel were not only costly, metal offended the Miners, who traded in crystal, not ore. "Get people killed," he muttered.

"What will, Lieutenant?"

The spear missed his mark, its momentum pulling his weight onto the bad leg. Pain spiraled outward; knee, hip, and shoulder smacked the ground and gravel scored his skin.

"Your Majesty." Instinctively, he grabbed Elekia's vision and found a gaze lingering on the dirt-streaked muscles of his chest and stomach. Coughing, he released her sight and hauled himself up the spear haft. "Did you need something?"

"An answer to my question. What will get people killed?"

Her breath huffed in soft, quick pants, and he recalled she

98

ran around the perimeter of the grounds each dawn. The idea of glistening skin and a heaving bosom quickened his blood. Cursing himself, he bowed his head and prayed she didn't notice the flush flooding up past his navel. "The lack of steel weaponry, Majesty."

"Ah, yes. I've been thinking on those lines myself. I've completed my morning exercise. Would you walk with me back to the Manor—if you're finished, that is?"

"Of course, Majesty. Let me get my shirt." He hobbled across the yard and patted the rail, her gaze like a poker between bare shoulder blades. His palms found fabric, and he wormed into the tunic. The collar chafed his throat. Laces tickled his spine. *Dundlehead, you put it on backward*. Heart pounding, he twisted the fabric the right way round. Thank Elesendar, dawn was hours away yet on the plains. By His grace, Ashel slept soundly while Geram stood here like an ass, struggling to don a shirt while the other man's mother leered at him. Or was he only hoping she leered at him? Shrine's bitch, ever since he'd learned she'd used her powers to keep him alive while the surgeons worked, he'd fought a mad desire to rub up against her like a tomcat licking scraps off his mistress's fingers. Of course she wasn't leering. She was the Ruler of Latha, a paragon of virtue, and he was a fishlicker from Alna.

With a final tug, he straightened his tunic and measured his steps to the graveled path, using the spear as a crutch.

"How is your leg?" Her scent wrapped around him, seeped into his lungs and blood like vapor in a bliss dive.

He pulled his shoulders back and stood at attention, clinging to a soldier's discipline. "It's getting stronger, thank you. I was told you . . . helped . . . when the Healers were stitching me back together. I'm very grateful."

"The Manor's Healers are, thankfully, discreet. I did not wish to lose the advantage of your abilities."

Gravel crunched beneath his limp. He didn't need her vision to know the way—he'd memorized all the Manor paths and could walk them unaided—but he gave into the temptation to *see*. Her eyes flicked over flower beds and shrubbery, paused on a cerrenil raising its limbs to greet the sunrise, then rested on him. Heat flashed up his neck, and he released her sight.

"What do you know about Fensin of Alna?" she asked.

"I imagine nothing you don't, Your Majesty."

"He represents your city. Did you vote for him?"

"There's never anyone else to vote for." Foreboding stirred. "You don't want me to—"

She laughed. "No, Lieutenant, I don't want you to challenge him. The Senator from Alna is by definition the monarchy's opposition—that is a matter of law, not merely custom, and I want you by my side."

He coughed. *By her side?* The odd phrasing stirred hope and dread alike.

"Are you ill? You keep coughing."

"It's the spring air, Majesty. Sometimes the blossoms make it harder to breathe."

"Hmm, that must have made spring campaigns very challenging during the war. You're right that we need steel to defend ourselves against the Kragnashians, and anyone else who might come through the Device with the Kragnashians' aid. Until now, the Miners' crystal blades have always sufficed, but the world is changing. There are rumors of ore discoveries in the Plenetor. That provision my daughter so blithely agreed to, about the Penance, I fear it may be Latha's doom."

He stopped walking and pulled the threads together. "Earnk Korng is Relmlord now. You believe he's colluding with his father and the Caleisbahnin to shut Latha out of whatever resources might be mined south of Relm? And you think Fensin is involved because of his ties to the Caleisbahnin."

"Yes—very good, Lieutenant. Earnk Korng may have denounced his father, but those two always find a path to reconciliation. What was your impression of my nephew?"

Geram swallowed bile. Elekia's adopted sister had been Earnk's mother, another knot in the tangle of jealousy and vengeance that had led to Latha's long conflict with Relm. During the months between the battles of Olmlablaire and Re, when Earnk had traveled with the Lathan army, Ashel's rancor toward him had faded into an almost friendly regard, but Geram still despised Lornk's son. He thought for a moment, composing a counselor's objective reply. "Earnk's actions seem driven by his emotions, the dominant of which is guilt. He lacks Lornk's ruthlessness, and I don't expect him to remain in the Seat of Relm. He is a Listener, though," he added. "Ashel and I were even more closely connected than we are now, for a time, and Earnk helped us to separate to the degree that we have."

"Out of guilt or mercy?"

"Both, I think. It was after Earnk tried to kill his father and Lornk imprisoned him for treason. We were all together in the prison hospital, put there by a fever that swept through prisoners and guards alike. It's what made me blind."

"I thought Lornk did that to you."

"Only indirectly. Ashel resided entirely in my mind for a while, and it drove me mad. I tried to tear out my own eyes. Between that and the fever . . ."

Fingers touched his temple, glided across his cheek. Nerves afire, he gripped the spear with both hands, his breath short and shallow.

"I'm grateful for everything you've done," she whispered aloud. "For your discretion, your loyalty, and your sacrifice. Is Ashel asleep now?"

"Yes." If he'd replied aloud, his voice would have cracked, like a youth meeting his first courtesan.

"Is he safe?"

His shoulders fell from his ears as he realized the emotion thickening her voice was for Ashel, not him. "He's still with the Herders. He thinks they'll enter Fembrosh tomorrow or the next day, and he plans to escape once he has the cover of trees."

"I hope Vic will find him before Lornk does."

"She will, if anyone can."

She grunted, and they traveled several paces. "I need you to go to Fensin's office and ask him for funds to buy steel spearheads in the Senate. You will appeal to him as a fellow Alnan and a disgruntled veteran who fears the Ruler's stubborn commitment to the Miners has left her guards in danger. Then you will cultivate a relationship with him. Do you understand?"

He bristled. "Being a Listener doesn't make me a spy."

"The night the Manor was attacked, you asked me what a blind Alnan fisherman could do. Now I've told you."

"I also resigned my commission that night."

"Yet you're still here. Lieutenant, however much you train, however lucky you were to survive your encounter with the Kragnashian, you are ill-suited as a Manor guard, just as you're not suited to be my aide or my clerk or even my Listener. Your talents transcend all those things, and I need you to fulfill your potential."

"You want me to be no more than a liar."

"Another one of your talents. You hid your connection to my son quite well."

His pulse throbbing, he expelled one hot breath after another. Elekia had cornered Ashel like this a thousand times and always gotten him to do what she wanted. Shrine, how he hated harboring those memories.

She clasped his arm. "I need you to help me save this nation by going to Fensin and learning what you can from him about the Caleisbahnin and Kragnashians who freed Lornk Korng. I need to know what else they have planned."

"What if he doesn't know anything?"

"Then I want you to remain close to him, in case that changes. In the meantime, Fensin is a wily and devious politician. Observing him is an education by itself."

He ground his teeth and thought of home. There was nothing in Alna for a blind, lame fisherman but a barstool and a tankard. A breeze wafted her scent—earthy and salty and sweet—and the mad desire to clasp her face had his palms itching to go back to the training yard and bash a pole with a stick until his hands bled.

"Do you understand your orders, Lieutenant?"

He swallowed a sigh—or perhaps it was a growl. "Yes, Majesty. I'll go to Fensin and present myself as a frustrated Alnan." That much, at least, was true.

THE CHALLENGE

The granite slab rose out of the forest like an anvil. As soon as they arrived, Febbin climbed to the top and came down claiming he had spotted Mount Mirkeldirk's snowy shoulders.

"It's just a thunderhead, boy," Erik said. Shaking an empty flask, the crew chief grumbled and pulled a small barrel out of the baggage. "Anyone seen the tap?" he asked.

"It's got to be Mirkeldirk," Febbin said. "Ashel, come up with me so you can vouch for it."

"You should bind them, not let them climb rocks!" Kelmair protested.

"Here it is." Erik pried out the bung and slammed the tap into the hole. "We're to wait here, Highness. Meet could be hours, days, or weeks from now, depending on what tribulations our patrons encountered along the way. It'd be uncomfortable for you and a bother for us to have to keep you bound. So as long as you don't try to run off, you can move freely about the camp. Joslyrn, keep a solid eye on Minstrel Melba."

The older outlaw assented, gaze scuffing the ground.

"Come up, Ashel," Febbin repeated, angling his head at a steep crevice in the rock face. Ashel followed the boy, finding good toe and handholds to the top, where moss filled the pebbly cracks around a single stunted geilmor, quivering in a stiff breeze. Shading his eyes, he looked to the southwest. The sky was clear, but he could see nothing but the expanse of Fembrosh.

Febbin grasped his arm. "The cavalry outpost is forty miles south. I'll take you there."

Eyebrows popping, hope twining with suspicion, Ashel stared at the youth.

"If you tried to ride Meager there alone, you wouldn't be able to stop her going back to the plains and the herd. But I can get you to the outpost by morning."

"Won't they come after us?"

"Erik brought a cask for the pirates, and you can see he's already started without them. Joslyrn will stay with the steeds."

"Joslyrn and Kelmair concocted this whole show."

"Joslyrn's only doing this because he's desperate to keep the herd and crew together. He feels real bad about it, and I don't think he'd be too upset if you and Melba escaped. Kelmair, well, she's another story. I'll take care of their mounts, make sure they can't follow." He swore softly. "It's not fair to the boys, but, well, it's got to be done. You'll know it's time to go when I water the steeds."

Ashel began writing as soon as they came down, quickly laying out a score, using a code of musical notes from his apprentice days. He hoped Melba remembered it. Marking the passage allegro, he took her the paper. "Can I get your opinion on this?"

She looked up, eyebrows cross. "I can't believe you're composing *now*."

The sinking sun streaked the cerrenils red. "The muse is upon me. Look at it."

She ripped the sheaf out of his hand, and Ashel strolled to his bedroll. Leaning on an elbow, he watched Erik squat near the fire, sipping steadily from his flask. Joslyrn diced with Febbin, and Kelmair paced, her neck shrunk into her shoulders. Their steeds clustered beneath the outcropping, heads low, manes twisting.

Hooting victory, Febbin snatched the dice off the gaming board.

"Go tend the steeds, boy," Joslyrn reached for the teapot in the coals.

"Next time we'll play for chores," the youth ventured. "I can't wait to see you hauling water, old man."

"Next time I'll win."

Chuckling, Febbin snatched up the water baskets and headed toward the stream gurgling past the other side of the outcrop. The sun sank. Shadows spread like molasses, flowing faster as they approached the fire. Purple melted across the sky, and Melba came over and handed him the score.

"It's one of the best things you've ever written." She glanced at Febbin, returning with the sloshing baskets. "The muse wouldn't be a water sprite, would he?"

"I think more a spirit of the wind."

Firelight streaked the steeds orange as Febbin set one water basket in front of his mount and Meager and gave the other to the remaining steeds. Ashel headed into a patch of hoarsgrout, aware of Kelmair's eyes hot on his back. In the bushes, he emptied his bladder, humming loudly to allay suspicions. Cursing, Kelmair stalked into the darkness, passing him with a fury of twig-snapping. Febbin sprang onto his stallion and snagged Meager's mane in one hand, held the other out for Melba. Clasping his wrist, she swung up behind him. Ashel crashed out of the thicket, taking a scratch on his cheek while he fumbled his gloves on. Erik stumbled up, shouting. Febbin paused while Ashel leapt onto Meager, and the steeds charged into the dark.

Gloveless, Febbin controlled the stallion with a blur of words. Melba's fists were locked round his waist, her face buried in his shoulder. Ashel gripped Meager's thorax with his thighs, struggling to keep her from turning back. Tentacles whipped, blistering the skin above the too-small gloves as he gripped the mare's mane. He sang, urging the steed and himself to trust the youth leading them into the black hollows of Fembrosh. Behind them, Kelmair screamed curses, and her steed crashed through underbrush.

"Just wait," Febbin shouted. "I put harlolinde in their water. The faster her steed runs, the quicker it'll knock him out."

The forest became a gauntlet of thorns as the steeds twisted around geilmors and ducked through vines. Tree limbs took aim at Ashel, bashed his shoulders, swung for his head. Leaning close to the mare's neck, he took a tentacle sting beneath the eye. Tears blinded him, the skin puckering. Melba bit off a sharp cry; blood brimmed from a gash in her thigh. Yet behind them the racket of pursuit died, and Kelmair's curses were left behind. Febbin slowed to a canter, Meager keeping pace with the stallion. "See," the boy said. "Like I said, you wouldn't have held her without me."

"Thank you," Melba gasped.

"When will we reach the outpost?" Ashel asked.

"Around sunrise—"

Febbin's stallion screeched, and Meager squealed and spun. Ashel squeezed her thorax, tugged on her mane, but he could not get her to turn around. Melba's voice, wailing Ashel's name, wove through Febbin's shouts as their mounts galloped apart.

Nose and eyes inches from writhing tentacles, Ashel clung to Meager and prayed. The mare crashed through a mass of grumelbury. Thorns scored deep across her armor, slicing ribbons out of his boots. She made a pealing kind of sound, her thorax shivering, legs tripping over roots. The mare twisted and jerked, slithering out of her saddle as she had that first evening on the plains. Jumping seemed a better option. A clear patch of ground ahead, Ashel held on until they cleared the thicket, then sprang. He slammed into the turf and tumbled like a fallen top. His head struck something hard, and the scents of grass and humus swirled into black.

Garbled voices shouted, the cadence and clink of steel a dread music. Ashel rolled onto his knees, trying to focus blurred eyes. His skull throbbed; probing fingers came away sticky with blood. *Geram*? he asked, but as if he were drunk, he could not sense the other man.

"Yo, Gustave, I've found him."

Boots stomped closer; a sword rang out of its sheath. Ashel staggered to his feet, vision reeling. A figure emerged slowly from the haze, a man as short as Vic, black hair slicked back from a high forehead, steel sword white in the starlight. Two others stepped into the clearing. One came nearly to Ashel's nose—tall indeed for a Caleisbahnin. While the pirate appraised him, Ashel tried to hold himself still, but the ground was rotating slowly, the trees tipping, tipping, and diving upside down. The grass swung up and smacked him.

"Wild ride?" The pirate grinned, a gap between his front teeth.

His sight going black, Ashel managed an answer. "Not wild enough."

† † †

The back of his head throbbed against a bandage. Someone was daubing scratches and welts with a citrus-scented salve— slotaen. His eyes flicked open; a woman's hand fuzzed into clarity.

"Stay with me, Shemen," Kelmair hissed. "You're worth nothing dead."

"Leave off." He yanked her wrist away.

She smirked. "Pretty shemen shouldn't have scars."

His thumb rubbed the puckered skin circling her wrist. "What about sea-mistresses?"

Scowling, she shoved her supplies into a pouch and stalked off. Dozens of Caleisbahnin lounged round fires or lay on bedrolls. A few clustered around Erik's cask; rumbling laughter filtered through the dark. Eyelids heavy, Ashel scanned for a golden head, but Lornk was nowhere among the dark-haired crowd. Woozy, he lay back, anger and regret churning into a vicious stew. His broken hand curled into half a fist. Why in the Shrine had he stopped Vic from killing the Relmlord? *Shemen*, he growled at himself.

A warm hand clasped his maimed one. "Ashel?"

His eyes sprang open. "Wineyll—what—" Hair ratted with twigs and leaves, she was pale and thin with dark crescents beneath her eyes. "Elesendar." He wrapped his arms around her, his heart turning hollow. "Have they hurt you?"

"No. No, they haven't."

His fury flared. "Has *he*?"

She pulled away from him. "No."

"Wineyll, go to bed." Lornk emerged from the trees.

She drifted away, and Lornk squatted, eyes glinting. A wild beard split into a vicious grin. "I'm glad to see you, son."

Hatred swelled out of Ashel's rage. That Mother might have—could have—with this fiend? He choked on the bitterness of it but forced his face into an impassive mask.

"I paid off your debt to the Caleisbahnin while you were still my guest in Olmlablaire," Lornk said. "I should probably have mentioned it before."

"Do you think that matters to me?"

"It matters to them." Lornk waved at the pirates. "In their eyes, you're mine."

"And what is it you want?"

Lornk studied him, lips sly. "I'd always meant for Earnk to take the Seat of Relm, so I could focus on other matters. When I next see your sister, I must thank her for facilitating my plans."

Hatred and fear surged, and Ashel sprang to his feet. The throb in his head nearly knocked him back, but he staggered toward the pirates gathered round the fire. "I claim the blood rite."

They stared. One man rose, his scabbard embossed with silvered feathers, marking him out as a captain. "You what?"

"The blood rite." Ashel held up his hand. "I demand revenge."

"Nonsense!" Lornk laughed.

The captain shrugged. "It is, Citizen. But if any man makes a claim to honor, it is my duty to uphold it. Gustave?" The tall fellow who was at the Cobblestone rose from the fireside. "Send the Kragnashian south to keep any cavalry from interfering. Citizen, you may choose a champion from among my men."

A Spook in the Forest

A snarl of hoarsgrout climbed up the earthwork walls of the bastion, half-hiding the outpost from passersby. Ahead, a vine-covered portcullis opened. Looking forward to a hot bath and news, Bethniel urged her mare to a trot. She had over a month's worth of correspondence to post, and she hoped for an equally thick packet of letters to read during a long soak. After that, there was a massive stack of homesteader charters to certify and file. Pride heated her cheeks, and she smiled at a job well done—so far, at least. An uncanny number of accidents had occurred among the would-be farmers and loggers she and her cavalry escort had found, the first stirrings of war between Fembrosh and the squatters. But Bethniel had managed to convince the squatters to undertake the proper rituals, and on their swing back toward the outpost, the newcomers reported no further hostilities. With proper respect for the land, peace was possible, and Bethniel would broker it.

"Welcome back, Highness," called a sentry as they passed through the gate. "The commander was just about to send a scout to find you."

"Is there news?"

"You'd better ask him, ma'am."

They clattered into a yard milling with troopers and horses. Grooms ran to and fro, bringing gear or checking bindings. In a high-walled paddock by the far wall frisked a steed, his carapace shining copper in the midmorning sun. Bethniel stared at the awesome creature and wondered why a single Herder would be visiting the outpost.

"Bethniel!" Melba burst out of a building and ran across the yard. Bruised circles rimmed her eyes, and worry etched amiable features.

The mounted patrol, their eager horses, the grim expressions on the officers' faces seized Bethniel's throat. "What are you doing here?"

"Highness." The commander's door banged open for Fieldmarshal Greldren. Bushy white eyebrows were tilted toward his nose. "The prince has been taken by Lornk Korng."

She felt like she was reliving a bad dream while Melba twisted her tunic sleeve into a knot and told a tale of steed rustlers turned kidnappers.

"We have to go now," Greldren said, "or Korng's party will reach the herd waiting on the plains. Once they do, we won't have a chance of catching them." He angled his head at the steed and shrugged. Bethniel's fingers tightened into fists.

"You need to stay here," he continued. "I'm not going to risk you falling into the Relmlord's hands as well."

"Lornk Korng is no longer Relmlord, Fieldmarshal. He's nothing but an outlaw, and I've been dealing with those for the past ten weeks. I will see this one brought to justice, whatever the risk." Grabbing her saddlebags, she slid off her mare. "Get me a fresh horse."

Greldren sighed and mounted. "There's no time to argue. Rustler!" A pair of troopers escorted a sandy-haired youth into the yard. Melba's face turned splotchy, eyes shying from the boy's bound hands as the troopers helped him mount a tan gelding. "If you lead us into a trap," Greldren said, "you won't live to know a hanging. Understood?"

The boy voiced a surly "Yes, sir," then leaned toward Melba. "He'll be OK."

Damn right he will, Bethniel thought, hoisting herself onto a stallion.

☦ ☦ ☦

As the sun topped the day, Bethniel maneuvered her horse close to the steed rustler. Lieutenant Lillem, the officer in command of her escort, shadowed her, handsome features bent in the same scowl he'd worn since they'd changed mounts at the outpost.

Brush hid most of the company as they plodded through thick woods. Hands bound, the rustler directed his gelding with knees alone, choosing a path wide enough for three mounts—his and his guards. Catching Bethniel's eye, he smiled impishly and twisted his knees. Snorting, his mount wheeled and hopped over a fallen log to her side. Cursing, the guards scrambled to flank him as the boy winked at Bethniel. "Have you ever been on a steed?"

Lillem snatched the boy's reins and reprimanded the other soldiers.

"It's all right, Lieutenant," Bethniel said. "He's just showing off. What's your name, rustler?"

"Febbin. You sit a horse pretty well. Think you could ride a steed? Ashel does pretty good for a Fembrosher."

"Is it really like Greldren said?"

His grin shriveled. "It's all Kelmair's doing. She's got Erik in her pocket, twists him round to her way. Joslyrn and me, we wanted nothing to do with any pirates, but we needed the mullas to pay the Guild fees, and Erik's still crew chief." He shrugged guiltily. "I'm sorry about Ashel. We were almost away when something spooked the steeds. Your brother is a good rider, but most Herders couldn't have managed a steed that scared, much less a Fembrosher."

A horse's scream ripped through the trees. Bethniel's stallion rolled his eyes, shying from shadow-dappled tree trunks. A trooper yelled in the distance. The boy's gelding snorted, and whinnies chorused all around them. "Lupears?" she asked Lillem.

Scanning the surrounding rocks and trees, he stroked his mount's neck. "Could be." Another shout echoed through the woods, the words garbled. "They don't usually hunt in Fembrosh, but could be they followed the steeds in."

A cacophony of curses, whinnies, and cracking branches spun around them. A woman screamed, her cry cut short by a sickening squelch. Lillem urged his stallion to Bethniel's side, his eyes shadowed with readiness.

"It's the same thing spooked Meager," muttered Febbin.

Snorting, Bethniel's stallion hopped sideways, haunches quivering. With pats and soothing noises, she brought him under control and they paced forward. Birds twittered. Sunlight shafted green and gold through the canopy, conjuring spirits out of shadows. A pair of riderless horses galloped across their path, reins flying, the whites of their eyes bright under the trees. People shouted in front, behind them, cries punctuated by panic.

Lillem touched Bethniel's knee with a long, brown finger. "You'll be all right, Highness."

Bethniel peered through the woods but could see only light and dark trunks, screens of leaves and clumps of needles. Her mount groaned, his steps hesitating. The rustler looked nervous, as if he'd never been astride before. The horse beneath one of his guards whickered and danced, ignoring the rider patting her neck.

A Kragnashian appeared on their flank, leaves whirling in its wake. Bethniel's stallion reared, front hooves pawing the air, a squeal vibrating his neck as she hung on with clenched knees and fingers twined through his mane. She glimpsed Febbin's gelding plunging into a thicket, his guards' horses fleeing pell-mell into the woods. Lillem was scrambling to his feet, his mount gone. Landing with a huff, Bethniel's stallion leapt over a gully, climbed swiftly up the opposite bank, hooves slipping in the depth of decaying leaves. There was a thwack, and a rancid knot hissed past her hair as the stallion topped the rise.

Withers foaming, the stallion careened around tree trunks, choosing his own path. The Kragnashian flowed after, branches snapping, plowing through hoarsgrout as if it were grass. Bethniel hugged the horse's neck and prayed. *Mother, give me calm. Elesendar, give the stallion speed.* A horn blew somewhere. With a piercing cry, the stallion veered toward the noise, Kragnashian on their tail.

"It's right behind me!" she yelled aloud and with all the mindstrength she possessed. The horn cut off mid-blow. Something splattered on the stallion's flank. Squealing, he skidded, bucked, his eyes rolling. She clung to his neck, screamed at him to *run*. The Kragnashian sauntered closer. Kicking, the stallion twisted round to bite a sizzling wound. She jumped out of the stirrups, stumbled for footing, putting the horse between herself and the Kragnashian. It swung around the animal and shot through a shaft of sunlight. Blood pumping, Bethniel scrambled toward a cerrenil. Branches whipped down and swept her into the canopy. Mandibles snapping, the creature screeched. She grabbed for a higher branch, one foot lodging in a crevice, and thrust herself up. The limbs quivered, shifting lower and higher as she climbed, boosting her beyond the Kragnashian's reach. Clinging to the old mother's trunk, she wept her thanks.

In the distance, the horn bugled a signal for the troopers to regroup. Below, a sulfurous pheromone squeaked out of the tracheae lining the Kragnashian's abdomen. Its antennae twitched. Bethniel's heart in her mouth, she watched it hesitate toward the horn, then ram the trunk with its head. The cerrenil shook, bark jamming under her fingernails.

"You are the Fulcrum," the Kragnashian clicked. Rearing back, it launched a wad of spit. Twigs and leaves rustled, and the spit splattered against a green shield. The old mother shivered as half-eaten leaves dripped acid into the leaf litter.

The Kragnashian backed up for another charge.

The Fulcrum was the name the Kragnashians had called Bethniel in the desert. "What do you want?" she cried, clapping and snapping the words, as humans did to communicate with Kragnashians.

The creature rammed the tree, and she clutched at thrashing branches. "The Fulcrum." It hit the trunk again and again, the tree convulsing with each strike. The armor between the creature's eyes became dented and scratched while Bethniel hugged the cerrenil and prayed. She coughed sobs at the fall, at her fate when she landed, at the thought of a wad of the creature's acidic spit hitting her—

Thunder banged overhead. The Kragnashian froze. Bethniel followed its gaze through the canopy and found a sky blue and clear. Another boom, loud as a lightning strike in the garden.

Hooves pounded the ground. A man roared, and a spear plunged into the creature's thorax.

Leaves whispered softly. A warbler trilled. At the base of the tree lay the Kragnashian in a heap. Lillem's horse huffed beside it; the rider peered through the branches.

"Are you all right, Highness?"

Blinking, Bethniel wiped a salty wet face on her shoulder, smelled the stink coming from her trousers. Laughing at the indignity of fear, she hugged the old mother, thanked it for its protection, as true as a genuine mother's.

"Are you all right?" the lieutenant repeated.

"I am," she said, climbing down. "I'm afraid I need fresh trousers," she added sheepishly when her feet hit the dirt.

He smiled sympathetically. "This day, you won't be alone in that."

THE PLEDGE

On stomach and elbows, Vic wormed through the hoarsgrout toward an eerie blend of spoken words and mindspeech. A dozen Caleisbahnin lounged beside a sheer granite face that towered out of the forest behind them. She bit hard on her tongue, stifling a growl. She'd asked the Kia to take her to Ashel, and it had brought her to these men? Bafflement and irritation twisted through worry that he was the pirates' captive. If so, she needed to grab him and *fly*. Holding her breath, she drew on the Woern. Pain lanced through her eyes, and she swallowed hard at her roiling belly. Shrine, what a time to be powerless.

One of the pirates nudged a fellow and jutted his chin at a shirtless woman, and they shared a jeering laugh. The woman spat a retort, and Vic's eyes locked on the scars round her neck.

"Come here, Kara," Lornk says. The hot afternoon sweeps through the window. Blood thick in her face, her knees weak, she slips off the bed and stands beside him. "Look there," he points. A Caleisbahnin struts down the street, one hand on a pommel decorated with a luxurious tuft of feathers, the other flourishing a hat to pantalooned Trainers. Behind him crawls a young woman, naked and muddied. Her head is shaved, her knees bloodied by the cobbles. "See her tattoos?" Lornk fingers the jeweled leather sewn around Vic's neck, nodding at the blue ink spiraling round the woman's. "She is a sea-mistress. What are you, Kara?"

116

She peers up at him, her shoulders tight. "I'm yours, my Lord."

He smiles, cupping her chin in his hand. "Aren't you glad?"

"I hate the Caleisbahnin," she hissed, needing to say it aloud.

A sharp call rang out, and the pirates rose to attention. Lornk strode into their circle, golden hair aflame in the sun. Leaves crinkled against her cheeks as she breathed in the scent of the earth. Her fingernails dug into her palms, and she fought to cool the blood gushing toward her eyes. In Olmlablaire, she'd put aside vengeance in favor of justice. *You let him live so you could free yourself. He has no hold on you whatsoever,* she told herself. *He means nothing to you.*

A Caleisbahn captain, his sword pommel decorated with silvered feathers, followed Lornk into the circle as another pirate, old but with muscles like knotted iron, climbed onto a fallen log. "A challenge among men is issued," the old one announced in a grizzled voice. "The challenged may choose a champion, and the choice of weapons is his as well. What say you?"

Lornk donned his cruelest smile. "For my champion, I choose Captain Thiellin. For weapons, I choose fists—I do not seek my challenger's death, only his defeat, so we can put this farce to rest."

The old Caleisbahnin conferred briefly with another pirate, then nodded his head. "It is agreed."

The woman cried, "Thiellin, no! This is *my* chance!"

"You'll get your share," the captain snapped. "It's done. Let's begin."

As the men stepped back, widening the circle, Vic wondered where the Kragnashian might be lurking. Lornk retired behind the line as another pair of men walked out from the trees. Ashel—his name in her throat, Vic swallowed a cry, instinct freezing her limbs as her worst fears were realized. Her gaze darted at his companion—Gustave, the pirate from the Cobblestone—then swung back to Ashel's bruised, swollen face and the strip of linen wrapped round his head. He marched into the circle like a man determined to meet death.

"Wagers!" the old pirate called and scribbled furiously while his companions shouted their bets. At a slice of his hand, they fell silent. Ashel raised his fists, a whole one and a half at the ready.

A vortex spun in Vic's chest. That half hand was hers to own. So was the fact he stood here at all. Before she could move to stop him, Ashel sprang forward and jabbed Thiellin's ribs, dodged a counterblow to his jaw. She watched in shock as the men engaged and broke off. Ashel used his greater height and reach to land blows and avoid them, his movements graceful and economical, just like Geram's. Did the other man guide him, or had Ashel tapped into his instincts? It didn't matter, either way. Thiellin was tough and wily, taking some punches but dodging the worst ones. He danced around, letting Ashel wear himself down, biding his time. No doubt the pirate captain had decades of experience in brawls and duels. Even with Geram's help, Vic doubted Ashel could win this fight, and she didn't want to watch him get hurt any more than he already was.

"Stop!" she cried.

Swords rang out of sheaths, and gazes sprang round the clearing, searching for an ambush. When she climbed free of the hoarsgrout, the pirates hooted with relief. Just a woman alone, mud on her nose, leaves in her hair. Only Gustave's eyes widened, and he grasped Thiellin's arm, whispering. Ashel's face rippled through surprise to sadness, his eyes flashing to Lornk. She shook her head. *Not Lornk*, she thought at him, as if he were Geram and could Hear her. This time, not Lornk. Surely Geram had told him she was coming for him. A breeze billowed, bringing a citrus scent, and Vic's throat clogged with something between laughter and tears. She just had to show him she was here only for him.

The Relmlord pushed into the circle, and she quickened her pace. Ashel's eyes flicked again to Lornk and back to her. She reached him, and the laugh burbled forth as she pressed her cheek to his chest, her arms tight around him. Lornk's stare was hot on her back, but her smile deepened when Ashel laid his hand on her hair.

"This little snippet is yours?" asked a pirate.

"She's mine," Lornk growled.

The Woern tingled along her skin, straining toward Ashel's. Rising on tiptoe, she brushed her lips against his, tongue darting for a whiff of his latent symbionts. A rough beard scraped her chin. "Kiss me and we'll go," she whispered.

His eyes sad, his mouth was flat. "They've got Wineyll too."

Lornk barked the minstrel's name, and Wineyll shuffled out from the trees, matted hair spilling over her face. She looked thin and worn, a shadow of the robust girl Vic had known. "Now hide yourself, Songbird," he said, and Wineyll disappeared. Hatred spiked, and Vic funneled all her loathing into a glare.

"My, my, Kara," he chuckled. "Who abandoned them to me?" Turning to the pirates, he raised his arms. "May I introduce Victoria of Ourtown, Destroyer of Olmlablaire."

Mouths fell open; eyes darted, but no one moved. A bird chirped, and a chorus of tweets accompanied the old pirate as he climbed off the log and walked toward her in a rolling gait that echoed the sea. A moment later, the woman sprang forward, fists on her hips. "It's my right," she grated.

"Step aside, sea-mistress," the captain sneered.

The woman turned to Vic. "Will you claim me?"

Vic stared at her, bewildered.

"Say yes," Ashel whispered.

Eyebrows drawn tight, Vic bobbed her head, though she had no idea what she was agreeing to.

The woman held out a hand to Thiellin. Scowling, the captain gave her his sword. "I am no sea-mistress," the woman hissed and knelt before Vic, sword tip in the dirt. "In honor of what was, I, Kelmair of Sect Dameron, pledge my life to yours. My sails and my sword are yours to command." She spoke, the words halting and thickly accented, in the language of the Ancients, the language of

Vic's childhood. The captain and the old man knelt and repeated the words in Vic's native tongue, followed by the other Caleisbahnin. Only one pirate stood. A bit of pink poked through his front teeth.

"You," Vic said. "You tried to burn down the Cobblestone."

"Yet it did not burn, madam."

"You nearly killed the cook."

"Yet he did not die."

She waved at the others. "What are they doing?"

He grinned. "You could have had this pledge sooner."

Her anger boiled beneath a tight lid, and she could feel the energy in the air, prickling the hairs on her arms. "That's not an answer."

"They think they see a legend."

"What do you see?"

"Someone who has yet to earn the honors they give."

A chill scurled down her spine. "What is this about?" she asked Lornk.

One corner of his mouth bent upward. "I once said to you that the day would come when you would hold the world in your hands."

"I want you to hand it to me, without reservation," he'd said. "This is not that day, Lornk. I wouldn't give you a dirty handkerchief."

He chuckled, his eyes resting on Ashel for a moment. "No, not today, but soon enough. I want you to be prepared, my dear, and to have the help you will need. That is all I've ever wanted."

"Whatever your scheme," she grated, "I don't care." She took Ashel's hand. "We're leaving, and not one of you is going to stop us."

"Oh, they won't stop you," Lornk said with a vicious grin. "But they'll follow you, wherever you go—to serve you, of course."

"Madam," Thiellin said, "we aim for Betheljin, where we will overthrow Commissar Parnden and raise Lornk Korng in his place. Your name means *victory* in the Ancient's tongue. With your help, we would be assured of it."

Harsh laughter tickled the back of Vic's throat, an aching

reminder of the absurd course her life had taken. She fought an urge to crush their skulls. "You're all insane."

Kelmair stood. "Commissar Parnden has committed insult and injury against the Archipelago, yet the First cannot declare war on him directly—"

"I don't care!" Fury boiling, she imagined them all lying among the needles and leaves, heads smashed, blood soaking the litter, just like the dead on the field outside Re. How many had she killed with wizardry? Elesendar, it shouldn't be so easy! The *wrong* of it robbed her breath, and she stood still, reaching for air that wouldn't come.

"Vic," Ashel said her name aloud, kissing her forehead and eyes. "Vic."

Her lungs filled, and his gaze melted into the warmth that had always been there but which she'd so long refused to accept. "I went into Fembrosh and got lost," she said. "Will you help me find the way home?"

Even the wind stilled for his answer.

"Of course," he said, tugging her into a fierce embrace.

"You can't!" cried Kelmair.

"The challenge," hissed the old pirate.

"Madam," Thiellin said, "we have pledged ourselves to your service. You must accept that pledge and—"

A scream sizzled out of her as an electric bolt sprang from her chest into the clear sky, throwing Ashel backward. Another bolt arched from her hand at the granite outcrop, blowing a spray of rock over the campsite. Ashel yelled her name, and she drew air across the face of the cliff like a curtain, thickening it. Rocks drifted toward the ground like pebbles sinking through honey. Kelmair gasped; the drunkard and the clay-haired man spun toward the outcropping, pointing at animals tethered there. A few Caleisbahnin sat frozen near the stone, their faces crumpling. Gently as feathers, the boulders settled, and Vic released the curtain. The pirates fell; the animals buckled, and an acrid stench plumed through the rattling downpour of dust and pebbles.

Vic dropped to her knees. Three more people were dead. "I don't ever want to do that again," she whispered. Ashel's arms encircled her as pain rolled through her, stopped her ears and blinded her. She fell into a dark well, then felt nothing.

A Sensible Man

I should just go, Geram thought, toweling freshly shaved cheeks. He gripped his washstand, quivering as imaginary fingers brushed his face. He fancied himself catching Elekia's hand, bringing her knuckles to his lips, tasting the skin of wrist and arm and shoulder, all the way to her mouth. The more time he spent with her, the more his blood throbbed at the thought of her. The awful scenario reeked of Ancient legend: the orphan who loved and married a queen, then discovered the bride was his long-lost mother. Shrine, that wasn't even his knowledge, it was Ashel's! A sensible man would just *go*. Yet Geram's sense had got up and left without him.

So far, Ashel, preoccupied with his own troubles, hadn't noticed the shift in Geram's feelings. At the moment, the prince slept, exhausted from the day before. Vic remained unconscious, and Ashel had carried her while the Caleisbahnin hustled toward the plains. Geram hoped she'd wake up soon and get them *away*. If she didn't . . . He imagined Elekia's reaction to news of her foster daughter's death: a single hoarse sob that would break his heart.

Stop. He butted his forehead against the wall. *Focus on your duty.* A spy's duty, the only job fit for a blind Alnan fisherman. Curse that woman, and curse his need to please her.

He fumbled into a silk shirt and brocaded coat and hobbled out of the Manor. Paving stones bordered the road to the city, and he tapped his staff along them to guide his steps as he limped through hot and cool spaces, the road's tells of sun and shade.

123

Sweat trickled through his hair, dampened his shirt. Leg aching, he stopped in a cool patch and removed the heavy coat, wishing he hadn't worn it. Wishing he had not attached himself to the royals in the first place.

Carriage wheels ground the track, and tack jingled as horses stopped beside him.

"Are you going to Narath?" asked Timny, Ashel's teenage cousin. "You can ride with us."

Thanking him, Geram felt for the toeholds to climb up beside the driver, but the youth invited him to sit inside the cab.

"Aunt Elekia won't let us walk to the Academy anymore," said Cimba, Timny's sister.

"The city's not very safe these days." Geram settled beside the girl. Twelve and fourteen, the royal cousins had been reared at the Manor after their parents died. Their father, King Sashal's older brother, had been Heir during their grandfather Rivern's reign. Geram chuckled whenever he thought about how he'd also been brought up by his aunt and uncle, but in a tavern instead of a palace.

"My friend Melandy's cook was robbed in the marketplace, right in front of other people," Cimba said as the carriage rumbled down the hill. "And nobody did anything to stop it!"

"An Eldanion boy in Fifth Year was killed when a mob attacked the wine market," said Timny.

"He wasn't *killed*. I saw that boy in school yesterday."

"There was a mob though."

The siblings argued over the details of the attack, and Geram shook his head over how the city's troubles had grown so fast. Beggars, robbers, and thugs seemed to have sprung out of the ground like weeds.

When the carriage arrived at the Academy, he thanked the royal cousins and walked to the Senate. The streets stank of offal, and he had to borrow the vision of passersby, swinging from one to the next, to navigate through the piles of refuse that spilled out of bins at every corner. The Haulers were on strike. The Miners were marching. The Weavers were refusing to pay their taxes, and each day only added to the midden heap.

The Senate building offered little respite from the stinking streets. The Opposition chambers were stuffy with tension and sweat, and when a junior clerk ushered him into Fensin's office, the breeze through the open window brought more garbage stench.

"Lieutenant." A hand shook his. "My apologies that my calendar prevented us from convening sooner, but let me assure you how honored I am to meet one of the heroes of Olmlablaire, especially one from my home city. Please have a seat. May I take this?"

Geram released his staff and settled into a cushioned chair. Tea things rattled, and a warm cup was placed in his hands. "Thank you, Senator. It's an honor to meet you as well."

"What district are you from?" A loud slurp followed the question.

"Southdock, sir. My aunt owns a tavern near Heretic House."

"I know the area well. There's a place on Shoal where they serve chowder in a bread bowl."

"Emalin's. Best chowder in the city, sir."

"Indeed! Regrettably the duties of state have kept me here this past year."

Geram Listened as they chatted about other favorite places, but Fensin kept his thoughts well muffled. A deeper probe could alert the Senator to the intrusion, so Geram set down his teacup and got to the point. "I came to ask for your help, Senator. We cannot allow another Kragnashian incursion, but as it stands, the Manor lacks the weaponry to stop them if they come back."

"Why did you come to me?" Fensin asked. "You have daily contact with the Ruler. Why not speak to her?"

"I did, sir, and afterward I concluded it would be more effective to ask you."

"Why is that?"

Here came the lie. "Her Majesty sides with the Miners and believes crystal blades should be enough deterrent. She blames the guards for the incursion, not our equipage."

"That sounds unlike her. She's always been a stalwart supporter of the military."

"Surely, Senator, you've noticed how the queen cloaks admonishments within blandishments."

Fensin laughed. "An astute observation, Lieutenant. If I may ask, what exactly do you do at the Manor?"

Geram sighed and told the truth. "A good question. I train with the guards but have no postings to the duty roster. Elekia has me sit in on various meetings, but she never asks for my counsel afterward—and obviously I'm not a scribe—so I don't understand my purpose there. She said once I should be grateful for having a comfortable position on her staff, so I suppose it's really just royal charity."

"And are you comfortable?"

"Frankly, Senator, I'm bored. A hundred times I've almost resigned, but the queen also sends my aunt and uncle a pension, so I feel obliged to stay, for their sake."

"I think I could give you a purpose, Lieutenant. And I promise you wouldn't be bored."

Geram sat straighter. "If it would help secure the Manor, I'll do it gladly."

The clerk opened the door. "The ambassador is here, Senator."

"Good, send him in. Lieutenant Geram of Alna, may I introduce Ambassador Breon of Sect Moyere of the Caleisbahn Archipelago. I asked the ambassador to join us."

Taking the Senator's sight, Geram stood. Silver wound round the Caleisbahnin's earlobes and coated the feathers on his scabbard. Gemstones studded the hilt of his sword. Geram shook the offered hand, but he didn't bother to temper his frown. "With respect, Senator, I do not think the ambassador should be part of our discussion, considering their role in Lornk Korng's escape and the murder of dozens of Lathans at the prison."

"The First has disavowed the actions of Sect Dameron," said Breon.

"But not denounced it."

"Lieutenant, please," Fensin said. "I believe the ambassador's assurances that Sect Dameron are rogues and their actions were neither ordered nor endorsed by the First. Besides, who knows how to forge steel blades better than the Caleisbahnin?"

"No one," Geram conceded, resuming his seat.

"There, you see? I suspected the Kragnashian incursion might have prompted your request for a meeting, and I asked the ambassador to come because he could arrange a supply of steel weapons at a reasonable cost. I will gladly work with the Prime Minister to overcome any objections from the Miners as well as secure funding from our Senate colleagues."

A pause grew into an awkward silence. He wondered if Fensin were after merely graft or if something else was afoot, and he felt very much out of his depth. He was a fisherman and a soldier, sometimes a counselor, but not a spy and certainly not a politician. Both men kept a thick layer of baffling over their thoughts as they waited for Geram's response. "I am grateful for your help," he said.

"If you wish to truly secure the home of your monarch, you shouldn't build it around a Device," said the ambassador.

"My friend," Fensin said, "the Manor has been on that site for hundreds of years. Let us change what we can." His mindvoice sharpened. "Lieutenant, what do you know of the history of King Sashal's ascension?"

He thought of the royal cousins, arguing in the carriage. "I know Navael was Heir, but the Senate gave Sashal the throne, some say because Elekia brokered a deal with the Kragnashians."

"Did the prince tell you that?"

"We had a lot of time to talk in Olmlablaire's dungeon."

"And I imagine he had much to say. Elekia did indeed convince the Kragnashians to demand that Sashal take the throne. It was a spectacular coup for a pair of seventeen-year-olds, fresh out of Fembrosh. At the time I was still young enough to be impressed by bold action, and I supported them. I regret that vote now."

He paused again, and Geram asked the question Fensin wanted. "Why, Senator?"

"Because Elekia of Reinoll Parish, Ruler of Latha, holds the throne through subterfuge and ill-intent. She must be deposed and Timnon of Narath declared Ruler. Of course, a suitable regent must also be appointed."

Geram's jaw fell open, and it took some effort to close it. The accusation—*subterfuge and ill-intent*—was the very language Lornk had used in a declaration he'd wanted Ashel to sign when they were imprisoned in Olmlablaire. Ashel's torments had culminated in those damn gauntlets, and Geram's cursed psychic link to the prince. "I don't understand, Senator," he replied.

"Succession in Latha is a funny thing. The Senate hasn't elected a child Ruler for over a hundred years, but there is precedent, and in this case it would be a relief to restore the throne to Rivern's legitimate line."

Alarm ticked up Geram's spine. "Legitimate?"

Fensin chuckled. "I believe the queen is an adulteress, and Bethniel of Narath is a bastard."

"What?"

"Inlander marriage practices are baffling, aren't they? In Alna, we marry whom we please, when we please, in a public ceremony. To Inlanders, a first bedding is a wedding. I have on good authority that the queen's first tryst was *not* with Sashal, which would make our late king the cad in a sordid love triangle. The cuckold is none other than Lornk Korng."

Geram pulled up every barrier he could to prevent Ashel from Hearing. "Who told you this?"

"The former Relmlord himself."

Geram rubbed his chin to hide rising panic. "What about Bethniel? She still has bloodright through Elekia, who was herself fairly elected Ruler."

"Alas, I regret my former clerk will never be elected to the throne she wants so badly. Her claim isn't strong enough to survive the scandal when Lornk Korng publicly announces Prince Ashel is his son."

"Many would prefer Sashal's daughter over a fourteen-year-old boy. Or the Senate could choose someone else altogether."

"This nation stands at a precipice, Lieutenant, and cannot survive the turmoil from a succession battle in the Senate, where every jumped-up guildmaster and junior Senator puts themselves forward as the next Ruler. No, for stability's sake, we must restore Rivern's line to the throne and choose the right regent to guide young Timnon."

"And you have yourself in mind for that role?"

"Elesendar, no! I'm the Opposition—I cannot be regent. I can, however, ensure the Senate chooses a suitably sober and thoughtful individual."

Geram eyed the two men, letting his suspicion show. "Why are you telling me all this?"

"Because we want you to do your part easing this transition. If I'm mistaken about you, and your loyalties in fact lie with Elekia, you will tell her everything you heard here today, and it will only make matters worse. While she tries to fight or squash the scandal, the guilds will continue purging members, making more beggars and robbers in Narath and the rest of the nation. But if you help us, we can stabilize the country before it dissolves into chaos."

"What is it you want me to do?" Geram asked.

"Bring me proof your queen is a wizard," Breon said.

"Is that all?" Geram guffawed at the absurdity of the request. Even if he were willing to betray Elekia, she never used wizardry openly.

"Lieutenant," Fensin tutted. "I'm told your injuries from the Kragnashian attack were very grave, and it was a miracle you survived. Elekia had a hand in that, didn't she?"

"Elesendar's grace is not proof the queen worked magic."

"Is that what saved you? Far be it from me to deny the Father's power, and you're absolutely right it isn't proof. That's why you must look, Lieutenant."

"And I can hardly do that, Senator."

"Oh, he is clever, isn't he, Breon?"

"Get close to the queen," Breon said. "Gain her trust and

friendship. Become her intimate."

Heat tore up Geram's neck.

"When the moment is right, you simply ask her to make something for you. A keepsake, which cannot be made by human craft. When you have it, bring it to me."

"To you?"

"That is the price of Breon's help with the weaponry you seek, Lieutenant. Will you do it?"

Geram snagged the sight of one and swapped it for the other's, so he could see them both. The ambassador's expression was sober and inscrutable. Fensin wore a leer, and his thoughts dallied with the seamier meanings of *intimate*. Shrine, he should just go home. But Fensin had just proven himself in league with Elekia's enemies. Curse that woman and his own need to please her. He cleared his throat and spoke aloud. "I suppose you'll want regular reports."

Fensin's grin sharpened. "That would be delightful, Lieutenant."

THE DECLARATION

Ashel jerked awake. Firelight painted Kelmair out of the darkness, her hand on his shoulder. "Go in with her," she whispered. "I'll watch for you."

Vic hadn't woken since raining boulders on the Caleisbahnin, and despite those deaths, Kelmair and the other pirates had hovered around, doing all they could to help him care for her. Kelmair was as solicitous now as she'd been spiteful before. "Why?" he asked.

"We pledged our swords—"

"She doesn't want pledges from you."

"It's true, isn't it? She was a mistress?" Awe thickened her voice.

"She was my mistress." Lornk emerged from his tent. Crawling out after him, Wineyll hugged her knees.

"You will not touch her." Flicking open Vic's tent, Ashel nodded at Kelmair. "He doesn't set one foot closer."

With a slow, vicious smile, she drew her blade. "Not a foot."

Inside, he lit the lamp and watched Vic's chest rise and fall in the flickering light. "Wineyll?" he whispered, hoping she Listened for him.

Leave me alone, Ashel. I won't go with you. Her reply drifted into his mind, almost like one of Geram's thoughts.

"When she wakes—"

There's nothing for me in Latha. There's nothing for me anywhere.

"What the Guild did to you was wrong. We can still fix it."

He Heard nothing more from her.

131

Beating back anger, he used his lone thumb to hook Vic's hair and tuck it behind her ear. *"You left them with me."* Lornk's taunt had rung all too true. In Olmlablaire, she could have saved him. He pressed the palm of his hand to her cheek, half-expecting her to recoil. Instead she sighed, the skin around her eyes relaxing.

> *The ceiling groans dust into their eyes, choking the room like mist. She stands in the doorway, her hair fanned out in a halo of static, his avenging angel. But he swallows her name, because she's staring at Lornk, not him. She saunters closer, casually slapping a jeweled dagger against her palm. He whispers her name. She looks at him, seems to see him for the first time. The dagger falls into his blood—pooling under the chair—and horror clouds her emerald eyes into jade.*

She couldn't have known Lornk's fury and desire stretched past her, measuring the length of Ashel's life. He brushed the lone thumb across her cheek. She couldn't have known.

Her eyes flicked open, and a tear leaked across the bridge of her nose. She laid her hand over his. "Can you ever forgive me?"

He withdrew the maimed hand. "I don't know."

"Where are we? How long was I out?"

"Two days. We're close to the eastern edge of the Kiareinoll."

Grimacing, she pushed herself upright. "Shrine, I've pissed myself, haven't I?"

Irritation tightened his throat, but he poked his head outside, asked Kelmair to help her clean up. As they walked off, the outlaw warned Lornk to stay away. With a satisfied grunt, Ashel reclined on a mat spread over the dirt. More than a thousand years ago, the Caleisbahn First had pledged the Archipelago to the service of wizards, but Lornk had made a mistake thinking he could bond Vic to these modern-day brigands. *"By your laws as well as Betheljin's, an escaped mistress is still the property of a Citizen,"* Lornk had argued. But Thiellin had replied, *"A wizard cannot be a mistress. Clearly she is a wizard."* The pirates believed they could convince Vic to help put

Lornk in the Commissar's seat, but the way they hovered around her with eyes full of hope and worry, it seemed half-likely she could order them to return him to Lathan custody. If only it were so easy.

The flap rustled and she ducked in. They sat with shoulders pressed into the canvas, away from each other.

"I'll be right outside," Ashel said.

She touched his arm. "Wait. I've been looking for you. Geram must have told you. I'm sorry I didn't find you before they did." Her voice full of self-recrimination, she told him how she'd set off for Mora but let herself be blown off course. Rubbing her temples, she added, "Every time I've used wizardry since the storm, it's made me so sick I can hardly breathe."

Chuckling softly, he squeezed her fingers. "I've heard I can help with that."

Her shoulders cringed to her ears. "I know. But it's wrong for me to ask."

Humor twisted into anger. "Then what was the point of coming out here? Shrine, Vic. I gave up—" He swallowed the rest and pulled in a breath, looking for a steady current in his own roiling emotions. Her small figure pulled at his blood like a magnet, the scent of her—sweat and woodsmoke and forest detritus and that essence of *her*—filled his nose and went to his head like a drug. He could see, hear, and smell her—he wanted to taste and feel and *know* her too. But threaded through his desire was a fury he couldn't deny and didn't know how to expunge.

"You gave up everything for me." Wet streaks glimmered on her cheeks. She sandwiched his maimed hand between her palms. "You let him do this to you to save me, and I let him do it, to save myself. Elekia ordered me to come find you, and I came out here hoping we could . . . we could start over, but it's not that simple, not with this pack of Caleisbahnin—"

"Shrine, Vic. The Caleisbahnin are just your latest excuse."

"I'm sick, Ashel. I want nothing more than to rescue you from these brigands, but I'm too sick—"

"I'm talking about us! You dangle hope like a lure and jerk it away every time. I wish you'd make up your bloody mind."

"I just can't."

"Why not?"

"No—"

He put his palm under her chin and forced her head up. "Why not, Vic?"

She jerked free of him. "Because I love you!" Eyes wide, she laid her fingers over her mouth, breathing heavily.

She'd said it. She'd admitted it like confessing a crime, but she'd finally said it. A silly grin pulled at the corners of his mouth; sunshine and the scent of wildberry blossoms colored the air.

"I can't, but I do," she mumbled, her breath jagged. "I shouldn't, but I do. And I'm afraid."

"Of what?"

"That you can't possibly love me. Or if you do, you'll come to hate me. *I* cost you this hand and everything you ever wanted. Sooner or later I'll be exiled for being a wizard, and . . ." She sucked in a sob. "You'll have to choose between me and the country and the family you love. Or maybe you'll just meet someone else who is, is normal—"

He grabbed her neck and kissed her, cutting off the vile forecasts. Trembling, she parted her lips; her tongue tagged his, drew back, and darted forward in invitation. His lips roved down her throat, and she gasped and clasped his head. Her hands grazed tender bruises and scrapes, but the pain melted in the rising heat of a need finally fulfilled. At last he tasted her, a salty tingle on his tongue like spicetarts at Winterfest. At last his fingers twined through hair like spun amber. His palms stroked hard muscles under silky pale skin. His heart pumped yearning to his pores, and the air grew hot and damp. He yanked his shirt off and dove after another kiss. His hands crept beneath her tunic, delighting in the warm, smooth curves—

She shuddered and dropped her arms to her sides. Smoothing her hair aside, he studied her eyes. In the dim light, he couldn't see their color, but he could see her earnestness. Her fingers crept around his wrists, and he felt the pulse in her thumb echo his own. He kissed her knuckles. "I can forgive, if you can."

Nodding, she wrapped her arms round his neck and pressed her mouth to his.

Each kiss restored her. The hammering above her eye ebbed, the churning in her belly eased. Aches melted away. Each caress brought bliss as his tongue explored her clavicle, his fingers brushed a shoulder, slid down a flank. Yet when his hands crept under her tunic, tracked up her ribs, doubt froze her limbs. Military life allowed no space for modesty, and killing sometimes called for a lover's intimacy, but the last person to know her like this was Lornk. She trembled at how much she had craved the Relmlord, even while she hated him. She'd longed for Ashel too—there was that pull, like iron to a magnet, she'd resisted every time they were together. Her desire for Lornk had *felt* like a parasite, but the need for Ashel really was an infection—

"I can forgive, if you can," he said.

Elesendar, had he Heard her? Did it matter? Whether it was the Woern's need or hers, she wanted him. Her arms flew round him, her lips tasted his, and life passed into her, washing away doubt. She shrugged out of her tunic, shivered and hugged his head as his tongue danced across her breast. An electric charge sparked from skin to skin, and they shimmied out of trousers and nested together, arms and legs wrapped round torsos. Fingers migrated below her navel; he murmured something, a bass rumble she couldn't discern over the rush of blood to her head. He found the point where heat roiled, stoked it into a blossoming fire that enveloped her loins and surged past her heart and lungs to explode in waves behind her eyes.

"How does a chaste Lathan prince know how to do that?" she gasped.

Kissing her neck, he chuckled. "A few tricks a courtesan taught a soldier from Alna."

"Shrine, is Geram with you now?" She drew back.

Laughing, he tugged her close. "He's asleep."

She grinned and straddled his lap, heart pounding, loins tight and dripping need. His breath gushed down her throat as she guided him inside her, but hers caught at the lancing pain.

"Did I hurt you?" He stilled, dark eyes shedding concern.

"No." She kissed him deeply. How that piece of her could be intact after years of jumping out of trees, dodging blows and taking them, she didn't know, but as their tongues darted and twined, the virgin sting faded. Her body wrapped him, contained him, shivers passing between them as they forged a bond through shared heat, tempering it in the sweat slicking their skin. Another pierce jabbed inside her, not pain but a burst of dark energy that shuddered up her spine, and as he swelled inside her, the love she felt for him, which had been withered and stunted, began to grow like a parched seedling exposed to light and water. Warm and green, it spread through her blood, cycled through her heart, blossomed and ripened in her mind. Beneath her, Ashel pressed his hips up, pulling hers down, his teeth bared. Then they collapsed into a heap, their arms tight as salvation around each other.

Dawn seeped through the canvas, sculpting Ashel's neck and shoulder like an artist carving life from polished wood. "I love you," Vic whispered, looping an arm over his chest, awed at the potency of the feeling now that she'd finally admitted to it. Admitted it, let it in, into her heart and her head. It wasn't just the Woern, she promised herself. She'd longed for him long before taking the Elixir, but her preoccupation with Lornk—her shame over the remnants of desire she'd felt for the Relmlord, and her need to purge those sensations through blood and vengeance—hadn't left any room for *love*. She swallowed a devilish giggle and hoped Lornk had heard them. In his tower in Traine, he had starved her, terrified her, manipulated, intimidated, abused, and pleasured her. He'd demanded every form of intimacy, except he'd never stuck his cock in her cunt. Why he had left that part of her untouched was a mystery, but she was glad to have shared it first with Ashel. "My love," she whispered.

And now, her *husband*. Among the Oreseekers, marriage was celebrated in public with feasting and dancing, and most people had sampled multiple partners before they matched to one. For Lathans, or inlanders at least, a first bedding was a wedding—a thing meant to last a lifetime. "I love you, and I can forgive if you can," she promised, thinking of all the people, like more than one of the pirates outside, who cast him admiring glances like fishhooks. Jealousy spiked, as strong as affection.

Ashel jerked and uttered a clipped shout. She rose on an elbow, pressed a palm against his thudding heart. "It's only a dream, my love." Shrine, it felt good to say that, to mean it and know the truth of it.

Eyes blinking open, he threaded fingers through hers. "Am I still dreaming?"

She kissed his cheek and pulled him round to face her. "I'm here. Me and two score pirates and the former Relmlord." She knuckled the black fuzz framing his jaw. "You're not quite as pretty with this beard."

"It's been a while since I've had a proper shave."

"I like it, and you're still the loveliest person I've ever met. You ready to leave?"

"Are you? Let's have another go to be sure." Eyes sparkling, he opened her knees and buried his tongue in the cleft between her thighs. Breath gushed from her lungs as he explored, lingering here and dancing there according to each moan and purr. It was as if they wove a symphony together, his tongue her conductor, she his muse. Heat waved up her nerves. Her fingers balled into fists. Her hips rose toward him, followed by her feet and shoulders.

When her back arched and body trembled in bursting ecstasy, his kisses climbed her torso and he pushed inside her. She wrapped her legs around him, pulled herself tighter onto him, while his thrusts sent starbursts through her blood. A final squeeze, and a gush from two throats melded into a single cry.

He settled them on the mat, where they lay with matched grins, skin pressed to skin as he slowly twirled her hair round his fingers. "You know," he said, "in Alna there are shops where you can buy a woman-shaped balloon. For lovemaking."

Her jaw dropped as she wondered just how much bawdy knowledge he'd acquired from Geram. "Your Highness, my ability to float does not make me a balloon."

"But the lovemaking does make you my wife, Marshal."

"Just marshal? I don't get to be a Highness too?"

"Only Beth's husband will get that title, if she marries before she's Ruler." His humor faded. "When she's queen, he'll be called Your Majesty, same as my mother was while Sashal was alive."

"I miss your father." She kissed the yellowed skin under his eye. "Why do you look like you've been beaten with a stick?"

"Many sticks, not to mention steed tentacles and a rock." He told her about the flight with Melba and a friendly outlaw. "It was the Kragnashian chasing us. Then Thiellin sent it to harry any cavalry that might be in pursuit. I hope Beth is all right—she's at the outpost, isn't she?"

"She should be, and I'm sure she's fine. I want to know what you were doing when I found you."

A corner of his mouth slid sideways. "I suppose you heard about the mess I got into with the Caleisbahnin."

"What mess?"

"It was in all the papers—a year ago last autumn."

"When I was at the front, preoccupied with blood and vengeance." She stroked his beard. "Just tell me, my love. Shrine, I like saying that: my love."

"Well, I lost a lot of money to some Caleisbahn gamers. Since I'm not Heir, I have no right to the royal coffers, so I asked the

Guild for a loan. Instead the Harmony got the Senate to banish the gamblers."

"And how did you end up here?"

"Lornk paid the debt, and he paid the Herders to bring me here. Joslyrn—he's the one with the clay-molded hair—he tricked Melba into introducing us, and then he lured me out on the plains by offering me a chance to ride a steed. They're beautiful and unimaginably fast, and I've wanted to ride one all my life. It was supposed to be an afternoon lark, but here I am."

"What does Lornk want with you now?"

"He told me something in Olmlablaire, which I haven't shared with you." A long sigh blew from his lips, and a tear rolled across his nose. "Lornk never married Earnk's mother—my Aunt Richelle."

She touched her lips to his. "I know. Your mother told me he seduced Richelle into living as a mistress rather than his wife."

"Well, the reason he never married Aunt Richelle, it wasn't . . ." He swallowed. "It wasn't just because he's depraved but because he was already married to my mother, by Lathan custom. They never declared, but . . . they wed, and there's a good chance he's my father."

Her love and the urge to protect him surged as she studied the shame writ across his face. "Sashal loved you, Ashel, and he bore as much pride in you as any father could for his child."

His eyes narrowed. "My mother wed *Lornk*. That makes Sashal a cad and Bethniel a bastard. If the Senate found out, they'd force Mother off the throne and wouldn't let Bethniel succeed."

She sighed at Latha's strange and strict moral customs, wincing at the pain they'd caused her, when every promotion and honor she'd received had been questioned because she'd once been Lornk's slave. Her fingers combed through his curls. "Lornk bewitches people. Look how deeply he has his hooks into Wineyll. Whatever happened with your mother, it was a long time ago, and she despises him now. Is this why you challenged Lornk to a duel?"

Darkness flooded his eyes. "He owns my debt now, and he threatened Bethniel. Challenging him was the only way I could see to shed the hooks he still has in my family. After you arrived, and fainted, the Caleisbahnin decided to postpone the challenge until they obtained your approval. They've decided I belong to you." He laughed again, the sound sharp as an obsidian blade. "But Lornk still owns the debt, so by Betheljin law, he owns me."

"What if I buy it?" Helara's guildbond was still in her pack. "The debt, what if I pay it off?"

"Do you have thirty thousand mullas tucked away somewhere?"

Her mouth fell open. "How much?" A season's provisions for the entire Lathan army cost less. "How did—" Her questions fell away in a bed of shock.

Grimacing, he slipped into his trousers. "It was a wild night in Alna, with too much drink and too many temptations. I thought I was wise, choosing a gaming house instead of a brothel."

A grin spread into a laugh, and she pressed her forehead to his. "My storybook prince is *not* perfect? Praise Elesendar!"

His echoing smile melted into a gentle kiss. "Last night, I wasn't thinking about how this affects you . . . Lornk might demand *you* work the debt off as a mercenary."

She tugged her tunic over her head. "And it will be a wet day in Kragnash when that happens. Thanks to you, I feel completely restored. We'll grab Wineyll and go, now."

Ashel cupped her face, draining the tension from the bridge of her nose. "How do you feel?"

Not a whiff of migraine lurked behind her eyes. "As if I'd never been sick—it's miraculous."

"We can't leave Lornk free. Could you carry me, him, and Wineyll without getting sick?"

"I brought down a mountain, my love."

"Could you take us all the way to the outpost," he pressed, "in one go, so there was no chance Lornk could escape? Could you keep Wineyll out of your head, keep her from doing what she did to you in Olmlablaire, when we almost lost you?"

She bit her lip. "You think she'd try again?"

"I love Wineyll; she's a little sister to me, but I don't trust her where Lornk is concerned."

She considered that Wineyll might be Hearing everything they said. *Do not betray us,* she begged, in case the girl was Listening. "I could take you out of here, then come back for them. I'll bring them out separately, so she can't try anything."

"Distance doesn't matter to me and Geram."

"Wineyll and I aren't linked, Ashel."

He sighed. "If you took us separately, there's the risk they could be gone by the time you returned to fetch Lornk. I think there may be a Device in this area. It's too risky to come east, otherwise." He quirked an eyebrow. "Would the Blade be up for some reconnaissance?"

"You want to stay?"

"If Febbin and Melba made it to the outpost, there might be a cavalry unit on its way here, and they could surely use your help. You should pretend you're still too sick to use your powers."

She chuckled. "My husband, Prince of Latha. Your mother and sister would be proud."

A sad smile bloomed and faded. "Let's say I'm doing this for my father."

When they ducked out of the tent, the breakfasting pirates stood and bowed, but guffaws and sniggers whisked around the fire too. They'd doubtless heard every gasp and moan. Mortification and annoyance twisted together, and Vic let that sourness show on her face, rubbing her temples in a mime-show of powerlessness.

Ashel grasped her hand and cleared his throat. Making a Lathan marriage official was beyond simple; they said the words together, speaking aloud: "We declare ourselves wed."

Openly laughing, the Caleisbahnin and outlaws gathered round, offering congratulations. Drawing Ashel to the fire, they slapped his back like comrades, not enemies. Blood heated Vic's cheeks, but satisfaction warmed her gut when she saw Lornk's eyes glowing blue as a flame's heart. She had seen him this angry, but never this impotent. "Never yours," she mouthed at him, feeling her vengeance was complete at last.

"Madam," Kelmair bowed and offered her a sliced citrus. "Would you like tea?"

At a nod, the woman darted to the fire. Vic stared at her scars, recalling the Herders' betrayal. Bastards, every one of them. She settled on a log and chewed a wedge while Ashel sat with the outlaws. The fruit caught in Vic's throat as she recalled the steeds crushed by boulders in the clearing where she'd found Ashel and the pirates. She hadn't meant to kill their mounts. Damn! So much she'd done that needed forgiveness.

"Vic?" Hand shaking, Wineyll held out a corona of wildflowers, another at her side. "In the southern Kiareinoll, where my father is from, a bride and groom wear these their first day as newlyweds."

"Thank you, but—"

"You don't have to. I know these aren't people you'd like to celebrate with. I just wanted you to know that I'm happy for you."

Taking the wreath, Vic squeezed the girl's fingers. So much that needed forgiving. "I thank you. And I'm sorry. I'm going to get us away from here, but"—she rubbed her temples—"I need a little more time."

Blinking quickly, the minstrel ducked her head. "Take this one for Ashel. Tell him I'm happy for him too. Be happy together." *I won't betray you,* she added in Vic's mind, *but I won't go with you or let you take him.* With short, quick steps, she returned to Lornk, climbed into his lap, and rested her head on his shoulder. The fruit sour on her tongue, Vic looked away.

"Anything else?" Kelmair laid a cup of tea and some dry cheese on the log.

"No, thanks." Vic fingered the flower petals.

"I've never met a mistress like you before." The pirate settled herself cross-legged on the log. "I mean, the ones I knew are sniveling maens and shemens, too google-eyed to look sideways at their masters, much less escape and go to Direiellene." She nodded toward Lornk and Wineyll. "Like that one."

"Wineyll has more courage than you," Vic growled.

Blinking, Kelmair slid off the log. "Yes, madam." With a bow, she fled.

Plopping a wreath on her head, Vic glared at Lornk, vowing to free Wineyll if it was the last thing she did.

ABDUCTION

Two score cavaliers—less than half the full company that had left the outpost—followed Febbin into the clearing where he said the outlaws had camped. A granite outcrop towered above the trees, its face shattered. A pyre smoldered amid fractured boulders. Bethniel shuddered, remembering the blasted rock of Olmlablaire.

"Why blow up the rock?" Lillem asked. "And how much sulfa would this take?"

"A lot." Or none. Dread and hope settled on Bethniel's shoulders. Both were old friends now, especially when it came to Vic. Could her sister be out here? She suddenly regretted not checking her mail before they left the outpost.

Febbin screamed and leapt off his mount, falling to his knees beside the pyre. As his sobs echoed off the stones, Bethniel studied the human remains smoking alongside three steed carcasses. Relief washed through her; the hands on the skeletons were whole, the frames too short for her brother and too tall for Vic. Dozens of footprints headed east out of the camp, the trail a clear sign the Kia wanted them to find Lornk and his allies.

Two days later, the horses picked their way through hoarsgrout and messernils toward broken echoes of laughter and song. Greldren signaled a halt as a trooper slipped out of the underbrush. Straining to Listen—wishing she had real talent for it—Bethniel leaned forward in her saddle.

"—killed their last scout. They'll have no warning."

Greldren issued orders, and the company split to flank the

144

pirates, the horses silent as stalking cats. "Keep her Highness safe," the fieldmarshal ordered Lillem.

Hefting a spear, Lillem brought his stallion alongside Bethniel's mount. She gripped her own spear and breathed deeply, wrestling her fear into the box, and drawing out her wrath. *Lornk Korng will be killed or captured today*, she promised herself, *and Ashel will be safe*. In Olmlablaire, she'd foolishly believed the Relmlord wouldn't dare harm her brother. Now she knew better.

A year ago, when rumors of Prince Ashel's imminent wedding to Vic the Blade swept through Narath, Wineyll had privately scoffed at other girls' late-night laments. That spring, her tears had spilled over her father's grave, not heart-littered diary entries about Latha's most desirable bachelor. Yet like the other girls, she had wondered what the artistic scholar-prince could possibly see in the caustic warrior.

"What about the *Elesendar*'s technical specifications?" Vic asked as the couple squeezed through a gap in the underbrush. They walked apart from the pirates but still close enough Wineyll could Hear them. "What scriptural meaning can you possibly glean from a manual on touchscreen maintenance?"

"The Logs are full of mysteries," Ashel replied sagely. "Do you know what a touchscreen is?"

"It's a glass plate you use to control the ship's functions."

"By touch. Very mystical and mysterious."

"The real mystery is how you people can believe we came from trees. What about cats and horses and cows? The mammals on this world are nothing like any other animal. Where did they come from? Did Elesendar mate with a bush?"

Ashel laughed. "What do you mean, '*you* people?' That's *our* people, Marshal Victoria of Ourtown, ward of the Lathan Ruler and bride to a Lathan prince. And please explain how arrival by spacecraft is any more believable than Elesendar's gift of life?"

"Well, for one thing, we can *see* the spacecraft!"

Wineyll sniggered behind a fall of her hair and soaked up her Guild-brother's happiness. Yesterday the newlyweds had walked together quietly, holding hands while Vic pretended to need Ashel's help to endure the long day's march. After another night of hushed moans and choked laughter, the couple had emerged bright-eyed and cheery. Vic's feigned illness evaporated in the enthusiasm of their scriptural debate.

Their delight washed away Wineyll's bitterness, and the chortles she secretly shared with them stirred up nuggets of hope, like gold in a stream. But the gold sifted from her grasp as the couple's conversation turned toward the Guild and the Harmony's purge.

"Silnauer wants to bury anything she thinks will promote heresy," Ashel said bitterly. "She doesn't want people questioning why a just god would allow evil like this"—he raised his hand—"or what happened to Wineyll."

"You look troubled." Lornk wrapped an arm round her shoulders.

She jerked away. "You—you told Silnauer about Olmlablaire." She'd never confronted him on her expulsion from the Guild, but spite suddenly oozed from that reopened wound.

His lips rolled down, the lines at his eyes deepening. "You don't need a guild to shine. In Traine, all the musicians freely compete for renown. The only politics are those of proficiency and talent." His hands grasped her shoulders. "You would triumph there."

"What would you know about it? You've never even heard me play."

Someone shouted, and a thunder of hooves rolled toward them, horses and soldiers screaming. Swords flew out of scabbards and orders from the commanders.

"Take cover, Songbird." Lornk pushed her toward a geilmor.

"I can hide you," she cried as cavalry crashed into the pirate ranks.

Shoving her away, he parried a spear thrust from a mounted

soldier. The horse reared, and Wineyll dodged into the swirling geilmor limbs. Arrows whizzed and thunked. The men afoot slashed at hamstrings and riders; the cavaliers thrust spears and threw them. Horses kicked and bit. Soldiers and seamen screamed. A pair of cavaliers harried Lornk and Thiellin. Swords and spear hafts clacked and clashed. Back to back, Lornk and the captain retreated toward a dense stand of trees.

Now would be the time to flee, but Wineyll couldn't take her eyes off Lornk. She ought to hate him, and she did when she thought about what he had done to Ashel. Yet he had always been gentle with her, even in Olmlablaire, and as they'd traveled east through the Kiareinoll, he'd given more comfort than the old mothers surrounding them. *"Rape is rape, even when it feels like seduction."* Geram had said that to her once, and it would be easy to call it that, absolve herself of complicity, go to Eldanion and play chamber music for silly nobles until she was reinstated in the Guild and could resume her old life. But she could never resume her old life; it had ended when her father died. Her breath caught as a spear plunged toward Lornk's heart. He ducked, and the spearhead glanced across his shoulder. Relief flooded through her, and she decided: she believed in him.

Pressing her lips flat, she wove the image of a thicket of vines around him and Thiellin. She couldn't see it herself, but she imagined them passing into it, imagined nothing but empty woods on the other side, and folded this image into the minds of their enemies. The Lathans drew rein and looked around in confusion. Thiellin thrust his sword through one cavalier while Lornk gutted the other. Wineyll winced and looked away. She'd just consummated a betrothal.

Cavaliers charged out of the trees, hooves thundering and horns blowing. Three passed them; a fourth stopped to lower his spear at Ashel's chest.

"Lieutenant," Vic scolded, batting at the haft, "get some spectacles! Do we look like Caleisbahnin?"

"I don't know who you are, but—"

"This is Prince Ashel. The one you should be here to rescue?"

The man immediately raised his spear, bowing awkwardly. "Highness. Uh, forgive me." He slipped out of his saddle, offered the reins to Ashel. "Please. Princess Bethniel will be pleased. She's waiting nearby."

"Is anyone *not* in this corner of the Kiareinoll?" Ashel grumbled, taking the reins and mounting. He held his hand down. "I need to get Wineyll."

"I'll find her. You find Beth and keep her safe. Can I borrow a dagger?" Vic asked the cavalier.

His gazed scraped over her. "For what?"

Ashel pulled a dagger out of the horse's trappings and tossed it to Vic. Catching it neatly, she flipped it into the other hand. "She's the Blade," Ashel told the soldier. Spinning the horse around, he laced an arm under her shoulders and pulled her up for a kiss. Feet dangling, she let Woern-bliss soak into her. "Be safe, wife," he said.

Her toes touched the ground, and she squeezed his right hand, holding the thumb and kissing the stump. His eyes tightened, but his lips stayed soft, and he brushed her cheek with his thumb. "See you soon, husband," she said, her chest tight. Flashing her a smile, he kicked the horse in the direction the cavalier had pointed, leaving the stunned trooper behind. With a gruff laugh, Vic thanked him for the dagger and dashed toward the sounds of battle.

She spotted Wineyll cowering against a geilmor and followed the girl's gaze to Lornk. He was hard-pressed by a pair of Lathans, and Vic's throat closed as she watched his end approach. The cavalier jabbed her spear, spun the haft around for a swipe, thrust the point at him again. Driving him backward, wearing him down, she didn't give him time for an attack of his own. Vic had dreamed for years of killing Lornk; it was strange to watch someone else deliver the death blow. She blew out a breath, reminding herself again that she'd given up her chance at him. Lornk was someone else's problem—

He vanished behind a wall of leaves. The troopers hesitated. One fell backward off his mount, blood spurting. The other slid from her saddle, and Lornk appeared above her, driving his sword into her belly. Vic's eyes snapped to Wineyll and the minstrel's gaze, locked on Lornk. Spewing curses, Vic charged out of cover.

"Madam!" cried Etien, the old gnarled Caleisbahnin. Yelling, pirates dodged spears and hooves, rallying toward her. Lathan mounts spun and charged. "Shrine's bastards!" She couldn't let any Lathans see her using wizardry. Sprinting to Wineyll, she grabbed the minstrel.

"Leave me!" Wineyll tried to yank her arm away.

The Lathans caught up to Etien and Gustave. One lost his spear to the blur of the old man's sword. The gap-toothed pirate pulled a sandy-haired woman from her horse.

"Madam," Kelmair stumbled to a halt, panting fiercely. "With your help—"

Vic flashed the point of her dagger under Kelmair's chin. "My help won't go to you. Let us pass." Battle sounds spun around them. A drop of Kelmair's blood trickled down Vic's blade. The pirate woman stepped back, and Vic yanked Wineyll away as a spear thunked into the geilmor's roots. Crying, the minstrel clawed at Vic's hand, twisting in her grip as Vic dragged her into a mesh of vines. She slapped the minstrel. "What are you doing?"

"Please, Vic," Wineyll cried. "I've made my choice."

Anger flared into a hammerstrike behind Vic's eyes. "Lornk isn't a choice; he's a dead man."

"Then I should die with him!"

"Bloody flaming Shrine!" An arm tight round the minstrel's waist, Vic rose a few inches off the ground and darted between stands of hoarsgrout and allenver toward a cerrenil that promised enough cover she could fly unseen to the canopy.

"Leave me, leave me," Wineyll repeated over and over. Each word knocked against Vic's skull and churned the contents of her stomach.

"That vile bastard dies today."

"No!"

Wineyll's cry drilled into Vic's brain, and she tumbled to the ground and retched. The girl vanished into the green, leaving only the cries of battle and the stench of failure.

† † †

Shouts and the clash of weapons filtered through the woods. Bethniel's hand tightened around a spear, foreboding worming out of the box. *Please keep Ashel safe*, she prayed. *Elesendar, please.*

Febbin's mount danced. "I've got to find Joslyrn. Fare well, Highness." His horse sprang into the trees and disappeared.

"Good riddance," Lillem muttered.

Whinnies, shouts, and the clash of weapons filtered toward them; their horses snorted and stamped in response. The noise of combat drifted closer, farther, closer again, dimmed to silence.

A scream erupted, and Bethniel's mare reared up, pawing toward a young soldier reeling from the undergrowth, blood streaming down his face. Bethniel jerked her mount aside as a Caleisbahnin sprang after him, sword high. Flipping her spear around, she rammed the butt into the pirate's breastbone. The blow jarred into her shoulder, but the man fell. Lillem's stallion leapt atop him, hooves grinding his guts into the dirt.

The air stung with acid, sulfur, steel, the stinks of death and fear. "Pull back," the lieutenant barked, and they cantered around a creeper-infested messernil and up a slippery bank of moss.

"Beth! Where's Ashel?"

She pulled hard on the reins, and her horse spun up a spray of leaves. "Vic?"

Stumbling away from a foul mess on the grass, her sister looked sick as a drunken Weaver. "Where is Ashel?"

Pirates broke through the allenver. Bethniel leaned out of her saddle. "Get up behind me."

Lillem's stallion skidded in front of the pirates, and cavalier and mount held them off with a whirring spear and slashing hooves.

Vic looked up with eyes as green as grass. "Where is Ashel?"

"I don't know! Now mount up or fly away!"

One of the pirates scrambled past the stallion's flanks, sword high. Screeching, Bethniel kicked her horse around to face him, but Vic ordered the pirate to hold. He stopped short, the glitter in his eyes as shrill as the silver rings in his ear. "You will not harm her," Vic said aloud. A greedy, gap-toothed smile ignited the Calesibahnin's face, but an older pirate pointed his sword at the ground and backed off.

"Hold, Lieutenant," Bethniel cried as Lillem hefted his spear. "You look like you can barely stand," she said to Vic.

"Then I look better than I feel." Vic's eyes mellowed to gray. "I lost Wineyll."

"Wineyll?" Shoving aside her surprise, Bethniel extended her hand. "We'll find her together."

"Gustave," ordered the older pirate, angling his head toward Vic. Grumbling, the other Caleisbahnin sheathed his sword and knelt, signaling that Vic could step onto his thigh. Bethniel's astonishment mounted as Vic thanked the pirate and took hold of his shoulder for balance.

"Well," Vic said, "are you going to move that animal closer?"

As soon as she was up, the old pirate rushed through the allenver toward the battle, but the young one touched Vic's boot. "I'll look for the snippet, if you wish."

"We'll find her. You'd better go before the lieutenant kills you."

The Caleisbahnin gusted a laugh and stepped back, saluting Lillem with his sword hilt under his chin. "Another time?"

Lillem nodded, his gaze murderous. "Which way did she go?"

"Try that way," Vic pointed at a hedge.

The stallion's ears flicked forward, and a Kragnashian barreled out of the brush and snapped its mandibles through the neck of Bethniel's mare.

The animal shuddered beneath them. Vic's arms cinched Bethniel's waist, and they hurtled backward, curses scoring

Bethniel's ears. Tree trunks and hoarsgrout rushed past the edges of her vision, but her eyes were stuck on Lillem's spear plunging into one Kragnashian as a second charged them. Vic spun around and rocketed into the canopy, her arms still locked round Bethniel. Leaves and twigs scored her cheeks; she threw her hands over her face and choked on a scream.

A hissing thwook cut past the whipping branches, the acrid stink dreadfully familiar. Vic jerked, the vise of her arms convulsing into Bethniel's diaphragm, driving the air from her chest in a violent huff. Vic's shriek was an awl in her ear, a terrible cry that chased their fall through crashing limbs. They struck the ground, and Vic twisted away, back arched, throat emitting an inhuman squeal. Sucking air, Bethniel struggled to hands and knees. The Kragnashian rolled toward them. Lillem's stallion screamed. Hooves scrabbled against the creature's armor as its legs enveloped Bethniel in shadow. Sharp spines raked her skin; the dense smell of grass stuffed desperate lungs, and then she could breathe. Turning in the creature's wake, she saw it sweep Vic off the ground.

Cursing, Gustave sprinted after it. He leapt aboard the trailing abdomen, and the Kragnashian fled with Vic and the pirate.

"Lillem!" Bethniel shouted. The lieutenant pulled her up behind him, and his horse raced after the abductor. The stallion's muscles surged as it leapt gullies and twisted around trees. Bethniel glimpsed Gustave fighting to hang on as the Kragnashian pulled ahead and disappeared.

Sweat foamed the stallion's haunches; his breath grew ragged. "I'm sorry, Highness," Lillem said, letting the horse slow to a walk. "It's just too fast."

Anguish squeezed Bethniel's chest—Vic was taken! The scent of cut grass—of hope—flared her nostrils, and she pointed at a bit of pale green ooze. "It's wounded; follow it."

The stallion trotted along the glimmering trail to an earthwork, densely covered with hoarsgrout and crowned with a gnarled old geilmor.

"You don't mean to go in there?"

"It has my sister!"

"Highness, I saw what she did—if the Kragnashians want her, let them have her."

"You don't have to come with me; just give me a spear."

"You're not going to fight those things."

"No, I'm going to negotiate with them. Give me a spear."

Lips flat and sour, Lillem pulled two from the trappings and fished a lantern out of his saddlebags. Hefting the stallion's reins, he scanned the nearby brush.

"Let him go. If another comes, he should be free to run."

"How will we get back?"

She studied the opening, the faint scrollwork on the supporting stones. "I don't think we'll be coming back this way."

Expelling a breath, he slapped the stallion on the rump and clucked it homeward.

They descended a steep ramp thick with cobwebs. Dust sparkled like fog in the lamplight. In a chamber at the bottom, Kragnashians' tracks swirled around the broad, shallow depression and gemstone-studded compass slots of a Device. She knelt next to the small knob stuck in one of the slots, between a pair of glowing blue gems. "Looks like it took her to Direiellene. Are you coming?"

His knuckles turned yellow around his spear haft. "What do I do?"

"Take my hand." Murmuring a prayer, she grasped the knob, and pinpricks sizzled over her skin.

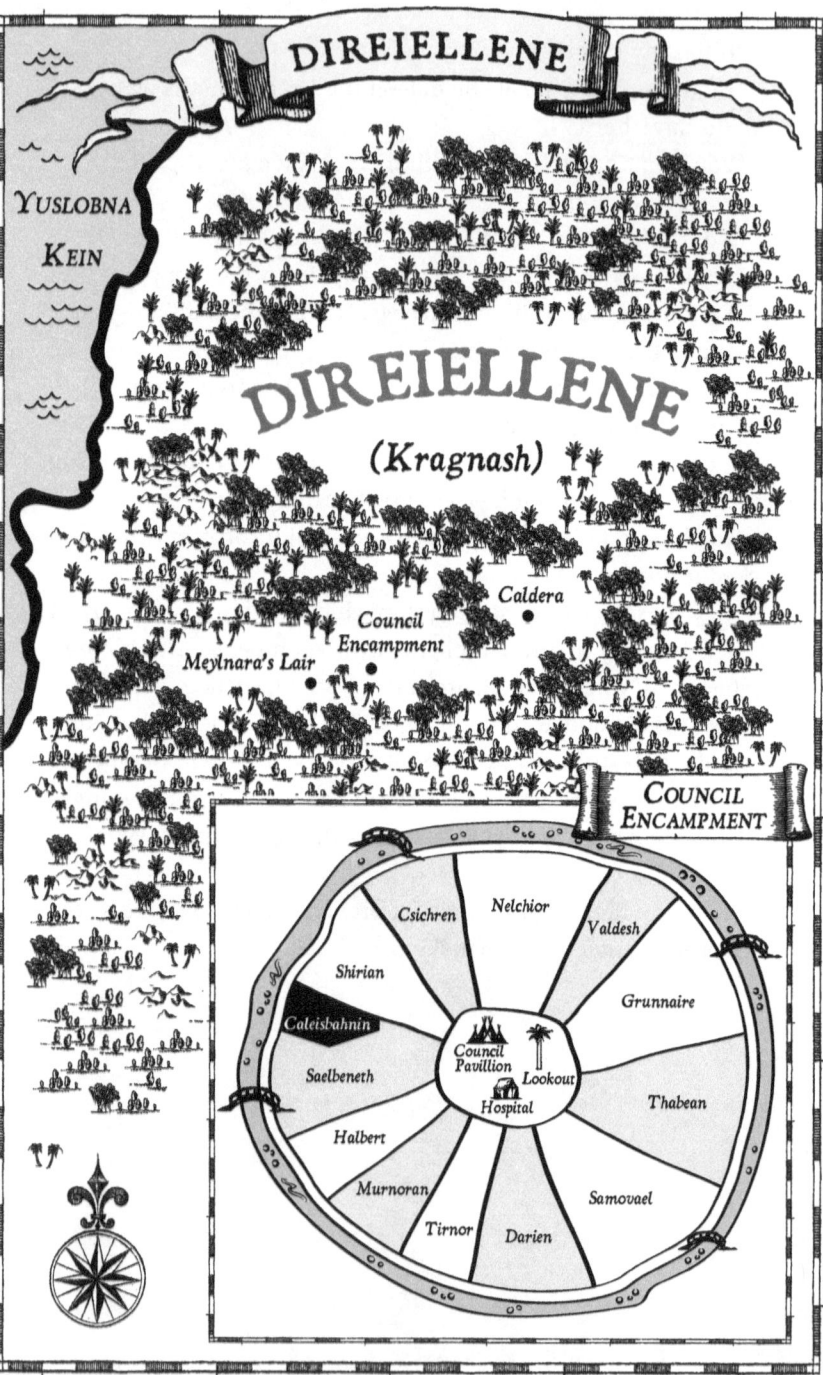

DIREIELLENE

YUSLOBNA
KEIN

DIREIELLENE

(Kragnash)

Caldera

Council
Encampment

Meylnara's Lair

COUNCIL
ENCAMPMENT

Csichren   Nelchior

Valdesh

Shirian

Grunnaire

Caleisbahnin

Saelbeneth   Council
Pavillion   Lookout
Hospital

Thabean

Halbert

Murnoran   Samovael

Tirnor   Darien

PART TWO

Personal Log, Captain Franklin T. J. Wong, United Mineral Mining Vessel, Registry LSNDR2237, June 30, 2153

Barb's report is in; nothing conclusive. We checked and rechecked and checked again all systems before launch, and I can't help wondering whether the saboteur is on board. Morale is low—an understatement. Barb's people are working on restoring the communication grid, but privately she told me there's not much hope. A thousand ifs are in my head. If we had set watch differently, if we had done more background checks. If UM had put more resources behind this op. Nine hundred and ninety-seven more ifs.

What would Jason say now? Eliza and Genny will be in college by the time they figure out we're not coming back. I wonder how long UM will wait before telling them. Lie to them and say everything's fine for two whole years before they 'fess up. Probably. Let people move on to other jobs, up or down the ladder, to other corps, and make some poor slob who wasn't involved deal with the inquiries from the families.

But I've got a planet to settle. Craig is down there learning to speak with the indigenous. Let's hope we don't have to kill them all. Let's hope they don't kill us. I don't want us to be another Roanoke.

155

THE WAY OF TREES

Carrion flies buzzed around the mare's severed neck, dove greedily into the Kragnashian's oozing thorax. Ashel stared at the gory feast and tried to make sense of the fieldmarshal's words.

"No sign of them, Highness," Greldren repeated.

He paced alongside crushed grass and scattered leaves. "There are hoofprints here, clear as day. I'm no tracker, and I can see them."

"Highness," the outpost commander's voice shook. He spoke aloud. "The tracks disappear. It seems Fembrosh—"

"Don't tell me about Fembrosh," Ashel growled. Greldren and a pair of cavaliers followed him down the trail to a wild hedge growing across the tracks.

"There's no trail on the other side," Greldren said.

Ashel's next breath stuttered past a spiraling madness like the one that had landed him in Lornk's dungeon. "That makes no sense."

"What can we know of the way of trees?"

The way of trees. A soldier quoted scripture to him while he battled helpless, hapless despair. "I—" he faltered. He was a prince of Latha, of this ground they stood upon, but what decree could he issue that would bring his wife and sister back? "I want them found," he said feebly.

"Of course, Highness. However . . . we must prioritize the recapture of Lornk Korng."

He glared at the fieldmarshal. "Could you spare two troopers to help me look for the *Heir*?" His sister, and Vic, his *wife*!

156

"Of course, Highness."

They searched all day and into the evening. In the gloaming, rocks and humus melted into a gray soup of lost signs. Ashel twisted round in his saddle and asked for a torch.

The cavaliers exchanged hopeless glances before the man pawed through his gear. The woman clucked her mount closer. "You should return to camp, Highness. We can resume the search in the morning."

Fatigue embossed circles under her eyes, and the other soldier swayed in his saddle. Ashel's limbs trembled. He'd had a few swallows of cold tea and a flatcake that morning and nothing since—nearly sixteen hours. None of that mattered. "I asked for a torch."

"The horses need rest and fodder too, sir," the man said.

Throat tight, Ashel slid to the ground. "Take them back, then."

"Highness, we cannot leave you. There may still be Caleisbahnin—"

"Go. Take the horses. I'll return on my own." The troopers hesitated, but when he repeated the order a third time, they handed over torch and flint and trotted off. The forest grew still. A gizzard hooted. Knees shaking, he resumed the zigzag pattern they'd followed all day, hoping the yellow torchlight would reveal a gleam of blood or other sign they'd missed in the dappled sunshine.

Don't do this again, Geram said. *Don't let your grief drive you into madness.*

There has to be some trace of them.

You know there doesn't. Not if the Kia doesn't want you to find them.

Why would it hide them from me?

What can we know—

"Shut up, Geram," he said aloud. "Geram Geram Geram."

The other man said nothing, but Ashel could feel his elbows on his knees, Hear him debating how best to tell the queen her daughter and Vic had disappeared and Lornk Korng had escaped. He hated that Mother knew of his secret connection to Geram and hated that her knowing couldn't help anyone right now.

A citrus draft filled his lungs, and a wealth of spring tresses blossomed in the wavering torchlight. Snuffing the fire to avoid harming the old mother, Ashel parted the flowered vines and knelt among gnarled roots. "Please lead me to them," he implored, pressing both hands against the trunk. "You led Vic to me. Help me find her now." He poured his fear and need onto the bark. "My sister. She came here to teach the squatters to revere you, and when she's Ruler, her duty will be to protect you as much as to govern the human and erin peoples of Latha. Please help me find her."

Limp branches rustled, and more citrus scent wafted over him. Elesendar winked through the leaves. His eyes soaked in the meager light, picked out a darker patch of ground snaking away from the cerrenil. A trail! Hope flushed fatigue from his limbs, and he loped down the narrow track. No stone or root hindered him; he moved swiftly, breath puffing, heart pumping, a shadow among shadows, down into gullies and up embankments, past outcroppings and meadows. He ran minutes, half an hour, an hour—the time seemed long, but no weakness of heart or lungs or legs slowed him until the trail led up a rise to another cerrenil. A figure slumped among tangled roots. Heart thudding, he crept closer. It was Erik. Cold stiff fingers clutched his flask, his life long since drained from a gaping wound. Grief and disappointment tore out of Ashel's throat.

She has to know, Geram said.

"No, no, no," Ashel sobbed. A helpless, hapless man's plea and prayer: no, don't tell her. No, don't let them be gone. Geram opened his bedroom door. Ashel ripped the flask from the dead man's grasp. Fingers tracing the wall, Geram headed toward the stairs. Ashel choked down the liquor, shivering as it burned a path to his stomach.

Geram grasped a bannister, stepped onto a riser. Falling cerrenil blossoms dusted Ashel's eyelashes and cheeks, recalling the tickle of Vic's hair. *Be safe, wife.* Harlolinde burned his tongue. Kill you fast or kill you slow, people said of har and the liquor distilled from it. He took another mouthful. It went down easier this time. Slower.

Geram's hand slid along the turning of the railing, and he ascended a second flight. A dance of Bethniel's laughter surrounded Ashel. His sister had always found joy where she could, like her father. "Like *our* father," Ashel muttered, sucking at the flask.

Geram knocked.

Harlolinde blurred Ashel's view of Elesendar winking through the intertwined branches.

Elekia opened her door. *"I have news,"* Geram said.

Ashel tipped back the flask, gulping until nothing but air drained into his mouth. Gasping, he staggered up.

"What is it?" Elekia asked, her voice taut with irritation.

Geram cleared his throat. *"There's been a battle . . ."*

"Geram," Ashel whispered, his tongue thick. "Geram. Geram. Geram." He repeated the name, crashing through a stand of allenver, slipping to his knees on a bed of moss. The liquor blinded him. The forest spun around him, but he still Heard Geram say the words that sealed a fate he dreaded. *No, don't tell her. Don't make it true.*

"The Heir and the Blade have been taken or killed. By Kragnashians."

In the silence that followed, he felt his mother's arms circling his head, Sashal's blood hot on his lap, her breath on his face as she murmured a lullaby. He imagined her now, pressing her fingers into her eyes, rocking herself because she heard this news alone and the only one to know her grief couldn't see it. But through this fancy, a hand pressed against his—no, Geram's—chest. *"Can he feel this?"* she asked.

An arm jerked under his chin, banishing his mother's touch. "You want to find your wife?" Lornk hissed. "Come with me."

Geram imagined Elekia's eyes, tight over the quivering corners of her mouth. A face to match the quaver in her voice, begging comfort in a year of death and loss. Ashel drunk and lost to him, he laid his hand over hers. Her flesh felt cold, brittle, like frozen glass about to shatter. "No, he can't feel me right now."

"Come in, please," she whispered. The urge to hold her, and hold her together, drove him across the threshold. The door shut. Palms found cheeks, clasped necks. Her lips were salty, her breath sweet. Her skin warmed, and she did not break.

THE WRONG SIDE
OF HISTORY

Black fire enveloped Bethniel, searing her flesh, stealing her breath. She had no mouth or lungs to voice the scream that vibrated in every molecule. She had no brain, yet she knew something was wrong.

After an eternity, the black fog of the Device cleared, and she collapsed to her knees, sucking air like a drowned woman.

"Highness," Lillem gasped, leaning heavily on his spear.

The last time she'd traveled by Device, there had been an uncomfortable prickling, not debilitating agony. Trembling, she climbed to her feet. A weird green light seeped through fibrous walls, and damp air clung to her skin. The Device's knob emerged from a complex web of slots.

"I've never been here before," she breathed. "This isn't the Device chamber in the Kragnashian capital."

Three of the creatures flowed through a doorway. Lillem lifted his spear and froze. Bethniel's feet were rooted to the ground, her arms and face stuck as if covered in plaster. Only her heart could move, and it was trying to hammer out of her rib cage.

A woman stood behind the Kragnashians. Hair hung in knotted mats; grime streaked naked skin. Vinegar and rot—the stink of a human body long unwashed—overpowered the springtime scent of the Kragnashians.

"They're not wizards." The woman clicked and chattered in an

161

unfamiliar dialect of Kragnashian, but she made no effort to hide her thoughts. Damp heat, green light, and the woman's matted red hair planted a seed, and comprehension sprouted like a weed. *It can't be*, Bethniel thought. *She cannot be Meylnara.*

The woman grasped Lillem's wrist. "A drudge," she clicked, her lips twisted in distaste. A Kragnashian swooped forward; long mandibles gripped Lillem under the arms.

Bethniel's scream squeezed through sealed lips. Lillem's shouts were strangled groans as the Kragnashian hauled his stiffened form out of the room.

The woman's fingertips grazed Bethniel's arm and sprang back. She smiled. "You're a . . . a . . . latent!" The words were slow, halting, and in a language Bethniel had never heard, but now the woman spoke rather than clicked. "Sister, why have you come?"

"Where is my companion?" Bethniel asked in mindspeech.

"He's a drudge." The woman flicked her hand dismissively. "Have you come to help me?"

Limbs free, Bethniel stumbled into her own balance. Worry for Lillem and Vic twined round her throat, but she pasted on a smile. "Yes, I'll help you. You're Meylnara, aren't you? What do you need?"

The woman clasped her hands. "Meylnara is the name my mother gave me. What do I need? More like you. The People say they can bring no more, but here you are. Can you bring more?"

Bethniel glanced at the web of slots and gemstones behind her. "I could try. Did someone come ahead of me?"

One of the Kragnashians chittered, and Meylnara's smile melted. "You did not come to help me."

"I will—"

"Liar! You want to take her from me!" Bethniel's skin tightened; her limbs stiffened. Even her eyelids felt glued open. A Kragnashian flowed toward her. A keen leaked past her teeth. Mandibles snapped around her; breath gushed and ribs groaned as the creature carried her outside. Its tendrilled legs swished through broad-leafed ferns, past tree trunks wide as houses. Knotted moss draped branches;

dew dripped like rain as the creature scrambled up a jumbled wall of lichen-mottled logs. Bethniel's limbs jerked out of paralysis, but she could not budge the creature's jaws. It plowed through a thicket of branches, heedless of her cries as twigs raked her face. At the top, the creature flung her into the green shadows beyond the wall, and she fell into a forest that hadn't existed for a thousand years.

Heroes and Scoundrels

Thabean parted the mossy screen and peered at the Lair. Far below, Meylnara's creatures moved in and out of an immense cone composed of shrinking layers, each a dozen feet high and gleaming white, even under the pregnant clouds. Roughly stacked logs served as a wall round the compound.

"My arse hurts," Dealn complained around a mouthful of nuts. "Couldn't you put more padding down?"

Thabean shifted on the branch, his own backside aching after the hours they'd spent lodged in the canopy, surveilling the Lair. "Next time bring a pillow."

"I would if you'd let me, Pip."

Thabean arched an eyebrow. His brother, who topped him by a head and had twice the breadth of shoulders, had teased him for being small as long as Thabean could remember. Eyes twinkling, Dealn dumped another handful of nuts into his mouth.

"Must you masticate like that?" Thabean asked as crunching ground against his ears.

"I must. You want some?"

"I want you to eat quietly."

"Is that a Caleisbahnin?" Dealn leaned forward. Below, one of Meylnara's creatures carried a man, limbs frozen stiff as a statue. Cresting the stacked logs, the minion dropped him. A loud oof followed a crack and a thump as the seaman tumbled into some ferns at the base of the wall. Staggering up, he pressed a hand to his ribs and scowled.

"Put feelers into the Caleisbahn camp," Thabean said. "Find out why they're sending emissaries to Meylnara."

"Looks like the fellow got an icy reception. Did you see how his limbs were frozen, and the bitch wasn't anywhere about?"

"Residual hold. It wears off."

Mingled disgust and worry tightened Dealn's mouth, and Thabean grasped his brother's shoulder. Ever since Thabean had received the Elixir, Dealn's concern had fringed all their private moments. Wizardry was a death sentence, even if it didn't always kill the wizard right away.

Below, the pirate roared and rushed the wall and kicked and hand-chopped at a protruding log. Bark flew from furious blows, but when the man retreated, hands and forearms bloodied, the wall remained solid.

"A barrage of boulders couldn't bring that wall down, sir pirate," Dealn said.

"He can't hear you."

"Ha ha, Pip."

The seaman settled on a fallen log, legs crossed, breathing slowly. After a time, he returned to the jumbled pile and began to climb with more composure but no less determination.

"Elesendar, there's another one."

A shout rang as a minion tossed a second man over the wall, this one with dark brown skin and a spear. "That's no pirate," Thabean muttered, wondering which wizard had sent secret emissaries. The Caleisbahnin paused to watch the newcomer land in the ferns, then resumed his climb. Rising, the dark one spotted the seaman, shouted again, and charged. The Caleisbahnin sprang clear just as the spear thunked into the wall. Dagger in hand, the dark one leapt upon the seaman. Unarmed, the pirate parried and struck with arms and legs. A crack echoed, and the dagger spun into the underbrush. The dark one staggered back, holding his wrist, teeth bared. The Caleisbahnin grinned, and the second man plowed through snaking undergrowth to slam the seaman into a tree. Roaring, the Caleisbahnin shoved him off, and the pair rained blows upon each other with fists and feet.

Dealn grinned and chomped more nuts. "Good fight."

"But who are they, who sent them, and what prompted their conflict?"

Whistling, Dealn shook his head. "I don't know, but now it's getting *really* interesting. Look at *her*."

A third creature stood atop the log pile, a woman struggling in its jaws. The combatants paused, their gaze following her scream. When she crashed into the ferns, the dark one yanked his spear loose and charged the seaman. The woman scrambled toward them, yelling.

"What language is that?"

"I know it not," Thabean replied. The woman put herself between the men, hands out. She was tall and graceful, a froth of black curls capping her head. Even with mouth and eyes taut with fear and bloodied from her fall, she was lovely. Thabean gritted his teeth; taking the Elixir required a vow of chastity, but a man still had appetites, even when he chose to go hungry.

"Shrine, I'd like to have that lady grateful to me," Dealn said, crunching another handful. "She looks threatened by those scoundrels. I think a rescue's in order, don't you?"

Thabean rubbed his ears, a buzzing at the edge of his awareness, like the nag of a forgotten word. "They're using mindspeech!" Only wizards and their ministers could use the Council's secret language, although the Weavers were rumored to have developed telepathy as well. "We'll move closer." Wrapping a cocoon of air around Dealn, he floated them down the greslet trunk. Pale green light melted into deep shadows as they descended through the canopy layers. When they stood among the roots, Thabean released the Woern and stepped out of the void he'd created to hide his power from Meylnara's awareness. Grinning, Dealn preceded him, and they stole through the underbrush. When they drew near, the strangers' silent speech resolved in Thabean's mind.

"Move, Highness!"

"Where do you think we are, Lieutenant? Stand down!"

Peering over a vine-draped log, Thabean found the woman staring down the spear-wielder.

"Listen to your princess, Weaver," the Caleisbahnin said. "She's clever."

The dark man sprang around the woman, brandishing the spear. Dodging, the seaman rushed the woman and locked his arm under her chin. "I'll snap her neck," he promised.

Dealn started to rise, but Thabean held him down, a finger to his lips. "Let's see how she handles this."

Ignoring the arms round her head, the woman splayed her fingers and gestured for calm. "He's only threatening me because you're trying to kill him, Lieutenant. Stand down—I command it."

The soldier hesitated, then lowered the spear. "If you harm her, I will gut you!"

Chuckling, the seaman stepped away from the woman. She expelled a breath and looked between them. "Gentlemen, we have come to this place on the wrong side of history. That was Meylnara." The pirate's grin widened at the soldier's gape, but the woman continued, "Elesendar has brought us here—it's His will that we are here, together. We need each other." The seaman flourished a mocking bow; the soldier glared. The woman swallowed, her face etched with worry. "Is Vic still alive, Gustave?"

The Caleisbahnin sobered. "She was sorely wounded, Princess, but Meylnara spoke of keeping her, so I do not think she intends to kill her. They took her deeper into the compound as they carried me out."

She surveyed the wall. "There are several hundred Kragnashians in there at least. Even if we can get back inside, I doubt we could free her without being caught. We need help."

"From whom, Highness?"

Dealn raised his eyebrows, and Thabean returned a grin. As boys they'd played heroes and scoundrels; as men they often were both on the same day.

"If that is Meylnara, the Council may be nearby," the woman replied.

"Agreed. The compound is fortified against attack," the seaman said. Reluctantly, the solider nodded.

"Then we find them, and we ask for their help."

Thabean cocked his head at Dealn, then rose out of the underbrush, using the Woern to pull Dealn after him. Hand on sword hilt and as tall as the soldier, Dealn struck an imposing figure, but the strangers' gapes fixed on Thabean as he alighted. "And if you found a member of the Council, what would you say?"

The woman donned composure like a veil, her lips curving, but she withheld a full smile like a crafty jeweler hides his best diamonds. "First, sir, I would ask his name," she said aloud in her strange language but letting him Hear her as well.

"Thabean Graystone, Second on the Council."

Her eyebrows shot up, dismay flickering over her features before she restored her courtier's mask. "Sir Thabean. My name is Bethniel."

"Princess Bethniel? Of what land?"

"One far from here, sir, in your Unknown."

"And why are you in Direiellene, Highness?" he said the title mockingly.

Pink stippled brown cheeks. "My sister and I, we heard of your war and came to help. These men"—her blush deepened, and he wondered how thick a lie she spun—"are with us."

"A princess, a soldier, and a Caleisbahn seaman. The soldier and the seaman might be useful, but you, Highness, and your sister—another princess, I presume? What help can you give?" And where on Knownearth were they from?

"My sister—she and I aren't blood sisters—she's an Oreseeker. Lieutenant Lillem and I are from even farther away. Commander Gustave is a Caleisbahnin, as you guessed. He . . . guided us here."

Thabean smirked, his curiosity piqued at her careful phrasing. He suspected she cleaved to the truth, but only in a barrister's sense. "You Heard a question I had, but you did not answer the one I asked."

She straightened her shoulders, raised her chin. She was tall; he had to lift his chin to meet her gaze. "Sir, in my country I'm heir to a throne. But my sister is a warrior, and I promise she can help you defeat Meylnara. We . . . where we're from, there's a sort of prophesy about her—"

He laughed. "A prophesy! My lady, you were doing so well. Captain." He turned to Dealn. "We'll leave these three to their fate."

"Wait, sir, please!" The veil shrank away, leaving her features taut with fear again. "Meylnara holds my sister captive. She's badly hurt, and we don't know what Meylnara intends to do to her. I will serve you"—she flashed a warning glance at the soldier—"however you desire to gain your aid."

He raked his eyes over the woman. Elesendar, what a beauty— before the Elixir he'd have enjoyed competing with Dealn in the wooing of her. His brother's size gave him the initial advantage, but Thabean's wit had often won the day. "My lady, even if I were willing to aid you, it's impossible. All the Council put together have been unable to penetrate this wall. I'm sorry, but your sister is lost."

"I do not accept that. Will you take me to Saelbeneth? I would plead my case to her."

"Saelbeneth does not grant such favors, my lady."

"At least point us in the direction of the Council!"

"I could lead them back," said Dealn casually. "Clear them through the sentries."

Thabean frowned at his brother. This so-called princess was stunning—he couldn't have her, but why deprive Dealn of his chance? "All right. I'll take you to our encampment, and I'll ask Saelbeneth if she will meet you."

FEVER DREAM

The flies were the worst. Rot and midden fouled Vic's nose. Wet heat cloyed her lungs. Her head ached as badly as ever, and fiery spasms shattered any attempt to move her left arm. A metal hinge—Shrine, metal!—bit into her right wrist, chaining it to the wall above. But the flies buzzed into her ears, licked the rims of her eyes, dug at the corners of her mouth. Whenever she roused herself to shake them off, the motion wrung her stomach.

Slithering footsteps pried her eyes open. Passing through shafts of green-tinged light, a filthy woman descended a rough stone ramp. Using the Woern, she nudged Vic away from the wall and examined her ravaged shoulder.

"Where am I?" Vic asked, blowing at a fly.

The woman cringed, and wide eyes shot to a cane grate overhead. "I'm sorry they hurt you, sister."

No breeze stirred the air, but the woman's hair writhed like red snakes over bare breasts. The throbbing in Vic's temples shifted in time with the twisting hair. Shutting her eyes to the seething, sickening motion, she could still sense it. "Where am I?" she asked again.

"The People brought you to me, as a gift."

Recognition squeezed through the flies and pain and stench. She had dreamed of this place years ago in Fembrosh, and the Kragnashians had told her she was the One—the savior who had freed them from Meylnara the Oppressor. But Meylnara had lived a thousand years in the past. Incredulity wedged past pain. How could she have traveled through time?

170

"Eat," the woman said, motioning to a Kragnashian bearing a bowl of blue gel. It tipped the rim against Vic's lips. A few sips drained the pain from her head, but her roiling stomach balked and she turned away. Gently pushing her forward, the creature nipped one of its filamentous legs and slathered her shoulder in grass-scented blood, easing the burning agony. Meylnara urged her to rest, and they left.

Savoring the respite, Vic took deep, slow breaths. *The People brought you to me as a gift.* She had been Lornk's treasured slave. She would not be Meylnara's. She reached for the Woern, and a fiery bolt stabbed behind her eye. Bile, acid, and blue gel erupted, splattering skin and stone. Whimpering, she hung from the manacled arm. Ashel's smile flashed in her mind like a beacon, and a lump closed her throat. She'd finally turned toward love and life, and now the Kragnashians had spun her about and shoved her back down a path toward hate and death.

Hours dragged through noxious agony and mourning. Night melted into the dungeon, and Meylnara returned, a faintly luminous ball floating behind her, casting more shadows than light. Vic gathered her legs under her, enduring the breath-splitting tendrils shooting from her shoulder. "Why don't you kill me?"

"You are a vessel for my future."

"What does that mean?"

"You are a vessel, to bear the child I cannot. The Council denies me. They denied my mother. I defy them!" The glowing ball bounced, jerking shadows as Meylnara mixed human words with grunts and clicks. Without mindspeech, Vic wouldn't have understood her. "I will have a wizard's child," Meylnara continued, "but I will not soil myself with a drudge."

"You should have kidnapped a wizard with a cock if you want help with that."

The woman inched closer. Flinching, she pressed her palm to Vic's belly. "Don't you feel it?"

Vic's heart lurched as she recalled the soft, fragile warmth of Maynon and Silla's child. "Feel what?"

"My mother took refuge with the People so I would be safe. But she went back to them. They'll kill you like they killed her, unless you stay."

"Feel what?" Vic repeated. There had been that jolt through her womb the night she and Ashel married.

"Save your child as my mother saved me. I will love it as my own."

Energy flooded her nerves, and the manacle snapped open. Pain lanced her brain and shoulder, but fury overrode it. Meylnara shrank away. Vic chased her to the opposite wall. "Is the Council in Direiellene?"

Eyes wide, Meylnara nodded.

"Send me home. I won't hurt you if you send me home."

"But they'll kill your child!" Meylnara's back struck the opposite wall.

"I have no child!" Vic seized the other woman's throat, and fire surged through her hands and up her arms.

"It's mine!" Meylnara cried as Vic fell back, her fingers cramped into claws, a sizzle clinging to her bones. Above, the grating slapped back. Heavy shadows swarmed down. Shaking the sting out of her hands, she shot upward, but a blue rope of energy lassoed her waist and hauled her back. Kragnashian legs wrapped round her neck and face. Her teeth tore into spiked filaments, and slick green blood oozed into her mouth, choking her with springtime sweetness.

Sprawled atop a fibrous mound, she blinked awake. It was utterly dark. Sweat crawled through her hair. Shit and piss jabbed her nostrils; the fetid air swept over a parched throat. Groaning, she tried to rise. The nest material swallowed her elbows; pain scorched her shoulder and hammered her head, and she flopped back to her belly, limp as a ragdoll. She had felt like a clockwork doll when she had been in Lornk's thrall—a thing wholly his, whose very breath and heartbeat he controlled. In a pique of irony, he had called her Kara, naming his powerless slave after history's most powerful wizard. A bitter chortle slipped out. She was Meylnara's doll now, and just as powerless.

A swish brought a spill of light and a Kragnashian. Working with mandibles and multitudes of prehensile legs, the creature rapidly stripped off her garments and washed her, dressed her wound, and placed her on a clean nest that molded round her. Supporting her head, the Kragnashian inserted a tube between her teeth. Gelatin slid past her protests, easing her thirst, and she gulped hungrily. Pain melted into darkness, and she dreamed.

Rosen blossoms fold into the scent of his ardor. She clutches his shoulders, her hair sweeping his chest as he draws her hips toward his. Her ears strain for footsteps, but he hums, the sound passing from his throat into hers.

Spent, he settles her next to him. The grass yields to them, prickly and soft.

"We should go," he mumbles into her hair.

She nuzzles his throat. "Audience is soon. We should go."

Ashel squeezes her shoulder, his right hand so strong, the calluses on his fingertips rough against her skin. Kissing her hair, he pulls his shirt over his head.

Sighing, Kara tucks sheer silk under the metal belt soldered round her waist. The belt used to pinch, but she's used to it after so many years.

Stamping his feet into his boots, he smiles at her. "You've got grass in your hair."

Blushing, she runs her fingers through it. "You look perfect."

His smile deepens. "Ever my aim."

Kara kneels at the edge of the dais as supplicants stream into the throne room: merchants, miners, minstrels, and weavers. Tradespeople and tinkers. A crew of Caleisbahnin, greedy eyes assessing everything. One smirks at her, stroking his mustaches.

The inner doors bang open, and the king and queen enter. Head bowed, Elekia walks stiffly, her hands clasped, her eyes hateful as they fall on Kara. Lornk flops onto his throne. Kara's muscles clench round her spine—she knows that tight smile all too well. Her breath catches, and she blinks fast to dam welling tears.

The crown prince saunters in and levies a smirk at the minstrels. His humor melts Kara's worries. If his father knew of their affair, Ashel wouldn't be so jovial.

"Citizens." Lornk nods to the courtiers who take their seats at the back of the room. "Guilders, seamen, before we hear your pleas, we must attend to some household business. Kara."

Her name is a hot poker between her shoulder blades. The courtiers stare, eyes wide. Ashel's beautiful smile twists into a sneer.

Holding her face still, she kneels at Lornk's feet. His hand rests gently on her hair. A silent moan clogs her throat as she struggles to keep her breathing even.

"You have stolen from me."

She was Lornk's distraction, his plaything, a possession to be displayed but never used by anyone else. It would do no good to lie. "Yes, my lord."

"And given to my son." Quiet rage soils the air.

She nods. "Yes, my lord."

His fingers tighten like a vise on her skull. A whimper escapes her throat. She waits for Ashel to stand and claim her, but she hears nothing but murmurs from the Audience. Behind the throne, two giant forms shimmer into being. Gasping, courtiers fall back, but Lornk drags her in front of the creatures. "Master, I ask of you a great favor." He bows, remaining bent until the antennae touch him on the shoulder.

† † †

Spray whispers past her face, drawing her skin into little bumps. Waves crash, a steady white sound with lumps of darker colors. Behind her, forest rises toward the sky, but the shade never reaches her. The sun melts into the sand, and she shivers as the breeze scrapes across skin burnt red as coal. Her wrists and ankles glued to stakes, her fingers and toes are numb. Her throat is dry as this bed of sand.

Ashel will come for her. Her eyes ache for sight of him. He'll come with cool hands that will wash away pain. He'll come.

She waits. The sun burns red through closed eyelids. He'll come.

Others lie staked to the beach to dry. Flesh for the masters. She shuts her eyes against the horror. She believes she's the only one still alive. He must come.

Sea spray stings her blisters. Sand grinds into her sores. Her ears hurt, listening for his footfalls. She dozes, wakes, dozes again, hope shrinking. Her tongue laps dry lips. Iron dribbles down her throat. He must come.

Burning pain shivers down her spine. Worse is the waiting.

Remembrance of
Things Lost

Water gushed, a solid stream, the splashing strong and heavy. A faucet squeaked as it shut off. Drips plunked. Plunk. Plink.

There was only one place in Knownearth where water came from faucets, not pumps or buckets. Prying open his eyes, Ashel thrust himself into a morning in Traine, capital of Betheljin. A fortuitous ancestry had made the Korngs rulers of Relm, but their wealth was rooted here.

"You're awake," said a woman aloud in Betheljin. "A servant is bringing up hot stones to heat the bath."

"Thank you." Temples pounding, he sat up. Sunlight edged the curtain hem, a hard, white bludgeon, threatening an agony of brightness. Carefully, he stood, head reeling. *Kill you slow*—harlolinde slowed everything, especially the day after. Until you became like Erik.

"You know where you are?"

He nodded. *You want to find your wife? Come with me.* He'd stumbled after that promise, slung between Febbin and Joslyrn, drunk but not surprised when they brought him to a Device.

"Well then, I'll find you some clean clothes." Tall with ash gray hair, the woman had a strong, handsome figure and a broad, plain face.

"You must be Elsa." Lornk's cousin had been his housekeeper, but she wore a well-tailored embroidered silk vest and pantaloons, not the shapeless culottes usually worn by servants here. "You seem to have come up in the world."

She stared at him, mouth flat. "This is my house now."

"And what does Citizen Korng think of that?"

A servant bustled through to the bathroom, two buckets, radiating heat, yoked over his shoulders. The hot stones plunked into the water, and steam billowed through the door.

"I am Citizen Korng."

They left, and Ashel hugged himself, wishing they were Vic's arms. Grief clogged his throat as his eyes fell on his reflection. The mirror was his own height, backed with silver and probably worth the Caleisbahn debt that Lornk had paid off.

"He doesn't own me," Ashel said, but his reflection sneered at the carpet pile bristling past his toes, the massive, soft bed, silk-upholstered chair, marble-topped desk. The steaming marble tub offered no respite from shame.

As he washed, pounding temples ground regret into disgust and mourning, and he wished he had followed the Lathan troopers back to their camp. He'd never have found Erik's flask and yielded to its temptation. If he hadn't succumbed to vice in a Caleisbahn gaming house, he could have avoided this entire mess. All the shouldn't-haves that led him here harried his steps out of the bathroom.

"You have his frame," Elsa said.

He jerked the towel off his head and whipped it around his waist.

"You favor your mother, but I can see Lornk's bones underneath. Yet you have your father's manner. Sashal was ridiculously modest too."

Pantaloons and a vest lay on the bed with a porcelain razor, an ivory comb, and a toothbrush. Ashel scooped it all up and retreated into the bathroom.

Elsa snapped back the curtain and blatantly appraised him.

"What do you want?" The towel in a tight fist, he arched an eyebrow and straightened his shoulders.

Her lips curved. "Now that's your mother. I remember her like yesterday. You're not the only one in this house to lose a wife to the Kragnashians."

"Lornk Korng is *not* my mother's husband."

"A first bedding is a wedding in Latha, isn't it? Well, here in Traine, we say bed your lover and wed your financier. Elekia was most certainly not the latter, but Lornk did love her enough to honor your quaint custom and consider her his wife. Because he loved Sashal, he never challenged their marriage. He wanted to spare Sashal the shame of being named a cad."

"Am I supposed to be grateful for his discretion?"

"You're supposed to acknowledge you don't know anything about who they were then or who they are now."

"I know my father is dead." He held up his hand. "And I know what Lornk did to me out of perverse, maniacal jealousy."

"If you're so sure of that, why are you here?"

You want to find your wife? Come with me. Rage vibrated through him. "To find out what he knows about the Kragnashians who took my wife."

"Well then, come have some breakfast, and maybe he'll tell you."

After he dressed, Elsa led him to a sunlit room where the outlaws forked eggs into their mouths, but Ashel's gaze fixed on the young man who stood to greet him.

"I am deeply sorry for your loss, cousin," Earnk Korng said. "Whatever aid I can give in finding Vic and Bethniel, you have it."

"Thank you," he said, using manners to carry him through surprise. "How did you get here? The Device in Olmlablaire was buried." Vic had cleared it so soldiers could take Lornk directly to Latha, but more rocks fell on it afterward.

"I had it dug out. It's too valuable as a conduit to the rest of Knownearth. Dear Elsa." Earnk turned into his cousin's warm embrace.

"Tea, Shemen?" Kelmair fetched a pot from the sideboard. A gray silk gown flowed from her shoulders, leaving muscled arms bare but sheathing the rest of her like water. Loosed from her topknot, hair sprayed over her shoulders in a fall of blue-black silk. She heaped pastries and eggs onto a plate and set it down with a steaming cup. His surprise at finding Earnk here drowned in shock at the Caleisbahnin's courtesy. Dumbly, he sat at the place she laid out.

"You all right?" Joslyrn asked. Washed free of clay, his hair flared around his head, gray twirling through black spirals.

"Why are you here?"

"Waiting for those Lathan soldiers to clear out." Kelmair slid into her chair. Sheepishly, she nodded at Elsa. "Thank you for the clothes."

"You'll have your mullas this afternoon," the older woman said, taking a seat with her breakfast.

Joslyrn's eyes fell onto his teacup. "I'm sorry for your loss, Ashel. We didn't . . . You try to do right in the world, but it hardly ever turns out like you planned."

Febbin put his fork down and covered his face. Kelmair rubbed the boy's back, and they whispered about Erik.

Blinking back his own grief, Ashel focused on the fresco on the ceiling—an image of the daylight sky, pale pink clouds, and Elesendar pulsing as brightly as the sun.

"Good morning." Lornk entered, Wineyll on his heels. She stalled at the threshold, eyes wide as they darted between Earnk and his father. Her face flushed, she ducked behind a spill of dark locks and collected a pastry and tea before sliding into a seat beside Ashel.

"The new cook is inferior to you, cousin," Lornk said, trying the eggs.

Ashel bit into a scone. It was dry. "I agree," he said, playing their game of polite small talk. "I had the pleasure of sampling your baking while in Olmlablaire's dungeons."

Earnk flushed, and Lornk grinned. "You can thank your brother for that."

"I don't have a brother."

"Elsa, look at this fine pair of sons I have," Lornk said. "A traitor and a sot."

Earnk bent over his breakfast, and Ashel felt a pang of sympathy for the younger Korng. Each evening on the road to Re, he and Earnk had split a wine bottle or three while Bethniel chattered away, gently prying information from Earnk about Aunt Richelle, while regaling him with amusing anecdotes of their upbringing. The ache in Ashel's hand and heart had rivaled each other during that trip, so he'd left it to Bethniel to charm an alliance out of their cousin. All that effort, and now she was gone. Ashel would not be in his own body—he might even be dead—were it not for Earnk Korng, but that didn't change the fact these people were his enemies. "I made a mistake coming here."

"I thought you wanted to find out what happened to Victoria. I am, by the way, content to let her remain your wife."

Ashel's lungs stoked a smoldering fury. "You have no say in what she does."

"The Buzzards' Roost is a stew of misery, filled with escaped slaves, bliss-addled whores, cutthroats, and starving urchins," Lornk said. "If not for me, Victoria might have been one of them."

Wrath flared. Fists clenched, he shut his eyes and latched onto Geram in the training yard.

> Geram's foot connects with Drak's chin. There's a scrabble
> of pebbles and a thud as the larger man's bulk hits the ground.
> "Well done, cuz," Drak laughs.
> Gravel crunches, and Geram feels a draft. Dodging a fist, he
> jabs, strikes leather, but a leg twists round his shin and he falls.

Ashel forced his breath to follow Geram's rhythm as the other man rose and circled Drak.

"The Buzzards are Victoria's people," Lornk continued, "Oreseekers and their descendants, and Parnden hangs half a dozen a week. He lets his enemies buy their way off the gibbet. All they have to do is pay a fee and supply a substitute. Anyone will do, so long as the fee is paid. And hence, of late, most of the bodies decorating the square are children from the Roost. It's quite clever, really. He makes the wealthy beholden to him and oppresses the poor. Two birds, as they say."

"And you care about the Buzzards?" Ashel sneered. He was shaking, imagining Vic dangling from a rope and furious with himself for letting his thoughts go right where Lornk wanted them.

"I do. Betheljin is a house of cards that must be toppled if civilization is to survive the next age. But we must be careful which card we draw out, or humanity will descend only deeper into misery and ignominy. Slavery, war, famine, plagues—these will become the daily bread of every human in Knownearth unless Parnden is ousted."

"You want me to help you execute a coup? What in the Shrine makes you think I would?"

Lornk's mouth tilted upward. "Because I'm your only hope to find your wife."

In Latha, Geram withdrew from the sparring match and stood beside the water barrel, nursing a cup and paying close attention. The ghosts of Ashel's fingers itched. This was why he followed Lornk here.

"Come to the library," said Lornk. "There's something I'd like to show you."

Only the Academy in Narath, and perhaps the Archive on Caleisbahnin, held more embossed and ancient volumes than the Korng library. The Device was in a chamber below, and last autumn, Ashel had stood here after escaping captivity in Olmlablaire, debating whether to take ship for Latha or return to Relm to protect his sister and Vic. He rubbed the severed knuckles, wondering what the cost of a different choice would have been.

Lornk retrieved a map and unfurled it on the table. It showed the southern half of the Isthmus, lands that included Kragnash, Relm, and Latha. Kragnash was painted in swirling greens, as if to depict the rainforest that once stood there. Near the compass printed on the blue-painted sea, someone had written, "In remembrance of shared nightmares."

"Sashal stole this map when we were twelve. The inscription is his," Lornk said.

Ashel's chest felt hollow as he studied the loops and slant. The penmanship echoed his father's style and could be the boy's version of the man's hand.

"As boys we traveled between Latha, Relm, and here as often as we could slip away from our studies," Lornk continued. "Once we used the Device between Olmlablaire and Narath, and it . . . slipped. We arrived in the Manor's throne room, but it was the wrong room and the wrong time.

"It was as if we were dreaming. We saw ourselves as grown men, and my elder self was king of a single nation encompassing Relm and Latha. Notice there's no border on this map, but the rivers and cities are marked." He chuckled. "Elekia was my queen, and you my firstborn and heir."

"Sounds like a fitting fantasy for an ambitious boy," Ashel snarled.

Lornk chuckled. "I met your mother three years later. She was the first person I encountered in this world whom I saw in that one; Victoria—and you—were the last. Your wife's destiny lies here." He tapped the X labeled *Direiellene*. "In this strange place and time, Sashal and I learned the Council had lost the war against Meylnara, and in the aftermath, the Kragnashians conquered and enslaved all of humanity. My older self was a king, but also a subject of Kragnashian overlords who kept humans as *cattle*. I watched myself give them Victoria to feed upon. That is the threat we face. The one she was born to stop, and the one I would have prepared her for had she stayed here, where she belonged."

"Only a madman would rationalize his depravities as a tactic to save the world!"

"There is method and purpose to everything I do. Victoria would have been far better prepared for her destiny, had she stayed with me. Elekia didn't tell her what to expect when she sent her to Kragnash, did she? Your parents told her nothing, taught her nothing, and they knew her fate."

"You're the one who sold her to the Kragnashians."

Lornk laughed bitterly. "Do you think I expected her to be in eastern Fembrosh?"

"Isn't that why you had me kidnapped?"

"No! You are my son and a man with untapped potential who will be vital to me in ousting Parnden."

Heart pounding, he struggled to keep his hands from Lornk's throat. "A Kragnashian tried to take her from the Manor the night the pirates broke you out of prison."

"The Kragnashian who took Victoria from the Kiareinoll was no ally of mine. I wanted her help overthrowing Parnden before she went to Direiellene to meet the destiny *I* would have prepared her for."

"This is preposterous."

"It is the truth. Since Sashal and I escaped from that place, I have researched the War of the Council and the other momentous events in Knownearth's history. There have been disparities between what the written histories say and what people claimed to remember, as if a change occurred in *time*. The Caleisbahnin call these changes *Concordances*. A Concordance occurred a thousand years ago when the historical Victoria of Ourtown slew Meylnara the Oppressor. The disappearance of the contemporary Victoria of Ourtown confirms we are approaching another Concordance now, in this time as well as the past. Your wife is the same woman who fought in the War of the Council, and I believe she is now there in that time and place. I also believe what happens here and now in Traine will determine whether we are free or slaves for generations, perhaps millennia, perhaps forever."

He is insane, Geram said. *Use the Device and come home.*

Lornk tapped the inscription. "Sashal knew the Concordance was coming. Why else would he have made Victoria his ward? Why push her into the military and turn a scholar into a warrior? And why did Elekia send her to Kragnash, where she knew Victoria would be given the Waters of the Dead? Your parents knew her destiny as well as I."

Ashel's voice shook in time with the blood pulsing through his neck. "Time travel is not possible."

"It's no less preposterous than trees birthing people or spacefarers settling this world. Or the miracles of mindspeech and wizardry. The Device is beneath us—I won't stop you using it to go ask your mother if I'm lying."

"All you do is lie."

"Son, that is one thing I never do."

"You just did." From a nearby desk, he took a pencil and paper. The Device in Latha was locked against incursions from Relm or Traine, but even during the height of the war it was checked once a day for messages. Finishing a note, he crossed the room and shoved books aside to reveal a hidden knob. A pull, and the bookcase swung open on a tunnel through the bedrock. Sconces flickered as he descended to a black knob set in a compass rose fashioned from porcelain and set with blue gemstones. He dropped the note into the shallow depression in the stone, shoved the knob into the southernmost slot, and stepped back. The note faded away like sugar in a glass of water.

"It may be some time before she picks that up," Lornk said, standing behind him.

"I'll wait." Crossing his arms, he glared at the other man. "Alone."

"We'll leave it open on this end. You're always welcome here, son." Smirking, Lornk took a few steps up the passage, then turned back. "This room will be guarded—in case Elekia gets any ideas about sending troopers, remind her the Device is a choke point."

I'll tell Elekia you're coming home. Geram's feet crunched on the gravel path back to the Manor.

Send a message back to me first. I don't want Lornk knowing about us. Geram agreed, and Ashel waited an hour for a note to appear beside the gems. He stepped into the depression, and pins prickled his skin, a feverish tingle that spread to his toes and his eyebrows.

All went dark, blacker than a lightless dungeon. His blood stopped, then gushed through his veins. Light flooded his eyes, and he stood behind Latha's throne. Half a dozen guards watched him step off the dais.

"The queen will see you upstairs, Highness," Selcher said.

Ashel glanced at the guards, most of whom he didn't know, and strode toward the doors leading into the Manor. Geram waited with his mother in her small parlor. *Tell her to meet me in Vic's room,* he said.

Hurrying after him, Selcher scowled, no doubt Hearing and disapproving of his making demands of the Ruler.

Reaching a landing between floors, he rounded on the housekeeper. "Did my father and Lornk go missing when they were boys?"

Her scowl deepened. "Nine days. King Rivern and the Relmlady sent soldiers everywhere looking for them. We thought they'd been taken by outlaws or a press gang."

"What did they say when they came back?"

"Your mother—"

"You were there, Selcher. What did my father say?"

She narrowed her eyes. "He said it was a nightmare. He dedicated himself to rearing you to be different."

His skin pebbled with cold. "Different from what?"

"From the vainglorious scoundrel he met in that other place."

He charged up the stairs two at a time, leaving Selcher behind, and burst into Vic's room.

His mother stood on a carpet woven into a pattern of flowers and rushes.

"Where is the rug showing the War of the Council?"

"It was ruined in the attack."

A trembling weakness washed through him. Gritting his teeth, he locked his knees. "Is it true, Mother?"

"Is what true?"

His heart beat his ribs like a prisoner striking the bars of a cage, a voice inside him yelling, *All of it!* He asked the most pressing question. "Is it true you and Father knew Vic was the One? Not that she simply bore the same name as someone who lived a thousand years ago, but that she is the same person?"

"We did *not* know that."

"Then why in the Shrine did you give her the bedchamber with that particular rug?"

Her lips twisted, but she didn't respond.

"Beth and I played on that rug when we were children. Where did it come from?"

"Sashal commissioned it after you were born."

Sorrow and fury warred within him. "He knew they might take her, and he did nothing about it except give her a Shrinejumping rug?"

Elekia's shoulders crimped, and she folded into a wizened crone. "We did everything we could to keep her safe."

"Safe? You made her become a soldier. You sent her to Kragnash so they could give her a power that is killing her, and now they've taken her!"

"I have requested an audience with the Center."

"An audience? You should be sending soldiers."

"You know nothing about Kragnashians if you think this nation could muster the force required to combat them in their own land. You didn't see the damage a single warrior did in this very room."

"Then why aren't you going to Kragnash yourself and tearing the place apart? You're a bloody wizard!"

"I cannot expose myself as one or I'd lose what leverage I have as Ruler. Negotiating the return of your sisters will take time, especially as we have little to trade. You must be patient."

Seething, he thought of Lornk's snide invitation to return, and his missing fingers ached to curl into a fist and smash the expectant smirk from the fiend's face. Yet his mother's plea for patience stung like salt in an open wound. "If you cannot help them, I will find someone who can."

"Lornk will not help your sisters," she spat.

"Vic isn't my sister," he grated. "Is Lornk my father?"

Her nostrils flared as she drew her shoulders back and raised her chin. "He is a villain."

Pain squeezed his chest. "Do you even know?"

"When Sashal died, you and I, we held him between us and wept together. That is the only knowledge that matters."

A sour breath gushed out, along with any trust he'd ever had in her. "You can never give a straight answer. Goodbye, Mother."

The Consequence
of Ignorance

Bethniel winced at each dab of the washcloth. Fiery welts webbed over her cheeks and forehead, striped her fingers and the backs of her hands. Everything stung, and she prayed the abrasions wouldn't scar. Rinsing the cloth, she swiped it once more over her face and looked in the mirror. "Lovely," she muttered, wishing for the pot of face powder on her vanity. Homesickness rose up, clogged throat and nose with longing, and she swallowed hard, squashing it all into the box where fear and anger belonged. Blubbering wouldn't help Vic.

Neither would a desperate wild woman. As she tamed rogue curls, her thoughts whirled through meager knowledge of the Council period: the Council had fought Meylnara, and their war had destroyed the rainforest of Direiellene, leaving behind the vast wasteland she and Vic had crossed to rescue Ashel from Olmlablaire.

Poor Ashel! He must be mad with worry, and if he were here, he'd know what to say and do to get Vic where she belonged. If only she'd taken his course on the Council! She'd always avoided his classes so she wouldn't have to endure her friends ogling him. Why hadn't those ninnies chattered about his knowledge instead of the fit of his damn trousers?

She shoved the if-onlys into the box with homesickness, fear, and anger. No point dwelling on what couldn't be changed. The woman in the mirror blinked the creases from her eyes, donning a semblance of confident serenity before she put on the clothes Thabean's servants had brought. Victoria of Ourtown was a member of the Council. Her deeds—whatever they were—were a matter of record. The Council would rescue her. History had deemed it so.

Clinging to that certainty, she shimmied into a clean shift, then stared at the bewildering array of sashes and slits on an embroidered silk overgown.

Someone cleared a throat, and she spun round to find Thabean eying her through a gap in the privacy screen. Mortification heated her cheeks—how long had he been there?

"Flagrant tardiness may be the prerogative of future sovereigns in your land, but it will not endear you to Saelbeneth."

Swallowing ire, she emerged from the bathing area, robe in hand. "I don't know how to tie this."

His eyes flicked over his own garment and its complex fastenings. "The flat panel goes in front. Slip it on." She thrust her arms into the sleeves, then shivered as a static charge crackled through the silk. Sashes wove through slits and round each other, binding the gown closed.

"Too tight?" His eyes grazed her figure.

She took a breath, working hard to keep it steady. "No. Thank you."

He looked over the spacious tent with its silk partitions and the bower where'd she'd spent a fretful, sleepless night. "I hope you found the accommodations suitable, Your Highness."

She ignored the sarcasm cloaking her title and copied his formal manner of speaking. "Please, sir. I would have you call me by my name only: Bethniel."

Smirking, he unstoppered a decanter and streamed pale wine into a cup. "Bethniel of . . . ? You haven't told me from whence you hail."

"Might I remind you of your warning against tardiness?"

"And I would warn my Council leader against spies and

charlatans. Saelbeneth agreed to meet you because she is curious why so strange a trio was expelled from Meylnara's Lair—more importantly, why you were there in the first place."

"Yesterday you refused to hear my plea—why do you want it now?"

He drained the cup and tilted it toward her. "Look at the hospitality with which you—a possible spy—have been treated. Perhaps you should respond in kind, with the truth."

Her brow knit. "I have not lied to you, sir."

"You mentioned a prophesy."

Squaring her shoulders, she raised an eyebrow. "I do not wish to be late for my audience with Saelbeneth. I will explain everything to her."

He twirled his hand in a mocking salute. "As you wish, Your Highness."

Lillem fell in beside her as she exited the tent. "What did he want? I tried to stop him going inside, but he froze my bloody limbs; then some barrier kept me from following him in."

"He wanted me to hurry up," Bethniel muttered as they followed Thabean down a narrow alley between tent stakes. "We are his guests, Lieutenant. Antagonizing him or any other wizard won't help us gain their aid."

"My duty, Highness, is to protect you."

"Where's Gustave?" she asked, teeth grinding.

"I sent him to his own people," Thabean tossed over his shoulder.

Regretting she couldn't consult with the pirate, Bethniel followed the wizard down a wide lane past neat rows of tents busy with soldiers, farriers, and smiths. The Council's encampment was huge. Minutes stretched and footsteps multiplied as they approached a central area occupied by two gigantic pavilions with a lone tree towering between them. One structure was plain white canvas stretched taut over a massive frame. Banners flapped from multiple peaks on the other, its walls a riot of color and patterns, from scrolling scarlet to rippling azure. "The Council hall," Thabean waved at the wildly colored pavilion. "The hospital, the lookout station. Saelbeneth's camp is directly opposite mine." He led them on into a wedge bustling with soldiers chattering in Old Lathan.

"These people haven't seen much action," Lillem muttered. "Everything's too clean and orderly."

"Did you talk to anyone last night?"

"No. I slept outside your tent entrance."

They came to a pavilion walled in elaborately patterned erinsheen. An aide led them down a fabric-walled corridor and into a room lit with dozens of glowing orbs that floated near the ceiling. Lillem stopped dead; Bethniel had to pinch him to get him to move out of the doorway.

A handsome woman with spiraling brown curls smiled from a table laid with tea and bread.

A man seated beside her sneered. "Are these the vagabonds you found near the Lair?"

"Madam," Thabean said, "this audience does not concern Nelchior."

"It must if you'd rather I not hear it," rejoined the other man.

Saelbeneth's benevolent smile remained fixed. "Nelchior worries you have a scheme that requires thwarting. Have you breakfasted?"

Red spots appeared on Thabean's pale cheeks. "We have, thank you." He paused while a Caleisbahn officer entered, Gustave at his heels. The pirate had a new sword and fresh clothes. Bethniel's nose twitched at Lillem's stinking uniform, and she wished he had been able to change.

Saelbeneth said, "Commodore, thank you for joining us. Your counsel is always welcome." She nodded at Bethniel. "Who have you brought before us, Thabean?"

Jaw bunched, he shot Bethniel a warning glance. "This is Lady Bethniel of the East Reach, a territory across the Senacna Kein. She and her sister Victoria led a force of two hundred warriors to assist us but were waylaid by Meylnara's minions and wiped out. Only Lady Bethniel, her retainer, and this Caleisbahnin escaped. Meylnara holds her sister captive."

"What nonsense is this?" Nelchior spat. "There are no territories on the other side of the Senacna Kein."

"It is a colony established by my forebears and Semena steed herders," Thabean replied.

Bethniel maintained her courtier's mask, but her pulse thudded as she wondered why Thabean had concocted this lie. Still, if it meant he'd help Vic, she wouldn't contradict him. "The East Reach is a distant place, known to few, madam," she said. "My father is liege-bound to Sir Thabean and sent us to join your cause."

Saelbeneth tilted her head sympathetically. "My condolences on your losses, my lady."

"Madam, my sister—I came to beg your help rescuing her."

"I'm afraid we cannot expend resources to rescue a single captive."

Bethniel swallowed. Saelbeneth had to see value in rescuing Vic. A glance at Gustave gained her no counsel but a slight shake of his head. "Madam, Meylnara kept my sister but expelled the three of us for a reason: my sister is a wizard."

"Treason!" Nelchior shot to his feet.

Saelbeneth's gaze pierced Bethniel's certainties. "Did the Purge miss the East Reach?"

Gustave's head shake was more emphatic, and Bethniel feared she'd made a terrible miscalculation. What in Shrine was the Purge? "Not that I know of, madam."

"The Reach was cleared forty-three years ago, in the last round of the Purge," Thabean interjected.

"Then how did your retainer get the Elixir?" Nelchior snapped.

"I know not." The red had drained from Thabean's cheeks, leaving them white as cerrenil bark.

Victoria of Ourtown was on *the Council,* Bethniel reminded herself, trying to slow her breathing. *They will rescue her.* Shrine, why hadn't she taken Ashel's class on the Council? Now there was no way through this morass but to hew close to the truth. "Madam, Sir Thabean knew nothing of my sister's powers. Neither does my father, or anyone else in the Reach. She acquired them on our journey here, from a tribe of friendly Kragnashians—"

"Preposterous!" Nelchior cried.

Thabean's eyebrows shot up, his forehead creased.

"Quiet, Nelchior," Saelbeneth ordered. "My lady, that story is absurd. There are no friendly Kragnashians. They all serve Meylnara. Do you as well? Have you concocted this ridiculous tale to sow discord among her enemies?"

Bethniel felt the wizard prying into her mind, a clumsy attempt at Listening that she might have laughed off if she weren't desperate for the woman's help. She dropped every bit of baffling she always held over her thoughts, allowing Saelbeneth to Hear the truth. "Madam, my sister Victoria obtained the Woern from Kragnashians who refer to Meylnara as the Oppressor, and these creatures claimed Victoria was prophesied to destroy her. But Meylnara's forces killed our troops and captured her. My retainer and I, guided by this seaman, attempted to rescue her, but we failed and were expelled from Meylnara's stronghold. We come to you with a sincere offer of aid in your war, if you will only help us free my sister."

Saelbeneth narrowed her eyes, glancing between Bethniel and the other wizards. "I Hear no lies, but not the entire truth, I think."

"We did not come to betray or harm you, I swear on the old mothers and Elesendar."

"Since the Purge the world has had twelve wizards serving on the Council. Twelve wizards *only*. We have come to this place to execute Meylnara for being a rogue wizard. If your sister has the Woern, she is subject to the same fate."

Bethniel's skin pebbled as the blood drained from her face. "We did not know there could be only twelve, Madam."

"Clearly you must remedy some educational deficiencies in the East Reach, Thabean."

He glared at Bethniel. "I will indeed, madam."

"In the meantime, we cannot risk Meylnara having another rogue wizard for an ally."

"No wonder you wished to speak to Saelbeneth privately," Nelchior said. "Did you think if you confessed your sins to her alone, you would dodge the consequences?"

Jaw bunching, Thabean placed a fist over his heart. "I will find and expunge the second rogue, madam. And if I can, I will kill Meylnara as well."

Nelchior laughed, and Bethniel's heart lurched. She looked desperately from Lillem to Gustave. The pirate whispered to the commodore, who bowed to Saelbeneth. "Madam, although twelve wizards sit on the Council, two are drained or nearly so. As your tactical advisor I suggest you consider the advantage of permitting this new rogue to live so long as she fights for your cause."

Nelchior's mocking laughter ceased, and Bethniel released a silent prayer of thanks. Saelbeneth raised an eyebrow. "The law is the law, commodore."

"During wartime it is not uncommon to suspend laws that impede victory, madam."

The Council leader's gaze landed on Bethniel. "Perhaps we should give the accused a chance to defend herself before the full Council. Thabean, this situation is yours to remedy. Go to the Lair, find the rogue, and arrest her; do not kill her. However, if you have a chance to dispatch Meylnara, do so. I miss the Kiareinoll and would be happy to return."

"Madam," Bethniel interjected, "Victoria was severely injured by Meylnara's minions and won't be fit to defend herself in a tribunal. I beg you, let me speak for her, but give me time to prepare her case."

"You have many requests, my lady. First, let Thabean find your sister. I promise you she will not face justice until she can bear the consequences."

THE SECOND ROGUE

Thabean settled into the surveillance blind, fury steaming his blood. Glowing orbs flickered over the minions bustling in and out of the Lair, but Nelchior's gloating sneer dominated his thoughts. Hatred seethed with each heartbeat, and he trembled with rage. At himself most of all. He'd claimed the self-proclaimed princess to keep Nelchior from building some scheme around her, and now he'd implicated himself in the emergence of a rogue wizard! A colossal blunder, all because he'd let a pretty face turn his head.

But another rogue wizard—the thought chilled his blood. For more than fifty years the Code had kept the world from chaos. If someone outside the Council had acquired the Elixir and was spreading it through the populace . . . Nelchior? No. The fiend was devious, but he wouldn't unleash a power he couldn't control. Yet if that scoundrel got his hands on the rogue? Thabean shook his head, tamping down his anger and shifting his focus to the mission. First, find the new rogue.

The night wore on, the milling creatures thinning until all but a few sentries disappeared into their hives. Keeping to the shadows, he drifted over the wall and released the Woern. Meylnara might sense his power, and her minions had proven remarkably resistant to direct assaults with wizardry. Crouching low, he crept to the dungeon. A rank stench of blood and excrement wafted from the pit—human odors, to be sure. The gigantic arthropods occupying this compound smelled *good*. Eyes darting for the creatures, he worked a puff of air into the lock, and the grate clicked open.

195

Down inside, a broken chain clinked against scorched stone. Rusty stains reeked of iron. No captive wizard now, but someone with power had been held here no more than a day or two ago.

He climbed out and stole toward the hive, freezing at every noise. A pair of minions exited, clicking and rustling as they passed. Hunkered in the folds of a tree, he suppressed a chortle. Since he'd received the Elixir, he had mostly forgotten how to fear, but now his heart thumped in his ears like a boy on his first lupear hunt. He felt *alive*. Swallowing another chuckle, he slipped through the arched doorway.

Inside, spongy walls shimmered with a sallow light. He could see no lamps; the walls themselves glowed dimly. Ramps ascended to his right, descended to his left, and plunged straight inside. He froze, eyes closed, ears sharp for some sense of wizardry. Nothing. A small ripple of power altered the molecular structure of the dyes in his robe, and the color changed to match the pale walls. Taking the ascending ramp, he followed a smooth, featureless passage as it wound up and up to a bulbous dead end. There had to be chambers along the corridor, but he could see no doorways. Puzzled, he retraced his steps. A click and a rustle pricked his ears. Pulse thumping, he ducked under his cloak and pressed himself to the wall. A panel slid aside and a minion emerged, shut the door, and headed down the ramp. Thabean exhaled and stole to the hidden door. His fingers slid along the surface, discerning no seam until at last he found a serrated edge and a slight indentation. He pressed the surface, and a narrow gap clicked open. Very slowly, he slid the panel aside. He imagined the chamber might hold a laboring queen, with attendants to remove the eggs and put them in cells, or a room stacked high with maturing larvae, but he found only a large volume of webbing piled together into a nest. He exhaled, and his heartbeat slowed.

Back in the corridor, he searched for more doorways. They were slightly more yellow than the wall, a difference so subtle he wasn't sure he found them all. Wary of traps, he strained his ears each time he cracked open a door. Inside the chambers, creatures lay curled into armored balls, slumbering atop the nests. The rooms provided a hiding place while minions shuffled past in the corridor. Sweat soaked his shirt as he searched, the fear of discovery rising with each chamber lacking a human occupant.

On the lowest level was a doorway streaked with faint, rust-colored smears. The chamber within reeked like a midden. Suppressing a cough, he swiped at watering eyes. Someone groaned softly, the sound dying to a whisper. Cautiously, he spun a light orb and sent it bouncing into the room. Upon coils of thick white webbing slept a woman, her face hidden beneath snarled red hair. Meylnara! Blood surging, he drew his dagger—then froze. Yellow pus and raw muscle ravaged her shoulder. The woman quivered in the grip of a chill; heat shimmered off filthy skin. "Rockfall," he breathed. He knew such wounds. In the last assault on the Lair, the minions had rained their spit on the troops scaling the walls. Screams scorched the eardrums as soldiers fell, their flesh melting off their skulls. Sheathing his dagger, he brushed aside a clump of hair, exposing pale freckles scattered across the face of a woman much younger than Meylnara. He stretched his fingers over her arm, watched the hairs stand and bend toward his palm. The rogue, as grievously wounded as Bethniel claimed, and Woernsick too. His anger ground finer, thicker, leavened with sympathy.

The young woman's eyes opened. Gasping, she clutched his arm. "You came! I knew you would." She climbed to her knees, her eyes glazed. "I waited so long—I thought you'd abandoned me. Forgive me! Forgive me for doubting you!" Shushing her, he backed away, but she stumbled after him, her voice rising as she switched to the language of the Oreseekers. "I love you. You came; I love you—" As his shoulders butted the wall, she collapsed into his arms.

Ears twitching, he held his breath. Hers came in heavy gasps, her skin bleeding heat into him. He pushed the hair off her face and studied the delicate nose, the pointed chin. Her lips were thin, her face gaunt. Not a beauty like the princess. Not likely to be Bethniel's blood sister either—from their complexions to their height and build, the women couldn't differ more, but the world was full of fostered orphans. He scooped up her legs—she did have a fine figure: a body small and slight, but solid and strong. *Shrine, get hold of yourself,* he chided. Lust had gotten him into this mess and would only make things worse if he got the rogue back to camp.

A shriek pierced the air, and he ducked the silver fire crackling from the doorway. Clutching the rogue, Thabean slammed a wall of solidified air into Meylnara and zipped past her. The corridor teemed with rattling minions. Raising a shield, he sent an electric jolt through the floor, frying the feet of his enemies. Wizard and minions faltered, and he sheared up through fibrous walls to reach the stars.

A Myth of the Ancients

Ashel slapped a book shut, setting dust awhirl, a sparkling dance above the tomes scattered across the table. For years, he had taught the Council history to pimpled adolescents, and he'd laughed at himself for pining after a woman who bore the name of a Council member. She even had red hair, like the woman described in the accounts. But that didn't signify a thing. Meylnara was described as having red hair too. Sashal had had red hair. A coincidence of name and coloration didn't mean his wife was a thousand years in the past!

Grabbing another volume, he flipped to a dog-eared chapter full of dates and events but not enough bloody detail to prove or disprove Lornk's claims. This ridiculous story of another world was a myth fabricated to cover some deeper machination. Yet dread niggled as he thought of the damn rug in Vic's room and its central motif: the duel between Victoria and Meylnara. The historical Victoria of Ourtown was an Oreseeker wizard who took the place of Darien, a Council member whose powers had faded. The War of the Council ended half a year later when Victoria met Meylnara in single combat, a battle so fierce it left the entire forest of Direiellene burned to ash and sand. Victoria disappeared afterward.

"My wife will not die there," he swore aloud, fists clenched. "Elesendar, she will not die in Kragnash!" A vow, a promise, and a prayer, he meant each syllable, but what could he do to fulfill it? Vic in the past was preposterous, her true location and Bethniel's a mystery. Not a single text even hinted at anyone resembling his sister, but that didn't prove a thing either. Traveling thousands of miles in the wink of an eye was preposterous, yet Ashel had done it three times within the span of a day.

You should do it right now, Geram said. *Why did you go back to Traine?*

Because Lornk knows where they are. And Lornk's library contained more volumes on the Council than Ashel had ever seen.

Those books are nothing but a madman's obsession. Don't fall into it.

Ashel rose and perused the shelves. Scanning spines, he strayed from history to mythology, where his finger paused on a title that was ancient to the Ancients: Orpheus. *Orpheus and Eurydice* was a favorite opera in the Guild, and a sacred one too. His heart leapt with sudden inspiration, and he rushed to another shelf and snatched a lexicon of Kragnashian signs to his chest. Hope flooded down his cheeks, into the beard she'd said she liked. By Elesendar's grace, she'd see it soon.

Breath short and pulse rippling, he checked the Kragnashian dictionary. He was fluent in every language in Knownearth, except the one he needed now. Making certain of the necessary phrases, he descended to the Device and shoved the knob into the southwestern slot.

Cool air washed away the Device-borne itch. Rising, he found himself upon a stone pedestal. A ramp sloped toward a doorway set in a dome constructed out of hexagonal cells, rising several hundred feet from a sandy floor. Outside, the Desert People swarmed past, as intent on their business as merchants on the docks.

Whistling, a sentry whisked up the ramp, and Ashel clapped a greeting. "I am Ashel of Narath," he spoke his name in his own voice, "and I come to trade."

The Kragnashian clicked something; he asked it to repeat itself while he scrambled through the dictionary. The clicks and snaps slowed, and he caught the meaning: what did he wish to buy?

"I will bargain only with the Center."

"All who enter Direiellene must pay the price."

He'd expected that condition and had a ready answer. "I already possess the Woern."

The sentry swept closer, antennae wheeling. It towered over him, its tattooed mandibles as long as he was tall. He breathed deeply, using his diaphragm, filling his chest with the creature's benign springtime scent to control the quaking fear stirred by pinchers that could snap a man in half. Geram's heartbeat raced alongside his, and his thigh muscles twitched as Geram knuckled his scarred limb. After a dozen long, slow breaths, the sentry ordered him to follow.

Outside, heat dug sweat out of Ashel's pores. Beneath a scorching sun that squeezed his eyes to slits, he followed the sentry to a shaded fountain decorated with statues of pipers and harpists. With a parting order to wait there, the sentry merged into the stream of Kragnashians flowing toward three mountainous white domes. Hope bolstered by the granite renderings of musicians, he dipped cupped hands into the fountain, slaking a dry throat and splashing his hair and clothes. *Look at the singer, Geram. It has to be a sign. They're here in this city. I know it.*

Maybe you're right, Geram said. *May Elesendar help you bring them home.*

The sentry returned, dwarfed by another Kragnashian wearing a coppery stole draped over its thorax. The fabric rippled alongside thousands of feet as the Center swept up to the fountain. Ashel had to crane his neck to meet its sparkling gaze.

"Dealmaker's Offspring," it said. "All aims are to me. What do you seek?"

A breeze blasted his shirt dry. *Orpheus,* he thought. *You have the power of Orpheus, and you will bring your love back from Hades.* He took breath and sang:

> *If you were lovers*
> *you would know for yourselves*
> *the burning desire*

which torments me,

which goes with me everywhere.

Not even in this

peaceful haven

can I be happy

if I do not find my love.

"What is it you offer?" the Center asked. "What is it you seek?"

"I wish to trade for Victoria of Ourtown and Bethniel of Narath, Heir to the throne of Latha. In payment, I give you Song." The Kragnashians were always hungry for human novelties—the Center's stole was erinsheen, dyed the color of Vic's hair. Yet another sign that he had chosen the right path. He sang Orpheus' lament:

Ah! You would be less harsh

to my weeping and lamenting

if for but a moment you could know

what it is to languish for love.

The Center reclined beside the fountain, eyes glittering as Ashel sang ancient lyrics that mirrored current grief. He threw himself into the performance, singing Hades' response, repeating stanzas that seemed to pique the Center's interest. He knew the creature couldn't understand the words, but as it leaned forward, head cocked, Ashel's hope crystalized into certainty as bright and hard as a diamond. The final note faded, and Ashel bowed, panting and flushed and expectant.

"This sound was new. This sound was good," said the Center. "You are the Voice."

"I wish to see my mate and sibling."

The Center rose to its feet. "The One and the Fulcrum."

"Yes."

The Center turned its back and curled its abdomen upward, flaring its tail segments. It turned its head; a single eye whirled over its thorax. "No."

The crystal core of his faith shattered, the shards ripping through his gut. He blinked as hope drained away, leaving only an ice-cold void. His legs jelly, he sank to the ground. "What do you want?" he clapped feebly.

"Nothing from you," the Center said as it swept away.

Restoration and Revelation

Worry needling Bethniel, she pushed Vic's arm straight over her head, then slowly rotated it forward, down and out to the side. Vic sucked sharp breaths, her fists clenched in pain as Bethniel pulled the arm up for another rotation. After nearly two months, a lattice of hard white scar tissue covered the wasted muscles of Vic's shoulder. The healers said she'd never regain full strength on her left side, but that was the least of Bethniel's concerns.

"You're too kind, my lady," Vic said, her voice soft, meek. Since Thabean had brought her back from Meylnara's Lair, she never used mindspeech and always addressed Bethniel with deference, not the grudging affection Bethniel expected from her sister.

"That's it for today," Bethniel said. "Time for your bath." Eyelids drooping, Vic shivered on a pile of towels while Bethniel quickly sponged the sweat from her skin and combed her hair. "Now back to bed." Bethniel pulled a clean shift over Vic's head, threaded her arms through the proper holes, and helped her totter the few steps to the bower. Despite the stifling tropical heat, Vic's teeth chattered as she lay down, her eyes glazed with fever. Bethniel tucked the blankets tight, and her sister sank into sleep.

Chewing on her bottom lip, Bethniel checked the contents of the chamberpot. Not a drop of red. Bethniel's own courses had come twice since they'd arrived. *It's because she's so sick,* she thought. Why else would Vic's monthly blood be absent? *It's normal for women with more muscle than fat,* she reminded herself. *And she's so sick.* Sitting, she stroked Vic's hair. "You will get better," she promised aloud. *Elesendar, she must.* History was written: Victoria of Ourtown had fought with the Council against Meylnara.

"My lady," Thabean sneered from the tent entrance.

"Sir Thabean." Bethniel stood and bowed.

"No change?"

"She's little better than the day you rescued her."

Lip curled in disgust, he scowled and pulled the flap aside to admit Saelbeneth. Dismissing the other wizard, the Council leader swept over and felt Vic's forehead. "I've never heard of anyone lingering this long," she said. "Your sister must be more compatible with the Woern than most."

Compatible, but not completely so. "She has been very ill, madam."

"Even so. Thabean informs me that you say she has not been herself? How so?"

"She . . . raves, madam."

Saelbeneth gave her an appraising look. "My lady, I lack your strength in mindspeech, but I am wise enough to know when someone withholds the truth. Speak plainly, please."

Bethniel cleared her throat, trying to expel the worry lodged there. "She—she is not my blood sister. She became my father's ward after she escaped from one of his rivals—an evil man who held her captive." She gulped, full of foolish prudery and horror at Vic's ordeal. "She became a fierce warrior in my father's service, but she has always carried the shadows of her former master's tyranny, and now she acts as if she still belongs to him." And as if Bethniel were somehow part of Lornk's household—an even more disturbing idea.

"Woern-madness takes many forms. Have you seen any glimmers of the woman you know as your sister?"

"No, madam."

"And has she used the Woern?"

"Not that I have seen."

Saelbeneth placed a hand on Vic's forehead again. "They're still alive within her; I can feel them straining toward my Woern. If mine were to mix with hers, it might restore her." The Council leader clasped Bethniel's arm, and her skin prickled beneath the woman's palm. "But it would be unseemly for me to give aid to a rogue. We'll have to continue our vigil and hope your sister recovers so she may stand trial."

The Council leader glided out, leaving Bethniel to stare at the place where Saelbeneth had touched her. *Any fluid of the body,* her mother had said. And Elekia had sent them to Direiellene together, expecting Bethniel to help Vic survive. "Oh, Vic," she whispered. "You're not going to get better, are you?" *Any fluid of the body.* She swallowed, then churned up some saliva with her tongue. How could she give it to her? Spit in her mouth? Disgust cinched her throat. Vic was so sick, how could a little bit of spit help? *Any fluid of the body.* Her skin flushed hot as she thought of the way fluid usually passed from one person to another. "I love you, sister, but you'd need my brother for that." *Any fluid.* Rubbing her fingers together, she felt her own pulse. Mother had used her blood. Blood was thicker than water, and surely thicker with Woern than spit. Fetching a knife, Bethniel sliced her thumb and slipped it between Vic's lips. Her sister stirred, coughed, then latched onto the thumb, sucking like a babe to the breast. "Shrine," Bethniel swore as the burning draw grew fiercer. Her oaths grew fiercer too, until at last she extracted her thumb and toweled the blood off Vic's lips and cheek. Her sister moaned softly and rolled back into a deep sleep. Wrapping linen round her injured finger, Bethniel gnawed on her bottom lip. *Elesendar, I hope that helped.*

In the middle of the night, Vic listened to the guard changing, the exchange of greetings, the briefing that all was quiet, complaints about the rain. She rolled over and slipped back to sleep, relishing freedom from guard duty.

She woke again, heard the wind rush through cerrenils, paused to wonder at the damp heat coating her skin and sopping her hair. She couldn't remember a summer so humid.

She tossed out of other nightmares. Lornk ruled over a Latha steeped in the vices of Traine. Ashel stood beside him, casually abetting his cruelties. Bethniel mopped her face; tears stained the princess's cheeks. A comely, dark-bearded man stood above her, his face contorted with disgust. Dust danced through light beams. Strange birdsong echoed. Bethniel sang to her, squeezed her hand too tightly. The night rolled on, not ending, the longest sleep Vic had ever known.

At last she woke to a dull ache in her shoulder, a pang in the pit of her stomach. Ashel's last words rang while her eyes brimmed with unshed tears. *Be safe, wife.*

She nestled in a bower shrouded with fine netting, a clue that fate had moved her from Meylnara to the Council. Dim light stuttered in floor lamps. A slope of canvas stretched from a center pole to a ring five feet above a thick blue carpet, scrolled in gold. A desk and table, a few canvas chairs crowded the floor. She crawled out of bed and stood on jittering knees. A silk shift tickled the tops of her feet. Woozily, she stumbled to a water pitcher, her mouth sour, her throat drier than Krag—she snorted. Drier than the sea. She didn't see any cups. Arms shaking, she raised the pitcher to her mouth. Water splashed down her chin, the pitcher stuttered against the wood, and she lowered herself into a chair, shaking.

Be safe, wife. Her skin felt brittle and hollow, like an eggshell. The ghost of his last kiss touched her lips, and something in her womb flinched. Her lungs drew in the hot, damp air; her head fell into her hands. *No, not that. Elesendar, no.*

Vivid dreams of a corrupted Latha haunted her: Elekia cowed as Lornk's wife. Ashel proud and vain as his son. Only a dream, but as real as—she gripped the arm of the chair. As real as this . . . time. The Ancients had a concept called Relativity, a kind of time travel. What would Martha say to this? Martha, Ourtown's ranking Logkeeper, the master who'd granted Vic her sash and sent her into the world, to maintain a tradition of knowledge old and useless as myth.

> *The Logkeeper's lodge is warmer than most, smaller than most. A pallet, a desk, and books, books. Vic looks up at Father. He tugs his beard and squeezes her hand.*
>
> *"She knows all I know," he pleads. "She's full of questions I can't answer."*
>
> *"Know all you know? Theodore, she's a child."*
>
> *"I'll be a good student," she swears.*
>
> *Martha turns cold blue eyes on her. "I don't want a student," she snaps. "Ours is not to understand, but to preserve."*

Seven years under Martha's tutelage, and she'd memorized every Log in Ourtown. An apprenticeship that prepared her for nothing. Certainly not this.

Outside the tent, voices hailed Bethniel. Bethniel?

"Madam, sir," the princess answered, her mindvoice as real as the chair. "Well met."

"Well met," replied a man. "Saelbeneth and I have just looked in on your sister."

"And how fares she?"

"She sleeps as yet," replied a woman, her mindvoice like velvet, "but her color is much improved."

"Yes, madam. Her fever broke last night. I have no doubt you will soon have the answers you seek."

The tent flap parted for elegant brown fingers. Vic winced at the shafting sunlight, but when the flaps closed, she blinked up at the tall, slender form of Latha's Heir. Hair grown to her shoulders, Bethniel looked for a moment like a young Ashel.

"You're up!" Beaming, the princess laid a hand on Vic's forehead. "How are you feeling?"

"I can't remember worse, not least because of where we are. This is Direiellene, isn't it?" Even in mindspeech, her voice lacked the strength to bridge a whisper.

"Elesendar, it's you!" Bethniel glanced at a bandaged thumb and flung her arms round Vic's shoulders.

"How did you get here?"

Her foster sister's lower lip folded under her teeth. "I'm always following you where I shouldn't go."

The urge to scold bubbled up through Vic's shock and weariness, but she swallowed it, said the other thing she felt. "I'm glad to see you. How long have I been here?"

"Almost two months. You've been very ill. What do you remember?"

Two months! *Be safe, wife.* Swallowing a new wave of emptiness, Vic shook her head. She remembered searing pain and loss, but she confined her account to Meylnara's dungeon.

Beth recounted her story, casting her eyes down as she neared the end. "The first wizard I met, and the one who saved you, is Thabean."

The one who'd loved Victoria. Something sunk into Vic's bowels, twisted itself into stale laughter that emerged in hoarse barks. "Elesendar," she cried, tears running down her cheeks. "Elesendar—they've planned it all down to the last, haven't they?"

"They?"

She felt a twinge in her belly, Meylnara's words sharp in her ears. *"Don't you feel it?"* No, please let that not be true. The laughter turned to sobs, hard, heavy. Her chest hurt, it was so hard to breathe. "I can't do it, Beth. I can't."

"Vic?" Bethniel's arms encircled her shoulders. "Don't cry. You're safe now. Please, you're safe."

"Safe! Safe!" Vic choked. Her head and shoulder throbbed; her body trembled, and she lacked the energy for tears. There were other matters to settle—Meylnara and Thabean and the Council and History—but the sobs came anyway, gagging her. Bethniel released her, and she bent over, slipped to the floor, still sputtering and moaning in a torrent. If there were a god, be it the spacecraft circling the planet or the omnipotent creator scoffed at in the Logs, if such a being existed, then her creation had been the cruelest of jokes. Dangling a *life* before her and then ripping it away just as her hand closed around it? If her destiny was to stay a soldier, what ironic madness could send her to a war so completely debilitated?

A decanter clinked, and a glass pressed cool and solid against the back of her neck. "Drink this. You're sweating out of your skin."

Hands shaking, she sipped. Sweet watered wine clung to her teeth. After another swallow, she could take a breath without choking. Groaning, she wiped her eyes with the backs of her hands.

"The Woern are doing this to me."

The princess swept a hand along her face. "I know, sister." One of the lamps flared, the light gilding her skin, like everything in the tent. The furnishings, the brass and crystal, the drapes with thread of silver could have fed an army for months. Something twitched in her gut. *Life.* How long? Two months? Forty days? She laid a trembling hand below her navel. Was it firm? A year was two hundred and twenty-three days long. Babies were born in just over eight months. One hundred sixty days, give or take. *"Don't you feel it?"* It was too soon to feel anything, if there was anything to feel.

"Beth?"

"Yes?"

She cleared her throat. "While I was sick, did I—" Her cheeks grew hot. Even as a soldier, her courses had come regular as clockwork. "I think I might—" Elesendar, no.

The princess clasped her hands. "What?"

Her touch jolted breath into Vic's lungs, made her aware that blood still flowed around bone under the brittle skin. She pulled in a long breath, then met Beth's eyes. Their creases conveyed a strength that belied the shallow vanity the princess wore like a veil. "This is the second time I've been taken from my home," Vic said. "Twice the ones I love have had to assume I'm dead." Bethniel winced, but she waited for Vic to go on. "First it was my father. Second—" She touched Beth's cheek. "Second, it was Ashel. I love him. I finally realized it."

"I've known it a long time."

"And now I think I might, possibly, be . . . pregnant."

Bethniel gasped, eyes tearing. "You married? I'm going to be an aunt?" Her arms flew around Vic.

Caught in the princess's embrace, sobs filled Vic's chest again. "I'm not sure yet, but if it's true, I know what I should do. What I *would* do, except . . . this may be all I'll ever know of him. And this war—I don't care. I don't care."

"You talk as if we're never going home."

"We're not."

The princess pulled back. "We got here, we can go home. No door doesn't let you through both ways."

"What do we know of the Kragnashians' doors? Aren't you frightened that they can do this? The Ancients flew through space, but they couldn't move through time."

Bethniel's mouth flattened. "I won't argue religion with you."

"Shrine, I'm not starting a debate. Whether they were born of trees or came from the stars, will you at least acknowledge the Ancients knew more of science than we do, that they had machines we don't have?" The princess gave a begrudging nod, and Vic went on. "Whatever they had, with the Device, the Kragnashians have more. That scares me. And whatever their intentions bringing us here, I doubt they plan to send us home."

"It seems you have a dilemma." A short man with eyes as bright and blue as Lornk's stood at the entrance. He carried himself like one used to command, but the relaxed tension in his shoulders and legs suggested he knew how to fight too.

Bethniel stood and bowed her head. "Victoria of Ourtown, this is our host, Thabean Graystone, Second on the Council of Wizards."

Thabean—the sight of him burned off Vic's tears. Using Beth as her anchor, she stood. "What did you hear?"

"I'll let your sister tell you, madam, though she's not much help to you, allowing me to eavesdrop so long. The Council has some questions for you."

"She's still too ill to meet them," Bethniel said, aloud in his language. "Look at her—she only just regained her senses, and she can barely stand. Saelbeneth said she should be well before—"

"She is well enough, my lady." He turned to Vic. "Madam, you have broken two of the highest laws. The Council will demand your death."

Bristling, Vic waved at the tent. "You treat your condemned prisoners very well. I understand I've been under your care for months—why not just let me die?"

Chuckling, he inclined his head. "The Council always prefers rogues to die on their own, and they usually do. Yet you recovered, and quite miraculously." He crossed his arms. "Two laws, madam. My lady, ready your sister to meet the Council."

The Business of Traine

Sunlight streamed through lead-paned windows, setting the merchant's stylus aglow and his pate agleam. Laying down the quill, he blotted sweat with a silk handkerchief before sealing an envelope and handing it to Ashel. "I wish I could do more, but . . ." He shrugged at the silver-embossed ledgers behind him.

Ashel swallowed protests and took the note. For weeks, he'd met dozens of slotaen merchants. Round women with bejeweled fingers, lanky men sporting silver-capped teeth, old ones, young ones, svelte, rotund, clever, and dense ones. All had an iron lock on their safe and a stalwart unwillingness to ask their supplier difficult questions and jeopardize their monopoly on Knownearth's most prized commodity: the healing ointment the Kragnashians distilled from their own blood. He looked at the envelope: *Lisette*, pier 4. "A Caleisbahn ship?"

The merchant nodded. "They're better able to help you than we are, Highness."

Dimming hope lured him down paved avenues and muddy byways toward the docks. Commerce swelled and ebbed around him: everyone after something, from the beggars who flicked a rag at his boots and demanded a penny-crystal for the shine, to the master courtesans who raised finely styled eyebrows and beckoned with gem-studded nails. At one corner, a coal wagon blocked half the intersection. A man and a skinny youth heaved at a wheel mired in sludge, while horses strained in harnesses, flinching beneath the lashing whip of a bone-thin woman.

213

A pair of constables strolled over, slapping clubs into their palms.

"Move this lot now," said one.

"You're blocking traffic," growled her partner.

"Soon," said the wagon driver. "We go when wheel free."

"Not soon enough." The first constable peeled back the tarp to reveal the load of glistening black chunks. "Where're your papers for this haul?"

The other officer grabbed the youth, pinned him against the cart, and fished a hand into his culottes. "Hey, pretty birdie, you got the papers? Or did you Buzzards steal this load?" The boy yelped and squirmed as the grinning constable churned his hips against him.

Buzzards. Vic's people. "Let him go," Ashel said.

"Don't trouble yourself over these birds, my lord," the first constable said, her eyes skirting over his embroidered silks. "They'll be on their way to the Commissar's gibbet soon enough."

"They're late delivering this load for me. Do not delay them further."

The second constable stepped away from the boy but kept a fist clenched round his collar. "You have proof, my lord?"

Ashel fished in his pouch. "What's the fine for missing paperwork? I'm afraid I left it up in the Circle."

The first constable named a sum, and he handed it over, watching in silence while the pair strolled away. After they'd disappeared into the crowd, Ashel nodded at the horses' scored withers. "Keep wearing them down like that, and they won't be pulling coal or anything for you."

The freckles on the woman's nose paled. "Horses good for draft, Citizen. You buy?"

"No, I want you to take care of them." He dug more crystals out of the pouch and handed them to her. "Get some gravel to put under the wheel and some fodder for the horses, and be gone before they come back."

Their eyes were fixed on his lone thumb, snagged through the pouch strings.

"You Prince Ashel?" asked the woman.

With yellow fingernails and furtive eyes, the trio looked like they might kill a wealthy stranger who stumbled on them at the wrong time and place. But he'd already stuck his foot in it. "Yes."

"For your loss." Together, they bowed their heads, placed their hands over their hearts, and extended their palms toward him.

The youth swiped a sleeve across wet eyes, smearing dirt over his cheeks. "I'm Fred, and he's Michael," he said, dropping the Buzzard patois for the Oreseeker's tongue. "We're from Cairo."

Michael looked up and down the block, then whispered, "The same ship brought us here, with her."

The woman handed Ashel back his money. "We'll take care of the horses. I'm Mary. I didn't know her, but we all revere her. She was our hope."

Was. "She's not dead," he said, his faith as solid as a cerrenil trunk. But a creeper of doubt grew among the roots of his convictions. Before it could flourish in their sorrow, he strode away.

In the square before the Commissar's palace, teahouses and booksellers crowded between guildhouses, all the buildings facing a teeming marketplace. Cafe tables buzzed with chatter. Market stalls bustled with haggling shoppers, laden porters, merchants, crafters, tradespeople, and laborers. In the center of it all was a gibbet decorated with four small bodies. A bitter, sulfurous reek coiled through the breeze.

Parnden lets his enemies buy their way off that gibbet. Ashel stared at the gallows, blood boiling as he watched the throng ignore it. When he'd visited Traine as a youth, he'd barely noticed the Buzzards and thought the scaffold was merely a stage, one where he'd performed the night he first saw Vic. A wide-eyed, timid girl, naked, alone, and collared. Property. Of Lornk Korng.

Throat tight, he veered toward the sturdy wrought iron fence separating the palace grounds from the market. The lane alongside was cleared of passersby, and there he moved swiftly, his gaze lingering on the Minstrels Guildhouse on the other side of the square. The day after his failure to get answers from the

Kragnashian Center, he'd gone to the Guildhousemaster and told her everything that had happened. Master Jovial had suggested he try the slotaen merchants. She'd also invited him to come and use the practice rooms any time he wished. Squashing the temptation to lose himself in music, he quickened his steps.

The palace gates squealed open, and the Korng carriage rattled out, Relman flags aflutter. Ashel crossed his arms as the carriage approached. The driver tugged on the reins, and the vehicle shuddered to a halt. Earnk leaned out the cab window.

"Are you headed to the docks? We can take you."

"I'll walk, thanks."

"You're awfully conspicuous with that murderous scowl, cousin." Earnk hopped out of the carriage. "Especially when you're stomping alone through the pomerium. Parnden keeps this lane clear for a reason."

"Why were you there?"

"I am a head of state," Earnk said drily. A subtle tremor marred the glib answer, and Ashel noticed the tight set to the Relmlord's jaw. Earnk's eyes flicked to the gibbet, and his larynx bobbed as death stench wafted over them. "Care for a drink?" he asked. "I know a place near the docks. Won't take you out of your way, and we can walk if you like."

Throat aching, he shrugged. "I suppose I'm thirsty."

A pair of guards dropped off the back and shadowed them into the market. Ashel fingered the note in his pocket as they meandered past brimming stalls. The crowd parted for their silks, some muttering respectful greetings. Most avoided Ashel's gaze, but the shabby ones who glimpsed his hand stopped, touched their hearts, and flashed their palms before hurrying off. For weeks Buzzards had signaled him this way. Weeks of dead ends, slim hopes, and sympathy from strangers. Slaves and former slaves, like Vic.

The noise of the square fell behind them as Earnk took them down deserted alleys into rougher districts lined with tenements. Squalling babies, banging pots and cutlery, bickering and lullabies filtered from windows as he walked beside this man who was enemy and ally, cousin and, possibly, brother. Oaths and prayers that Lornk was not his true father whirled and settled into the dank and foggy moor of his grief.

"Why do you support him?" Ashel asked in mindspeech. "From what I can tell, you've suffered more than most at his hands."

Earnk's jaw bunched. "My father is cruel and utterly without remorse for his actions. But . . ." He chuckled bitterly. "But he protects those things which, in his eyes, belong to him. He thinks the world belongs to him, and he is determined to save it."

"By ousting Parnden?" Ashel sneered.

"He will be in a much better position to defend humanity if he controls Knownearth's foundries and smithies and is officially allied with the Caleisbahnin. But this coup is also an act of vengeance."

"For what?"

"For me." Red tinged the tips of Earnk's ears, and they quickened their pace to the pier. As they walked past the slips, Ashel looked for the *Lisette*, but he felt hollow inside, devoid of hope. On the north rim of the bay, shanties snarled over marshland like a wart on a gangrenous finger. The Buzzards' Roost, where Vic's people lived short, miserable lives. What did Fred, and Michael, and the rest want from him, when they offered their condolences? He was empty. He had nothing to give them.

An alehouse sign creaked overhead: *The Logkeeper.* A dry laugh cracked his throat. An Oreseeker establishment.

Earnk pulled the door open. "This is the place, and there's someone here you should meet."

The barwoman gave half a smile and nodded them toward the booths in a far corner. Scattered patrons murmured over drinks in pairs and threesomes. As they slid onto a bench and the guards settled at a nearby table, the barwoman brought over a tray of frothy steins. She served the guards first, then slid onto the bench beside Earnk.

"This is Ellen Storund," Earnk said, raising his mug to their host before drinking.

The lager had a mild, sweet flavor, but it was strong. A few swallows and Ashel's head felt like it was floating off his shoulders. He offered his left hand to the woman and introduced himself.

"Your Highness, I'm so pleased to meet you." Young and handsome, Ellen had a strong grip. Blonde hair wound into a bun atop her head. Spectacles magnified blue eyes with pale lashes.

"The Storunds are important allies to the Korngs," said Earnk. "Have been for years, since my father was a boy."

"I married into the family," Ellen answered Ashel's raised eyebrows. "I've lived in Traine for only the past seven years." Her forehead creased over a wooden ring she wore on her third finger. Meeting his gaze again, she touched her heart and laid her palm on his chest. "I came here with Vic, from Cairo."

He stared, trying to breathe through the blood pounding up his neck. What were the odds, in this city of half a million, that he would meet three people who had known Vic within the space of an hour?

"Slim odds," Earnk muttered, and Ashel remembered he was a Listener.

"I was incredibly lucky," Ellen said, responding to Earnk. "The man who bought me from the slavers was kind, and his goal was to set me free. The Storunds don't believe in slavery, you see, and they have a tradition of picking someone from the slave markets and becoming their patron."

"Would there were more Storunds," Ashel said, trying to work out how his encounter with Michael and Fred could have been set up.

Speaking directly in Ashel's mind, Earnk said, *Does it matter?* For Ellen's Hearing, he added in mindspeech, "If my father succeeds, he will ban slavery in Betheljin. That's why the Oreseekers support our rebellion."

"How will he keep his Caleisbahn allies if he eliminates their main source of revenue?"

"They'll be compensated."

Ellen clasped Ashel's hand. "My husband Alek and Lornk

Korng have spent years planning this uprising. They began long before Vic or I arrived. I know Lornk was not kind to her, as Alek was to me, although I believe him when he says he did what he thought was necessary."

"Necessary?" Ashel's mug smacked the table, ale slopping over the polished wood.

"Please, Highness." Ellen's eyes darted toward her customers. "Our children—Oreseeker children—are dying. On the gibbet, on the street, in galleys, in mines. My good fortune leaves me aching to help them. I knew your wife only a few weeks in a pitch-black slave hold, but I've never forgotten how she helped me endure it. For her sake, do what you can to help her people by supporting Lornk Korng."

His left fist curled tight round his stein, he fought the urge to throw the thing.

Earnk gazed at him calmly. "Whatever you think of my father, I assure you Parnden is worse."

"That may be so." He stood. "But my only purpose in staying here, in this accursed city, is to find Vic and my sister."

Outside, people swarmed the quay, empty carts rattling along the wharves, full ones creaking into the city. "Hoy theres" peppered the air. A crew of porters trotted past, burdens strapped to their heads, a litter borne on their shoulders. All the business of Traine. Ashel leaned against a wall, his face in his hands, wishing he could fold time backward to the scent of the flowers wreathing her hair. The grip of her hand, the robust, hearty music of her laughter.

Come back to Latha, Geram urged. *Lornk is mad. Insane, and you're becoming infected with his obsession. It isn't helping you find them, Ashel, it's only making you lose the best parts of yourself.*

And what are those? I can do nothing at home, and apparently, neither can Mother. At least here . . . if she is alive, I know Lornk wants to find her. You Heard Earnk—Lornk protects his own. That sick, mad bastard of a man is the only one in Knownearth who wants to find her as much as I do, and he's the one person who might have a chance of succeeding.

You cannot remain there, Geram said. *People are saying you helped Korng escape. Fensin is stirring that pot, and there is talk of charging you with treason. Elekia won't be able to protect you—you know Fensin is trying to push her off the throne. Come home before things get out of hand.*

Ashel stood with head down and fists clenched. A tempest raged within him, swirling around a well of grief for all he'd lost: father, sister, wife, music. Different parts of his soul had been ripped away and cast down that hole, and he couldn't find the means of dredging them up and stitching himself back together. His right hand, its four fingers butchered and thrown away, butted against his forehead. *Tell my mother I cannot fix what she broke.*

New World, New Enemies

A path arrowed past rows of sharply staked tents, from a black and white scrolled pavilion anchoring Thabean's camp to a massive edifice bedecked with banners and striped in patterns of scarlet, verdant, azure, violet, black, and white. A fancy silk robe enveloped Vic, dragging on the ground and snagging underfoot. Leaning on Bethniel, she hobbled down the lane with the vigor of an ailing crone. A few paces ahead, Thabean's cloak billowed as if caught by a breeze, but there was no wind and they moved slowly.

"Are you doing that?" Vic asked.

Thabean stopped. The cloak undulated. "I'm doing many things, madam. Thinking, breathing, talking to you. I was walking—would you like some other means of transport?"

She realized the cape floated just above his shoulders. His hair looked fresh and dry, while everyone else's locks clung to damp foreheads. She stepped closer. "I've been sick ever since I got the power. Is that what I've done wrong? Meylnara's hair moves on its own, like serpents. Your cloak billows, and you don't sweat." Using the Woern, she lifted her hair off her neck, swallowing nausea while tingling spread up her torso and into her head.

His lips toyed with a smirk. "Come to the Council. Think, breathe, madam, and *do* just enough."

Dropping back to Bethniel's side, she held her hair off her shoulders. Blood pounded behind her temples, and she gnawed on her tongue to keep from falling to her knees. But that small thing—holding her hair off her shoulders, walking behind that billowing cape, drawing each breath into her lungs and blowing it out again in concentrated effort—wrung black starbursts out of her nerves, and with each pulse, the pain in her temples faded a little and the shaking began to leave her limbs. By the time they reached the Council's pavilion, her head was floating, and Bethniel's arm, twined around hers, felt as distant as a cloud.

A guard drew aside the canvas flap, and Thabean nodded an aide toward Bethniel. "Fainend will take you up to the gallery. Victoria?"

She took the arm he offered, felt a little jolt when she touched him. His smirk shifted to a grin. "Brace yourself."

Inside a small anteroom, the air was dry and cool. Thabean's aide led Bethniel toward a circular staircase while another guard parted a fabric doorway for Thabean. Vic followed him into a narrow passage carpeted with plain knotted wool. Thabean waved at undyed canvas walls. "It's a nod to Samovael. He paints."

She glanced at his floating cape. Mild nausea clung to the back of her throat, but the headache was gone. "What do the others do?"

"Grunnaire spins. Nelchior twists. Csichren floats—but he's lost to the Woern. Don't do too much, only enough. Darien sings and is lost as well as bothersome. Saelbeneth does nothing, but she is immune."

Swallowing, Vic held him back. "I knew the Waters might kill me when I took them, but I thought it would happen immediately, or not at all."

His sneer softened into a bitter frown. "We all die, Victoria. In time. Saelbeneth is fifty-two. The rest of us are . . . younger." He shook his head. "You can't be more than twenty. Too young for the Woern. You hadn't yet lived. I'm sorry."

A laugh burbled out of her throat. "I've lived enough," she said, starting for the next opening. "You can't guess."

"Madam, protocol!" He rushed ahead to beat her through the doorway.

Be damned, she thought, stepping through before him. He slid into the hall after her, cheeks red. Murmured conversations died, and nine faces round an oblong table turned toward them. Two wizards did not look; one stared blankly ahead, the other at the ceiling. A buzz nagged at the edge of Vic's hearing, and she felt the hairs on her arms stand on end.

A handsome woman at the head of the table stood. Saelbeneth had a mass of dark brown curls that framed a symmetrical face, her skin the same color as her hair. The other wizards blended together—dark and light—as Saelbeneth held Vic's gaze. Vic bowed her head slightly, trying to copy the way Thabean greeted the Council leader. Saelbeneth frowned. "She hardly looks better than she did this morning, Thabean."

"She's well enough." Directing Vic to stand at the end of the table, he took a seat on Saelbeneth's right. The wizards exchanged glances up a chain leading to their leader, then back down to the last of them, the one who stared at the ceiling, a soft round man reclining in the air above his chair, his eyes half-closed. They wore no uniforms, but their places at the table showed their ranks as clearly as the stripes on a trooper's sleeve. Vic straightened, recognizing a martial court.

"Tell us why you're here, Victoria." Saelbeneth sat.

Dread crept over Vic's skin, and she fought the shudder gripping her spine.

Vic. Bethniel whispered in her head. Vic glimpsed shadows in a gallery above them—all the aides assembled, Listening. She couldn't be sure some wouldn't be as strong as Geram or even Wineyll. She couldn't be sure, so she couldn't lie. Fine. At least the headache was gone. Steeling herself, she opened her mouth and spoke to them in the Ancients' tongue. "I was born in the North, in the Unknown. Among the Oreseekers."

"What? What's she saying?" One of the wizards, a beige woman, her hair and eyes as pale as her skin, jerked her head up toward the gallery, then at Vic again. The buzzing grew sharper, louder, her throat vibrating hideously.

Shrine, Vic breathed, but met the woman's stare. "I'm an Oreseeker, madam."

"You're looking here? There's no ore—what's this woman want?"

"Darien," a voice intoned from the gallery, silencing her. The gleam leaked out of her eyes, her mouth turning down into the same frown the rest of them wore.

Shifting her gaze to Saelbeneth, Vic continued. "I am trained as a Logkeeper—a historian of the Ancients' knowledge—and as a soldier. I did not seek the Elixir, but the circumstances of war left me without a choice."

"So you came as a mercenary?" asked a broad-shouldered man. Behind him, painted ivy unfurled across the colorless wall before bursting into flame and dropping into a river of molten earth.

"I'm not here for metal or mullas, sir, but to find a purpose," Vic replied. "In my homeland, we have no wizards. My power incites fear but fails to inspire awe. What can a wizard do in a land that does not want one?"

"Vic—" Bethniel hissed.

"Saelbeneth!" cried a woman with blue gems spinning beneath each ear, her chestnut hair woven with ribbons.

A hand up for silence, the Council leader motioned Vic to continue. Thabean scowled, his eyes dark as storm clouds. The spinning woman—Grunnaire—and the painting man—Samovael—bore matching expressions of disgust and outrage. Shrine's bitch, Vic cursed silently as pain lanced her temple. She'd barely said ten words, but every one of them seemed to be wrong and she had no idea why. What did she need to say to end this tribunal and get on with the business of killing Meylnara so they could find a way home?

The wizards stared at her, faces composed into masks of judgment.

She decided on the simple truth. "News of your war came to us. I was sent to help."

"Outrage!"

"She condemns herself with every word!"

"This is insufferable!"

Vic's eyes jolted from face to face as wizards stood, shaking fists and banging them on the table. Others sat with crossed arms and stormy features. Thabean, the one who'd risked his life to rescue her from Meylnara, covered his eyes and shook his head. Her hair dropped flat against her shoulders. Her stomach sank as they called for her death. "What have I done?" she asked in mindspeech, so her words would carry over the shouting.

The Council leader stood, and the others fell quiet and retook their seats. Saelbeneth had kind eyes and a soft mouth, like a mother who would hold you to her bosom in warmth and safety. Vic wanted to walk round the table and enter that promise and ask forgiveness. Instead, she set her chin. "I come with offers of help, and you respond with threats and accusations?"

"You *came* from Meylnara. You obtained the Elixir illegally. You carry a child. Any of these three would incriminate you. All three together condemn you."

In the silence that followed, Vic opened her mouth and shut it again in dumb surprise. It had been just over two months—how could they know? How could Meylnara have known after only a *day*? Regardless, the Council would kill her for being pregnant. And yet, she had awakened in the room of a queen, not a prisoner. They wanted something from her, or she'd be dead already. Grabbing hold of that, she began again. "I was Meylnara's prisoner—"

A bugle pierced the air, echoed by shouts. Aides rushed in, and the Council stood to receive messages. Saelbeneth called for order and asked for a report.

"Meylnara's minions are entering Csichren's wedge," replied an officer.

"This tribunal is recessed," she said. "Victoria, you have a chance to show your allegiance. Thabean, you will guarantee she does no harm."

"Madam—" a wizard protested.

"Do not defy me, Nelchior," she snapped. The Council adjourned swiftly, some running through the passage, others diving beneath the canvas walls. Nelchior and Grunnaire shot through a hole in the pavilion roof, captains in tow. Saelbeneth strode out, leaving Thabean alone with Vic.

"Shall we go, madam?" Thabean asked.

"She can barely stand!" Bethniel appeared at the threshold of the Council chamber.

A chance to show your allegiance. Vic grimaced at the sick pressure behind her eyes. Her knees trembled, and she felt as if they might collapse beneath her. "I don't think I have a choice, Beth."

"You don't," Thabean said. "Come with me."

Outside, a garbled roar soaked the air. In the distance, bugles wailed. Entrusting Bethniel to Lillem's protection, Vic followed Thabean into the air, swallowing hard as hot pain tore into her skull. "It's the same as before," Thabean said, gripping her shoulder. "Do only enough; you do not need so much Woern to fly—only enough, Victoria!"

She banked the power flowing out of her into the supporting air molecules. The pain mellowed, and she followed Thabean to his camp, where they alighted near a knot of officers. A servant brought him a tunic of steel links while he listened to reports. Vic's jaw fell, and Thabean paused with an arm halfway into a metal sleeve. "I have none for you, madam."

Shaking herself, Vic tore off the hem of the robe, shortening it above the knees. "It's all right; that thing looks heavy and I can barely stand as it is."

They took to the air again, sailing after the soldiers dashing eastward. Kragnashians swept over a trench filled with spikes and tar, their wedge formation a dagger that plunged toward the heart of the encampment. The tip was blunted by heavy fighting, but the Kragnashian warriors swept through the humans like a knife through legumes. Thabean's troops ran down the wide lane stretching between camps, the archers splitting off to join the artillery assembling along the flanks of the wedge. Thumb-thick arrows darkened the sky. Flaming boulders sailed toward the crush of chitin while ear-splitting trills and human cries of battle and pain and terror rose like swamp gas.

A cluster of wizards floated above the fray, casting lightning and fire. The bolts glanced off the Kragnashians' carapaces, channeling into the dirt or the soldiers defending the line. A few scattered Kragnashians lay like lumps of stone, but many more troopers sprawled on the ground. The creatures flowed over the corpses, elongated mandibles snapping at the living, cleaving through arms and necks.

Vic formed a block of hardened air and smashed a knot of the People. The creatures flinched, then surged forward and savaged the soldiers attacking them.

She looked at Thabean in consternation. "That should have flattened them!"

"It was an impressive blow, madam, but the Kragnashians are resistant to direct attacks with wizardry."

A catapult thunked. Boulders crashed and tumbled into the invading wedge, and springtime scent plumed thick from the carnage. Soldiers spilled into the hole, working in teams to strike with pikes and drive the creatures back, but the Kragnashians regrouped and tore through the human defenders.

Safe above, the wizards continued to shoot electric volleys that did more damage to their own troops than the Kragnashians.

"If direct attacks with wizardry don't work, why are we wasting our time up here?" Vic asked. Steeling herself, she opened herself to the Woern. Power plunged into her. The icepick grinding behind her eyes became white hot, the pain its own focal point as she dove headfirst toward the churning mass. A dropped pike flew into her hands as she swooped beneath a slashing mouthpart, slipped between the rows of tendrilled legs, and thrust the point up into the creature's thorax. Keening, the Kragnashian reared, its blood a torrent of cut grass. She yanked the pike free and shot to the underside of another, killing it. A third went down, and a fourth. She evaded the crushing mandibles, but spine-laden legs raked her skin, tore her garment. Giant, deflated corpses accumulated around her, sinking into the stew of crushed and mangled troopers. Bathed in blood and offal, Vic's heart thrummed with energy. The Woern sang within her, enhancing her strength and sustaining muscles wasted from illness. Her left arm seemed nearly as strong as her right.

It went on, for seconds, for hours—she lost all sense of time in the rhythm of killing. She glimpsed Thabean in the fray as the Kragnashians' wedge broadened and thinned, and the creatures wound between tents instead of plowing over them. Able to fight individuals instead of a chitin-armored mass, the soldiers brought down more and more of the Desert People. Flying up, Vic gazed over the vast sea of green, taller and denser than Fembrosh, extending to the horizon in every direction. "I guess I can't call them Desert People here," she muttered.

Thabean joined her, his hair and mail soaked in green ooze. "They've never attacked with such numbers before," he said suspiciously.

She glared. "I'm helping you."

Meylnara shot out of a writhing mass of Kragnashians. A fireball whizzed toward them, veering after Thabean as they flew apart. An invisible net cinched around Vic. The breath gushed from her lungs; she sucked and gagged, but there was no air to refill them. Heart desperate for oxygen, she gathered all her power and rammed it against the force holding her. There was a feeling of stretching, then a burst, and she hurtled high above the camp. Gulping air, she paused to watch Thabean and the others converge on Meylnara, shooting lightning and fire, driving her back under the cover of her People. The rogue disappeared under armored wing covers, and the creatures retreated like a fast-running tide.

Vic flew down to the cluster of wizards, now arguing. Grunnaire urged caution, while Nelchior advocated pursuit.

"What is your counsel, Victoria?" Saelbeneth asked.

A fierce throbbing behind her eyes, Vic peered at the Kragnashian retreat. The Council troops followed, still hot with battle but their arms sluggish. The bodies left in the Kragnashians' wake were mostly human. "You follow them into the forest, into *their* forest, they'll destroy you."

"They're in retreat!" Nelchior cried. "We have the advantage."

"I've lost too many," Thabean replied icily. "Do what you wish, but I withdraw."

"Coward," Nelchior spat.

"I concur with Thabean," Saelbeneth said. "To follow now would be too costly. Victoria, your method of killing was effective. May I ask your assistance?"

Vic grinned sardonically. "I can't help if I'm dead, madam."

The Council leader nodded serenely. "No, you cannot."

Triumphant shouts rang outside. Bethniel put down the *Order of the Council*. She'd been reading it—well, looking at the words—while she waited and worried.

Lillem ducked inside Vic's tent. Green ooze and sticky red splattered his clothes and caulked his hair, but his eyes gleamed. "We drove them back. It was like no battle I've seen, Highness—the carnage . . . but we drove them back."

"Where's Vic?"

"She was with the wizard."

"She's barely able to walk, Lieutenant. You should have been with her!"

"And how could I do that? She was *flying*."

Vic slipped in and trod silently to the bower, where she curled into a ball, her lip folded under her teeth.

Bethniel felt her skin. "Shrine, you're hot. Lieutenant, bring some water."

"You may depart," Thabean said, angling his head between Lillem and the flap.

Lillem's jaw bunched, and he did not leave until Bethniel waved him out. To Thabean, she said, "You needn't stay, sir, unless you can help her." It took all the self-control she had learned as Elekia's daughter and Fensin's clerk to keep her voice calm.

"I wish I could, my lady," he replied, pouring himself some

wine. Mud and Kragnashian blood caked his face. A rent in the mail shirt revealed a shoulder scored and bleeding. His hand shook as it brought the cup to his lips.

"You'd be better off with water," Bethniel scolded softly, fetching Vic a drink. "Wine will dry you out."

"Ah, but I'll feel better dry."

Vic coughed and doubled over, groaning fiercely. Blood melted into the sheets beneath her pelvis.

Bethniel clutched Vic's arm. "A midwife? Is there one in camp?"

"It's better—"

"No! A midwife!"

Vic moaned again, hugging her knees. Bethniel clawed some green ooze from Vic's hair and squelched it between her thighs. Her sister yelped and shuddered, then her muscles loosened and some of the tightness left her eyes. Bethniel held up her hand, smeared red and green. "She helped you defeat them today—you owe her."

Thabean languidly sipped his wine. "You are both here by my charity."

Furious, Bethniel thrust bloodied fingers under his nose. "Do you see what you've done to her? Do you think she was in any condition to fight today? This is your fault, Thabean. If she dies, it will be your fault."

He grabbed her wrist to shove her away, then froze, his eyes wide. A static tingle razed her skin. Satisfied she had won her point, Bethniel yanked her arm free and toweled her hands clean. "Get her a midwife."

The wizard sat still, his mouth twisted in horror. "Where . . . who are you?"

Vic's eyes flickered open. "We told you—"

"No," he spat, raising an accusing finger at Bethniel. "She has the Woern. She does not use their power, which frightens me more than all your ill-got strength, madam. Tell me how you acquired it, or I will kill you both here and now."

Bethniel stared at him, cold gripping her spine. Shaking, her eyes glassy, Vic pushed herself up. Her voice was solid, fearless. "You will not harm her."

Fury darkened Thabean's features, and Bethniel stood between the two wizards. "I don't have any power, but my mother is a wizard."

Thabean's head jerked as if she'd slapped him. "And the babe within her was fathered by your brother? Elesendar, do you know what you're saying?"

"Vic told you the truth: she's an Oreseeker. I am not. I was born in Latha. In the future, Thabean. That's where we come from—the future."

His face changed again, brows furrowing in bewilderment. "What?"

"You want to know more? Get a midwife."

CAMP LIFE

Article Fourteen, Paragraph Eight

> *No one may take the Elixir without the knowledge and approval of the Council of Wizards. The Council shall administer tests of knowledge, strength, wisdom, will, and discipline to all Candidates, which must be passed before access to the Woern shall be sanctioned.*

Article Fourteen, Paragraph Nine

> *The Council shall consist of all living Wizards but at no time shall exceed the number Twelve. Each Council member shall designate, by will or by declaration before peers, a replacement Candidate. Said Candidate shall be trained in Law and Governance and must exhibit a temperance of spirit and manner so as to predispose him or her to a place on the Council.*

Article Fourteen. Paragraph Eight. No one . . . Groaning, Bethniel threw her head back, stretching her arms behind her. These were the laws that sentenced Vic to death. *And me.* Thabean's revulsion when he'd grasped her arm the night before stirred fear in her belly. She didn't feel the Woern. She didn't *want* them. But soon, she'd have to answer for having them.

She had to focus—the law was the only way they would get

232

out of this. Twirling her hair, she bent over the text, looking for a loophole. The Council had granted Vic clemency, but how long would that last? Of course, it had to last—History said Vic would kill Meylnara. But History had never mentioned anyone named Bethniel of Narath, nor did it record anything about Victoria of Ourtown being pregnant.

She rose and paced. Last night, Thabean had grudgingly called a Healer. The woman had tutted and shook her head, claiming nature would have to take its course. Thank Elesendar, the bleeding stopped and Vic slept until morning, when Thabean came and took her off to battle again. "Saelbeneth and I will require a full accounting when we return," he'd promised.

She wore a path in the carpet until the shouts and noise of soldiers pervaded the camp. At the mirror, she tucked frizzed locks back into curls, then rushed to Vic's tent through knots of green-slimed soldiers, joyfully slapping each other's backs and recounting their deeds.

"Highness!" Lillem called. He was filthy with mud and blood, but most of the latter was green.

"I'm glad you're well, Lieutenant. How is Vic?"

His smile soured to a scowl. "It's corporal here, Highness. The Blade fought well. I can't fault her courage."

"You find other faults with my sister?"

"She isn't your sister."

Eyes narrow, she pulled back her shoulders. "She was my father's ward and is my brother's wife. That's twice my sister, and you will give her the same respect you give me."

His lips twitched toward a sneer, but he smoothed his expression and gave a respectful nod before turning toward the barracks.

In her tent, Vic was bent over the chamber pot, retching. Bethniel pulled her braid clear until the final, empty gag, then fetched a damp cloth.

Vic mopped soot, sweat, and splattered blood from her face. "They seemed surprised we retaliated—I don't know why they weren't prepared, but we were able to tear down one of the defensive walls and left a good number of the People dead. But then they formed up into a kind of mass, hundreds of them on top of one another in a ball, with Meylnara in the middle. We couldn't get at her. The Kragnashians have some kind of resistance to wizardry. What we do mostly just bounces off them."

"I don't care about that," Bethniel said. "How are you—how is . . . ?"

Vic rolled her head around to blink at her. She looked about to pass out, but she fished under her skirt, brought out bloodless fingers. "No worse."

"That's a surprise." Prenlin, the Healer, pushed through the tent flap and began unloading beakers and vials from a basket. "Get her into bed, then go order a bath and clean linens for her."

Bethniel blinked at the Healer.

"You heard me, girl," the woman snapped.

"Go fetch me a bath, Your Royal Highness," Vic teased as she slid onto the mattress. Bethniel stuck out her tongue, but it turned into a grin as she left to find a servant.

When she returned, Vic was alternately swallowing and coughing as Prenlin tipped a potion into her mouth. Pounding Vic's back, the Healer handed her brown slivers of dried fruit. "That'll ease the stomach. It's the same we give the wizards in the first weeks after the Elixir. It'll help with the brooding sickness too, for as long as that lasts." The woman frowned. "Sick as you are, were you a normal woman, I wouldn't give the babe a week. With the Woern in you . . . I can't say."

"It's the Woern that are making me sick."

"They're healing you too—giving you unnatural endurance, no? Tell me, before, could you have fought for hours if you felt like this?"

"The soldiers fought just as long today."

"They're not sicker than a cat either. There are limits to what a body can do; the Woern stretch those limits, even while they're killing you. They're parasites; they want their host to live. Like as not they kept that babe alive during your fever. Now eat."

Vic nibbled a brown sliver, grimaced, but kept at it.

"We need help at the hospital," Prenlin said to Bethniel.

"I'm not a Healer."

"You're a pretty face. You'd find a use for yourself, helping to cheer the wounded."

Thabean entered, holding the flap open for Saelbeneth. Both wizards wore clean garments, their skin and hair as fresh as their silks. Gustave and the Caleisbahn commodore followed them; Gustave's hair was plastered to his head, his shirt stained green, but his commander had washed. Next battle, Bethniel vowed, she'd have hot water and soap ready for Vic. Her sister needed to be seen as the wizards' equal, not a dirty outlaw.

Prenlin gathered her things and left, with a final order for Vic to keep eating the fruit and to drink as much watered wine as she could.

"I understand you have a new story to tell, about your origins." Saelbeneth sat with Thabean next to her, like a pair of judges. The two Caleisbahnin stood silently behind the Council wizards.

Bethniel settled beside Vic on the bed. "Why should our story matter?" Vic asked. "If you've granted me clemency, why not Bethniel?"

"Because you have proven yourself able in battle," Saelbeneth replied. "Your sister, on the other hand, presents only a threat and offers nothing of value."

"I speak Kragnashian," Bethniel said.

Saelbeneth and Thabean exchanged dubious glances. "My lady, your insistence that Meylnara's creatures are more than dumb beasts is absurd. You have the Woern. Explain how this can be."

Vic squeezed her hand. "I think you should tell them."

Bethniel took a breath, heart thudding. "Madam, I speak the truth and will mask none of my thoughts if you choose to Listen. We are from the future. My mother traces her descent through almost thirty-five generations to your daughter, Taelniel of Narath."

"Taelniel is no wizard. I bore her before I received the Elixir, and as my daughter she is excluded from receiving it now."

Bethniel nodded. "My mother is your descendant, madam, but she acquired the Woern from the Kragnashians. In our time, they are a civilized race with whom we exchange goods and live in peace. They also guard the only known supply of the Elixir."

"If this is true, your time must be rife with chaos."

Bethniel offered a diplomatic smile. "No more than any other time, madam. The counties of the Kiareinoll united with the lands west of the Lathalorns some four hundred years ago, and Latha has been one nation since. The Relman counties united within the past two hundred years. Wizardry is exceedingly rare, but it made the difference in a twenty-year war Latha won against a Relman tyrant who sought to conquer us. Victoria risked her life to acquire the power to defeat this monstrous man, and she risks it still, as you can see."

"Why is wizardry rare if there is no Council to control who may become a wizard?" Thabean asked.

"Look at me, and you see why," Vic said. "People fear the effects of the Elixir more than they crave its power. Most who risk it die."

"Your mother did not?" Saelbeneth asked.

"She seems to have inherited your immunity, madam."

"And if she has the Woern, why did she not use their power to defeat this tyrant?"

Cheeks hot, Bethniel glanced at Vic. What Mother had done—condemning Vic to this dreadful illness, and eventual exile, when she herself remained safe in the Manor—how could Vic ever forgive her?

Flashing a hint of a smile, Vic replied, "Queen Elekia assumed Latha's throne when Bethniel's father was murdered. As commander of the Lathan military, she directed battles; she didn't fight them."

"My sister is trying to spare my mother's honor, but in truth,

Victoria's power—her infection with this condition—was not a thing she sought but which was forced on her."

"That makes no difference to her status under the law in this time," Saelbeneth said. "Or yours."

"I had no idea I had the Woern until recently. My mother never told us we might inherit it, and my brother and I have never manifested any power."

"For that you can be grateful, but in this time, being a carrier of the Woern puts you in grave danger."

"I understand I am now subject to the same penalty as Vic."

Thabean's scowl softened. "Not quite, but it is dangerous for you nonetheless. In the age before the Council, some wizards would take latents such as yourself captive, to keep as a reservoir of healthy Woern. They would bleed them like cattle, or use them in other unsavory ways to gain their Woern."

Bethniel shivered, and Vic narrowed her eyes. "I would kill anyone who harmed her."

"You say the Kragnashians of your time are a civilized race," Saelbeneth interjected. "Why did they bestow the Woern on you?"

Vic replied, "The War of the Council was a momentous event for the Kragnashians. When they gave me the Elixir, they called me the One and said it was my destiny to kill Meylnara. We thought they spoke metaphorically, and that it was a coincidence that I have the same name as a woman mentioned in Lathan histories of the Council. I never expected to actually *be* here."

"Nonsense," Thabean spat.

Saelbeneth glanced at the commodore. "I believe they speak truth. Our Caleisbahn allies have made similar claims regarding the Kragnashians. Perhaps we erred in dismissing any possibility that Meylnara may have enemies among them."

Scowling, Thabean leaned forward. "How did you become Meylnara's prisoner?"

"What I told you before was true," Bethniel said. "Kragnashians allied with Meylnara attacked us, although this happened in our own time. They captured Victoria and took her through a Device to Meylnara's keep. Gustave, Lillem, and I followed."

"Meylnara wanted me to join her, and when I refused, I believe she kept me prisoner rather than kill me because she wanted the child I carry." Vic cleared her throat. "Thank you for rescuing me."

"This is preposterous," Thabean cried. "Time travel? How?"

"A Portal," the commodore said.

A tickle in her gut, Bethniel asked, "You don't know about the Devices?"

Saelbeneth's brows drew down. "There is a Portal in the Archipelago and one in Narath."

"There are others, madam. Did you never wonder about the spokes round the knob?"

"Of course, but they lead nowhere, except death."

"The master Device is here, in Direiellene," Vic said. "In Meylnara's keep. Whoever controls it can control Knownearth."

"And we know the location of three more Devices, or Portals, as you call them," Bethniel added.

Gustave nodded, lips curved, and Vic squeezed Bethniel's hand. "We'll tell you exactly where they are," Vic said, "if you permit us to leave via the Device once I've killed Meylnara."

"Once you've killed her?" Thabean guffawed. "Madam, I found you in her thrall."

Vic's lips pressed together. "Don't underestimate me, Thabean."

Saelbeneth stood. "I am satisfied. Thabean, see that Bethniel's condition remains secret."

"Madam—"

"Let us not throw away what providence has given. Continue to protect them, treat them well, and begin training Victoria in the power. She almost burned herself out today." Signaling the Caleisbahnin to follow, Saelbeneth ducked out of the tent.

Thabean scowled after the Council leader, then turned to them, lip curled. "We will begin immediately. My lady, the lesson will be better learned if you . . . gave your sister some assistance."

Pink bloomed on Vic's cheeks, and Bethniel's face warmed. What she'd done the other night, feeding Vic her blood—it had felt so intimate, it was mortifying to consider doing it in front of Thabean.

He reclined in his seat, a boot across a knee. "We find the exchange of Woern best accomplished through the eyes. A moist kiss upon the tear duct for a wizard only slightly out of sorts, but bloody thumbs may be best for one so ill as Victoria."

"Blood in the eyes?" Vic asked. "That's . . . disgusting."

Thabean smirked. "There are other ways to exchange fluids of the body, madam. From your condition, I assume you know them well, but Lady Bethniel cannot help you in that manner, and I will not."

"She could ingest," Bethniel said.

"She could," Thabean replied. "But ingestion is the least efficient, as many of the Woern do not survive the digestive tract. Hence, the Elixir is first delivered by spinal infusion."

"Painful," Vic said. "My first time, I drank it."

"And how was it?" Thabean raised an eyebrow.

"Disgusting." A corner of Vic's mouth tilted upward, and a smile ghosted across Thabean's face before he turned toward the wall. Bethniel retrieved a knife and nicked her thumbs. Grimacing, Vic lay back. When Bethniel touched her lids, Vic jolted up and jammed Bethniel's thumbs harder against her skull, gasping. Bethniel's thumbs tingled, as if candle sparks landed upon her skin, and a tremor traveled up her arms to her chest.

"That's enough," Thabean wrapped his hands around hers and pulled them away from Vic's face. Gently, he kissed each wounded thumb, and she shivered. "There, sealed with a kiss," he said, his eyes meeting hers before he released her and returned to his seat.

Vic sat up, toweling off her face and Bethniel's thumbs. Sliced skin had knitted together, the knife sting gone. "How did you do that?" Vic asked.

"One of many things I have to teach you, madam," he replied. "We should begin. My lady, you will excuse us."

Vic smiled wanly. "I'm better now, Beth. You can go."

She returned the smile and left, her footsteps strangely light on the grass, and her thumbs still tingling where his lips had touched them.

† † †

Thabean's eyes followed the princess, their color turning darker, a shade closer to Lornk's. Vic took another bite of the sour fruit. The ache in her head had drained away, and her stomach growled with hunger. Her shoulder was sore, but it was a normal, expected soreness, considering half the muscle was eaten away.

Servants hauled a steaming tub through the flap, and Thabean allowed them to place it behind the privacy screen. Knowing very well how the elite viewed a dirty face, Vic dunked herself into the tub, blushing as she washed off sweat and Kragnashian blood while Thabean paced on the other side of the screen. Shrine, he was supposed to fall in love with her, if you believed the songs and stories. Thinking of Ashel's baby, she wondered whether it was wise to get herself presentable. Perhaps a little contempt from this wizard might not be such a bad thing.

Yet when she emerged wearing a clean shift, braiding damp hair, he gave a perfunctory nod. "How long have you had the Woern?"

It had been the beginning of autumn when they'd met the Kragnashians in Direiellene, and now it was nearly midsummer. "Almost nine months out of twelve."

His eyebrows went up. "That you've survived nine months with no training is a wonder. You must be more resistant to the Woern than many."

She grimaced. "I've been sick the whole time."

"Evidently." He sat and waved her into a chair. "And how much of the Elixir did you drink?"

A foul memory of the slimy, grainy brine scalded her throat. Choking, she lunged toward the chamber pot, but Thabean caught her and kissed each of her eyes, his tongue brushing her tear ducts.

She shoved him back. "What do you think you're doing?" She'd been alone with the man ten minutes and he already couldn't control his passion?

Blue eyes paled, and his mouth struggled to remain straight until a laugh burst out of him. "Not what you imagine, madam! Trust me, I would not violate the Council's laws for *you*." He swallowed another snigger. "How do you feel?"

She paused, realizing the nausea had subsided and every muscle in her body had relaxed. "How does it work so quickly? Elekia—Bethniel's mother—told us, any fluid of the body, but why does that work?"

He licked his fingers; saliva glistened in the lamplight. "Just as you are sick, madam, so are your Woern."

"But why? Elekia said it was a matter of compatibility."

"She is correct. Everyone who receives the Elixir risks death, and most die within days. A very small few remain hale and gain power, and fewer still are entirely unaffected and their Woern become dormant. The small plurality of us who become ill and yet survive have an intermediate compatibility with the Woern, and the only way to coexist with them is to feed them a steady stream of our power. When we fail to do so, they sicken and die themselves, and our symptoms worsen. A small infusion of healthy Woern eases our suffering as well as theirs. We must treat our friends well, feed them properly, give them rest. As I've already told you, *do* just enough. Now, please answer my question."

She framed the size of the cup with her hands. "About this much."

His mouth fell open. "Elesendar. You drank all of that?"

Sheepishly, she nodded. "Afterward, I learned most people manage only a sip."

"You are lucky it did not poison you. Yet—" He frowned. "You appear quite strong, perhaps as strong in the Woern as Kara. She nearly destroyed Knownearth."

Heat flashed into Vic's cheeks, and she heard Lornk barking

that name, the one he'd called her while she was his slave. Shrine, would she ever be free of those vicious memories? "I was taught she died fighting an evil wizard who wanted dominion over the world," she said to cover her distress.

Thabean snorted. "Kara was hated and feared, her power nearly limitless and unconstrained. You at least are not immune to the Woern, and even should you learn to control it, I fear your lifespan is much shortened. But Kara *was* immune—an entirely compatible host. She inherited the Woern, as did nearly all wizards in the age before her. It was because of her that the Council formed and established the Code."

"What did she do?"

"What do all those who seek power and dominion do? She built a fortress and sent armies to subjugate all the peoples of Knownearth. Even the Caleisbahnin feared her, and they made an alliance with Shamar of Alna, who led a group of wizards against her. Together, they created a phantasm that defeated her, but in doing so, they all burned themselves out and died soon thereafter."

"Burning out—I can guess what that means, but suppose you tell me."

His face resumed its mask of composure, unreadable. "You have seen Darien?"

"The one who floats, or the one who sings?"

"Sings. She burned herself out and has no real power. We did not expect her to live so long without it, but you can see what it has done to her—she is an imbecile. Meylnara blocked you from your Woern for the three or four days you were with her, and it took you two months to recover. Once you have the Woern, madam, your fate is theirs. They remain healthy if we feed them a little all the time, by using the power they give us in some small way. And we are able to do larger tasks with their help, but just as the glutton kills himself slowly, they will sicken if too large a feast is forced upon them. Particularly when they are made to fast for long periods between the uses of power. Mayhap many of your Woern have died, and you do not have all the power you had once, nine months ago. In any case, even with your sister's help, if you do not begin to control what you do with their power, your Woern will all die, and then so will you."

"But you said I'm going to die soon anyway."

"It's a choice between years spent in comfort, or months as you are now."

During their conversation, Thabean's boots had slowly shifted in color. Vic lifted her braid, holding it off her neck. After a moment, a tightness she didn't know was there melted from her temples. She placed her hand on her belly, thinking about Ashel and his child. One way or another, she'd find a way back to him, and she'd do whatever it took to get them as many years as she could. "So what do we do first?"

INTERLUDE

Wineyll jolted awake when her book slapped the floor. Rubbing a sore neck, she retrieved it and sat up in the chair, hunting for her place.

"You don't have to stay with me," Lornk said from a desk piled high with documents and ledgers. He tapped the quill on the ink jar and scratched out a note.

"Is there anything I can help you with?"

"Not at the moment. Go into town. Amuse yourself while you can."

She left his office and dithered along the first-floor gallery. She'd taken a few walks round the quiet, pretty streets of Citizens Circle, but the city below was too daunting. *It's not like you've never gone anywhere before*, she chided herself. With her father, she'd traveled to every city in Latha, and he'd even taken her with him to perform for the Eldanion royal court. She'd been to Kragnash, Olmlablaire, and Re. But Traine with its Citizens, mistresses, merchants, thieves, slaves, and beggars . . .

Boots on the stairs drew her to the foyer where she caught Ashel halfway out the door.

"Let me come with you," she said.

His scowl shifted into a forced smile. "I'm just nosing around today."

"All the more reason to let me help—"

"I—I'll bring you when I get a solid lead and need your skills."

He was gone, and Wineyll's shoulders slumped.

"Shemen leave?" Kelmair asked, hurrying down the stairs. She was out the door before Wineyll could answer. Kelmair shadowed Ashel wherever he went, working with the Buzzards and her sect to put Oreseekers in his path and build his sympathy for them. Wineyll gnawed on a ragged thumbnail, squashing guilt about keeping that information from him. If he would only stop stubbornly hunting for Vic and Bethniel, when they couldn't be found. When. She shivered a little, wondering what it must be like in the rainforest of Direiellene. A wet heat pressed down upon her skin, and she sank into a chair, feeling inexplicably weak, as if she'd been very ill for a very long time.

"Hello, Wineyll." Earnk stood in the hall. A close-trimmed goatee sharpened his chin, but his golden hair was all wild soft curls. Her gaze scrolled over pale arms, shadowed with lean muscle, and the narrow waist encased in an embroidered silk vest.

Yanking her eyes to the floor, she stood and bent her shoulders to him. "My lord."

"Are you busy?"

She straightened. "No."

"Will you have luncheon with me? I'm going back to Relm for a while, and I thought I'd stop by a favorite cafe before I go. I'd love some company."

Eagerness radiated from her heart. "Then I'd love to come."

Cutlery scraped and porcelain clinked. Voices murmured beneath sprinkles of laughter. Buttery pastry crackled as Wineyll bit into it; it melted as it touched her tongue.

"Do you like it?" Earnk asked.

She nodded, brushing flakes off her blouse. "I do, but it's messy."

"If you can eat a crescent bun without making a mess, it's not a good crescent bun."

"I've never tasted anything like it—how do they get it crunchy and soft at the same time?"

"Baker's magic?"

Her smile widened as she realized genuine feeling, not stagecraft, bent her lips upward. She leaned in for another bite, and flakes spattered her plate. "I wonder if my mother could bake these. She's a tavern cook in Re."

His eyebrows rose. "Your mother's Relman?"

She nodded. "My parents met in South Market. I lived with her there when I was very young, but Father took me back to Latha once they realized I was good at music."

"Did you stay in touch?"

"Letters. Not many, because of the war. They had to go through Mora, so it would take a long time."

"Did you see her when we were in Re?"

"No."

His eyes narrowed, whether in judgment or sympathy, she couldn't Hear.

She added, "It felt too awkward to contact her, when I was there with a conquering army."

"And a wizard?"

"That too." Her smile mirrored his, and again she *felt* it.

"It was a little awkward for me too, arriving there with a conquering army and a wizard." A soft, sardonic laugh caressed her ears.

"Your father meant for you to be Relmlord all along."

"Which is probably why I still hold the Seat. Far be it from Father to let attempted patricide interfere with his grand scheme."

She looked down at the fists curled atop her napkin. She had given herself entirely to Lornk, but in the weeks since they'd arrived in Traine, he'd mostly ignored her except when he took her to meetings with the Citizenry, so she could Listen for him. She'd been given her own bedchamber, and he'd visited only twice, the lovemaking distracted and perfunctory. When she'd told him she was going off with Earnk, he'd only wished her an enjoyable afternoon. The lack of jealousy hurt, but she reminded herself that everyone was just a pawn on his chessboard.

Earnk sipped the last of his tea. "I could take your mother a letter, if you'd like to let her know where and how you are."

"When are you leaving?"

"Tomorrow. Father may have meant for me to inherit the Seat, but I could still lose it if I stay away too long."

Disappointment pulled her mouth down. It was as if she stood outside herself, watching her own facial expressions and feeling astounded that they reflected genuine feelings. Perhaps she was astonished at feeling anything; she'd been hollow inside for so long. She covered the frown with her napkin. "That was delicious. Thank you, my lord."

"Shall we walk?" he asked as they left the pastry shop. A pair of guards hopped off the waiting carriage and shadowed them as they ambled along the cobbled sidewalk.

"This city seems so small to me now," he said. "More people live here than in Re, but in such tight quarters. I've grown used to the expansiveness of Relm. It seems more familiar to me, as if I dreamed my childhood here."

"It can't have been easy."

His eyes darkened the way Lornk's did when he was angry.

"I'm sorry, I shouldn't presume. It's just that I know how cruel your father can be—of course, he has always been kind to me," she added hastily.

He guffawed, a bitter, angry sound. "No, Wineyll, he has not."

They continued past elegant shops selling silk, silver, and other luxuries. "Yet you're here," she said.

"I had to gain Father's blessing—show the Council I have his endorsement. And I had to meet with Parnden. I couldn't not meet with him, considering our positions." Rancor tinged his mindvoice. His expression grew more thoughtful. "It's impossible not to admire my father. He transformed Relm from a rustic backwater into an economic power. South Market has trebled in size since you were born there. The war bankrupted Latha, but Relm thrived, and the people are better fed and educated and live in much greater health and comfort, which makes them far less likely to protest my rule, however it came about. It is quite a legacy Father left me."

"And now he wants to do the same here."

"He loves a challenge."

A glint drew her to a shop window where a silver flute gleamed. Tiny springs propped open pearl-inlaid keys. Whistling softly, she wondered how it might sound.

Earnk pushed open the door. "Let's go in."

Her chest hollow with longing, she backed into the bodyguards. "I—no. No, thank you, my lord."

His brow furrowed. "I loved hearing you play on the journey to Re."

"That one would sound different from my old flute."

"Would it?"

"It's entirely silver. The flute you heard was hollowed crystal." And one no Trainer silversmith could match, her father had always said.

"I'm still curious to hear it. Indulge me."

She let her hair fall between them as they went inside and Earnk spoke to the shopkeeper.

"It's sterling." The woman placed the smooth, radiant metal in Wineyll's hands. It was lighter and slimmer than her old flute. She blew softly across the embouchure hole, adjusted the headjoint, and played a quick scale. The tone was a pure, clear single line, lacking the inherent harmonies of the crystal instrument but full and beautiful nonetheless. Closing her eyes, she began a bright little march, delighting in the swirling, swooping stutters and glissandos. The shop door scraped open while she played, but no disruption could diminish the pure joy of playing music again. As the last note trilled, she turned to the shopkeeper, her skin tingling with warmth.

The woman's eyes were big and staring over Wineyll's shoulder. Earnk's features were preternaturally composed as he gazed at a bald, wizened man who smacked his palms together in slow applause. The copper baubles on his sleeves rattled with each clap. "That was delightful! Lord Earnk, my dear boy, who is this charming magician of sound?" The man's head, perched on a thin and wrinkled neck, emerged from a silk caftan dripping with gemstones and copper scrollwork. A thickly muscled woman with short, iron-gray hair stood by the door, a hand on the pommel of her sword.

Earnk gave a polite nod. "Commissar Parnden, may I present Wineyll of Narath."

Wineyll donned a courtier's smile and bowed her shoulders to Betheljin's sovereign. "It's an honor, Commissar."

"Of Narath you say? Then you're a minstrel?"

"Wineyll has joined our household as a retainer," Earnk said. "And I'm afraid we have an appointment. We'll leave you to your business here."

Parnden nodded at the flute in Wineyll's hands. "I've had my eye on that instrument for some time and came in when I noticed it had been taken down from the window. My Horst is very fond of music, and I thought I'd get him a present."

Wineyll offered the flute to him. "It's magnificent. It would make a very fine gift."

Parnden leered, but his eyes slid from her to Earnk. "It seems to me it's found its master already. I couldn't deprive a magician of her wand, could I, my lord?"

Earnk's lips spread in a thin smile. "As you say, Commissar." Earnk named a sum and asked if the shopkeeper would find it acceptable.

"Very satisfactory, my lord," she replied in a small voice and hurried away to pack up the flute.

Parnden grinned and pointed at a large brass horn with looping pipes and silver keys. "What do you think of this monstrosity, my dear? Would Horst like that, do you think?"

"Any instrument can be learned with enough practice, sir." She looked up at Earnk. "I'm afraid we'll be late for that appointment, my lord."

"Indeed. Commissar, we must take our leave." Earnk handed the shopkeeper a stack of bank notes in exchange for the case.

"When do you leave for Relm, my lord?"

"Tomorrow."

Parnden's eyes rolled over Earnk. "Well then, until you return, I shall have to content myself with dear Horst. Perhaps I'll invite your divinely handsome cousin to dine with me. I'd love to hear how a prince of Latha has come to reside at the Korng palazzo. You should come too, my dear." Parnden swept up Wineyll's hand and pressed wet lips to her knuckles.

"Thank you." Wineyll bowed again, and Earnk steered her out of the shop. Blocking the street, the Commissar's litter was surrounded by mounted guards. The bearers—beautiful, young men, all of them nude—squatted on the cobbles, each wearing a collar of gray steel with a chain bolted to a ring on the litter. Wineyll touched her throat as the sensations of Vic's captivity skirted through the shadows of memory. Relief and shame prickled under her fingers as they found only skin, no collar.

Lips pressed into a bloodless line, Earnk strode swiftly up the posh avenue until they reached a flight of carven stone stairs rising up a hillside toward Citizens Circle. Halfway back to the palazzo, they stopped at an overlook to catch their breath. The city unfolded below them, a landscape of gray stone ringing a blue bay that merged with the sky far out at sea.

"Who were those youths, the bearers?" she asked. "They didn't look like Oreseekers."

"They're not." He grasped a wooden railing, breathing with deliberate steadiness. "They're all the sons of Citizens or guild leaders."

Her eyebrows drew together. "Their sons? How? Does he force them? How do their families tolerate it? I haven't Heard a whiff of resentment from any Citizens Lornk has met with—much less any desire to overthrow Parnden. At best, some seem indifferent to his rule."

"Fear and greed drive allegiances here, and fashion is a

powerful tool. Parnden has groomed each of those young men to be his willing chattel. He has no heir, and his current favorite, Horst, doubtless thinks he'll win that title."

She began to ask why anyone would allow themselves to be degraded that way but swallowed the question. For Lornk, she'd abandoned every principle her father had taught her. Her gaze rose from Earnk's white knuckles, tight round the railing, to bloodless cheeks. "Did he . . . do that to you?"

"Did he make me one of his bugger boys?"

Wineyll winced, "I'm sorry, my lord—"

"He asked me. He always *asks*, and I wanted to do it, because it's such a Shrinejumping honor to be asked. Father made me decline." Red stained his ears as the cords in his neck stood out. "There are always consequences when you refuse an offer from the Commissar of Betheljin. He killed a friend of mine, the son of a tradesman whom I loved as a brother. Sliced his throat right in front of me."

"Elesendar," she breathed.

"For years, I blamed Father, thinking nothing would have happened to my friend if I'd only said 'yes.' That may be true, but after I met Vic and saw what living like that was like for her, I realized what Father had saved me from. It's ironic. And shameful."

She watched a cloud sail over the bay, its shadow darkening the bright waters beneath, until his breathing slowed. "Do you still love Vic?"

He crossed his arms and leaned against the rail. "No. I pined for that smart, arrogant, frightened girl who was my father's slave for years, but when I met the woman she became—the real woman who saved herself, not the fantasy girl I'd hoped to rescue—I realized it wasn't really the girl whom I loved but rather the idea of a star-crossed romance with my father's mistress."

They stood in silence as more clouds drifted across the bay.

"Do you like the flute?" he asked.

"It's magnificent. But I can't accept it. I know you only bought it to escape Parnden's company."

"No, he was right—you are the right master for that instrument, and it's my pleasure to give it to you. In fact—" He pulled in a deep breath. "I'd love to have you come and play for the Council. When I reach Relm tomorrow, I have some business with the nomads, but when that's done, I hope you'll come with me to Re."

"I can't." Her chest grew tight, and she had to clear her throat.

"My father doesn't own you, Wineyll. You can go where you like."

She flushed. "It's not that. The Guild expelled me, and the Guild rules forbid me from playing in Relm, as in Latha."

"If you appeared as my guest, they couldn't stop you. It would be one friend sharing her gift with another." His lips tilted slyly. "The invitation would give you a better reason to be in Re, and you could see your mother."

"I don't think the Council would welcome me, my lord."

He wrapped her arm around his and started up the stairs. "I think the Council could not object to a friend of mine. But first, we do have to be friends. Call me Earnk."

Her skin where they touched felt hot and her breath short, though they'd only climbed a few steps. A desire to flee warred with a need to let him continue to hold her hand, to lean on him as they walked away from his past, and she found herself hoping the stairs they climbed led toward a better future for both of them.

THE RICHES OF TRAINE

The final note died on Ashel's lips, and his companions clapped him on the shoulder and exchanged congratulations on a well-played rehearsal.

"We have a regular gig on at the Piper's Reel on Thirddays," Romner said, stowing his lute. "We'd be honored to have you join us."

"It's honor enough you let me practice with you," Ashel said.

"Master Romner's always better when his attention's fixed on his strings, not his vocals," Paeln teased.

"Lucky Master Paeln became a drummer, seeing how she's tone deaf," Romner returned.

Master Londsaen chortled as he snapped shut his fiddle case. "The pair of you bicker like chicken farmers. We would be pleased if you'd make it a quartet, Ashel."

"I'm afraid that won't be possible." Jovial stood in the doorway, arms crossed. "Ashel, come with me."

The musicians exchanged frowns, and Ashel followed the Guildhousemaster to her office, where she handed him a Guild proclamation. It declared his expulsion.

"I asked that your Guildhouse assignment be transferred here, and this was the Music's response. I'm sorry. It's the Guild's loss."

"The Guild cannot expel you, Prince *Ashel,"* Melba had said. She'd been wrong. He sank into a seat, rubbing the severed knuckles. "Maybe the only surprise is that it took them this long." He felt as if he stood at a crossroads in the dark, holding the frayed end of a guideline he thought would always be there.

Jovial sighed. "Allying yourself with Lornk Korng hasn't helped."

"I haven't . . ." The protest died. "Thank you, Master."

"You're welcome to continue to practice with Master Londsaen and the others, but I'm afraid performances are out of the question."

The offer felt like a kick, but what more could she do? Thanking her again, he left.

The bang of the Guildhouse door echoed through the square. His gut hollow, he sat on the steps, head in hands.

"Prince Ashel of Narath?" A soldier stood on the sidewalk, hand on the pommel of a longsword. Iron medals decorated her chest.

"Yes?"

"Bribery is outlawed in Betheljin, Your Highness."

"I believe it is generally outlawed everywhere."

"Yet you interfered with an investigation into the illegal transport of some coal."

He glanced round the square. She was alone. "Are you arresting me?"

"The two constables have been disciplined. In light of your station, the Commissar has decided a warning is sufficient, and he would like to return your money. I am Major Demsch, commander of the Commissar's personal guard. Follow me, please."

She led him straight across the square, into the heart of the death-pall shrouding the gibbet. The nearby merchants wore cloths tied around their noses; their buyers kept theirs buried in nosegays. Ashel coughed into his sleeve.

"We leave them up three days," Demsch said. "Make sure the thieving Buzzards see what's coming to them."

"They're children," Ashel said, eyes on the little feet dangling above.

"Chicks grow into birds. They'll come down tomorrow, and a new flock will go up on Endday."

"Did these little ones hang for their own crimes or someone else's?"

She cocked an eyebrow. "They're all lawbreakers, Highness."

"Are they? It seems the law is applied capriciously here in Betheljin."

"And you should be grateful the Commissar's mercy is applied to you."

At the gate, guards snapped to attention. The major returned their salutes, and they crossed a wide span of cobbles to a marble portico and a bowing servant. The man ushered them inside.

In the entry hall, a pair of staircases curved around a mechanical lift box. The shaft rose toward a dome of crystal and iron, glittering gold with reflected light. Ashel stared at a chandelier adorned with glowing bulbs, not flickering candles or even gaslights. "Are those electric?"

"Most people think it's magic."

His eyes traced the braided lines anchoring the fixture to the ceiling. "What are the wires made of? Silver? Gold?" Either conductive metal was more common than iron or copper, but they were still costly. He noticed the wall sconces and other lights also glowed rather than flickered. "This must have cost a fortune. How is it powered?"

Major Demsch gestured at the lift. "If you please, Your Highness."

On the third floor, they trod carpeted hallways to a pair of guarded doors. Inside, Demsch invited him to sit. "The Commissar will be with you shortly."

Eldanion tapestries covered the walls, dense erinwool rugs the floor. Woven cerrenil chaises bore silver-threaded upholstery. Each polished granite table supported an electric lamp, each bulb glowing behind colored crystal. The major leaned against a wall, watching him like a cat. Minutes passed, a mantle clock softly ticking. There were few clocks in Latha—the royal Manor had only two—but they were commonplace here, just like running water and iron. All the riches of Traine.

A door opened, and Commissar Parnden emerged with his arm slung around another man's shoulders. "I promise, you will be paid, but you must know for a cost so exorbitant, even a sovereign needs time to amass the sum."

The second man's pantaloons were frayed, his vest threadbare, his shoulders hunched and head bowed. "We had an agreement, Commissar."

"And you'll be paid. Here." Parnden dug into a pouch and dropped some crystals into the other man's pocket. "For the service you performed this morning. Should tide you over. Major Demsch, see my friend out. Ah, Your Highness! Welcome back to Traine."

The stranger glanced at Ashel as Demsch led him out. Black hair, straight and thick, capped features tight with mortification.

Ashel bowed to the Commissar. "Pleasure to see you, sir."

"What has it been? Five years?"

"Nearly seven."

"Oh, indeed. You were such a lovely youth—I'm pleased to see that beauty has matured so splendidly, but why are you hiding it behind that beard?" Parnden's grip was oily as he clasped Ashel's hand and drew him into the inner chamber. At the sight of a rumpled bed, Ashel's pulse quickened under Parnden's leer. He'd been an odious little man when they'd met before, and he was still wrinkled and bald as a young bird.

"Let's confer on the patio," Parnden said, passing through a glass door and taking a seat on a padded chaise. Servants appeared, poured wine, and left. Parnden dropped a small bag of crystals on the table. "There's your—or should I say, the Korngs'—mullas."

"Thank you." Ashel pocketed the crystals and kept his features smooth.

You should assume there's a Listener nearby, Geram said.

Parnden continued. "I'm curious why you're in Traine, residing at the home of your enemy, and spending his money to get Buzzards out of trouble."

Ashel sipped his wine. "The money is Elsa Korng's, sir."

"Don't insult me, Highness. We know who controls the Korng fortune, whichever name is on the Citizen's registry. Why are you here?"

"My sister is missing. Elsa Korng has offered to help find her."

"Your sisters, if I'm not mistaken. Marshal Victoria of Ourtown was Sashal and Elekia's ward, was she not?"

Ashel inclined his head.

"Your people call her the Blade, and in merchants' offices here, you call her your wife. Are congratulations in order?"

"Yes, Victoria and I declared ourselves wed."

Parnden's leer widened. "Marrying one's sister is a bold choice."

"Vic is my foster sister, Commissar."

"Of course, that makes all the difference. I understand she's not such a beauty herself, but I'm certain she has other charms, which certainly captured the interest of Lornk Korng."

His smile fixed, Ashel set down his wineglass. "It's been pleasant seeing you again, sir. Thank you for the return of the mullas. I won't make that mistake again."

"Stay and enjoy the wine, Highness." Parnden's fingers locked around his wrist, the grip strong. "Among your bride's many skills, I'm told she has acquired powers not seen in Knownearth for generations—that is, assuming your mother's powers are merely a gossip's fancy."

"Gossip always runs thick after a conflict."

Parnden chuckled. "Thick as blood, yes. There are other rumors. Older ones, which have reemerged now that you have taken residence at the Korng palazzo." Tutting, he dropped his gaze to Ashel's maimed hand. "I suppose the scandal can only harm your mother, while you stand to gain from an alliance with your enemies."

Ashel sipped his wine. "Is this from the Eldanion royal vineyards?"

"King Matthian sends me several cases a year."

"With a request for your intercession with the Caleisbahnin, no doubt. Commissar, my only purpose in Traine is to find my wife and sister. The Korngs have offered their help, and I am taking it. It's that simple."

"As a sovereign, I may be better placed to help you than a family of iron mongers."

"One of those iron mongers is Lord of Relm, a nation that shares a border with Kragnash."

"But which shares only the smallest trickle of trade with them. Although there are rumors—it's always rumors, isn't it?—of newly discovered riches south of Relm, in the Plenetor. Just the other day I witnessed Lord Earnk make a very costly purchase without blinking an eye." Parnden's lips curled enigmatically.

Ashel gazed at the golden wine, debating whether he should bite at Parnden's lures. He'd wondered at the flute Earnk had bought Wineyll, although his thoughts had lingered on the rationale, not the expense. *Elekia mentioned the same rumors about the Plenetor*, Geram said.

"Lord Earnk left for Relm," Ashel allowed. "If there were discoveries to the south, the nomads would control the trade routes."

"Indeed they would, Highness. I have always been very fond of your . . . cousin, and so very pleased to see him assume his father's Seat in Relm. I would very much like to foster an alliance with the younger Korng, but alas the elder stands in the way. I suppose my old school chum and that rabble-rouser Alek Storund have plans I must confront first."

"Rabble-rouser?"

"I understand you met his wife Ellen some weeks ago, a young woman who knows not only your wife but those same Buzzards you helped evade the law."

Ashel's pulse thumped, but he flung an arm along the chaise back and sipped the wine. His glass was nearly empty. "Have you been following me, Commissar?"

Parnden chuckled. "Not me! I could hardly skulk about the shadows, could I? My predecessor hanged Alek's father for publishing a seditious journal called *The Abolitionist*. Rumor says Alek has relaunched the publication, but no one has seen any copies."

"You seem to rely a lot on rumor. But I assure you, I haven't seen, or ever heard of, this publication."

"I believe you, Highness. But I would be grateful if you brought me any evidence, should you come across it. A copy would be particularly valuable."

"How valuable?"

The Commissar grinned. "As I said, I hold some sway with the Kragnashians, and I think it may suit us both to eliminate Lornk Korng. It pains me so, to think how he harmed you, and I can only imagine the bile you must swallow every moment you're in his presence. You must ask yourself, is selling yourself to this man worthwhile?"

Ashel placed his empty glass on the table. "The wine was very fine, Commissar. Thank you."

Parnden did not stop him when he rose, and Demsch escorted him out of the palace grounds without a word. He left the square, eyes avoiding both gallows and Guildhouse as he pondered the Commissar's offer. The man was vile and malevolent—qualities Lornk shared—but he was grotesquely venal too.

If that seasnake wants to find Vic, it's only so he can kill her, Geram said. *Any power he doesn't control is a threat to him.*

And Mother has still done nothing to bring them home.

The Center refuses to see her, and she's concluded there is nothing she can do except preserve the throne for Bethniel. We have to trust Elesendar will bring them home safely.

So she's given up?

Shrine, Ashel, come home. Today. Elekia will have to take action unless you come back and show unity with her.

My Guild expelled me. There's nothing left for me in Latha.

Your family is here. Don't abandon them.

My family is gone. Stale ale and laughter drifted out a tavern door. Kneading the bag full of Korng crystals, he went inside, his only hope to fill the void.

Royal Favors

Dawn warmed Geram's face. A breeze wafted through the window. Savoring the comfort of fine linen, he stretched. His hand grazed smooth skin, and Elekia sighed awake and snuggled into his arms.

"Tell me it's not today," she murmured.

He traced her shoulder with a finger. All her limbs were bone, sinew, and muscle, as sleek as a racing sloop. "I wish I could."

Pinching one of his nipples, she growled, "You never do as I command."

His mouth found hers as his fingers swept into the soft cleft between her legs. She swelled toward him, tasting bitter and salty, but her skin smelled sweet as citrus blossoms and his ardor rose. When her angles melted into curves, he slid inside her. "Command me now," he whispered. Her hands clutched his buttocks and pulled him deeper. They moved together in like rhythm, passion culminating in arched spines and quiet groans.

Rolling back onto the pillows, he stroked her braids while tears washed his shoulder. She'd gone so long denying joy and grief alike. Now, in the privacy of her chamber, one followed the other in furious bursts that dashed against him like waves on a bulkhead. When they were apart, the counselor in him nagged like a scold, urging him to break off this affair. *Your feelings are nothing but the warped perversion of Ashel's longing for the affection he never got. A little boy who misses his mama.* But when they were together . . . Drawing her scent deep into his lungs, he hugged her closer, wanting only to be the shield against the tempest raging within and around her.

"We could declare," she said. "I can still bear a child."

He stroked her arm, wishes stirring a fancy of an infant held between them. "You know what the Heralds would say about the widowed queen wedding the blind Alnan tomcat who took advantage of her grief? That would only bring more trouble."

Chortling, she nipped his ear. "Tell Fensin I asked; I'm curious whether he'd instruct you to declare or not."

"Elekia," he murmured, her name bitter on his tongue, his throat choking with longing and regret. "This . . . you know we will have to stop when Ashel realizes—"

"Where is he?" she snarled, her body suddenly sharp and hard again.

Geram released her and felt along the chaise, hunting for his clothes. "Sleeping off another bender."

"I suppose I should be grateful. The more he drinks, the more I see of you," she said bitterly.

He tugged on his breeches. "He's desperate and filled with despair."

"And I am not? I want my daughters home as much as he does."

He faced her direction. "Then why do you have to be so prideful that you can't share your grief with him? You should be consoling each other, crafting a plan together, and you've done nothing but drive him away."

"I didn't make him follow that villain to Traine!"

"Nevertheless." Nevertheless, the actions she took today would widen the rift between them, perhaps irreparably. It was exactly what Lornk Korng wanted. She knew that. Ashel knew that, and they plunged into that darkness without a look backward.

He shrugged into his shirt. "I'm due for practice in Olivet's yard."

"Go," she said, her voice like steam from an icicle.

† † †

The Haulers still on strike, piles of rubbish festered, reeking in summer's heat, the stench following the royal coach all the way into Senate Square. There, cobbles were clean and colonnades festooned with summer garlands, but the fetid miasma plaguing the city clogged the throat.

Eager to escape it, Geram hopped out of the coach and handed Elekia to the street. Seen through Drak's eyes, she looked magnificent in the trappings of her office: her braids woven through a steel circlet, a copper coil draped over her shoulders. Her face was serene as she led Timny up the stairs.

Geram held his arm out to Cimba. "Will you guide me in?"

The girl's hand clasped his. "You can use my vision if you like. I promise I'll watch the stairs carefully for you."

At the Senate entrance, Prime Minister Velbaor bowed first to Elekia, then to Timny. Red blooming on tan cheeks, the boy shook the officials' hands before the party went inside. The shaded foyer felt hot as an oven, and sweat tickled Geram's spine as Elekia's heels clopped across the tiles. The echoes shrank as they passed into the Senate Hall. Guards sweated at every door and under every window. Waving fans, the Senators stood and bowed as Elekia strolled to her seat at the front of the chamber, Timny three paces behind.

"Geram?" Cimba whispered. "What happens if Bethniel comes back?"

"I don't know."

She's robbing her, Ashel snarled. The prince rose in a dark room, filled a glass with harlolinde.

You'll kill yourself with that stuff.

To her, I'm already dead, and so is Bethniel.

The queen and Timny sat, and Cimba led Geram to stand with Drak and Olivet before she took a seat beside her brother. Above, observers—merchants and tradespeople—filed into the galleries. On the floor, Prime Minister Velbaor called for roll. Senators usually spent most of the summer at home; many seats were empty, but they managed to meet a quorum. Velbaor announced they could continue.

Heat swept past Geram's throat as Ashel slammed down a draught.

"I come before the Senate begging two favors," Elekia called out to the floor. "To assuage a loss in my family, I ask that Timnon of Narath, son of Navael of Narath, who was son of Rivern, Ruler of Latha, be named Heir to my throne."

Velbaor stood and asked formally, "The designee has the claim of Blood. What can he offer the people as King?"

"The schooling of a Lathan. The wisdom of the Loremasters. The justice of the Arbiters . . ." She listed the courses Timny had taken at the Academy and promised that once he was out of Fembrosh, he would take a clerkship in the Prime Minister's office.

Like Bethniel? Ashel hissed, swallowing more liquor. Geram's throat burned. He felt like a man balancing on driftwood, a sea serpent on one side, a whirlpool on the other.

Elekia stepped away from the podium. Striking his gavel three times, and three times more, Velbaor called Timny forward and tied the Heir's diamond round Timny's brow. The jewel Bethniel had worn had been lost, but the Miners had supplied another in a bid to win royal favor and keep the Manor's weaponry contract. The new gemstone was large and ungainly on the boy's head.

Timny bowed, then turned to the Senate. "I, Timnon of Narath, grandson of Rivern, Ruler of Latha, accept this honor in my fifteenth year with reverence for the old mothers and Elesendar and gratitude to the people of this nation. If elected to the throne, I vow to be a just and wise Ruler. Like my Uncle Sashal before me."

Gasps and murmurs rippled through the Senate and gallery, hushing as Timny cleared his throat. "I am designated Heir today because my cousin Bethniel, who was Heir before me, is missing. Bethniel has the same right of Blood as I to the throne. I vow that I will relinquish the Heirship to my cousin, should she be found well and alive. I command every effort be made to find her."

A babble erupted as the boy left the podium, his jaw set like he expected a whipping.

Velbaor struck his gavel and called for the Senate to approve Timny's proclamation, the only one he'd be allowed until elected Ruler. While the ayes rang through the chamber, Timny retook his seat. Cimba clasped his hand. "It wasn't fair," he whispered. "Who cares who Ashel's father was? It's got nothing to do with Bethniel."

Elekia scowled, and Velbaor called her back to the podium.

"I ask that the Senate try Ashel of Narath, Recorder of the Minstrels Guild and Prince of Latha, for the treasonous act of aiding Lornk Korng's escape." She swallowed, but her voice rang clear and loud. "Should he be found guilty, I ask that the Senate banish him from Lathan soil, on pain of death."

Roars cascaded from the gallery while Senators nodded their heads or shook them. Velbaor pounded his gavel for silence.

"This is highly irregular, Prime Minister," Fensin declared. "A trial in absentia goes against every custom of honor and fairness this body was designed to uphold."

"The people demand justice," Velbaor replied. Protests filled the chamber, and several minutes passed until the gavel knocked them out. "Prince Ashel has refused multiple summons to return home and answer these charges."

"He should at the very least have representation," Fensin replied. "I would be happy to speak for his Highness."

Velbaor agreed, took another vote, and declared the trial would begin that afternoon.

Outside the Hall, people jammed the foyer with sharp elbows and angry voices. Manor guards formed a phalanx, shoving a path toward the door. In the press of bodies, Geram felt a papery hand clasp his wrist. "Inform Elekia she will have a guilty verdict," Fensin murmured before slipping away.

NE'ER-DO-WELL

Ashel stared into his glass as epithets swirled like liquor and spit: Spendthrift. Ne'er-do-well. Coward. The Lathan papers had been full of those names for years. Now, they were true.

Spendthrift. He kneaded a pouch full of Korng mullas. Could he drink enough harlolinde to bankrupt them? He'd heard Lornk's mother had done a good job of it, smoking bliss. He slid another crystal across the bar. Frowning, Ellen topped his glass.

Ne'er-do-well. He had not done well finding Vic and Bethniel. He had sung for the Center in a wild fit of wishful thinking and been soundly rebuffed. He had seen every slotaen merchant, spoken to every ship captain and customs officer involved in the slotaen trade, and gained the help of none. He'd searched every volume in Lornk's library and found not a single bit of evidence to refute Lornk's claims and not one hint of how to bring his wife and sister home, if they were in the past. Every chronicle pointed to the same outcome: Victoria of Ourtown had died dueling Meylnara the Oppressor.

Coward. All his boastful vows that he would find his beloveds, that Vic would not die in the past, withered in the face of his growing terror that they were beyond his reach. Or already dead. He wanted to shrink into a corner and drown his promises and his fears in drink. Like a coward. A shemen.

Traitor. A new epithet for the headlines, and one just as true as the rest. He hadn't helped Lornk break out of prison, but he hadn't stopped him from escaping Latha, and he'd done nothing to stop his rebellion here in Traine. Inaction was collusion. Small feet dangled in his memory. Parnden was a vicious tyrant who deserved to be brought down, but surely Lornk would do no better. A blunt stump butted his forehead. "I gave these to bring him to justice," he muttered at the missing fingers. Now he'd lost everything and achieved nothing.

"Did you say something?" Ellen asked.

"I'll take a bottle."

He moved to a table in the corner. Liquor scorched his throat but couldn't burn away memories of amber tresses sliding through his fingers, or erase that crooked half-smile, or drown the rare and cherished laughter. Dispel the scent that would send his heart racing, his blood rushing hot and urgent; banish smooth skin and firm muscles from his touch. Hours ago, before he'd Listened to his mother banish him, his dreams had turned into a nightmare when he realized the sensations he'd thought were fancies of his wife were real couplings between Geram and his mother! He filled the glass and slammed down another draught.

A man rushed through the tavern door and leaned over the bar, speaking urgently with Ellen. Threadbare clothing and thick black hair tugged at his memory—it was the same man he'd seen with the Commissar. Ellen angled her head at Ashel. They argued a moment more, and the man came over to his table.

Glancing back at the tavernkeeper, the man made the Oreseeker condolence sign. "For your loss, Highness." He spoke in Betheljin, his diction crisp, but with an Oreseeker's accent.

Ashel filled his glass and shoved it at the man. "Just Ashel. You're another one?"

"Another?"

"Someone who knew my wife," he said in the Ancient's tongue, speaking slowly through his brimming inebriation.

The man's shoulders relaxed, and he answered in the same language. "My name is Samson of Cairo, and yes, I knew Vic. I was a teacher, and she was my supervisor." He loosed a sardonic chuckle. "I didn't like taking orders from a teenage girl, not that I was much older."

"To the Logs," Ashel swigged from the bottle, and Samson sipped from the glass. "I saw you at Parnden's."

Samson flushed. "Yes."

"You don't look like an Oreseeker."

"My mother was Caleisbahnin."

"That must be quite a story."

"It is. I . . . Ellen suggested I talk to you. I'm an inventor . . . or, a re-inventor, actually."

The glowing bulbs hazed into Ashel's memory. "The electric lights. Is that your work?"

The man smiled and raised the glass. "Yes! Unfortunately, the Commissar hasn't paid the bulk of my fee—"

The door banged open, and a trio of toughs barged over and yanked Samson out of his chair.

Ellen protested, and a hard woman said in the Buzzard patois, "Take Kinseller outside, brothers. No stains on pretty floor."

"No seadog keep you safe," one of the men sneered as they dragged Samson out.

"What did they mean by Kinseller?" Ashel asked Ellen. His tongue felt thick and ungainly, his head like it might roll off his shoulders.

Brows knitted, she slid into Samson's seat and leaned close. "Some from Cairo blame him, say he betrayed us to the Caleisbahnin."

"Did he?"

She shrugged. "He went on the auctioneer's block like everyone else from that ship."

Traitor. Inaction was collusion. Ashel took the bottle and stumbled out. Thumps and groans leaked from the alley. He followed the sound into the shadows, where the men held Samson pinned to the wall, a target for the woman's boot.

"Stop," Ashel said.

The woman paused mid kick, her foot suspended. "Leave, silkie, or you be next." Her heel jabbed Samson's gut. The Oreseeker groaned.

Rage fired Ashel's heart, and he cracked the butt of the bottle against the woman's head. She dropped. Glass and liquor sprayed as he smashed the bottle against the wall. The men cursed. A knife slashed. Ashel batted the blade aside, slashed the wielder's forehead. The savagery of his own attack shocked him as blood drowned the man's eyes, but the heel of his hand followed Geram's instincts and slammed into the man's chin. He finished him with a kick. Bone crunched, and the assailant collapsed. Samson released a loud "Ha!" as he rammed a fist into the other thug's nose. His knee rammed the man's groin, and the trio lay groaning on the ground.

"You're bleeding," Samson panted, pointing at Ashel's maimed hand.

He sucked at welling blood, the pain dull within the dizzy fog of harlolinde. He hadn't even realized the blade had sliced him.

"Thank you," Samson added. "I thought you were drunk."

"Not that drunk." Not drunk enough. Geram's instincts and skills for a street fight had once again prevailed. *The blind Alnan tomcat taking advantage of a queen's grief.* Shrinejump, it wasn't simply lust—he *knew* Geram genuinely loved his mother, which only twisted the knife in the wound left by Vic's loss. If only he could be free of the other man—all his thoughts, all his sensations. What would it take for the pair of them to be something other than a twisted manifestation of an Ancient tale about a blind man who fucked his own mother?

Palm afire and oozing blood, he stumbled out of the alley. Samson limped after him, a hand pressed to his side. "You should go home," the Oreseeker said. "Those people have dangerous associates."

"Who are they?"

"They work for my creditors."

Ashel chuckled bitterly. Ahead, an ironwork arch sported a dozen bent-backed, winged figures among filigreed leaves and thorns, obsidian eyes glinting in the setting sun. The gate to the Buzzards Roost. Spendthrift. Ne'er-do-well. Coward. "Show me to a place where I can buy bliss, and I'll help with your creditors."

Samson shook his head. "You don't—"

"Show me."

Samson hesitated, eyes darting down the alley and toward the Roost. His gaze shifted to the bay, his expression wistful as the sun sank into the mountains behind them. "You're not the only one to lose someone in the Kiareinoll," he said. "Gustave is my . . . Gustave of Sect Dameron is with your wife and sister. You must believe they'll come back."

Ashel snorted. An Oreseeker, speaking about faith. "Are you going to show me or not?"

"No."

A man in the alley stirred, then fell prone. Ashel rubbed his chin. "Come by the Korng palazzo Thirdday evening. We'll talk about debts and creditors, faith and lost loves then. But tonight, I'm going to forget all of it."

Inside the Roost, filthy, sharp-toothed children ran about, flinging mud and insults. Sour-faced women and old men scowled from doorways. Framed in lank, stringy hair, every face was dirty, and every one was pale, like Vic. The only brown complexion was his own. Pale skin was uncommon in Latha, though not unknown. Sashal had had red hair and a propensity toward freckles, like Vic, so Ashel had never thought of her as belonging to a *people*. Yet here were yellow-haired children shouting in the Ancients' tongue, proving the Oreseekers were not an abstract idea of a lost tribe but flesh and blood people from a culture rooted in heresy, stolen from their homeland and sold into slavery. Like his wife. *See you soon, husband.* The Buzzards' glaring misery dug at him, pricking his conscience as he took random turns, nose twitching through air laced with smoke, rancid meat, and chamber pots, but his need to forget his troubles squashed his sympathy for the suffering around him.

The slum was bigger than he expected; he wouldn't find what he needed wandering aimlessly. A knot of filthy waifs clustered in a shanty doorway; he flicked half a mulla into their midst. A dozen greedy eyes turned to him, and a girl rose laconically. She looked younger than Timny. "What you want, silkie?" The youths cackled as she sidled up to him. "You want sweet? Come inside. Better sweet than fine silkie flop."

"Bliss." He slid another crystal into the girl's hand. "Take me where I can get it, and you'll get twice that when we're there."

Eyes alight with greed, the girl led him along slime-slicked paths echoing with shouts and squalling babies. She stopped at a grimy door. "Emily will do for you. You want sweet to follow, you stop by my flop." She pocketed the remainder of her fee. "Pretty silkie like you get twice the sweet for half the price."

"No, thank you." He entered the place and slammed the door in the girl's face. A saccharine reek pervaded a dark corridor. He trod toward flickering light. Floorboards creaked. The hall opened into a chamber where shadowed figures sucked on hookahs, their exhalations a yellow smoke that swirled into clouds under rough ceiling boards. Other figures sprawled on mats, grimy faces bearing slack grins.

"Come." An old woman rose from a stained chaise and beckoned him into another room. "Very clean. Very private." She waved at a bed covered with a moth-eaten blanket. "Top grade for Citizen," she said as she filled the hookah and wiped the mouthpiece with a rag. "You like? Twenty mulla."

He raised his eyebrows at a price that would buy a fine meal and refined company at an elegant brothel, but he handed over the crystals. *Spendthrift.* The crone rolled the stones in her hand. "Whole night yours, now. I send you girl? Boy?" At the shake of his head, she patted her chest. "Emily bliss monger long time. You come right place. Whole night yours."

Shaking, he sat on the bed. His head still reeled from har, but he could sense Geram, sipping soup at the state dinner celebrating Timny's designation as Heir. Bethniel, robbed. Robbed and gone and no one did a thing about it. Least of all him. *Ne'er-do-well.* Ashel swiped the hookah's pipe and sucked the smoke. Yellow scalded the back of his throat, and he broke off, spluttering.

A sob gripped him. Cheeks wet, he tried again, suppressing the desire to cough, sucking the heat deep into his lungs. Warmth spread out from his chest, traveling up his neck, into his face. Anguish melted into relief. He took another toke, and elation rose through his blood. *Coward.* Elesendar, it felt good to forget. *Traitor.* A third inhalation drew joy deep into his chest, and bliss—bliss indeed!—bloomed behind his eyes. A wave of oblivion broke over him, washing away pain and awareness. He sank onto the mattress, his lips curved in beatitude.

Voices echoed, hard consonants and soft vowels, uttered in rhythms he knew but with sounds stretched out, as if he floated beneath the ocean's surface and the speakers stood above the waves. A tug pried open an eyelid, and a light shone. It hurt, but his limbs were too heavy to flinch, and the eyelid snapped shut. A white circle scarred the darkness.

Every particle in his body longed for the beautiful wave that had washed memory and sensation away.

Someone picked up his right hand. Fingers palpated the blunt flesh covering his knuckles, traced the scars, hissed at the new gash in his palm. "What happened here?" The echoing voices resolved into words. "Hand me the slotaen and clean dressings from my bag, please." A cooling balm masked the hurt, and a bandage wound over the wound.

"The stumps have healed well, considering," the stranger concluded.

"Said without a trace of judgment." Lornk's voice.

"Disappointment. You refused every lesson I ever tried to teach you."

"I learned better than you think—kindness has its uses, but that night I needed a sharper edge."

"That night you failed, and you ruined this man's life and livelihood for nothing."

"A tactical setback, Moralen, but success is within my grasp. As for my son, he doesn't need a livelihood."

"Or a grasp? Is he your son?"

Ashel's heart lurched into a faster rhythm. The probing fingers held his wrist, moved to the pulse in his throat as Lornk said, "I doubt Elekia could answer that question with certainty, but look at him, sprawled here, just like my mother. Bliss-lust runs in families, doesn't it?"

"It does, but—" Moralen squeezed Ashel's shoulder. A weight pressed upon the bed. "Every man has his breaking point. I met mine, and I know how hard it is to resist the forgetting that comes from that pipe over there. Even after all these years, every bit of me yearns for it."

"That's why I called you, to help me steer him from this path."

"If that's your goal, you'd better put up some guide rails. Rumor has it, he's been cooling his heels in merchants' offices for months."

"He visited with Parnden too. Will you talk to him? You've been where he is, in this very room."

"I could never afford this room, and this is your problem to fix."

"All right, my friend. I'll take him home with me."

The door latch clicked.

Ashel pried his eyelids apart. "Who was that?"

"My physician," Lornk said. "Can you sit up?"

Ashel levered himself up on leaden elbows. His gaze fell on the hookah; desolation yawned deep and wide.

Lornk grimaced. "I hate this place. Mother used to come here, and Elsa and I would have to fetch her home. We had only one servant—besides Elsa—and he was almost as useless as Mother."

"I couldn't care less about your rags-to-riches story."

"Never rags, Ashel. We had no servants. The palazzo and mines carried two or three mortgages apiece, and my mother sold heirlooms so she could suck on that hookah over there. Yet we still were far better off than the wealthiest family in this slum. Get up. We'll walk to the Circle—exercise is the best purgative for bliss."

"I will not help you become Commissar."

"Yet you haven't stopped me, have you? You could have betrayed me to Parnden, but here I am, fetching you from this place instead of swinging from the gallows. The last time he executed a Citizen for treason—the last time a Citizen refused to buy a way out of the noose—her body hung there a full month. I wonder how long he'd leave me up."

Ashel shrugged, thinking of small dangling feet. "I don't care which of you holds the Commissar's seat or swings from a rope."

Lornk laughed. "You don't? Well, that's progress."

A pain like icy fingers gripped his heart. Tears ran into his beard. He scrubbed a sleeve across wet cheeks. "I'm not going anywhere with you."

Lornk pulled a note out of a pocket. "Seems you have nowhere else to go. This came for you through the Device."

Official notice of your banishment has been posted all over Narath, and couriers have taken it to the rest of the nation. Your refusal to return home has sealed this fate and done nothing to secure the return of your sisters.

There was no signature, but it was his mother's hand.

"Elekia used to send me nasty notes through the Device. Now she's sending them to you. Let's go. If nothing else I'm sure you want your pouch filled."

On shaky knees, Ashel followed Lornk into the main room, where Emily snored on her chaise. Lornk curled his lip. "That fiend hasn't changed in thirty years." None of her customers woke as they stepped through sprawled limbs. Outside, morning fog obscured coastal range and bay alike, the mist curling ahead of their steps. Fish reek pervaded the alley; pops and sizzle of fry grease crackled through paper windows. Buzzards filtered out of doorways and joined a growing procession heading for the Roost gate.

"Citizen," a woman called and pressed a bundle into Lornk's hands. "Thank you, sir."

He buried his nose in the cloth. "Smells delicious. How is your son?"

"Much better now. Thank you for all you've done." The woman curtsied to Ashel and returned inside her hovel.

Lornk extracted a dumpling and handed it to Ashel. "She's a very good cook. Eat, you'll feel better."

The Buzzards' scowls softened as Lornk greeted them by name, always speaking in the Oreseeker tongue. Many thanked him for favors, gave him small gifts. One old man handed him a satchel in which to carry the ungainly collection of foodstuffs and handicrafts. Some flashed condolence signs at Ashel, a few even coming to him and pressing their palms to his chest; all of them turned to Lornk afterward and expressed their gratitude or approbation.

They passed beneath the iron filigreed Buzzards onto the wharves, and Lornk pointed out a tenement where the physician Moralen had been born. "He saved my life when I was a boy. I'd fallen, and a broken bone opened a vein. Moralen found me, but bliss-lust ran strong in him at the time. He robbed me and left me to die."

Ashel's remaining fingers bent into a fist. If Lornk had died then, Ashel would be whole now—or he might never have been born. The paradox left him seething. "What changed his mind?"

"His conscience and his compassion." A sardonic smile tilted Lornk's lips. "Just like yours. Moralen gained a purpose that night, which filled the void he'd packed with bliss. He made a project out of me, showed an angry, resentful boy what real suffering and injustice looked like."

Rage washed the last vestiges of bliss from Ashel's blood, and he shook his maimed hand in Lornk's face. "This is what your benevolence looks like to me!"

Shrine's bitch, you're finally sober, Geram said.

Over the bay, wind tore the clouds apart, and the color of the sea shifted toward blue. Ashel turned up a flight of limestone steps leading toward the Circle, concentrating on his breath and thudding heart as Lornk trod after him.

I thought you liked not Hearing me.

Geram didn't respond as townhouses morphed into palazzos with marble walls and iron gates. The ascending footpath took them across streets noisy with peddlers, cooks, and housekeepers, then past leaf-draped walls where the shouts and murmurs of traffic faded into the plop and gurgle of hidden fountains. The ocean breeze died under the rising summer sun, and the walk sweated the night's excess from his blood, leaving him with a vicious thirst and a throbbing head.

Lornk grabbed his arm when they reached a terrace. "Ashel, wait." Huffing, he waved at the Commissar's palace, far below. "Everything I do is calculated, whether the kindnesses I bestow on Buzzards or the horrors I unleashed on you. All of it is so I can claim that palace as mine. Thanks to your parents' failure to prepare Victoria, I have no control over the outcome of the coming Concordance, so all my planning may be for naught."

"You really are mad if you think telling me this will convince me to help you!"

"Yet, you should. The difference between me and Parnden is my ambition. I seek glory as the sovereign over a just and prosperous nation, not ignominy as a selfish tyrant who rewards his toadies and hangs his critics, along with the children of a despised underclass in order to cement their oppression. Nor do I want to be that craven king I saw when I was a boy, the one who allowed the Kragnashians to feed on his people so he could save his own skin. I have no natural conscience or compassion—this is an imperfection I freely acknowledge. Therefore, I surround myself with people who have these attributes. They are my moral lodestone."

"Is that what you want from me?"

"In the main of it, yes. But I cannot use you if you're lying in your own piss at Emily's feet."

Shrinejump, bliss? That's why I couldn't Hear you last night? said Geram.

You think I'm asleep when you go to her, but I'm not. Ashel charged up the stairs, his blood churning with a cascade of outrage and Geram's lust.

I can't help it—I love her, the other man replied.

She is my mother!

Geram raised a Listener's baffling between them, dampening his feelings. *I will shield you as best I can.*

You told Mother you'd stop if I found out. Well, I've found out!

I . . . I have a duty.

To spy on Fensin for her? You're making that your excuse?

I will not leave her, Ashel, unless she tells me to go.

Reaching the palazzo gate, Ashel stopped and shut his eyes, wanting nothing more than to turn around and go back to that filthy room and sink into oblivion.

Lornk staggered up behind him, mopping his brow. "And I thought I was fit." Grooms and gardeners hailed them as they passed through the courtyard. In the foyer, Lornk grasped Ashel's arm again. "The Commissar has invited us to a dinner on Thirdday. He has specifically asked that you and Wineyll attend. I want you to stay away."

Ashel sneered. "That makes me want to go."

"You won't. That night, I will launch the coup, and I need you to remain out of it, in case it fails. If it doesn't, I promise I'll explain the bargain I made with the Kragnashians for Vic, and how we're going to get her back."

"So, you did sell her."

"I traded her services for the greater good."

"Whose? Yours?"

"Knownearth's!"

"And where were your conscience-bearers that day?" Striding into the parlor, Ashel took a bottle from the cabinet and retreated to his bedchamber. He needed to forget.

THE LONG BATTLE

Chewing a piece of Prenlin's sour dried fruit, Vic studied the half-dozen buildings in Meylnara's compound. The Direiellene she knew was—or would be—comprised of thousands of structures swarming with tens of thousands of Kragnashians. Perhaps a few hundred People passed in and out of the handful of hives below. Meylnara had thousands of troops at her command, but they didn't all live here—they wouldn't be able to fit.

"In this entire rainforest, this is the only Kragnashian settlement you found?"

"It is the one where Meylnara lives."

"You mean it's the only one you cared to *see*." She leaned forward. "There, do you see them? Coming out of the fourth building, southeast of the main one?"

Thabean peered through the vines screening the surveillance blind. "Two of the bigger creatures, with the longer mandibles. So?"

"Look at the tattoos. Those are warriors."

"Clearly, madam. Meylnara marks them to keep track of them."

"They do it themselves. What will convince you they have sense?"

"Structures such as these are made by the crawlers on the Semena plains. Everything else in this compound was manufactured by Meylnara."

"By herself? How could she have learned to make these things if someone didn't teach her? You said the Council executed her mother twenty-five years ago."

277

"She would have been twelve, madam. Old enough to have learned all she needed to survive. And with wizardry, one can accomplish much more than a drudge. Her minions appear quiet today. Shall we resume our lesson?"

Exasperated, Vic followed him as they stole away from the Lair. Once on the ground, they used no power until they'd walked a good mile. Finally, Thabean signaled the start of a new exercise, and she waited while he moved off and hid. After a count of twenty heartbeats, she floated up above the canopy and held herself there, *feeling* for him. Her breath silent, her ears perked at rustling leaves, chirping insects, the calls of larger animals, even the distant clicks and whistles of Kragnashians. Detritus and blossoms flared her nostrils; a breeze prickled her skin. And then she felt it, a ripple in space, not the wind but a passing wave, like the surf's ebb. How often had she felt Elekia's waveform? Every shudder she'd ever suppressed in the queen's presence had new meaning. Remaining still, she waited for Thabean's next pulse. Each wizard felt different. Grunnaire had the shortest wavelength, Meylnara the longest. Saelbeneth pulsed unevenly like a cipher; the current of Nelchior's power stayed with you, thrumming with your heart.

Thabean's waves were steady, stable, neither short nor long but solid, predictable, like him, and Olivet. Two men who trained her to become what she was. Blade. Wizard. *Mistress.* Her eyes snapped shut, and she felt Lornk's hand on her neck, his thumb on her windpipe, his scent thick in her throat. Inhaling deeply, she drew in the hot moist air of Direiellene, reminding herself she was beyond his reach. Her palm pressed a stretched belly, and she remembered the defeat in his face that morning she and Ashel emerged as a wedded pair. She was beyond his reach the moment she'd found Ashel in the Kiareinoll.

Her heart suddenly ached for the depth of compassion and wisdom in those dark, beautiful eyes. "I'll come to you, my love," she whispered. "I promise." But the Device in Meylnara's keep was the only way back to him, and the only way to reach that was to kill Meylnara.

Another ripple passed, reminding her of the lesson. She sank deeper into the canopy, following the waveform north and east, staying hidden in the understory. Thabean's path arced toward the north gate. She neither rushed nor dawdled as she followed, matching her speed to his while circulating a layer of cool air over her body. *Do only enough.* A month had passed since she'd awakened to herself, and she still had bouts of nausea, but the headaches were rare. *Do only enough.*

Prenlin said that in a few weeks the brooding sickness would end and she'd feel better than she ever had in her life. "It's called the bliss," the Healer had told her, scowling. Vic grinned as the baby bumped against her womb. Prenlin also said she shouldn't be feeling the baby yet, but the Woern had opened her senses to all sorts of unimagined perceptions. *Like another wizard's power*, she thought, realizing Thabean's waveform had stopped.

Now the hunt was on. Chortling, she descended to the ground, taking in every bit of bark, every scatter of humus, every snapped twig. A forest was a three-dimensional space where enemies could ambush from the canopy above or a gully below, but Thabean was reared on the plains, and his woodcraft was no match for hers.

"Madam!" he whispered in her ear.

Polarizing the surrounding ions, she spun, aiming her boot at his knee, but her kick caught only air.

Floating upside down, Thabean laughed. A net of lightning crackled over her ion barrier but did not touch her skin. "Good shield."

Creating a vacuum, she sliced through the lightning. "You're using the Woern. How? I can't feel you at all!"

He alighted on the ground and swept up a stick near his feet. "You've learned to follow the waveforms of a wizard. Now it's time for you to learn how we hide within them. Here." He tossed her the stick.

She caught it and yelped, dropping it. The stick hit the ground, and she shook an electric sting from her hand.

"What the Shrine?"

"Are you certain you were a successful assassin in your own time?"

She returned a wry grin. "You're the first wizard I had for quarry. Why did the stick sting me? And how did you hide?"

"To the first question. Never grapple with a wizard during a duel. Why?"

"Why?" She thought back on their training sessions. "A wizard's weapons—lightning, fire—are best wielded from a distance. You don't want to get caught in the backlash. Or is it simply part of the Code, as a point of honor?"

"No, madam, this prohibition is for your safety. When a wizard is engaged in battle, the Woern shift into a defensive state. Direct, skin-to-skin contact between wizards when epinephrine or cortisol are elevated can trigger a surge of energy through the nervous system that may burn out the wizard."

"By what mechanism?" She filed away the unfamiliar medical terms—something to look up later. Thabean had trained as a Healer before he took the Elixir.

"When we are peaceful, our Woern long for each other, which is why it is pleasant, even stimulating, to touch another wizard. Yet during battle, the Woern repel each other. The worse the fear and pain, the stronger the defensive response. Usually the attacker comes out the worse."

A sigh huffed out as she remembered the vicious stinging that had cramped her hands when she tried to throttle Meylnara. "Well, that explains something that happened when I fought Meylnara in her Lair." She frowned at the stick. "The stick isn't a person, Thabean. No skin, no epinef-whatever, no Woern. Why did it sting me?"

He sniggered. "True. That was merely an electric charge. How did it get there?"

Kneeling, she studied the stick. Bark pitted by decay, it looked ordinary, but she felt it pulse in a rhythm that echoed the beat coming from Thabean himself. "You put your waveform on it somehow." She met his eyes again. "But you stopped using the Woern. I know I didn't lose you."

"I did not stop using the Woern. I imbued the stick with my waveform, then positioned myself opposite it and used my power pulses to counter the current from the stick. You happened to follow the wave to the stick, and then found yourself in the pocket where its waves and mine canceled each other. We call it a void. It is a good way to hide from another wizard while you continue to use the Woern. I routinely use one when we surveil Meylnara. Why do you think she never detects our presence?"

"I assumed she was simply ignoring us, so long as we weren't attacking her keep."

"Really, madam, when she wants *you* so much?"

"Her attacks have been less frequent. Perhaps she's realized it's more sensible to bide her time until the baby's born."

He snorted. "We have no definitions of sensible where you and Meylnara are concerned. In any case, back to the lesson. The imbued waveform fades. Touch the stick."

Tentatively, she touched the bark. A faint tingle passed along her nerves to her elbow, but the stick was quickly becoming just a stick. She raised an eyebrow at him. "You enjoyed that."

He grinned. "I did."

Chuckling, she hopped onto a fallen log, letting her feet swing. Sunbeams slanted through the canopy, but a line of deeper forest shadows approached them, heralding rain. "You asked me about being an assassin in my own time. Do you believe us now?"

He joined her on the log. "In the month I've trained you and fought beside you, I suppose I've come to trust your word. Besides, the Elixir is closely guarded and has been here, with the Council, since we began this campaign, its supply undiminished. However you acquired the Woern, it was not by stealing from us."

"That sounds like a *sensible* conclusion. And Saelbeneth seemed to trust the commodore's word, vouching for us, from the beginning."

He inclined his head. "With a Portal in Narath, she has frequent relations with the pirates." His mouth quirked. "Rumor would have one believe *very* close relations."

"Thabean, are you gossiping with me?"

His smile broadened. "I am a man of honor and would not spread innuendo."

"Of course not," she intoned, then added, winking, "though the Caleisbahnin are sworn to *serve* the Council."

"As it suits them, yes. They bring steel to a fight. I value that, but their pledges mean a grain of sand to me."

She snorted. "Me too." The coming rain spattered nearby leaves. Drops plopped onto shoulders and heads. Copying the wizard, Vic pulled a thin shell of matter around herself to keep dry. "They kidnapped me from Cairo, in the north," she blurted, her words smacking like the rain. "Then sold me as a concubine to a Citizen of Traine. I don't suppose that sort of thing happens now."

His smile faded, the light dimming in his eyes. "Bethniel had told us something of this. The iron merchants in Traine are well known for their vices, madam. I'm sorry for your troubles."

She nodded her thanks, studying him. He was not so much what history had made him—a cad, a tyrant, but one turned to good by the love of Victoria.

> *The duo on stage plays the last note, and she swipes her cheeks dry, feeling a fool for crying over a ballad about a pair of sorcerers ending an affair.*
>
> *"Is it strange for you, hearing that song?" Ashel asks.*
>
> *"Why would it be?"*
>
> *His teeth gleam at her, his eyes creased with mirth. "You, Captain, have a famous wizard for a namesake."*
>
> *Her mind pounces on the name Kara, and her cheeks turn icy with mortified anger. Ashel's face falls, and he stumbles into an explanation about a Victoria of Ourtown being a member of the Council that defeated Meylnara.*
>
> *Her anger evaporates into a chagrined smile. "That is absurd."*

"What amuses you?" Thabean asked.

She liked Thabean as a comrade, but as a lover? *That* was

absurd. "Nothing here is what we expected, least of all you. Thank you for being . . . not what history made you out to be."

He guffawed. "That sounds ominous, madam! You must tell me what flaws history has recorded, so I can remedy them."

"I would not presume, sir. How about the next lesson?"

Horns echoed through the trees. Mirth vanished, and they tore over the canopy. Only an hour ago, Meylnara's People were peacefully going about their business, not marshaling for an attack, yet Kragnashians marched upon the encampment, tattooed mandibles and shining carapaces aligned in even rows.

"I don't think Meylnara's with them," Vic said as she and Thabean joined the Council above the assault. "She always hides within an armored mass of Kragnashians, and there is none."

"She must be here," Nelchior spat. "The creatures are attacking with great precision. See how they have chosen to breach the weakest point in our defenses."

"Csichren's camp will soon be overrun," Saelbeneth said. "There is no time for arguing. Let us to our tasks."

The Council broke, and Vic flew to Thabean's artillery unit.

"Ho, Victoria!" cried Dealn as she landed.

"What'd you bring home from market?" she asked.

"Madam." He gave a shallow bow, his grin matching the one Thabean had worn earlier. "You will not be disappointed in our fine selection of boulders and sulfa."

Chuckling, she eyed the carts, some filled with rocks and others with sulfur-rich clay. "I'll get started then. You'll find Thabean at the armory."

"By now I'll find him on the line. Fare well, madam!"

"You too!" She lifted a pair of boulders, rolled them in the sulfa, and dropped each into a catapult's basket. Flying up to fix the aim, she signaled the direction and tension, and the ox teams dragged the catapults into position. The gunners lit the sulfa, and Vic chopped her hand down. A beam thunked forward, launching a sizzling, spitting fireball. Vic boosted the ordinance's trajectory over the Council's troops.

The first rock exploded, flinging Kragnashians into the air, and the next catapult released its fiery load. Other wizards' artillery launched blazing rocks. Thumb-thick arrows rained, and massive bodies crumpled. Screeches and whistles echoed as obsidian fell in glistening black hail. Pockets opened in the shining rows of chitin. Down on the ground, Shirian and Halbert had erected a dome over Csichren's mess. Vic diverted artillery away from them, but elsewhere flaming debris smashed into barracks and pavilions, setting them aflame. The Kragnashians tore through the canvas, ripped apart anyone seeking refuge in the tents. Another volley exploded among the creatures, followed by the ballistae's load of spears, thick as a man's thigh.

Crawling over the dead, the Kragnashians plowed into the pikemen, swinging their mandibles like scythes and sweeping aside the troopers like grain. The pikemen dodged and parried, slipping beneath the mouthparts, stabbing upward, emerging from the corpses covered in green blood. Springtime scent wafted upward, stained with the iron stench of human blood, offal, and charred hair.

The battle dragged deep into the afternoon. Rain, then sun showered the combatants as the invaders crushed toward the camp's center. Troops became concentrated around the blunt point of the Kragnashians' wedge; all the wizards were on the ground or flying near it, exploding the earth beneath the Kragnashians' feet, shielding the pikemen or directing the archers. Mail glinting in a passing sun shower, Thabean and Samovael dove and struck with whirring pikes while their troops strove to hold the People at bay. Vic felt a twinge of guilt that she floated far above the fray, but contrition drowned in determination to protect her child. Ashel's child. A palm pressed against the small, firm bulge of her belly, she scooped the last rocks out of the cart below and loaded the catapults.

"That's the last of it, madam," the commander called up to her.

"There are no more carts?"

"No, ma'am! We're nearly out of ammunition for the ballistae too."

"Stand by." She flew up and surveyed the other artillery squadrons. Everyone was out or nearly so. Cursing, she dropped down and informed the officer. As he ordered his troops to grab pikes and head to the line, a horn sang an alarm. Vic hurtled into the air and saw another tide of Kragnashians flowing into the ditch bordering Thabean's wedge. At the trumpet's call, Thabean shot out of the melee. His troops broke ranks and streamed down the alleys between the tents, leaping stakes and lines to defend their perimeter. The guards already there tossed buckets of burning pitch into the ditch.

"Bring that sulfa!" Vic shouted. The gunners whipped the oxen into a run and hurried toward the new front.

"Help me erect a shield," Thabean cried as he sped past. His hair matted with green blood and red, his skin sallow—even from a distance she could tell he'd overused his power. Rushing after him, she pushed her own Woern to their limit. Her throat and temples tightened, heralding a migraine. Thabean was surely already feeling one. But soldiers did what had to be done, as true here as in her own time.

Along the rim of the ditch, Thabean thickened the air into a viscous glue. She flew to the edge of the Kragnashian advance and erected another barricade that surged toward Thabean's position, nearly a mile away. Seconds later, the ground shook with the impact of the two shields. The People clambered up the side of the ditch, crawled alongside the barrier, antennae batting solid air. More came behind, climbed over their fellows, building height, antennae hunting for the top of the shield. Vic raised the barrier as new ranks mounted old ones and a living ladder spanned the ditch and extended up the invisible wall.

A long-limbed girl ran up, panting. "Madam, Sir Thabean wishes you to collapse the barrier on his signal. He said to use the force of it to slam the creatures into the pikes."

"Acknowledged," Vic barked. Near the base, some creatures began to push through slowly, as if they swam through tar. A horn sounded three sharp blasts, and power churned through

Vic's nerves as she tilted the barrier and smashed it down. The mound of Kragnashians crumpled. Screeches pierced eardrums as bodies were crushed into the pikes, but the People nearest the base tumbled beneath the barrier into camp. A double rank of pikemen stood against them, spear butts ground into the earth. Rising on their curtain of legs, Kragnashians steamed over the soldiers and rushed into the alleys. Another rank of infantry burst out of the cover of the tents, dodging under the mandibles to bring their pikes home. Hundreds more People clambered over the broken bodies in the ditch; others wormed out of the crush, and Vic escaped into the air.

Thabean flew to her side. Grunnaire's camp and Samovael's were in similar peril. Smoke billowed as the remaining gunners lobbed buckets of burning pitch at the Kragnashians. It did little against their carapaces, but it did light the canvas barracks afire.

"Rockfall," Thabean swore and shot toward his pavilion. Through a break in the smoke, Vic glimpsed Bethniel with a pike in her hand, surrounded by Kragnashians.

"Shrine's bitch!" She hurtled past Thabean. An enormous warrior, twenty feet tall with tattoos thickly scrolled across its carapace and mandibles, loomed over the princess, antennae twitching furiously. Eyes wide, Bethniel scrambled backward on hands and feet. A dozen other Kragnashians, smaller and with many fewer tattoos, formed a circle around them. Vic swooped down, grabbed Bethniel, and launched herself upward, but the big warrior leapt up and grabbed her ankle. Bones crunched in the chitinous grip, and Vic's limbs and spine cracked as the creature flung them back to the ground. Rolling, she grabbed Beth's pike and jabbed at the warrior, erecting a shield around them to block the others. The warrior screeched, snapped, and swung its mandibles. Dodging the blow, she thrust up at the creature's thorax. It reared back, grabbed the pike, and ripped it from her grasp.

Thabean landed, Dealn beside him, and the brothers attacked, pikes whirling, jabbing, stabbing. Somehow, Dealn matched his brother's wizardry-boosted speed as they scored the giant's thorax and swiped it off balance. The other Kragnashians pushed through Vic's shield, and more were surrounding them, mounting each other, building a living dome and blocking escape by flight.

Vic hobbled over to Bethniel, her foot twisted at the wrong angle. It didn't hurt. Not yet. "Can you talk to them?"

Beth's eyes were big as saucers. "When they first surrounded me, I tried that. It just seemed to upset them. The warrior started clicking something about you—about 'The One,' and then something about the life of the trees, but their dialect is different, and I couldn't really make it out."

Dealn roared, entangling his pike in the warrior's legs. He yanked. The creature stumbled, but it landed a blow to his skull, and he tumbled back. Thabean shouted, struck with renewed fury, but he was wheezing, his face gray.

The pike flew into Vic's hand. Skin stretched around her ankle, blood filling her foot like a bag, but she immobilized it in a cast of hardened air. It felt like a brick, but she could stand on it. Beth stood, eyes locked on Thabean as he thrust and parried, each breath a hollow gasp while the Kragnashians chittered all around, a constant hum. The light died beneath the thickening mass of creatures. Vic filled her lungs. Her Woern thrummed. She'd once blown a hole in a mountain—could the Kragnashians' immunity to wizardry withstand the same force?

The warrior knocked Thabean to the ground and flowed on top of him, pinning him, its antennae dancing toward his head. Half a dozen Kragnashians burst through the shield, mandibles snapping. Vic swooped under the thorax of the first, shoving her pike deep into it, yanking it free as it fell. She dove toward the second, but a third had its mandibles around Bethniel's neck. Antennae tapped her forehead, and the creature shrieked and backed away. The giant warrior atop Thabean threw back its head and keened, flowing off the wizard. The surrounding Kragnashians peeled back, daylight blazing as the dome melted. The creatures rushed toward the forest, ignoring the troopers standing with slack jaws and idle pikes.

Thabean shook his head, blinking, then scrambled to Dealn. Blood pooled beneath his brother's skull. The wizard placed his palms on Dealn's cheeks, trembling and rocking. Bethniel knelt beside them, touched Thabean's shoulder. "I'm sorry."

He swallowed, and the lines above his forehead eased away. A hand on his knee, he shoved himself upright and watched the last of the Kragnashians disappear from view.

"Did you feel it?" Bethniel asked, her voice thick.

"It was monstrous, my lady." He handed her up, and their eyes lingered on each other, the corners of her lips curving into a whisper of a smile, his features softening in response. Vic marveled at the energy sparking between the pair, as if they were alone in all the world.

Soldiers rushed around them, crying praise to Elesendar.

"Highness!" Lillem pushed through the ranks, gasping, blood oozing from a gash in his forehead. "Are you hurt?"

Gustave followed in the lieutenant's wake. "Madam, you live!"

The sense of wonder vanished in the tumult of soldiers. "I live, Gustave," Vic said. "What do you make of this?"

The pirate glanced toward the empty perimeter. "It would seem they got what they came for. Did they touch you?"

"No." But they had touched Bethniel and Thabean, then retreated. *Got what they came for.* She frowned. "Why do you ask?"

Gustave grinned, the gap in his teeth sharp as his incisors. "Legend, madam. To be touched by a Kragnashian, and to survive, is to be blessed."

Searching for a reply to this baffling bit of faith, she stepped back, and pain exploded from her ankle.

Gustave shouldered her arm. "I'll help you to the hospital."

"Victoria," Thabean barked from the circle of his advisors. "What happened to our artillery support?"

She gulped back a groan. "They ran out of ammunition, sir."

Thabean glanced at Dealn. Eyes twitching, he pressed his lips together, then turned to his officers. "Have the men collect what stones they can from camp. We shall need to quarry more, in case there is another attack such as this. I shall speak to Saelbeneth about more sulfa. In the meantime, madam, the Council will meet—we must prepare. Fainend, attend me while I dress."

Bethniel followed protocol and bowed her shoulders as Thabean departed, but she still felt the ghost of his fingers clasped round her hand. Soldiers scooped up Dealn's body and hurried away, and her heart ached in sympathy.

"Highness," Lillem repeated, "are you hurt?"

"No, but Vic is." And the Council would be meeting. "Help me get her to her tent."

"I'm all right." Vic floated away from Gustave. "Lieutenant, get that gash looked after. Beth, let's go."

Servants had readied water and laid out a red silk gown, just as Bethniel had ordered. In the past month, Thabean's household had come to provide for Vic's needs as promptly as his. She stripped off her clothes and hopped into the tub, dunking herself completely. Water streamed off her shoulders and hair as Bethniel handed her the soap before stripping off her own blouse and trousers. She felt gritty with sweat and dirt, but there wasn't time for them both to bathe, so she slipped into a clean shift and the silk dress she kept in Vic's tent. Tying off the laces, she pulled the combs out of her hair and set to work getting it back into shape.

Well soaped, Vic submerged again and climbed out of the tub. Handing her a towel, Bethniel winced at her ankle, grown twice its normal size. "That looks really painful."

Grimacing, her sister pulled a comb through wet hair, the tines leaving dry strands in their wake. "It smarts. At least I can float."

Vic wove her hair into a neat braid while Bethniel helped her into the robe and tied the sashes together. When finished, she stepped back for a last look. Vic was always likely to forget some detail—leave her hair snarled or a fold of her gown awry—but today she looked well for all the speed with which they'd changed.

"All ready," she pronounced.

"What happened, when it touched you?" Vic grabbed her arm.

The tingling where their skin met was a shadow of the electric surge she'd felt when Thabean clasped her hand, a feeling which itself was leavened with the inexplicable wash of emotion she'd felt when the Kragnashian's antennae grazed her forehead— wonder and awe, followed by the briefest flash of joy. The tingling subsided, and Bethniel's blood rushed up her neck as she realized all these feelings were just the Woern! Bloody useless parasites, turning her into no more than a silly twit! She scowled. "I thought I felt something, but looking back, I think it was relief that the warrior wasn't killing me."

Vic's eyes narrowed. "Beth, this is important. They *retreated* after they touched you. They didn't say anything to you?"

Pushing her irritation aside, she thought back. She knew she must have been terrified when the mandibles clamped down around her neck, but she couldn't remember being scared, just the wonder and the awe and then, the joy. It was bizarre. She shook her head—in Direiellene, when various Kragnashians had touched her, she'd felt nothing odd. It must have been just shock and relief. "Like I said, I couldn't really understand their dialect—if they said something beyond what I've told you, I didn't catch it. I don't know why they left."

"All right; let's go." Lips pressed tight, Vic glided out, her robe sweeping the ground, covering her swollen ankle and foot. Heading toward the Council pavilion, they passed the artillery, drawn now into neat rows.

"I liked Dealn. I'll miss him," Vic said, touching both hands to her heart, then splaying her fingers.

"What's that gesture?"

Her sister snorted softly. "Oreseeker condolence sign. Not sure why it came to me now; I haven't used it in years."

"You saw enough people die in Fembrosh."

"I did. I—I guess I just said goodbye the same way as everyone else: 'May she go into the trees.' You don't hear that expression here."

"You do among Saelbeneth's troops, and Dealn was a believer, but I think Thabean is a heretic." She copied the sign. "What's it mean?"

"Basically, 'I feel your grief.' You touch your heart and then put your palm on her chest if you're standing close enough, or extend your hand in his direction if you're not. If you mean to express your own loss, you just open your fingers."

A wave of cold descended from the roots of Bethniel's hair as she recalled how Thabean had caressed his brother's face, and she realized he had shared an intimate secret, letting her see the anguish he masked to his retainers. She knew all too well the boiling within of feelings that cannot be shown. A royal was supposed to remain a picture of calm no matter what happened. She'd collapsed in a dead faint when the assassin's blade struck her father's throat and lost the throne to her mother as a result. "I'd have been utterly lost without Elesendar's guidance when Father died. How do you heretics stand it?"

Vic threaded an arm through hers. "Your loved ones draw you through it."

"What if you have none? Wizards are supposed to hold themselves above and apart from other people."

The skin around Vic's eyes tightened. "Like troopers in our time, why we weren't permitted to marry. You can't put your spouse or children above your duty."

Sympathy thickened Bethniel's throat. Vic had been sent here to kill a woman whose only crime was being born a wizard, as Vic's child would be. She squeezed her sister's hand. "Whatever I can do, I will," she said.

Vic's mouth tilted upward. "I know."

A GRAND SOIREE

Rapping, soft but insistent, drew Ashel out of a deep slumber. He rolled onto his back, massaged sleep out of his eyes. His head ached and his mouth tasted foul. In the mirror, the man sprawled on the bed wore stained, rumpled clothes. In the room, the one slouching upright stank like Emily's bliss dive. He hadn't been back there, but only because he'd been diligently working to empty Lornk's liquor cabinet first.

The rapping intensified, and he dragged himself over to the door. Wineyll stood there, clothed in gossamer silk. The neckline met the collarbone, the opacity dense enough for modesty, but the slits that rose from the hemline to the waist would have had eyebrows popping in Latha, even with the linen trousers swathing her legs.

"What are you wearing? It looks like a handkerchief."

Her nose wrinkled as she came into the room. "Elsa had it made for me. I insisted on the trousers, though."

Shame heated his face. "I wish you wouldn't go tonight."

"Lornk needs me there, and the Commissar asked me to bring my flute and play for him, so how could I refuse?"

In the Minstrels Guild, playing for the Commissar of Betheljin was considered a sweeter booking than performing for Latha's monarchs. "It's dangerous, Wineyll."

"It won't be the first time I've gone into the enemy's stronghold."

He scowled, and her eyes flicked to his butchered hand. Color stippled her cheeks.

"Did you need something?" he asked.

"I—I just thought I'd come by and see you. In case . . . just in case."

Regret dredged up his affection for this girl, one he'd taught and tutored and reared like a little sister, pulling love out of the morass of despair and self-loathing that stained his soul. He opened his arms slowly, hesitatingly, not expecting her to want to touch his stinking clothes, but she rushed into his embrace, her arms tight around his ribs. "I'm sorry you were dragged into this," he said.

"He's going to save Vic's people, Ashel. He's going to save us all."

Anger lanced the moment like a boil, and he pushed away from her.

Lips quivering, she dropped her eyes to the carpet.

He sighed, wishing he could spare her. "I've heard you rehearsing Arpeggio in D. Is that what you're going to play?"

"No, that one's just for practice. I think it's too esoteric for a general audience, don't you?"

He couldn't help but smile. "I do. What will you play?"

She listed several popular tunes and asked his opinion on some others. Offering suggestions, he paced past a window and noticed Samson of Cairo standing across the street, scribbling in a notebook. "Shrinejump," Ashel muttered. "I'd forgotten I'd told him to come by today."

"Who's that?" Wineyll studied the Oreseeker. "He's . . . he's someone from Vic's homeland, isn't he?"

His eyebrows rose. "You didn't Hear that from me, did you?"

"No. I snagged a lot of Vic's memories when—well, you know. It's not the same as you and Geram. I can't talk to her or feel her feelings, but sometimes I have these odd sensations, or one of her memories will pop into my head. I guess it's my punishment."

"No one blames you."

She blinked fast, her bottom lip folded under her teeth. "I need to go."

He glanced down at the inventor. "I suppose I should go down and invite him in."

Wineyll wrinkled her nose. "You should wash. I'll bring him inside to wait for you."

After he bathed, he found Samson in the parlor with Kelmair, their heads bent together over his notes, talking in hushed but excited tones. Combed silk, thin as smoke, glided off Kelmair's shoulders. Gold links hid the scars round her neck and wrists.

"Do you two know each other?" Ashel asked.

"His mother was from Sect Dameron," Kelmair said. Her lip curled. "You cleaned up."

Ashel ignored her. "What's in the book?"

"Plans for my re-inventions." Samson handed over the little volume. "I thought you might like to see them."

He sank into a chair as he leafed through schematics and musings, awe growing with each turn of the page. "Impressive, truly. You're like daVinci."

Samson smiled. "You know your Ancient history."

"History that was ancient to the Ancients was a particular indulgence of mine. Do you want to get a drink?"

"I'll come with you." Kelmair linked arms with Samson, and they walked out the palazzo and downhill. Her dress rippled like rain, flowing over her breasts, swishing over her hips—shaking himself, Ashel directed his gaze at the city's spires, glowing mauve and orange against a lavender sky. Samson jested, and Kelmair laughed, a low, throaty sound. Her hips swayed like a dancer's. Swearing silently, Ashel looked at cornices, sidewalk flags, other passersby, anything but her, and the small, taut nipples that were all too obvious beneath the thin, supple fabric of the damn dress.

"Where would you like to go?" Samson asked as they left the Circle.

"The Piper's Reel," Ashel said. "I know some people playing there tonight."

The music hall dominated a prosperous block halfway between the Circle and Commissar's Square. Patrons filled all the tables but the ones closest to the stage, where jugglers flung flaming torches at each other. Judging the performers sufficiently adept, Ashel took a table that abutted the boards, and Samson signaled for ale and food.

"How much do you owe?" Ashel asked as they tucked into sandwiches of roasted meat and vegetables.

"What the Commissar owes me—a ruler's ransom. I should never have taken the job, at least not until the Concordance had passed."

"Do you really believe that nonsense?"

"It isn't nonsense, Shemen," Kelmair snapped. "Your wife is in Direiellene, a thousand years ago, with Gustave. Samson and I want them home just as badly as you."

"Why, who's Gustave to you?"

"He's my cousin, and he helped me escape bondage." She flicked the gold necklace covering her scars.

"He freed me too," Samson said, the color in his cheeks high. Kelmair squeezed his shoulder, whispered that they'd see each other again.

"You're lovers?" Ashel asked.

Samson nodded.

"See—you're not the only one missing someone," Kelmair hissed. "For months you've done nothing but bang your head against the mast, while the ship sailed on, its course unchanged. It's time you realize there is nothing you can do to help your wife except prepare the world to receive her when she comes home. You have no idea what Victoria means to us, the ones who have been in bondage. She escaped and rose to heights we cannot *imagine*. The mistresses revere her. The Citizens revile her. The songs of her are forbidden, so they're sung everywhere. Every slave, every servant, every stevedore and Buzzard knows her name, and they know that name means *victory*."

He felt Vic's fingers, small and trembling, entwined in his the night they married. A fear gripped him that she would never come home, that without his Woern, the parasites would sap her strength. He saw her corpse half-buried in sand, drained of its blood, shorn of its hair and everything else the Kragnashians could recycle and sell. In that vision, she was in the *desert*, but Lornk and everyone else insisted she had been sent to a rainforest that hadn't existed for a thousand years. That fate was inconceivable.

The jugglers performed their last trick to cheers and table thumps. Beneath the applause, Ashel Heard Geram, walking alongside the Manor wall with Timny and Gaston, an elderly guard who had joined the Manor's detail during King Rivern's reign. *"A Ruler's got to have guts, got to have metal,"* the gruff old man said. *"Your father didn't have what it took, boy. Do you?"* Geram followed them in silence, living in Ashel's memories of Uncle Navael's hatred. Sashal's brother had always suspected Ashel might be a bastard, but he'd been wrong. By Lathan custom, Bethniel was the bastard.

In the Manor garden, Timny said, *"My father was jealous that he didn't get to be Ruler. I don't want to be king. You're not supposed to want it, right?"*

Romner's trio swept onto the stage, apprentices rushing to set up Paeln's drum kit. Twirling his instrument, the lute master stepped to the edge of the stage and addressed the audience, while Londsaen hopped down to their table. "Ashel, good to see you. Would you join us?"

"I thought I'm not allowed."

With a wry grin, Londsaen looked around. "I don't see any Guild monitors. Come on up!"

Ashel sprang on stage and bowed as Romner ceded the center with a twirl of his lute. The first chords signaled "Silly Sounder," a good tune to warm a cold voice, and to warm an audience, all its energy in Paeln's drum and Londsaen's fiddle. At its finish, the crowd cheered.

Ashel turned to Romner. "'Exploits' next?"

"That one? Are you sure?"

"Let's give them something they'll like. Then let's do 'Olmlablaire,' as something they'll remember."

Whither she wanders the Relmans will know.

The crowd slapped the tables as soon as the words hit them, some of them standing and singing along. He laughed, his voice swelling, the fiddle teasing, the lute rippling with defiance and mirth.

> She'll tweak Relman noses and tickle their ribs
> And run a blade up their arse, she's a quick little nib.

When they finished, the audience jumped to their feet, the stomping and cheers deafening. Samson and Kelmair clinked mugs as the masters laughed and bowed. The applause filled him like lifeblood, and the notoriety possessed him like passion. To be known, not as somebody's brother, son, or husband, but as himself, for himself. Bliss from a pipe was nothing compared to this. This was *real*.

When the applause died and the audience sat quietly sipping their drinks, Londsaen's fiddle moaned into "Olmlablaire." Romner strummed out the first mournful bars, and Ashel let the music carry him out of himself, as it always did. When Paeln struck up the martial beat, he sang:

> A nellowlem sings a song of joy,
> But the son of one learns to sing of sorrow.
> A harrier is small, hides in shadow
> Until her lover's in the lupear's jaws
> And pulled into the sunlit fallow.

The high style wasn't used much anymore. People found the metaphors hard to follow, and if you didn't know the history behind the song, all you heard was a fable about animals, trees, and monsters. But the history here was fresh, and the allegory glimmered like glass. By the second verse, people sat stunned, hearing the nellowlem's son himself, and Ashel sucked up their awe like a thirsty traveler at a well. Even the staff edged the walls, the scullions creeping beneath the cooks' feet. Sometimes when he sang, the notes colored his vision, and tonight he sang in blues, the fiddle in ruddy red moans and leaps of green, the lute like the sun and rain, the drums indigo and violet. Ribbons of color snaked through the crowd, binding audience and performer into one perfect note of resonance.

A tone, dire gray, arose. It began as a nagging at the ears, crept into a whining din, like the roar of a distant machine. Ashel glanced at Romner; the lutist's brows knitted. Londsaen's fiddle screeched. The singer's line paused, and while Ashel caught his breath, the noise grew. Patrons' eyes left the stage to fix on one another. The colors gone, the roar swelled. As Ashel sang the next phrase, his throat sour, his voice went ragged. But going on like this, when it had gone bad and the audience was lost and you had to fight to bring them back—that too was a kind of bliss, better than the sort that came in a toke.

The roar outside loud as thunder, the theater doors burst open, and the tumult drowned the minstrels. Outside, a mob hustled down the street, screaming, threatening the night with torches and clubs. Londsaen faltered, lowered his fiddle. Romner stopped strumming. Paeln kept beating her drum, madly accompanying the crowd. A youth broke from the marchers and stamped into the hall, screaming slogans, greasy hair casting a spiky shadow on the floor. Theater patrons scrambled up. Chairs toppled over, the lines of class sharp as the wealthy clustered away from the poor, and everyone tried to jam through the side exits.

Ashel jumped down from the stage. "What's happening? Why is there a mob?"

Kelmair folded her arms, smiling like a cat. "The coup, Shemen."

"You swore to Vic," he grated. "You swore to her."

Pupils dilating, Kelmair nodded.

"Then for her, tell me why there's a mob outside."

"They're going to take the palace. How did you think we were going to do it, especially since Victoria cannot help us?"

Wineyll. The truth of what was happening hit him like a sledge. He had been so obsessed with his own loss, he couldn't see Wineyll's danger, even when she'd come to his room to say a Shrinejumping farewell. "We need to get down there, stop them from . . . from hurting the wrong people."

"We're nearly a mile from the palace," Samson said. "The mob's well ahead of us."

"There are Dameron men in the crowd; we'll get you to the front," Kelmair said. Her face took on the glow she'd worn for Vic. "After tonight, Ashel, as the Commissar's *son*, you can get anything you want from the Caleisbahnin *and* the Kragnashians."

Gall clogged his throat, and his eyes lingered on the lute, sitting forlorn in a spotlight. Music, not politics, had been his mantra all his life. Scowling, he strode toward the door and the crowd streaming toward the Commissar's palace.

Wheels clattering, the Korng carriage clove through teeming crowds, beneath flapping banners and past steaming sewer grates. Nestled in the crook of Lornk's arm, Wineyll kept her breathing steady, trying to quell the nervous thumping of her heart while he chatted with Elsa, Thiellin, and Etien. His remarks were confident and cool, but she Heard his misgivings. He had bribed guards and rallied supporters, but he had not anticipated the Kragnashians would abduct Vic. She wasn't ready, and now his uncertainty about the outcome in the past left him unsure of the outcome in the present. When Vic was bringing Olmlablaire down around their ears, he was less worried.

"Perhaps you should call it off tonight," Wineyll whispered as they passed the Commissar's gate.

He waved at the iron grills closing behind them. "It's too late, Songbird. Stay alert for me."

When the carriage stopped in front of the palace, Wineyll gazed up at the marble portico, drawing calming breaths. She should be thrilled to mount these steps and enter the grandest building in Knownearth, but dread squashed relish.

Inside, a chandelier cast a clean, steady light on the entry hall, and she realized the globes held not flames but glowing bulbs. Thiellin whistled softly and muttered with Etien about tungsten and copper. The light fuzzed dimmer, then brighter, hardly steadier than a good oil lamp but a wonder nonetheless. Despite the foreboding in her belly, Wineyll absorbed the moment with all her senses—the glimmering of the light, the faint buzzing of the bulbs, the crisp, naked freshness of air unclouded by oil scent.

"I won't hoard this like he does," Lornk said so only she could Hear it. "Do you believe in me?"

"Yes." She laced her fingers into his. "If things don't go well, trust me."

He squeezed her hand as Major Demsch emerged from the lift. "Welcome, Citizen," she said to Elsa. "Minstrel Wineyll. Captain. Elder Etien." She ignored Lornk, turning back to Elsa. "Where is Prince Ashel?"

"He's been ill and was unable to join us."

Scowling, the major led them up the stairs. Wineyll Listened, sifting through the woman's thoughts, but Demsch was as skilled at baffling secrets as a Lathan royal.

On the second floor, the major led them past doors plated in gold, silver, steel, bronze—the value increasing the further they went, a grotesque and breathtaking extravagance. Opening a copper door, the woman announced them: "Citizen Elsa Korng. Lornk Korng, her cousin, deposed Lord of Relm. The former Minstrel Wineyll of Narath. Captain Thiellin of the Sect Dameron of the Caleisbahn Archipelago. The Elder Etien of Dameron."

Reclining on a sofa, Parnden sucked a bellowfruit dry and delicately licked long-nailed fingers. A circlet decorated his scalp, sapphires and rubies hanging around a pair of large ears. Aside from the jewels, he was dressed simply, like a Lathan gentleman in leather breeches and a linen shirt with its laces untied. He greeted Elsa curtly but took Wineyll's hand. His grasp was moist and light, and revulsion swelled her throat. "The magician! Did you bring your wand, my dear?"

"I did, sir."

"You're Winder's daughter, yes? During my Academy days, your father curated my education in music and other delights. Do you remember, Lornk?"

"Indeed, Commissar."

"Although as I recall my old schoolchum here was too busy wooing Elekia to follow Winder on romps through Narath's hidden brothels." He chuckled cruelly as Wineyll snatched her hand back. "And where is the prince, old friend?"

"Ashel felt unwell and sends his regrets."

"I regret to hear it, although I'm not surprised. I understand the wayward young man has lately spent most of his time in taverns on the wharves, and even made an excursion into the Roost last week. That sort of revelry does take its toll. Let's have a drink."

Servants emerged from a screened doorway and set trays of canapes and cream-colored Eldanion on the table, then disappeared. When everyone had taken a glass, Parnden raised his. "A toast, to my old friend and the prince he'd make heir to the Korng fortune."

His eyes glacial blue, Lornk lounged on the chaise. "Elsa holds the Citizenry and will designate its heirs."

"Sadly, she will not, my friend."

Guards banged through hidden doors, crossbows cocked. Caleisbahn swords rang out of scabbards. The major ordered everyone to drop their weapons, and three of the soldiers took a step closer, motioning with their crossbows.

Lornk stood slowly, palms up. "Major Demsch, I'm pleasantly surprised to find an officer with unwavering loyalty to the Commissar."

The woman glared, and Parnden chuckled. "You thought Demsch was in your pocket, but mine are bigger."

Lornk's lips curled upward. "Now I'm certain Ashel will be sorry he missed this."

Parnden cackled. "Indeed yes. Major Demsch, take them all into custody."

Etien leapt toward the soldiers. Crossbows thunked, and the Elder crashed onto the table. Wine and crystal sprayed everywhere.

Lornk snatched Etien's sword. More bolts flew, and he pulled Wineyll down behind an overturned table. Blades clashed, steel slathered and scraped as Thiellin engaged the guards. Elsa shrieked, and Wineyll peeked out and glimpsed a guard dragging her away.

"I need to get out of this room," Lornk said, eyes darting between a stone bust and a window.

"You need to appear to get out of this room," she whispered.

"A ruse. Well done, Songbird." His eyes glinting with dark humor, he sprang up, grabbed the bust, and hurled it. Glass shattered, and a furious roar, thousands of voices strong, poured into the palace. A trio of guards converged on Lornk, and his sword slashed and jabbed like a steel whip, driving them back.

Drop, she said to his mind alone. He hit the floor, but every eye in the room saw him whirl and dive through the broken pane, arms crossed over his face.

"After him," Demsch shouted, her sword tangled with Thiellin's.

A guard looked out the window. "Where'd he go?"

"Find him, fools!" Hilt to hilt, Demsch and Thiellin wrestled while guards rushed out.

Stay near me; they won't see you, Wineyll said, and Lornk wrapped his arms around his knees, making himself as small as he could. She Heard no shame or chagrin from him, having to curl up and hide in plain sight of his enemy. His trust strengthened her resolve. It was like her father's absolute confidence in her abilities, and she fought a smile that threatened to disrupt the terror stretching her features.

Demsch twisted away from Thiellin, and the remaining guards surrounded him, swords pointed at his throat. He dropped his weapon and surrendered.

"Put the captain in the dungeon overnight, and then return him to his ship in the morning," Parnden said. "Captain, my alliance with the First prevents me from hanging you, but I will communicate my displeasure to the Caleisbahn ambassador. You and your crew are banned from Betheljin henceforth."

Major Demsch yanked Wineyll to her feet.

"The minstrel may stay, Major," Parnden said. "She's here for a command performance, after all."

"One I want to hear." A youth sauntered into the room. Soft brown hairs scurled up a bare abdomen and chest. Sheer silk pantaloons draped around a silver codpiece, and jeweled metal bands circled his neck and wrists. The boy slouched onto the sofa, and Parnden, his fingers twined through the boy's black curls, reclined beside him.

Trembling, Wineyll picked up a glass and swallowed the contents. The wine felt warm as it went down. She'd always been a good actress and had used that skill to project whichever emotion best suited her musical performances. Now, she amplified the vestiges of her fear as she retrieved her flute case and assembled the instrument. "What would you like to hear?"

"Horst, you choose," Parnden said, kissing the youth's shoulder.

The boy turned hard brown eyes on her. "Something joyful, to match the spirit of the evening, now that Lornk Korng is out of the way."

"Play well for us tonight, my dear, and I'll remand you to your Guild in the morning. Then you will take the first ship out of Betheljin and never return. Understood?"

"Yes, sir." Wineyll lifted the flute and began with the happy march the Commissar had heard in the shop. Lornk hunkered by her feet, hiding a grin behind his knees.

Wineyll. Her name pushed at the small of Ashel's back as they wormed through the crowd and hurtled down alleys, then back into streets packed with fists and torches. Kelmair in the lead, his good hand was locked round her wrist; Samson's grip was iron around his other arm as they plowed through clumped torsos and tangled legs. *Wineyll.* She was in this mess because of him. Beneath his feet, the tenor of the streets changed from cobbles to flat paving stone. *Wineyll.* Her name shoved harder as they approached the Commissar's square, where the heads of the mob thickened into a single bubbled mass. Samson lost his grip, and bodies surged between them. Torches blotted the stars, singeing Ashel's hair, filling his eyes with smoke. Pushing forward, Kelmair called for her people, and he thought of his. *Wineyll.* His wife and sister might well be dead. *Wineyll.* His Guild-sister, she was as much his family as they were, and she was *here.*

He plowed ahead, passing Kelmair, funneling his anger into his glare, into legs and arms that shoved bodies out of his way. Shouts crackled around him, but when people faced him, they dropped back. Kelmair moved into his wake, fingers locked on his belt, still calling for her sect. They pushed through into Commissar's Square. Samson caught up, and Caleisbahnin gathered round them.

"Clear a path," Ashel said, and the seamen shoved into the screaming horde. A few had climbed the ironwork; one shook his fist, mouth stretched open, his voice lost amid other shouts for the Commissar's head. Yet as the Caleisbahnin pushed forward, the people—Buzzards, stevedores, liveried servants—fell silent. A woman, her face creased and dirty, pantaloons smudged and torn, touched his arm with a single finger. A hefty odor of stale legumes attacked his nose. "For Victory," she said. The reek of the crowd mingled with hers—sour ale, vinegar and musk, smokeweed and bliss. Nostrils flaring, he yearned to turn round and leave the unwashed mob to their misery so he could drown his own. But the other odors gripped his throat and shook him, a scolding reminder that their desperation was akin to his. These were Vic's people. Oreseekers, slaves, the desolate and the despised, and they stood here, just as she had stood in this square almost seven years ago, alone and terrified. He'd been blind to her need then. He could see her people's need now.

The woman raised a cudgel and shouted, "For Victory!" Others echoed her, and the chant spread, rippling through the mob until it sounded in a single cry. "For Victory!" A bitter laugh slipped out. Vic had been Lornk's slave, and he'd managed to twist her bondage into a rallying cry for freedom. "For Victory!" Lornk could convince a bird it was a cat. "For Victory!"

The chant his herald, the crowd parted for him. The palace gates were a latticework of fluted diamonds, the spaces in the iron grille big enough for a man's head. More a show of wealth than defense. That task fell on the guards waiting there, swords sheathed, crossbows cocked but pointing at the ground. The rabble-rouser who perched halfway up the ironwork fell silent as Ashel approached. It was Michael, the coal-smuggler.

"This is Michael of Cairo," Samson said. "Mike, this is—"

"I know who he is, Kinseller." Michael's scowl softened as he signed his condolences. "For your loss, Highness."

"It's just Ashel." He turned to the Commissar's guards. "Let me in. I have an invitation."

Stepping forward, one spat, and a thick, black wad splattered the pavement. "Tell this rabble to clear the square, or *we'll* clear it."

There must be guards massing somewhere beyond the crowd, said Geram. He sat alone in the Manor garden. *They'll come up from behind the mob to disperse it.*

A guttural howl burbled through the crowd. Kelmair pinched Ashel's arm. "They were supposed to let us in!"

The guard chortled and spat again. *Wineyll.* Ashel stared at the line of crossbows and heard Wineyll's cackling laugh echo through the Academy hallways, the way it always did after a prank. He hadn't heard that sound of joyous mischief since her father died. He lunged through the bars, grabbed the guard's jerkin, and yanked him against the grille. Kelmair plunged her dagger into his belly.

Michael scrambled up the ironwork, other Buzzards swarming after. Crossbows fired; gate-climbers tumbled back. Behind them, whistles blew, catapults thunked, and screams ripped the air.

Topping the gate, Buzzards flung themselves over. Michael led some into the guardhouse, others charged the crossbow line.

Kelmair slammed into Ashel, dragging him down as bolts zipped overhead, squelching into chests and faces. A coppery, musty stink mingled with screams. Michael sprang from the guardhouse, keys in a bloody hand. He snapped back the iron bolt, and the mob sprayed through the gate like the sea through a cleft. The Commissar's guards fled.

The Caleisbahn seamen gathered around them; one shoved a sword pommel at Ashel. "Take this."

"I'm not a swordsman."

Kelmair grabbed the blade. "We need to go!" Burning rocks showered the crowd. Smoke swarmed the streets. Behind them in the square, catapults had been pulled from hiding places between buildings.

"They've trapped us," Samson said.

"No, look how they run." Michael pointed at the palace guards, retreating round the building, the mob pelting after them, cudgels and torches waving like banners. "Tonight, we triumph!" he cried. "For Victory!"

Wineyll's flute song danced in Ashel's mind as the palace grounds absorbed the horde. *Wineyll*. Not Vic. Victory would not come tonight, and they could not save Wineyll either. If they went inside, they'd be dead or imprisoned before morning.

"For Victory!" Michael cried again.

Ashel gripped the Oreseeker's arm. "Vic isn't here. They're *driving* you inside the gates." Another volley of embers and rocks pelted the square, and more people rushed by them. "They're driving us, Michael."

"He's right," a Caleisbahnin said. "Thiellin never gave the signal, and all the streets are blocked."

Michael looked around again, dread twisting his features. "Retreat!" He broke through the Caleisbahn guard, calling his people to follow. Ashel echoed him, using his singer's voice to spread the order into the mob flowing like a river into the palace grounds. Few turned, and they shoved against the current, leading a thin line of allies past the gate and along the fence. The catapults thunked again. Fiery boulders struck the pavement, and a scatter of shrapnel stung bare skin with little smacks of fire. "Here," Michael cried, pointing into a sewer. A wiry little woman, her skin as tough and yellow as bark, helped him pry open the grate. The woman jumped down, splashed a second later. Two Caleisbahnin went in. Michael looked at Ashel. "For Victory."

In the square, the shreds of the mob scrambled among the twisted, bloody, screaming remains of Lornk's rebellion. *Elesendar, what we've done.* Nodding at the others, Ashel jumped down.

CENTER ALIGNMENT

The mattress ticking shifted, and Geram blinked awake. His arm swept across warm sheets until his fingers found smooth skin.

"Go back to sleep." Elekia nuzzled his ear. Her weight left the bed, and silk rustled over her shoulders.

"Where are you going?"

"Not to worry."

The dismissal rankled, and he rolled out of bed and found his trousers. "I do worry. What is it, Majesty?"

"I thought we dispense with titles in my bedchamber?"

"Elekia is frank; the Ruler inscrutable, Majesty."

She chuckled. "Cheeky love."

"Where are you going?" He pulled his shirt on and faced toward the noise of cinching laces. Her thoughts were baffled as snugly as if she were meeting with the Senate, but he sensed the store of secrets she kept, the lifetime of machinations that had driven Ashel away. His awareness swung to the prince, scrubbing sewage-stained trousers in someone's dingy hovel in the Roost. Ashel muttered Geram's name, repeating it over and over.

Leather rasped as Elekia slid bare feet into shoes. Outside, a breeze rustled through shrubbery. A gizzard hooted in the garden. "Put your boots on, Lieutenant."

The pinpricks resolved into darkness. The air damp, it smelled of mildew and earth. A candle flared, and Geram released Elekia's vision.

"You may keep using my eyes."

Cheeks heating, he faced away and took her sight again.

Elekia walked in front of him and grasped his shoulder. "Don't you like what I see when I look at you?"

He watched himself grimace. Even that expression was suffused in an unnatural glow. Was it real, this lens of love through which she saw him? She shared her bed but not her secrets. "Where are we?"

"Tell me Ashel's sleeping."

"What if he's not?"

"Just tell me he is." She kissed him softly. If he could see her, she would shine like the sun. He shoved Ashel's awareness away and wrapped her in his arms. Breath hot on his cheeks, she pushed him against the wall and tugged at his laces. Heat soaked into his skin, and his mouth pulled her into him as she took him into her.

Stop, stop, please stop. Ashel's protest scored his conscience, but Elekia threw back her head and he followed the line of her throat with his tongue. Geram's sense of the prince steamed away, and his desire to bond with this woman swelled and burst, showering every nerve with bliss. She collapsed against him, and they clung together, panting.

"Elesendar forgive me for stealing these moments while we can," she breathed.

He stroked her face, kissing her lightly, wishing the moments could stretch into a life. Gingerly, he felt for Ashel, but he'd vanished. With drink or bliss or something equally strong, the prince had shut him out. Shoulders hunched, he relaced his pants. "Where are we, Elekia?"

She snorted softly. "The woman is frank, the queen inscrutable—so you ask the woman. We're in the eastern Kiareinoll."

"This is the Device Lornk and Ashel used to go to Traine?"

"And through which I believe the Kragnashians took Vic and Bethniel. The Center is meeting us here."

Mortification choked him as he imagined the creature materializing while they were rutting in the corner.

"No worries of it popping in on us, love. This is the signal." She placed a stone in his fingers, let him weigh it, feel its shape, before she took it back. There were scratching noises near the Device, then a faint buzz. A moment later, the buzz changed frequency, and she announced the Kragnashian was coming. Her hand wrapped around his, and they stood with backs to the wall. Taking her sight once again, he watched a bright shimmering resolve into the same creature to whom Ashel had sung. The horns on its tail gleamed in the dim light of Elekia's candle. Lifting its stole out of the dust, it flowed away from the Device.

Elekia stepped forward and clapped out a greeting.

The Center's wing covers chittered. "What deal would you make now?"

"I seek answers to the questions you have refused to answer. I asked you here so we could speak freely, without concern for what our retainers may hear."

"The Slayer is here. The Slayer will hear."

"You have violated the terms of our previous agreements, and if you do not provide the answers I seek, I will advise the world that the Center has reneged on its bargains."

"Ask."

"When the One and my offspring came to Direiellene, why did you not take them?"

"You had paid for their safe passage to Relm."

"Yet you did not provide them with safe passage. They were lost and nearly died in your lands."

The Center made some humming noises that did not translate in Elekia's mind. "They passed safely into Relm. We did not renege on our agreement."

"The terms stipulated my daughters would remain safe until Latha was secure."

"You have defeated the Stonecutters; the Weavers' land is secure."

"The throne of Latha is not secure; it cannot be secure while its Heir is missing."

"The People did not take the Fulcrum," said the Center.

"Fulcrum?"

"The Dealmaker's offspring."

"Why do you call her that?"

"Events turn about the Fulcrum. The People did not take the Fulcrum."

"Did you take the One?"

The Center hummed, its wings extruding from beneath its carapace. "The One was taken by one of the People, but the People did not take the One."

"So there is not unity among the People?"

"Each lineage has its own aims. Some are misaligned and do not point to the Center."

"And what is the Center's aim?"

"What is the Dealmaker's aim?"

"To secure the future. What is the People's aim?"

"To secure the past."

They talked in riddles for some time. Elekia tirelessly clapped questions, rounding the Center's queries like a seasnake circles its prey. At last the Center admitted, "The Fulcrum returned with the One."

"Returned? Where?"

"The One is a maker of history, but the outcome is uncertain."

"Do you confirm the One and Fulcrum have traveled to the past?"

"Yes."

"And this uncertain outcome—does that mean history can be changed?"

"Yes."

"And if history changes, will the present change as well?"

"The outcome is uncertain. Past, present, and future are in

flux because the Fulcrum returned to the past in the wake of the One. Events turn about the Fulcrum."

"Is there anything we can do to secure the past, present, and future?"

"The past is what it was up to this moment. Each breath of the future is open to new possibilities as we approach the Concordance."

"That is the event Lornk told Ashel about," Geram interjected.

Elekia scowled and waved him to silence while she asked the Center to explain its meaning. It spun more riddles while Elekia paced, asking more questions. At last she said to Geram, "I believe it means that Vic and Bethniel have returned to the past, but they are, in essence, moving forward through time on a parallel track with us. Each day passing for them is a day passing for us. If only we had some way to speak to them!" She clapped that question to the Center.

"To communicate may be possible. To bring them back to this time is also possible. The One was not meant to return so soon."

"What do you mean?"

For once, the Center gave a clear answer. "The One of prior history was years older than the One that was taken. The One that was taken was transported with an offspring; the One of prior history transported alone."

"Offspring!" The queen whirled, beaded braids clattering. "Do you know anything about an *offspring*?"

Geram felt the wake of her motion and the heat of her stare. "Ashel and Vic . . . married."

"Why didn't you tell me?"

"It was private."

"Did they declare?"

Wincing, he nodded.

"Then it wasn't private." As if she'd slammed down a window, her thoughts went mute. He had to strain to Hear her reply to the Center. "You can bring my daughters back? How?"

"Your offspring can be returned to you. First you must help the People."

Something shifted—the air became both denser and colder, and Geram sensed doubt, fury, and fear in equal measure. Stepping toward the warmth of her body, he laced his fingers through hers. She squeezed his hand, then clapped a response.

"What would you ask me to do?"

"The People must have the Dealmaker's allegiance."

"My allegiance? As a wizard?"

"Your allegiance as Center of the Weavers."

Elekia stilled. Taking her sight, he found it fixed on the stone floor, her thoughts a maelstrom, and his skin prickled as he recalled Lornk's story about the strange realm he and Sashal had visited.

"I am not a despot," she said, craning her neck to meet the Center's gaze. "I cannot take this decision without the consent of my people."

"If you wish to see your offspring again, you will convince them."

"A threat?"

"A promise." The Center grasped the knob and disappeared.

Silk sifted against stone, and a choked cry rose from the floor. Geram knelt, and Elekia crawled into his embrace. Tears wet his shoulder, and his arms tightened into a shield.

"I want nothing more than to bring my daughters home safe and well."

"I know," he murmured. "This demand for allegiance . . . Lornk told Ashel a bizarre story—"

"I thought he and Sashal had fabricated that wild tale until the morning Vic appeared in the throne room. Sashal recognized her at once. But then again, he had recognized Ashel long before that, and he poured himself into making his son the opposite of the vain, venal scoundrel he'd seen in that other place. He half-succeeded."

"He did succeed, Elekia. I've never met anyone more courageous or self-sacrificing."

She cupped his ears, her lips brushing his brow. "I have."

He expelled a breath, guilt a hard cold knot in his bowels. "We need to stop. He knows about us. He's *felt* us."

She breathed an oath, and he touched his lips to her knuckles, rubbed his thumb over them, memorizing each peak and valley. "When he wakes tomorrow, he'll know everything I Heard here. And it will only convince him that Lornk is Vic and Bethniel's best chance to come home."

She climbed to her feet. "I wish you'd told me I'm going to be a grandmother."

"I didn't know. How could the Kragnashians? Vic and Ashel married only a few days before she was taken."

"I was less than a week pregnant when I went to Direiellene, and they knew. I suspect it has something to do with the Device."

Apprehension gripped his throat. "What did you sell the Kragnashians to gain Sashal the throne?"

"I will not hand over control of Latha to the Kragnashians, even if it would mean my daughters' lives."

"That's not—"

"However, I want you to tell Fensin the Center has made this offer. This threat. Let the Opposition think I want to capitulate; let him be the defender of the nation. It will help us stall for time while Vic does what she must in the past."

Just like that, she had become the inscrutable ruler, and his only response was to be the good soldier. "I understand, Your Majesty."

RECONCILIATIONS

Shadows danced on the wall, birthed by single flame. Flickers skated across the puddled floor, borne by ripples beneath dripping pantaloons. Ashel's nostrils twitched. Filth had seeped through his pores. This city—this world—was rife with corruption.

Geram and his mother materialized in the dank and dusty Device chamber. Groaning, he swiped and rubbed at lips and cheeks as his mother kissed the other man. *Stop, stop,* he pleaded, but Geram ignored him.

Kelmair ducked past the curtain with a basin. "I've brought clean water. Sit down." She squished a sponge over his shoulders. Suds ran into borrowed culottes. In Latha, his mother wrapped a leg around Geram. "I need to go," Ashel said, bolting for the door.

"Shemen, no." Kelmair's palm pressed into his chest. "No liquor, no bliss tonight."

Elekia's sweat was acid on his tongue. "I can't—I need to *not* feel . . . everything."

"Feel this." Hot fingers inched across his heart, slid over his shoulders. He grabbed her, meaning to shove her away, but she gripped his arm. "Feel me."

Reflected candlelight flickered in dark eyes. In Latha, Geram's ardor rose.

"Feel me," Kelmair whispered. He let the light in her eyes draw him down. His mouth met hers, and he forgot the taste of his mother.

From a window in the Minstrels Guildhouse, Wineyll watched undertakers clear the Commissar's square. She'd meekly played silly songs until Parnden let her go, long after midnight. Lornk tiptoeing behind, a guard had escorted her from the palace grounds and locked the iron grate behind her.

Lornk's grin had shifted to a glower at the smoldering corpses. They'd picked their way to an open sewer grate, where he had thanked her and promised he'd send for her when it was safe. Then he'd dropped into the dark, reeking tunnel, and she'd waded through carnage to the Guildhouse.

Master Jovial herself had opened the door, pulled her inside, wrapped her in blankets and put her to bed, showing more concern and tenderness than any Guild leader since Winder's death. But Jovial's compassion had fallen like raindrops into a dry well. The lively thrill Wineyll had felt while hiding Lornk from Parnden evaporated the moment he disappeared down the sewer shaft, eaten away by the same hollowness she'd felt after her expulsion from the Guild.

Knocking, an apprentice poked her head through the door. "You have a visitor—Master Jovial said to bring him up."

Wineyll unfolded her legs and stood, anticipation pouring into the emptiness. Had Lornk sent for her already?

Expectation twisted into bafflement as Earnk crossed her threshold.

"Hello," he said.

"Good morning, my lord," she stuttered. "I wasn't expecting you."

"I thought we agreed, I'm Earnk to you. I know you had a difficult night. Outside—it's horrible."

"It is." The bloody jumble of limbs and faces slapped her, and she suddenly realized what the failed coup meant for all the people who believed in Lornk. Fear, anger, and shame gripped her. A cry filled her lungs; she swallowed, determined not to let it out. Her cheeks flamed. Her vision blurred.

An arm wrapped around her, drew her into an embrace, and another memory swamped the fear.

Shoulder-high surf thunders, and white foam prickles round her shins. Father's hand grips hers.

"Wait for it, wait, wait, now!"

They run after an ebbing wave. Cold water swirls around her knees, her hips, her waist. A swell approaches, hulking higher and higher. Foam curls, a white line arrowing toward them.

"Jump!" Father yells. Her feet push off the sandy bottom. Father lets go, and her body is lifted up and up, feet dangling above the earth, laughter ringing over the crashing surf. They descend like leaves. Her feet touch the sand. Water sucks out, tugging her garments. Father shouts, she looks up, and a frothing monster slams her onto the hard, gritty surface.

Earnk's embrace was dry and warm, not cold and wet like the sea, but Wineyll's feet dangled over the earth while an irresistible force loomed, ready to pummel her into a hard and unforgiving place. Stunned, she waited for the wave to recede and leave her steady on her feet again. When she caught her breath, she looked up at him.

"Hello," he repeated, his lips a soft curve.

"You're back." The maelstrom surged around her again; she took deep breaths until it subsided. "Why are you here? At the Guildhouse?"

"Looking for you. I'll look for Father in the Roost tonight."

"He said he'd send for me, but I've been ordered to leave. Jovial is arranging passage to Eldanion."

"Come back to the palazzo with me. From there, you could go almost anywhere. You'd be welcome in Relm."

Face hot, she looked at his boots. Earnk had his father's blue eyes and golden hair, but he was otherwise his opposite—measured and compassionate where Lornk was forceful and ruthless. Another wave seemed to lift her from the ground.

"I did the Penance," he said.

"What?" She smashed down onto the hard, gritty earth.

"I am half-Lathan, and I need the nomads' support to hold the Seat, so I offered to serve the Penance. I hauled water for three days."

"What if you'd drawn a longer term?"

"Being a sovereign carries some advantages; out of consideration for the office, and the offer, they gave me the youngest infant's lifetime."

Three days. Sorrow for the murdered babes welled, and tears ran to her chin.

"A great tragedy for the nomads, I know." Earnk pulled a folded handkerchief from his pocket and pressed it into her hands. "It wasn't so bad for me. It gave me time to think."

Dabbing her nose, she imagined him sweating under heavy burdens in the Badlands, earning the nomads' trust and loyalty, earning the Seat delivered to him by inheritance and terror.

"Will you come with me to the palazzo?" he asked.

Wineyll's feet swung out from under her again, and hope lifted her upward. "Yes."

FOR VICTORY

A crier passed outside, announcing the arrival of the Caleisbahnin. Ashel lay still, staring at the ceiling as Kelmair yanked on a pair of culottes and bolted out. *Shemen.* She had never stopped calling him that name. Not on the plains, not in the Korng palazzo, not here, when they'd woken together at dawn, when she'd brought him bread and salted fish, when she'd lain with him again, to keep him from seeking other ways to forget, to not feel, to not Hear every time Geram reached out to him. *Shemen.* Affection tinged the name when she said it now, but the word still meant coward.

Nearby, a squeezebox, a guitar, and a singer tumbled through a song rhythmic and driven and mournful. A hand beat against the guitar's soundboard and a bell clanged on the upbeats, a mesh of noise that should have hurt his Guild-trained ears. Yet the falsetto, wailing in a minor key, rang in synch with Ashel's heart. *"Feel me, Shemen."* Her heat suffused his blood, an intoxication harder than harlolinde and stronger than bliss. He didn't love Kelmair. He damn near hated her. But he'd wanted her since the first time he'd seen her.

She thinks herself a surrogate, Geram said.

I don't need your explanations or advice. It's late; shouldn't you be with my mother?

Not tonight. Ashel tasted the breeze stirring the air in Geram's room, sweat mulched with blossoms. Geram fumbled with the water pitcher and filled a tumbler. Ashel's heart thumped against his ribs. Across the alley, the musicians clapped at tambourine

319

speed, the singer urgent and pleading. *Last night Elekia met with the Kragnashian Center. It confirmed Vic and Bethniel are in the past, fighting in the War of the Council. They're both alive.* His thoughts clogged with sympathy, Geram stopped articulating them and shared the memory of the encounter with the Center.

The darkness squeezed together, a vise around Ashel's forehead, a constriction on his chest, a tourniquet around his limbs so that his breath did not come and his blood did not flow and life leaked from his pores. Victoria and Thabean—their coupling was the source of a dozen romantic epics. Like a hideous monster, jealousy clawed through his anguish, for a moment pushing back the darkness with a blind and fiery rage. But white hot circles of betrayal spun, caging the monster in the irrational hope that her infidelity would make her forgive his. The darkness clamped down again, closer, more suffocating than before. Moaning, Ashel dug his thumbs into the flesh of his calves to feel some other kind of pain. Forgive. Forgive! History said that in the end, Victoria had spurned Thabean for her husband.

And that husband had betrayed her. Vic's heart would be driven toward Thabean's by history, but nothing more than lust had driven him to Kelmair. The music outside cut off, and Ashel coughed out a noise, something between a laugh and a moan.

His wife and his sister were alive, but gone and betrayed. Elesendar, what he'd done.

Vic is alive! Geram said, muffling Ashel's ragged grief with forced calm. *That's what's important. The Center's threat—it means they can come home. And there's the fact Vic is pregnant—all these things should give you hope.*

Pregnant? In the midst of everything, his mind hadn't grasped that detail. He sprang up, nerves, bone, and muscle thrumming with the need to go to her, to shove continents aside and part the seas to reach her. *She's pregnant? That's a death sentence for a wizard in the time of the Council!* He reached within himself, seeking to stir his latent Woern to life and fling himself across the ocean of time separating them. But nothing moved within or without, and darkness poured in, filling his mouth, his nose. He was drowning in impotence.

Ashel, stop. Breathe. The Center said it would bring them home.

Only if Mother gave over control of the nation, which she won't. Elesendar help him, he wouldn't want her to, even if it meant he'd never see his wife or sister again.

The Center wouldn't have offered if it weren't possible for them to come back. Hold on to that. Hold onto the fact Vic carries your child and the certainty that if anyone can find a way to survive attacks from Kragnashians or other wizards, it is her. Hold onto these things and live, Ashel. That's all you can do, all you must do right now. Kill yourself with drink or bliss or by getting involved in this insane rebellion against the Commissar, and you'll kill your wife when she comes home.

Pregnant. His child. The thought was a beam of light in the darkness. The music began again, and someone was calling his name. Cramming grief into a box, Ashel stood and dressed. *Home. Pregnant. That sounds so simple.*

It can be that simple. Hang on to hope.

Hope. Splashing water on his face, Ashel took slow, deep breaths. An image rose of a headsman's axe hurtling toward Vic's neck, and he collapsed to his knees, swallowing vomit. Deep breaths again. The rumpled pallet slid into his vision, and a cold sweat slicked his skin. Deep breaths. He pushed aside the canvas covering the hovel's doorway. An intricate riff lilted off the guitar strings. Clapping hands fell silent, and the singer sang one elongated turn around a single note. The guitar chords scaled up and died. Stinks of feces and rot coated the heady, fishy salt of the harbor. Hearing his name again, Ashel looked at a boy jogging toward him, a skeleton with skin scraped and bruised, eyes hard as glass.

"Oi, silkie! They wait on you!"

Vic . . . his child. An Oreseeker child. Simply by being here, among her people, he promised . . . help. Lornk wanted to rule the world. His only ambition was to hold his wife again.

He followed the boy, stepping over muck streaming slowly

toward the bay. Shanties lined the path, their walls stretches of canvas, sheets of bark peeled from millers' wood, held together with more wishes than nails. Down the alleys, Ashel glimpsed two moored boats. The hulls knocked together, the sound creeping up the foul streets like a thief. The boy flashed Ashel a grin, his teeth sharp and blackened. It was the Buzzard children you had to be wary of, people said. With no more remorse than the Citizens, they scoured the streets of Traine in the wee hours, taking what they found, and they'd kill for a crystal or a harsh glance. It was Buzzard children that decorated the gibbet in the square. Small feet dangling; small bodies reeking and dripping corruption. Why hadn't he noticed the stains when he'd stood there and sung for a square full of revelers all those years ago?

Atop a low hillock, driftwood columns supported a roof of mismatched tiles. A bonfire blazed in the center. Round it the feathered shadows of the Caleisbahnin leapt and danced like demons. As Ashel approached, the Buzzards lined his path, a gauntlet of loss, each delivering the Oreseeker condolence sign as he passed. Lornk and a Caleisbahn captain stood near the fire. Ashel stopped. Buzzards closed behind him: Michael, Fred, Mary, Samson, Ellen, and others he'd seen hailing Lornk, but there were many more, all with the same look of hope and desperation.

Wineyll came to him, copied the Oreseeker sign and clasped his hand. *Hold on*, Geram urged.

Wineyll. Guild-sister. He'd known her since she was small, tutored and looked out for her, then left her to languish in a pit of death and loss.

Lornk held out his arms and spoke aloud in the Ancient's tongue, the language of the Oreseekers. "Ashel of Narath, beloved of Victoria of Ourtown, it is time for you to lead her people."

"To what?"

"To Victory," shouted the crowd.

"The Concordance approaches," said the Caleisbahn captain. "Parnden must be brought down."

"He must!" echoed the Buzzards.

"He must." Earnk shouldered past Michael and Fred, and Geram's hatred waved through Ashel. "Are you with us, brother?"

Ashel scowled at Earnk. "I've never cared for politics or the rise and fall of nations, *cousin*." He turned and met the eyes of the crowd. "I have never known what it is to be a slave, or poor, or sick, or hungry. But my wife knew these things. She was one of you." A whiff of raw sewage burped through the columns. Small feet dangled. "I was born a prince, but I'm not a statesman. I hold the rank of captain, but I'm no warrior. I trained as a minstrel and as a Loremaster. I do not know how I can help you, but you are my wife's people, so I will do what I can."

One of the sea captains sank to a knee. "In honor of what was, my life and my sword are yours, as the standard-bearer for Victoria of Ourtown." The other seamen knelt and made the same pledge.

The Oreseekers glared at the Caleisbahnin, and Ashel wondered at their alliance in this rebellion. "Victoria of Ourtown is an Oreseeker first," he said. "A wizard second. As you swear to me in her name, I command you to cease all raids on Oreseekers and stop trading in slaves, forever."

The lead captain bowed his head. "We speak only for Dameron, but Dameron will comply."

"Nicely done," Lornk said in mindspeech.

Ashel's shoulders itched with the memory of a companionable embrace, the first time he'd met Lornk, before he knew his name and thought him only an ordinary Citizen and a kindred spirit. The same arm had held him while torturers had burned his flesh and Lornk had whispered the secret of his birth in his ear. He faced this man whose kinship revolted him. "Prove to me you're a better choice than Parnden."

Lornk grasped his arm. "The corruption in this city will bring down the world if it continues to fester and grow. Think of what is happening in Latha—the guilds are purging their rolls, seeding poverty as thick and dire as what you see here. Chaos and savagery will follow, and then the Kragnashians will come, Ashel. We will be *their* slaves. Help me stop that from happening."

"Your only goal is to gain power for yourself."

Eyes glittering, Lornk scanned the crowd. "I will share that power with you and all those allies gathered here. If I don't, Betheljin has a long history of coups and rebellions. Perhaps with the Caleisbahnin sworn to you, and these good people ready to die for a cause, you could bring me down."

"And what about Vic?"

"I swear, before all these people, that if it can be done, I will bring her, and your sister, and the others lost in time with them, back to the here and now. Haven't I wanted Victoria as my ally all along? What say you, Ashel? You've agreed to lead these people. Will you do so as my son?"

Torchlight and shadows played across desperate, hopeful faces. Could he sacrifice his name and his homeland for them? For Vic? There was only one answer. "If it will help the Oreseekers, I will accept your surname," he said. "But my father died a year ago in my arms."

Latent Potential

Rotten eggs jammed Thabean's nostrils, the stink wedging deep in his sinuses. Mucus gummed his eyelashes, and sweat streamed like tears. Mopping his face with a stained sleeve, he sucked in another choking breath. He could spare no Woern for cooling skin or clearing eyes; every joule went into the bubbling, sulfurous mud in the channel below. Around the perimeter of the camp, the earth heaved and steamed as the Council dug deep, crushing sulfur into basalt, hammering through rhyolite hard as granite, drilling vents down into magma. Siphoning lava into the perimeter ditch had been Victoria's mad idea. After the last Kragnashian attack, not a single wizard had argued against it. And here they were, six at a spell, barbecuing themselves over a pit.

Yet the plan seemed to be working. On the first day, when they'd barely begun the work, a force of Kragnashians had come as far as the treeline and halted. Horns had blown, troops had assembled, but the stink of sulfur was already thick enough to drive the creatures back into the forest. Six days later, camps had been rebuilt and troops rested and restored. The hospital staff had washed linens and rolled bandages. Farriers made new supplies of arrows and spears, and the artillery crews had restocked their stores of stone and obsidian. But the Council was worn to a frazzle. Saelbeneth no longer worked on the moat, saving her Woern to restore the others, and even she was weary and spent.

Shrine, his nerves sizzled. A shiver twisted his spine; nausea clogged his throat. His temples pounded. Grunting, he ignored the hammering and poured energy into the mud. His lungs ached, stuffed with mucus thick as wool. Coughing, he drove Woern at the earth. Below, a bubble oozed to the surface and popped; spray hissed on charred grass lining the channel.

"Ho, Thabean!" Victoria flew to his side. "You look like shit."

Bile churning, his gaze slid from her swollen belly to her ankle, splinted and tightly bandaged. One day, the Council would have to confront the hypocrisy of permitting her to fight alongside them while she committed the very crime that had brought Meylnara into this world, but that day would not be today, or soon. "I feel worse than I look," he replied.

A hard laugh cut the air. "I've said the same more times than I can count." Her mouth softened. "And how many times have you told me, don't do too much, only enough? You're violating your own rule, sir. Let me take over."

"Your shift begins in two hours—you should rest while you can."

She raised an eyebrow. "If *you* don't rest, you'll be taking a dip in scalding mud."

He glanced at her belly again. "The vapors here cannot be good for the babe."

A hand stroking her abdomen, she grinned proudly. "Look what I've learned to do, Master." A shimmering membrane formed around her head, and an iridescent hose snaked toward the forest and fresh air.

His eyebrows rose. "You can maintain that while you dig?"

Her waveform surged toward the rocky sludge, turning it over like cake batter. "I set it, just as you taught me to set light globes, so I don't have to think about it."

He shook his head, chortling softly. "Madam, you may be the strongest wizard Knownearth has seen in a long while."

Her pride melted into a frown, and she clasped his arm. "Please, Thabean. You're our haven—don't burn yourself out and leave us friendless here."

"I have no intention of self-harm." He ceased pouring his Woern into the mud, and dizziness rolled over him. His head lolled backward, and he blinked at his feet firmly planted on the ground, Victoria's arm around his shoulders.

"Shrine, you almost did have a very hot dunking. I'll take you to Saelbeneth."

"No, no, thank you, madam." He stepped away. "Saelbeneth is severely taxed—I'll be fine with some rest."

"Well, come here, at least." She palmed his cheeks and brushed her tongue against his eyelashes. Energy spurted between them, and his knees steadied, but she scowled as she released him. "You taste . . . sick. Not just tired, but sick. You should go to Saelbeneth. Or Bethniel," she added.

His eyes flashed at the tents surrounding them, but they were alone. "That, madam, is a crime. Not only by Council law—it was outlawed long before the Council's existence as a deed no less wicked than rape or murder."

Brows knit, she hissed, "She *helps* me all the time."

"I know, madam. But you must understand, a carrier such as she cannot defend herself should the wizard's need become greater than the wizard's will. Your love for your sister enables you to resist harming her, but someone who did not care so deeply for her might do so."

Her mouth quirked, she patted his arm. "Well then, I'm not worried about you. Rest up." Waveform blooming, she shot upward, and the earth boiled.

Cheeks hot, he walked fast to wring the giddy feeling from his gut. He had no time or inclination for forbidden fruit. Bethniel's mien was a pleasant distraction, her conversation an engaging diversion, but affection was out of the question. Still, he regretted the rude disdain he'd shown her during the months Victoria lay ill and helpless. He'd spent that time full of anger and resentment—and shame—at having been ordered to play host for people who ought to have been imprisoned. Yet he'd come to welcome Victoria's courage in battle, and her strength in the Woern was undeniably useful, especially at times like these.

His heart laboring, his steps slowed. Fatigue descended on him like a sledge, and the air felt thick as liquid earth as he forced one foot before the other. By the time he pushed aside the draperies covering his doorway, his muscles and bones trembled beneath the shell of his skin, and he had to use the Woern to hold himself upright.

"Sir, you are ill." Fainend rose from a table littered with open volumes. Bethniel stood too, a single finger marking her place in a book.

Thabean's Woern vibrated, their need for succor driving him toward her. "Leave us, my lady," he said hoarsely.

"Fainend was tutoring me in the nuances of Council law," she replied, slipping a ribbon into the leaves of her book.

He fought the Woern itching for her touch. "That is well, but I must rest."

"Of course. My apologies, sir."

As she passed, his Woern shifted toward her, like iron to a lodestone. He braced his backbone against the pull, but rigidity torqued into a rictus. Every muscle clenched at once. His head jerked back, his hands became claws, and furnishings and draperies spun. His head smashed the floor.

A paper crinkles. Teeth crunch and lips smack. "It's a shame, Pip."

Thabean nods, eyes glued to the furrowed brow, the hand urgently gesturing at the twisted body on the floor. "I brought her here for you to woo, brother. Yet you never spoke to her, so far as I know."

Dealn chuckles. "Pip, don't lie to yourself. I know what you did and why you did it—which is why I never sought the lady's favor. Now, look at that."

Fainend motions Bethniel out, but she shakes her head and points toward the camp center. After a moment's hesitation, Fainend ducks through the tent flap and is gone.

"And oh, now, what's this?" Dealn says. Bethniel pulls a short dagger out of her pocket. Yanking off the sheath, she slices her thumbs. "Oooh," Dealn teases. "She likes you too."

Thabean's gut clenches in terror as Bethniel kneels beside his body.

Wet heat stung his eyes. Fire flooded past his eyelashes, seeped through his tear ducts and into his sinuses. His spine relaxed, arms flopped still. *No*, the word formed in his mind, but he lay prone, his muscles released from contraction but heavy as lead. *Stop*, he begged, but the blood—her blood—ran down the sides of his face, into his ears, while his protest bloomed and popped like the molten earth. *No. Stop*, he said, trying to remember how to translate thought into speech. "No, stop," he said silently, hunting for that clarity of purpose that would permit her to Hear him. "No," he mumbled aloud, his tongue and lips finally obeying. Gentle fingers pressed his skull, her thumbs still nestled into the hollows around his eyes. He strained to lift his hands and move hers aside. "Stop, please."

"Is that enough?" she asked.

"Yes." Swallowing a groan, he pushed himself up and clasped her thumbs. Thriving Woern pulsed along his nerves as he probed her wounds, drew the tissues together, and knitted the skin closed. "Thank you." He pressed her hands between his. "Don't ever do that again."

Her brows drew together. "Why?"

He closed his eyes and expelled a breath. Woern fizzed between them; the hairs on their forearms stood straight as grass, ripples echoing each other's motions. Each moment, he grew stronger, more hale, but touching her, he only wanted *more*. "It is too much a temptation."

"Thabean! I'm glad to see you well," Saelbeneth said.

"Your steward interrupted a private conference," Nelchior drawled, entering on the Council leader's heels. "Elesendar, is that blood?"

All eyes locked on the red smears staining her skirt and his face, and Fainend snatched a towel from a cupboard and tossed it to him.

"I had a seizure and bit my tongue," Thabean said, mopping his cheeks. "Lady Bethniel was kind enough to pillow my head, until the fit passed." Standing, he handed her up. "Thank you, my lady."

"Who'd have guessed Thabean's mouth would contain something sharper than his tongue?" Nelchior raked his eyes over Bethniel. "How fortunate you were on hand, my dear."

"Sheath your wit, sir," Saelbeneth said. "You were retching into my commode not half an hour ago. I thank Elesendar Thabean recovered so quickly without my help, as I have few Woern to spare these days. My lady, how are your studies progressing?"

"Well, madam."

Saelbeneth nodded. "Good. Thabean, rest. I saw that Victoria has taken your place, but we must keep a close eye and be sure she does not overtax herself as well. Nelchior, let us return to my pavilion, so we may resume your restoration."

They left, and Thabean stared after them, blood boiling at Nelchior's temerity.

"I'll let you rest." Bethniel bowed over an armload of books.

He expelled a breath and relaxed his scowl. "Thank you, again."

She paused at the threshold. "What did you mean, it's too tempting?"

A tightness seized his throat as he met soft brown eyes. "You possess the gift of life, but it is a forbidden treasure, both for you to have and for us to use."

"In the Purge, they killed people like me, didn't they?"

"They did. It was a horror, but a necessary one to prevent Woernplague from covering the world once more."

"They had no other option?"

"At the time, they felt they did not."

Swallowing, she looked at the books in her arms. "I

understand." When she met his eyes again, hers were haunted. "Sometimes the only way to stop one horror is to commit another. Rest well, sir."

CITIZEN

Yelps, charred flesh, and insidious whispers drove Ashel upright. Panting, he took in the silence. He sat upon a soft bed, wrapped in fine linen. Peeling off a soaked nightshirt, he lay awake while black air melted into gray. Dawn on Landing Eve—midsummer. A year since he'd sat howling while Sashal's blood soaked his clothes and skin. He'd been howling inside since.

The door creaked, and Kelmair slipped into the room. Footsteps brushed the carpet. Her robe dropped into a silken puddle, and she wriggled between the sheets. Her body warm and firm against him, her fingers combed through the hair on his chest, circled his nipples, slid down his belly. His cock rose to meet her hand, and she straddled his hips and nipped his ear. "Would you like some comfort, Shemen?"

He pushed her off, but his body followed, desperate for the solace she offered. Her legs slid along his flanks as her eyes lured and taunted him.

"Why?" he asked.

She stroked his beard with the backs of her fingers. "People are depending on you now. You cannot help them if you sate your longing with drink or bliss."

Gall tainted his breath, but every exhalation exchanged disgust for desire. His cock was alive against her belly, aching to thrust into her. Kelmair squirmed her hips and caught him, drawing him deep inside. "You cannot let despair rend you," she gasped. "She needs you whole."

Vic. Shrine, what was he doing? He yanked out and flopped onto his back. "Why do you care? What is she to you?"

Tears glistened in the growing light. "I was a maen in the First's harem when I first heard of Vic the Blade, the mistress who fought a war of revenge against her master, and I wanted to go and fight with her! But to be chosen as a concubine of the First is a high honor and comes with a large dowry for your family. Everyone despised me for wanting to forsake my duty, but I thought of nothing else. My family would not return the dowry, so I could not leave, but I tried to go anyway. I was caught three times. The last, the First sold me as a sea-mistress." She stroked the scar around her neck. "The tattoos are a sign of great shame." Two streams trickled down the shaved sides of her head. "Gustave helped me escape when we put into port at Alna, and I took asylum with the Weavers. Along with refuge, they gave me their contempt. Judgment is the warp within the weft of their kindness. I left them and tried to join your Lathan army. They would not take a Caleisbahnin, so I went east until I met Erik. The herders never despised me for my scars, and they wanted to use me for my muscle, not my loins. But until I pledged myself to Victoria and she agreed to claim me, I always had to fear that I would be caught and returned to my captain."

"And that was Thiellin?"

She shook her head. "No. Thiellin is a cousin."

"You have a lot of cousins."

"We have big families in the Archipelago." The last vestige of hardness melted away. "I want to comfort you. Please."

Tears spilled down his cheeks. "I can't betray her again, Kelmair. You can sleep here if you like, but I want nothing more from you."

She kissed his palm. "As you wish. Ashel." Flopping down, she closed her eyes, and her breath fell into a steady rhythm while the dawn bled through a crack in the curtains. The light swelled, gleaming lavender, rose, and orange. A finger of amber crept across the carpet and kissed the door. He imagined Vic's light in his arms again, the room bright with Bethniel's merriment. His palm cupped an infant's head. A tiny fist clasped his finger. But these fancies evaporated when Kelmair sighed and shifted, and he looked around this room, with its silk draperies and brass fixtures. If he ever saw Vic again, would she forgive him?

A sharp knock interrupted his thoughts. Cursing, he opened the door a crack to find both Korngs in the hallway.

"We need to talk," Earnk said. "Can we come in?"

"I'll meet you in the library," he said as Kelmair rose on an elbow behind him. The muscles of Earnk's jaw quivered, and Ashel wondered if his cousin Heard her.

A vicious smile enlivened Lornk's face. "The palazzo isn't yours yet, but you're already giving orders. Well done, son."

"I'll meet you downstairs." He slammed the door and went into the privy chamber. His stomach churned, worse than a hangover. Vic, Bethniel, and *his child*. The towel snagged on the ragged beard. His eyes lingered on the frizzed spirals capping his head. How long since he'd even combed his hair? "You've really let yourself go," he said to his reflection. *And you've no idea how to get yourself back.*

In the library, a small coil of copper gleamed upon the table, as bright as Vic's hair in the sun. Ashel blinked, trying to keep his eyes in his head. Copper! More valuable than gold, silver, or iron. One of the ores Vic's ancestors had sought and never found.

He looked at the Korngs. "That's what you're doing in the Plenetor—mining copper." His mind leapt from astonishment to possibility. Heat, light, freely available. Electricity—how the Ancients had lamented its loss.

> *The lamp burns and sputters*
> *Its smoke blears*
> *Eyes squinting, blinking*

Head aching

Memories of clean, pure white light at my command

Like God's hand.

Samantha Farrak had written those lines before she went to the Shrine and finalized the Erin Alliance with her own blood. Some scholars considered it a suicide note.

"The rights came at great cost," Earnk said, his face and neck turning red.

Suspicion boiled into ire, and Ashel grabbed the coil. "You sold Vic for a bit of metal?"

"Not the metal. The power," Lornk said, placing a shallow porcelain bowl on the table. White and adorned with gems, it resembled the sconce of a Device. "The Commissar has an engine he stokes with charcoal night and day to generate the power for his lights." Setting a small glass globe inside the bowl, he pressed a gem and a light shone forth, bright as a hot lamp. "I didn't trade Vic for economic or political power. I traded her for energy."

"You admit you traded her!"

"It was supposed to be a mission—a task—not a sacrifice, Ashel. Do you think I would give up a wizard and her power? My agreement with the Kragnashians was that she would return once she'd achieved her objective, but the lineage with whom I made this agreement is not the one that took her. I can no longer say whether she'll find a way home." He scowled. "This debacle is entirely your parents' fault—not just your mother but Sashal too. They knew who she was, and they did nothing to prepare her."

"They didn't want her taken by Kragnashians in the first place."

"Are you sure of that? It was Elekia who sent her to Kragnash."

He choked on his response. He'd blamed his mother for Vic's power and illness, but everything that had happened to her was rooted in Ashel's own mad decision to try to avenge Sashal's death. "How do we know which lineage did or didn't take her? Everyone believes the Kragnashians never lie or renege on a deal, but what if they have? And if there are multiple factions at work here, how do we know one from another?"

"Good questions." Lornk rose and retrieved an old tome from the stacks. While he flipped the dusty pages, Earnk took the globe out of the porcelain object, replacing it with coiled copper. He unwound a long length of the metal, stretching it across the table. Lornk lay the book flat, tapped a page showing drawings of Kragnashian tattoos. With half an eye on Earnk's doings, Ashel scrutinized the pictures.

"The markings on their mandibles identify each Kragnashian's clan and caste," Lornk said. "The trouble is, the differences can be subtle, and it takes expertise to discern them."

"Can you tell the difference?"

"Yes, but I did not see the Kragnashian that took Victoria."

"So, you cannot know your Kragnashian partners weren't the ones who betrayed you."

He scowled. "What we do know is that she had better accomplish her objective, or none of what we do here and now will matter."

"And what, exactly, is her objective? Killing Meylnara?"

"That, and saving the forest of Direiellene."

"But the forest was destroyed."

"My allies want it saved. If she manages to undo the destruction of Direiellene, this is what we will gain." Lornk placed globes along the wire; each shone with white light. Ashel whistled softly—the light was bright and steady, revealing every spine of every book in the surrounding stacks. The globes bore little resemblance to the Commissar's yellow flickering bulbs.

"The entire city of Re was wired for electricity five years ago," Lornk said.

Scorn squashed Ashel's awe. "There would have been rumors—we would have known about it from my father's spies."

"We? Was Sashal really so free with secrets, Ashel? Perhaps he simply declined to share his knowledge with you or your flibbertigibbet sister."

"Father, please," Earnk said. "Princess Bethniel is an astute and clever politician. I owe her my Seat."

"You owe it to *me*."

Earnk's jaw bunched. "To both of you. Ashel, the grid is underground and hasn't been extended to the houses yet. We dug up the streets, improved the sewers, and at the same time installed the wires. The Works Guild has kept it quiet because they don't want people ripping out the copper to sell it. So, it will remain secret until we install the globes."

"The river Re will provide the energy," Lornk said. He pointed to the porcelain object. "The Ancients called that a power cell. There are mills set up at eight different stations along the river, but we need the cells from the Kragnashians to store the energy we pull from the flow."

"You told the Buzzards this is all about keeping humanity free, and yet you sold my wife for a few lights!"

Lornk rolled his eyes. "We do not have the cells, Ashel! I did *not* give her to the Kragnashians. How many times must I explain this?"

"If she changes history, who knows if any of us will even exist to worry about your wires and lightbulbs," Ashel spat.

"Stop fretting over what you cannot control, and start doing what you can, *brother*," Earnk said. "We can do nothing about the past—all we can do is try to improve the present, and right now we need you to assert your claim on the Korng holdings. This morning you and I will go to Parnden and offer him a mine for Elsa and Wineyll. Afterward, you will use your skills and charisma to build support among the Citizenry until the miners arrive."

"Miners?"

"From the Elgrion," Lornk said. "We must wait for them to filter overland into the city, where they'll harbor in the Roost and the docks. It may take several months to build a force large enough to mount a successful assault, since we will not have help from Parnden's forces. The previous fiasco was instructive in who cannot be bribed, and we will be more judicious with our mullas and our plans. We must also sway the Citizenry; letting them remain neutral is no longer viable. This is our contingency plan. We cannot allow it to fail."

A cool breeze gusted lazily off the sparkling bay, spinning drifting clouds into ribbons as a butler ushered Ashel and Earnk up the final steps to a rooftop terrace. The Commissar took Ashel's hand first. "Highness! Oh, my, why do you retain that ragged thing covering half your face? My father was a barber, you know, and I was trained in the craft. I could remove it for you and reveal the perfect mien beneath." Before Ashel could reply, the Commissar turned to Earnk. "Your beard, on the other hand, is very sharp, my lord. It strengthens the chin, and now I can hardly tell the new Lord of Relm from the old. Now come, let's break our fast."

Earnk's expression was mild as they took their seats, but the blood had drained from his cheeks and he hid clenched fists under the table. While servants brought fish and fruit, cheese, breads, tea, and sweet wine, Ashel wondered what Parnden had done that Earnk had endorsed his father's coup as an act of vengeance.

The servants left, and Parnden waved at the Caleisbahn frigates anchored in the bay. "Two more arrived since yesterday, and my dungeon is already brimming with seamen caught with the mob. If I didn't know better, I'd think the First was trying to interfere with my rule. What do you think, Highness?"

"Aren't those cargo boats ferrying goods between the frigates and the docks?" Ashel sipped his wine. "It looks to me like the alliance between Betheljin and the Archipelago is as strong as ever."

"Appearances can be deceiving, as a man with two fathers well knows." He pointed his knife at Ashel. "Will you forsake the Ruler's kinship for the outlaw's?"

"My cousin despises my father, Commissar," Earnk interjected.

"Ho, I believe it! Yet despite and loyalty can twine together—

just ask my Major Demsch. She despises me, yet she is utterly loyal. After all, it was she who betrayed Lornk's coup." Parnden's larynx bobbed as he eyed them suspiciously, his gaze resting on Ashel. "What about your wife? A warrior and a wizard would be a valuable mate for a Citizen of Traine. Too valuable, I think, when the rabble that attacked my palace chanted her name."

"She could be a frightful enemy, Commissar, or an indispensable ally. You should know Victoria *hates* Lornk Korng."

"And, she is lost, isn't she? If she should be found, what guarantee can you give that she would not seek to harm me?"

"She's never met you, Commissar, so she has no reason to harm you."

Parnden's grin sharpened. "As you say, Highness—or shall it be Citizen? Do you or do you not declare yourself a Korng?"

He swallowed some wine to clear the gall from his throat. "I would be pleased to take the surname and the properties, if you approve the change in registry, of course."

"But do you claim kinship with Lornk Korng? I can hardly bestow the Citizenry without a blood tie."

Ashel kept his face still. "Lornk is my marriage uncle; we share kinship through Earnk's mother, my aunt."

Parnden snorted dismissively. "Richelle and Elekia were sisters by law, not by blood."

Earnk said, "Since Elsa was arrested, the Korng holdings revert back to me, and I choose to adopt Ashel into my family, to honor my mother, who was adopted by his mother's family. Property may be passed through adoption and designation, Commissar. May I remind you how you came to your own Citizenry?"

"Both of you," Parnden sneered, "came to your positions by birth. I became Commissar through the craft of politics. Don't insult me. Lornk Korng sent you here to keep me from confiscating all his holdings."

"We are here," Ashel said, his indignation genuine, "to negotiate for my place in the world. To ask for the release of Elsa Korng, who is merely a housekeeper and incapable of intrigue, and to beg you to rescind the deportation order for Wineyll of Narath, who is only an innocent young girl. I despise Lornk Korng." For emphasis he held up his right hand and let his voice shake. "I despise him, and I will not pledge allegiance to a tyrant."

"You've chosen your words very carefully," Parnden rejoined. "Yet my old friend always had a long and subtle reach, and a particular talent for turning enemies into allies. What assurance— beyond your word—can you give me that he is not behind this ploy?"

Ashel took a breath and squared his shoulders. "You can search the palazzo."

"No," Earnk interjected. "I'm sorry, Commissar, but my cousin is unaware of Betheljin law. A Citizen's palazzo is sovereign territory."

"I'm very much aware of it," Ashel said. "You grant me the Citizenry, and I grant you permission to enter my home and search it."

Parnden snorted. "Where I will find no evidence of your father's presence, I'm sure." A sly smile twisted his lips. "Will you permit me access to the Device?"

"Yes."

"To go where?" Earnk asked, shooting a glare at Ashel. He had to admit, his cousin was a convincing actor. The conversation was going exactly where Lornk predicted.

Parnden said, "Oh, a few places, actually. I believe there is a Device in the Elgrion, near several of the Korng mines. I would like Major Demsch to secure that location and search for Lornk in the mountains. I would also like to inspect the palace at Olmlablaire, to ensure he is not there. I remind you, my lord, that there is still an extradition treaty between our nations. Finally, I would like to visit Latha. I never properly congratulated Elekia on her election to Ruler."

"A visit to Latha will take some time to arrange," Ashel said, "and only my cousin can grant you access to Olmlablaire. But as for the Elgrion—the Device is at your disposal."

"Now, a final question." Parnden looked at Earnk. "What are you mining in the Plenetor?"

"We thought you might ask." Earnk pulled out his copper coil. "Copper. We've found it."

Parnden whistled, his eyes glittering. "After three thousand years—a miracle."

"It seems the Plenetor is loaded with opportunity," Ashel said.

"So it is . . . Citizen." Parnden clasped Ashel's hand, his grip as flaccid and honest as their deal.

THE LEGACY

Skin tingling, Ashel stepped away from the stone platform and raised a hand to shade his eyes. Above, a glacier clogged an alpine pass. The sun glared off the ice, and a frigid breeze whistled through the trees, dusting his clothes with conifer pollen.

Major Demsch and a pair of guards hazed into view. One shivered and cringed, feet dancing as she rubbed her skin.

"Shake it off, soldier." Demsch eyed the woods suspiciously. "If your father's rebels attack here, or anywhere, you're dead."

"Lornk Korng is not my father."

Lips twitching, her eyes scraped over him. "You have the look of him."

More guards came through the Device in pairs. The major ordered them to take defensive positions round the platform before tossing a blue stone into the shallow well surrounding the knob. The stone disappeared, and Parnden took its place a moment later.

He sucked a long, loud breath through his nose, let it out of his mouth with a longer, louder sigh. "Mountain air is so refreshing. When we've caught your father, I think I'll give him back to your mother. Hasn't she sentenced him to the Shrine?"

"He escaped before his trial."

He snickered. "Yet she tried you in absentia. Why do people favorably compare your nation's justice to ours? I think a quick, clean hanging more merciful than starvation and exposure, don't you?"

"I no longer claim Latha as my nation, Commissar."

Parnden patted Ashel's cheek. "I do not like this beard, Citizen."

A shudder rippled up his spine; he tensed his shoulders to hold himself still. "Are you satisfied Lornk is not in the palazzo or hiding here?"

Parnden nodded. "I will be, so long as Major Demsch has free access through your home to hold this position and search the environs."

He inclined his head. "I'm at your service."

Geram's heel thumped the floorboards in time with his pulse. It irked him that he marked the rhythm of heel and heart, but bonding with Ashel had infected him with all sorts of abilities and inclinations he'd never possessed before. Like his devotion to Elekia. A warped perversion of a son's longing it may be, but his yearning had only worsened since he'd stopped visiting her bed. Elesendar, he missed her.

"Lieutenant! This is a pleasant surprise," Fensin said, coming into his office.

Geram rose. "Your clerk told me I could wait here."

"Of course. I'll have tea sent in."

When they were settled with warm cups behind a closed door, Geram said, "Elekia met secretly with the Center."

"Well done! You must have gained her full confidence if she'd tell you about such a meeting."

"I was there."

"Were you now? Well done, indeed. What did they discuss?"

"She asked about her daughters, and the Center told her they had traveled to the past."

"So Victoria of Ourtown is indeed a wizard, and the Kragnashians' One?"

"Yes."

"This is something you've known all along, yet never mentioned. I'm disappointed, Lieutenant."

Geram's fingers curled toward fists, but he spread them flat on his thighs. "Vic is a friend, Senator."

"Did the Center say anything else?"

"It promised it would bring them home if Elekia pledged Latha's allegiance to Kragnash."

"Elesendar! How did she respond?"

"She said she would consider it. She claimed it was a delaying tactic, but Senator, I think she might agree." As he lied to Fensin, he Listened intently. The Senator's surprise seemed genuine. "Her husband died a year ago. Her son has abandoned her for her worst enemy. Her daughters are missing. She is distraught."

"Do you really think the Ruler would betray Latha's sovereignty?"

"I don't know, sir. She collapsed when the meeting ended, and I know she is grief-stricken. I thought if you and the Prime Minister spoke to her together, reminded her of her duty—"

"Oh, of course. We cannot betray the nation!"

"I would say she never would, but she . . . she is distraught." Shrine, how he hated painting Elekia as a besotted, emotional fool.

"Have you had any success obtaining Breon's proof?"

"No, sir. She pretends she doesn't have any magical abilities."

"She let you witness a meeting with the Center but does not show you her powers?"

"She wants to appear ordinary in this regard," he said truthfully. Elekia had not used wizardry for months.

Fensin's teacup clattered, and the old man's feet shuffled between the desk and sitting area. He kept his thoughts well baffled, but Geram Heard him wondering how he could use this information to remove Elekia from the throne. "I will speak to Velbaor, but we must approach the queen delicately. I don't want to give you away."

"I could suggest she consult with the Prime Minister about the Center."

"Yes. Do that. Is there anything else?"

"I've heard from Ashel."

"You remain close with the prince?"

"I do. Lornk Korng attempted a coup against the Commissar and failed. Afterward, Parnden granted Ashel the Korng surname and Citizenry, and Ashel is cooperating in the hunt for his father."

"So we're all calling him that now, are we?"

"Elekia insists it isn't true."

"She would, but she also knows that cat has slipped out of the bag and captains the ship sailing away from port. She'll never repair her reputation."

"She is still Ruler."

"For now. This meeting with the Kragnashians could seal her fate, but we must have more proof than the word of her blind lover—no insult meant, Lieutenant."

"None taken, Senator. Parnden wants to meet with Elekia and asked Ashel to facilitate. Obviously, that's difficult given the rift between them."

"Does she know you communicate with him?"

"Yes."

Smug satisfaction ebbed through Fensin, so clear and loud Geram wondered if he broadcast it. "Then you should tell her about Parnden's request. Latha will need all the allies we can get in the days ahead."

Geram left the Senate filled with the dire certainty that Fensin would twist the meeting with Parnden into Elekia's downfall.

Shouts and clattering hooves signaled the arrival of the prison wagon. From a library window, Ashel watched Elsa emerge. Earnk helped her climb down, and the pair went inside, arm in arm. Ashel returned to the library table and his study of Kragnashian markings, making his own drawings of the pictures. He'd never been a particularly good draftsman, and renderings with his left hand were crude, but they still helped to fix the intricate patterns in his mind.

"May I have a word, Citizen?" The physician Moralen stood on the threshold of the library.

Ashel beckoned him in. "How is Elsa?"

"As well as can be expected. She is dehydrated and bruised but says the guards did not harm her otherwise. Have you returned to Emily's, my lord?"

Irritation and shame percolated through a craving for blissful oblivion. "No."

"Good. Grief and despair can damage the mind as badly as a sword to the gut. Liquor and bliss can relieve pain, but they don't heal agony, they only prolong it."

"I haven't been back there."

"The temptation will fester like a wound, especially while the Commissar's troops occupy this house. There are cerrenils in the parklands ringing the city, if you want another source of peace."

"You're counseling prayer?"

"I wouldn't presume to advise a scholar of the faith. However, I once found my path away from bliss in the same park. It might help you to seek solace from an old mother, and it certainly won't hurt you. My lord." With a curt bow, Moralen left.

Ashel shook off the sour feeling the title *my lord* gave him and returned to his drawing.

"May we speak, my lord?" Hair damp from a wash, Elsa wore an apron over clean, plain clothes.

"Please don't call me that. You're not my servant."

She quirked a shrewd eyebrow. "There are some papers we must sign together. Please come with me."

He followed her to a door leading outside. "You know this is all a sham."

"The papers are in my office." She stopped on the threshold, scowling as a pair of Demsch's aides hurried across the courtyard and out the gate. "They have the run of the palazzo?"

"By necessity."

The creases around her mouth deepened, and she crossed the flagstones to one of the two towers anchoring the north and south wings. Inside, stairs climbed the walls, sweet-scented sconces aglow along the square shaft.

He stalled at the first step. In all the months he had been here, he had never ventured into either tower. "Is this where he kept her?"

"I used it as my office. I'll move my things back to the den by the kitchen."

"Elsa, please—"

"Come, my lord."

His stomach twisted in knots, he trod the winding flights. Lornk and Vic. All he had ever imagined, had ever tried *not* to imagine, had happened in this tower. Geram's attention was fully occupied in Olivet's training yard, leaving Ashel to face this trial alone. A blessing, to feel neither Geram's soldierly judgment nor counselor's compassion, yet terror snagged at Ashel's bowels, and his thighs shook harder with each step.

Near the top, he stopped, wheezing. Elsa disappeared through a doorway. Sunlight cast a square upon the landing. "It's just a room," he said, taking a deep breath and tightening his abdomen. *It's only a room.* His feet settled onto the last steps as if taking him to the gallows.

The bookshelves startled him. Along every wall stood cabinets and shelves, filled with ledgers. A secretary's desk sat beneath a window, warm sunlight falling on tidily filed papers and quills. A couch and two well-stuffed chairs surrounded an Eldanion carpet patterned in grain stalks.

"I'm grateful they left things as they found them," Elsa muttered as she rummaged in a cabinet. "I suppose it was Lornk's idea to let them in?"

"He thought it would rouse the Citizens."

"That it will." She pulled out a sheaf of papers. "He drew these up after you came to Olmlablaire."

A sardonic chuckle escaped Ashel's teeth. "You make it sound as if I'd been invited for a holiday in Lordhome."

Scowling, Elsa collected quill, ink, and a writing board and sat on the sofa. "Here. Please sign to formalize the title transfer."

His head fell into his hands as he remembered the last document Lornk wanted him to sign.

I, Prince Ashel of Narath, wish for peace between the people of Relm and the people of Latha. I call upon my mother, Elekia of Reinoll Parish, elected Ruler of Latha, who came to her position through subterfuge and malicious intent, to end hostilities and withdraw all Lathan troops from Relman territory.

He had refused to sign that statement, and Lornk's torturer had burned his flesh with the same gauntlets Vic had used to extract Relman signatures on the peace treaty. After his hands had healed, Lornk had chopped off his fingers, severing him from everything he *was*. Another bitter laugh slipped out. "So, this is the room where he changes you." When Lornk had kept Vic here, he'd stripped her of all she was so he could make her into something else. Yet in the end, she had remade *herself*. Could he do the same—create himself anew when he signed this paper, rejecting his Lathan heritage for a Betheljin one?

He swallowed a lump that felt like salt and sand. "Do you believe him, that he saw that other version of our time?"

Elsa's lips tilted thoughtfully. "Parnden's troops have been very courteous in their search—that wasn't the case thirty years ago. Soldiers came from Latha *and* Relm, ransacked this house, tore through tenements and dives on the docks, looking for the two young princes. When no one asked a ransom, we feared they'd fallen afoul of a press-gang and were pumping bilges aboard a smuggler's scow. They'd been missing for nine days before they reappeared in Latha's throne room. We didn't see Lornk for more than a year after that because he refused to come home via the Device." She snorted. "The Relmlady was incensed and almost disowned him because he wouldn't visit her either. When he finally did come home, he had terrible nightmares. So yes, I believe him.

"And I believe *in* him," she added after a long moment. "I know him to be true to his word. He has promised to do all he can to bring home Victoria and your sister; he will do it, if it is possible."

Elesendar, let that be true. His fingers tight round the quill, he signed his name wherever she pointed.

"I don't know the first thing about running a Citizenry," he said when they finished.

Her lips twitched round a smirk, her eyes appraising. "Lornk's mother squandered a legacy six generations old, and it took him almost twenty years to restore the fortune she lost to blissmongers and gaming cartels. Do not waste it like your grandmother did." She restored the papers to the cabinet, handing him the key. "I'll have my things cleared out by tomorrow. Let me know if you want the furnishings moved to another room."

The door shut behind her, and he expelled a heavy breath. One window overlooked the courtyard, deserted in the midday sun. The city's spires shimmered through the other, the bay glittering beyond. "Lornk is not my father," he whispered aloud, like a prayer, a wish. But only a wish. He bore the Korng surname now, and the Lathan Heralds would name his sister a bastard, his mother an adulteress, his father a cad. *A legacy six generations old . . . do not waste it like your grandmother did.* He sank to the floor, too desolate now for tears. He'd resisted Lornk in Olmlablaire at the cost of his hands, his talent. Here, he had capitulated, all for half a hope that by sacrificing one family, he could restore another. His wife. His child. Forehead butting his knees, he uttered a growling moan, voicing the resentful fury that still raged in his heart. What sort of resentment had Sashal carried, knowing his wife loved another man, especially one like Lornk? Yet Ashel had known only affection and pride from Sashal. How had he done it, loving a child so well who might not be his own? An ache seized his gut as he thought of Vic, facing Kragnashians, wizards, and other dangers while their child grew inside her. He had to purge the rage from his heart, or he'd never be half the husband and father Sashal had been.

The only way to purge resentment was to forgive. Forgive them all: Lornk. Earnk. The Harmony. Geram. His mother. But he couldn't do it. Not without Vic. Not without her here, so first of all, he could forgive her.

Performances
and Proposals

The treacly soprano should have drowned beneath the strings and horns swelling from the orchestra pit, but the theater's acoustics captured and amplified the soloist, bringing her thin voice to every seat. Elbows on the box railing, Ashel soaked in the music like a hot bath on a cold day, and the wild thought crossed his mind that with the Korng fortune, he could buy this theater and employ better singers.

Eyes alight, Wineyll clasped his hand, her nod eager.

Behind them, Earnk whispered with a page and dropped another white card onto a growing pile. "You should be talking to these people," he hissed after the box door shut.

"You can't bring me to a theater and expect me to ignore the music."

"They do." Earnk flicked a hand at the jeweled coifs and sparkling garb stuffing the tiers. Gazes alighted on the Korng box and sprang away, like glowflies on a summer eve while gossip susurrated behind gloved hands and silken fans. Few eyes were aimed at the stage, and Ashel wondered how it would disrupt Betheljin politics if a gifted singer stood there.

At last the curtain fell to desultory applause and another knock on their box door. The page announced the Storunds.

Ashel stood as Ellen entered with Moralen and another man Ashel assumed was her husband. Lornk's friend had a plain, dark face with sharp eyes.

"I thought it was time you two met," Ellen said. Elegantly attired, she bore little resemblance to the dockside tavernkeeper he knew, though she appeared as comfortable in bejeweled silks as an apron. "Ashel Korng, may I present Alek Storund."

He bit his tongue at hearing his name paired with the Korng surname. Alek gamely offered his left hand and said, "I understand you know Moralen already. He is a dear family friend. A surrogate father, after my own died."

"You and Lornk gave me what I needed at the time," the physician said gruffly. "I'm not certain this is what you need," he said to Ashel.

"Music is always a welcome distraction. Does the Commissar ever come here?" Ashel waved at the Commissar's private balcony. Occupying the entire first tier, it was empty.

"Rarely."

"The intermission isn't long," Alek said. "Let's meet some people."

In the foyer, a servant offered Eldanion in sleek goblets as a wave of avid gazes broke over them. Alek waded into the throng and Ashel followed, trading names and witticisms.

A woman with rich chestnut spirals appraised him, tapping an index finger on pouting red lips. "I met you at the Commissar's palace some years ago. You were only a youth, but you set Traine on fire that night."

"I did?" He beamed and for the span of a breath allowed her fluttering eyelashes to stoke his ego.

"Be careful of setting any more fires, Citizen," Major Demsch said. The crowd peeled away from the officer, and she walked a clear path to Ashel.

"I should have guessed your love of music, Major, when we met outside the Minstrels Guildhouse."

Her lip curled at his companions. "Citizen Storund. Doctor. Are you aware, Citizen Korng, of the history of sedition surrounding these two?"

"I'm merely following the Commissar's suggestion I get to know Citizen Storund and his literary endeavors."

Alek took a pencil out of his pocket and scribbled on a napkin. "Here, Major. There's a bit of my work you can pass on to our dear leader. It isn't seditious, but it is salacious, so I think it should match his taste. Shall I recite it? There once was a barber from Traine—"

"Careful, Citizen," Demsch said, crumpling the napkin in her fist. "Or you might follow your father up the gallows steps."

Chimes sounded, and the audience melted into the tiers. Demsch glared at them, hand on her pommel.

"Would you like to join us in the Korng box, Major?" Ashel asked.

She blinked at him. "What?"

"I don't want to miss the second act," he replied. "You're welcome to join us, or please excuse us."

Scowling, she stepped aside. "No, thank you."

"That was well done," Alek said as the box door shut.

"I'd love to hear the rest of that limerick."

Alek chuckled. "Moralen tells me you've been going out to the cerrenil grove to pray?"

"I have. The trees are young, but they still give solace."

The older men exchanged wistful glances. "My father is buried in that grove. He'd approve of us using it as a place to meet, if it wouldn't interfere with your prayers."

Regret pinched Ashel's heart. He'd never visited Sashal's grave, finding a thousand excuses not to. Now it was too late. "In Latha we say, 'What can we know of the way of trees?' The answer is, nothing, but I don't think the cerrenils will mind hosting a gathering."

When they reached the palazzo, Wineyll paused in the foyer and Earnk hesitated beside her, the pair of them swaying like chimes in a breeze. Smirking softly, Ashel bade them goodnight and headed off to the library.

"Would you have a drink with me?" Earnk asked.

Her heart sped, and she pulled in a long slow breath. "Yes, of course."

In a parlor, Earnk poured them each a harlolinde and sat beside her on the sofa. The liquor scalded the back of her throat like fire made from ice.

"I can never seem to get used to that," she coughed, eyes watering.

"It just takes practice," he said, and they shared a fleeting smile. "I'm going to Relm tomorrow morning."

"Elsa mentioned it."

"The invitation to play for the Council still stands. I could use a lovely bit of music, to drive out that soprano's saccharine voice."

"She wasn't very good."

"Come with me." His fingers caught hers.

Her breath stopped, snagged on the cusp of longing and terror. "I can't."

"Your Guild rules don't matter to me, nor should they to you."

"It's not that." She inhaled with great deliberation, exhaled slowly. "I want . . . I can't go with you. I need to stay here—Ashel needs a friend here. I can't abandon him."

He brought her knuckles to his lips. The kiss sent fire up her arm, and her breathing became staccato whistles that grated on her ears. She thought he would shrink away, but his fingers grazed her temple and cheek, tucking her hair behind an ear. "What do you want, Wineyll?"

"Jump!"

Her feet push off the sandy bottom. Her body is lifted up and up, feet dangling above the earth, laughter ringing over the crashing surf.

Her mouth fell open, but words wouldn't come. He sat still, watching her with deep blue eyes that looked black in the flickering lamps, but his hair shone like gold. Clearing her throat, she forced an answer out. "Three years ago, I was touring with my father. We were in Alna. It was summer, and he took me swimming in the ocean. When the waves lifted us up, it felt like flying. It was the same sort of joy I felt every time we performed together. It was magic. All I want is to feel that again."

"I would give that to you if I could."

"Why?"

His lips curved upward for a moment. "I have a soft spot for wounded things."

"Especially when they're your father's?"

He laughed grimly. "I suppose it seems that way. I told you, I don't love Vic. I hope she comes home safely and she and my brother find some happiness together." Expelling a breath, he sat straighter. "I have a proposal for you."

Her skin pebbled over, she struggled to hold herself still. *I can't I can't I can't* echoed, but beneath was a whispered *please*. Please what? She could not decipher her own hopes.

"I spoke to Father about this—the choice is entirely yours, but there are political implications to everything I do, and in this matter it was better I obtain his consent. I want to make it clear, you don't need his permission, but I do. Understood?"

"I don't know yet what you're asking," she said.

Her body lifts up and up, feet dangling above the earth, laughter ringing over the crashing surf.

"I'm sorry. This is awkward and will seem sudden, but it's something I've been thinking about since the journey from Olmlablaire to Re, and I thought of little else while I was hauling water for the nomads. You have abilities that could help me, Wineyll. Even with Father's endorsement, even with the nomads' allegiance, my hold on the Seat is tenuous. I could use a partner I trust, particularly one who's a Listener. I'd like you to be my First Councilor."

"That's the Relmlord's spouse."

"Yes."

"You're asking me to marry you?"

"I know, it's sudden. Think of it as a business proposition. I don't expect you to . . . you don't have to do anything you don't want to."

She met his gaze, her pulse fluttering like butterfly wings. "And if I did want to?"

He gulped and pulled away from her. "There's a condition." Many silent heartbeats passed while he stared at his feet. "It's audacious of me to ask, but here it is: you'd have to do the Penance."

A frothing monster slams her onto the hard, gritty surface.

"The Penance." Screams and the foul stink of burning flesh. Sobs and harsh orders. Fury and hatred and the pillaging of one boy's knowledge and memory. Three weeks, she'd mined Mane Thrushwind's thoughts so Vic's company could thread through the Badlands unseen, and at the end of that journey, she'd killed him. A boy her own age, and she'd slit his throat.

"I can't," she whispered.

He stood, his face red. "Of course. I understand. I wish . . . I wish you a good night."

He left, and *please please please* rang like a bell in her mind.

A Touch of Knowing

Hefting a jug of water, Bethniel scanned the rows of wounded and pasted on a bright smile. Kragnashians no longer crossed the moat into camp, but they still tore through supply lines and ravaged perimeter patrols, leaving few empty cots in the hospital. Moving pallet to pallet, she filled troopers' cups and waited until each took a few sips. Some refused, and she knelt beside them, asked about their homes, their families, their faith or lack thereof until they took some water. Few of the soldiers had mindspeech; Listening was easy, and many found it a comfort that she knew their minds without them saying a word. Some had grievous wounds and would be lucky to live beyond the night. That she hid from them.

Jug empty, she returned to the curtained corner where a hand pump dripped into a sink. The handle cold wrought iron, she marveled at the intricate scrollwork and the ease with which it drew water out of the ground.

"Have you anything like it in the East Reach, my lady?"

She started at the oily voice but fixed her lips into a pleasant curve as she turned to Nelchior. "No, sir. In my father's house, the pipes are ceramic and the pumps enameled wood, but many of my people carry their water from wells, in buckets."

He nodded. "So it is in the southern Kiareinoll. Murnoran supplied most of the iron and steel we have. His army includes more smiths than soldiers."

"I believe your alliance is the first Knownearth has ever seen, sir."

357

He inclined his head. "So it is."

His gaze raked her, his lips stretching into a leer as an awkward silence lengthened. Face heating, she took a cup from the shelf and splashed water into it. "Were you thirsty, sir?"

The leer shifted into a malicious grin. "I was, thank you." As he took the cup, his fingers grazed hers. A shock snapped between them. The cup smashed, water spraying boots and hemlines. A jolting heart pumped fire up her neck. Ducking, she picked up the porcelain shards and offered apologies.

"It's only water," Nelchior said, glee edging his voice as he filled a new cup for himself. "We must be more careful next time. Until then, my lady."

The curtain fell into place behind him, and she slumped onto the floor. Her heart thudded, and worry stuffed the space behind her eyes. *He knows.* He'd seen her with Thabean, and now he'd touched her. Thabean had felt her Woern almost instantly, and he hadn't been looking for them. Elesendar, Nelchior knew!

"Ow!" Vic yelped as Prenlin's fingers probed her ankle.

The healer grunted and began wrapping fresh linen around the splint. "It would heal faster if you would stay off it."

"I do." A wave of dizziness swept over her, and she had a sensation of floating, her feet kicking for purchase as dark cold water swirled around her. The sensation had hit her from time to time over the past month. More than mere wooziness, it felt peculiarly specific and, for some reason, reminded her of Wineyll.

"Are you all right?" Prenlin asked, sharp eyes roving over Vic's face.

Vic waved the feeling away. "Fine. Just a spot of dizziness. As for the ankle, I can't lie in bed all day. I have duties."

"Do your duty as you must, madam, but do not stand on this foot." Prenlin pressed a tube to Vic's belly, the other end to her ear. "The babe's heart is strong. How do you feel?"

Her lips curled around a soft chuckle. "Good. Actually, good. My head hasn't hurt in weeks, and I can hardly remember what nausea feels like. The brooding sickness—or Woernsickness, either one—they're gone."

The healer smiled, a rare sight. "I always felt my best in the middle of a brooding term. You'll tire more easily, though, and your appetite will increase. Feed yourself with whatever you wish, but make sure to eat red meat when you can. Horseflesh is best, if you can get it."

"I think I'll have to settle for goat." Whatever horses they had in camp were for hauling, not feeding rogue pregnant wizards.

"Perhaps so. Good day, madam." Prenlin stalled her exit as Bethniel swept inside. "Did you finish your tasks already?"

"Yes—I got permission from one of the other Healers to leave early. We're burying Dealn today."

"Of course. My condolences, my lady. Madam." With a nod, the Healer left.

Vic hopped out of bed and shrugged into the robe Beth had laid out for her. "I suppose it's time to get ready." She blinked at the princess's stained hospital smock. "You're not wearing that, are you?"

Bethniel glanced down. "Oh! Oh, no. No." She ducked behind the privacy screen; water splashed into the basin and dribbled on the floor while Vic threaded her robe's sashes through its slits. "My hair's a mess," the princess said, emerging in one of the formal gowns she kept in Vic's tent.

Vic picked at the silken snarls knotted across her waist. "If you can fix this, I'll take care of your hair."

A smile ghosted over Beth's face as she knelt and tugged the sashes loose. While Vic tucked curls into place, the princess relaced the robe and gnawed pensively on her lip. "This is getting tight— we need to ask the tailors to add a panel."

"What's wrong, Beth?"

Her foster sister laid a palm flat on the finished weave, her eyes glistening. "Do you mind?"

Vic covered her hand. "Of course not . . . wait . . ." She shut her eyes and imagined the baby in her womb, reached out and gave him a gentle nudge. The babe awakened and jabbed a foot at Beth's palm.

"Was that her—or him?"

"Him," Vic said. Warmth flushed over her skin as she imagined Ashel's dark eyes shimmering while he held his son, and she grinned at the Woern-borne certainty that it was a son.

Tears spilled down Beth's cheeks.

"What is *wrong*?"

"I think Nelchior knows about me. He saw me helping Thabean recover. He knows you're the only wizard who didn't take ill when you were all making the moat. And in the hospital just now, he contrived a way to . . . to touch me, and a spark passed between us. I think he felt the Woern."

"Touch you? How?"

"Just a brush of the fingers as I handed him something."

"Why were you talking to him?"

"He spoke to me—just some trivial observation about Murnoran's iron. It's not as if I can ignore him—here, the wizards are the nobility, Vic." Her breath caught round a sob. "And Thabean said . . ." Shivering, she cleared her throat. "When I think about how Woern can pass from someone like me to a wizard, and what Thabean said about how the wizards of old would hold latents captive—Elesendar, I think about what you went through with Lornk Korng and—"

Vic pulled Bethniel around to face her. "Nelchior will *not* harm you. I will kill him before he does."

"He could tell the Council."

"Saelbeneth will keep him under control because she'd have to explain to the others why *she* kept your secret. But if it gets out, we'll leave."

"And go where? What about history—we can't go home unless we can get to the master Device in Meylnara's keep."

"I know, but I will *not* let them harm you." *I hope you protect my sister better than you protected my father.* Ashel had said that, the day after they'd all watched Sashal's life drain from his throat.

> *The crowd roars. She issues orders. The Dagger pelts off the stage into the audience, searching for a faceless assassin. Silk sifts against her skin as she steps toward the prince, but his suffering halts her advance, and she stands paralyzed while Elekia wraps her arms round his head and mother and son weep together, the man who was husband, father, and king held tight between them. Vic's head is stuffed with helpless, hapless awareness that she can do nothing to remedy the pain of this family she has come to love as dearly as her own. Suffused with rage and impotence, she stands apart as Ashel mourns.*

Groaning, Vic sank onto the bed, the heels of her hands pressed into her eyes. Water splattered, and a moment later a damp cloth cooled her forehead. Beth bared her knife.

"No." Vic pushed the blade back into its sheath. "It's not the Woern—just a bad memory. One of my failures."

The lines eased out of Bethniel's forehead. "My sister never fails—that's why she's called Victory."

"I wish that were true. Ashel's fingers, your father, Wineyll, you being stuck here with me . . ."

"None of those were your fault."

"They feel like it." Her throat tightened. "Three hundred and thirty-seven, Beth. The dead at Olmlablaire—those are *all* mine."

Bethniel's arms sprang tight around her. "I love you, sister."

Vic returned the embrace, her face pressed into Beth's curls, her mind reaching across time to Ashel, wishing she could comfort him, relieve him of the worry he must be feeling. She couldn't imagine how she'd bear the impotence of being able to do absolutely nothing to save him, if their places were reversed. The only hope for all of them was for her to kill Meylnara and figure out how to use the Device to return to their own time.

Rest Among the Trees

Traine's east gate had an iron portcullis and steel-plated doors that shone like silver. Wineyll's hand gripped the case strap while panic whipped her heart into an uneven rhythm.

> *I'd like you to be my First Councilor.*
> *Her body is lifted up and up, feet dangling above the earth.*

What does he want from me? she thought as she trod past bored guards and out into the parklands surrounding the city. Nannies pushed prams along graveled paths. Children flew kites on wide lawns. Lovers snuggled in flower-draped arbors.

> *You'd have to do the Penance.*
> *A frothing monster slams her onto the hard, gritty surface.*

Earnk had left nearly three weeks ago, and her mind had buzzed with his proposal ever since. Clutching the flute case, she trekked across a verdant swath toward a clump of trees crowning a knoll.

What do I want from him?

She was sick of asking herself that question and just wanted to be alone. Utterly alone, with no one around to hear her lose herself in music or weeping.

As she came to the wooded slope, voices crushed her hopes for privacy. A smattering of laughter and applause, then a single deep voice—Ashel's—filtered through the trees. So this was where the cerrenils were? She paused, looking around the park for another clump of bushes where she could find privacy.

Ashel began a hymn, and homesickness drew her toward him. She followed a path through dense underbrush, beneath a thick canopy, to a clearing where several dozen people sat on the grass. There were three cerrenils young enough that Wineyll could have encircled the trunks with her arms. As she came among the crowd, Ashel finished singing and began speaking about the comfort of the old mothers.

"I'd give him all the comfort he desired," one woman whispered to another.

Her friend leaned close. Elaborate coifs mingled, bejeweled locks clicking softly. "I met him once."

"When?"

"Years ago. He was the sweetest young tom you could imagine, but when I tried to pet him, he scurried off like a frightened kitten."

Cheeks burning, Wineyll sidled away from the tittering courtesans and stopped beside some soberly dressed Weavers. Ashel's gaze flitted to her as someone asked about the difference between the Kia and the old mothers.

"The mothers are our mothers," Ashel answered, patting the white trunk. "They receive our prayers and pass them to Elesendar. They give us a place of peace and solace when our hearts are troubled. The Kia is the spirit that connects the mothers to all life. And Fembrosh is the will—the mind—that pervades the forests of Latha, particularly those east of the Lathalorns."

"Is it true the trees walk there?"

"The trees themselves don't move so much as Fembrosh reshapes the forest around your perception."

"But don't Lathan forests kill people?" That fear echoed among the Trainers, prompting indignant mutters from the Weavers.

"Fembrosh will protect itself when roused," Ashel replied. "Fire and clearcutting always bring some kind of retribution, but we can live safely within the Kiareinoll so long as we respect it.

Elesendar and the old mothers will guide us—not just Lathans, but everyone—to a mutual understanding rooted in mercy and compassion, if only we'll listen."

The Weavers gave satisfied nods, but a gaunt man stood and spat, "Rubbish." Filthy culottes sagged off a skeletal frame; dirt stained a bald head and calloused hands. "No mercy but in ground."

Ashel scooped up a handful of soil and dropped it at the man's feet. "Mercy is within you, friend; it begins with forgiveness."

"You forgive him did that?"

Holding up his butchered hand, Ashel shared a sardonic smile. "Not yet." Drawing the Buzzard to the tree, he placed the man's palm on the trunk and laid his fingerless hand beside it. "That's why I pray with her."

"What about justice?" a woman cried out. Dirty yellow hair jabbed out of her scalp like wheat stalks after harvest. "We won't get that praying to trees."

"No, we won't." His gaze roved round the onlookers, pausing at a knot of city guards and again at a trio of Citizens. "Justice is the product of power and mercy. Mercy without power begets pity, and power alone births only oppression."

"Or vengeance!"

He nodded. "Or revenge—it depends which side of the gate you're on, doesn't it?"

Suspicion, rancor, and admiration—a cacophony of opposing thoughts assaulted Wineyll's Hearing and jabbed at her temples. The pain eased as Ashel held up the blunted hand again, recapturing the onlookers' attention. "The price of vengeance is high, and the sacrifice usually comes to nothing. I lost these fingers half a year before they were butchered, on the day my father—or the man I knew as my father at the time—died, and I vowed revenge."

The crowd roars. She issues orders. The Dagger pelts off the stage into the audience, searching for a faceless assassin. Silk sifts against her skin as she steps toward the prince, but his suffering

*halts her advance, and she stands paralyzed while Elekia wraps
her arms round his head and mother and son weep together,
the man who was husband, father, and king held tight between
them. Vic's head is stuffed with helpless, hapless awareness that
she can do nothing to remedy the pain of this family she has come
to love as dearly as her own. Suffused with rage and impotence,
she stands apart as Ashel mourns.*

Wineyll slumped against a tree, an odd sensation stuck in her
mind, of Vic reclining on a soft bed in an ornate tent.

She shook off the strange fancy as the crowd climbed to their
feet, some heading directly down the path out of the copse, others
pausing first to rub their palms against the cerrenil's trunk. She
Heard more doubt than conviction, but the Weavers broke into a
hymn as they ambled away. Grinning, Ashel rubbed his ears as he
came over. "We won't ask them to join the choir."

"Choir?"

He chuckled grimly. "I suppose I'm mixing some conversion
into the subversion. Alek has been spreading the word, and the
crowd's been growing little by little. Some actually come for the
sermons."

"I thought people already worshipped Elesendar here."

"They do, in chapels with Loremasters intoning scripture, the
sort of worship Silnauer would make common in Latha, I expect."
He gestured at the case slung over her shoulder. "Did you come
here to pray or to practice?"

Wincing, she stared at her feet and thought of all the people
she'd failed: her father, Mane Thrushwind and his tribe, Ashel, and
Vic too. Her sins jeered at the hope that lingered like a guttering
flame within her. She swiped at welling tears. "Not to pray. I'm
beyond forgiveness."

"Come here." He led her to a cerrenil and pressed her palm
on the trunk. "No one is beyond forgiveness, and Elesendar
knows you deserve compassion. I'm just as lost as you are, just
as surrounded with bitter roots and shadows. I've lost my entire

family—everyone but you, Wineyll. You're my sister, and I don't think any of us will come out of this Concordance unless we cling to our loved ones the way a sailor clings to a mast in a hurricane."

She sank to the turf and drew her knees to her forehead. "What if we don't have any loved ones?"

"I love you." He tapped on the case. "I think he does too."

"Did he tell you that?"

"No, but I can recognize the signs."

"He asked me to be his First Councilor, but he said it was a business proposition and I'd have to do the Penance. If he loved me, he wouldn't ask *that* of me. And then if I did it, became his wife, the joke would be on him. Every time I've used my abilities—in the Badlands, in Olmlablaire—it's been a disaster. People died or"—she grasped his maimed hand—"they lost everything."

Ashel rubbed the knuckles on his stump. Leaves rustled above them. Some creature scratched and skittered through the underbrush. "Earnk has been broken and mended many times over. Most people like that are steeped in cruelty, but it filled him with compassion. I think you need that, Wineyll, more than all the iron in Traine."

"Why would he ask me to do the Penance?"

"Because it's the only way you can be together."

"He could leave Relm."

Ashel chuckled bitterly. "He could, but it's not so easy for a ruler to walk away from that responsibility, especially when there's no clear succession. Think of it this way. Earnk has offered you a chance to leave the darkness behind. The Penance is a very old custom among the nomads, and I believe it's intended to bring the perpetrators redemption as well as the victims solace—it is a path to forgiveness, one a lot clearer than most of us ever get. If you agreed to do it, I expect your term of service wouldn't be too long. That's something Earnk would make sure of. The Relmlord would need his First Councilor sooner rather than later."

Anguish spilled down her cheeks. "I don't deserve a short Penance. Every nomad in that camp died because of me, and I murdered the last one myself." She choked. "I sliced his throat. I'm a murderer. Mane wasn't even the first! I killed my own father—"

He folded her into his arms. "We cannot change what we've done, Wineyll. I wish you hadn't been forced to hurt a single nomad, but it was my sister who ordered that raid and Vic who commanded it. Neither of them would have had to kill anyone if I hadn't let my rage carry me to Olmlablaire in the first place. As for Winder, Silnauer put you both in a terrible position. I remember how sick he was, how much pain he was in, and if he were my father and I had no other way to relieve his suffering, I might have done the same."

Her shoulders heaved, breath wheezing through clogged passages. "He was . . . It was unbearable."

He held her until her sobs stilled. When she finally grew quiet, he touched the case. "May I hear it?"

Sniffling, she pulled the flute out of the leather and fitted the headjoint on the body. Filling her lungs, she blew softly across the mouthpiece. The flute answered with a whispered D. Just a single note, but one that rang pure in tone and pitch.

"I'll never forget your father's last performance," Ashel said, then sang,

Forgiveness is the dream of those who love

"Will you accompany me," he asked, "to honor Winder?"

"You want to sing 'Wizard's Last Embrace'? That song? About Vic and—"

"It's just a song, one I want to sing with you because it was the last thing Winder did, and it was brilliant. Please play it with me, so we can sing him to the trees, here in the shade of these old mothers."

Tears streaming, she took deep breaths to clear her throat. She tongued the first notes, coughed, and tried again. After the first bars, Ashel came in, his voice an octave lower than her father's tenor but just as full of love. High and low, the weaving melodies spun around her like the warm sea on a summer day in Alna. Her back arched; her feet left the ground. Floating above the earth, she released her father. She let go of Mane. Wrapping them in music, her one true joy, she finally laid them to rest among the trees.

The One, the Fulcrum, and the Sacrifice

Lillem entered the tent and stood at attention, his uniform neatly pressed. "The procession is starting, Highness, Marshal."

"Thank you, Sergeant," Vic said, acknowledging the new stripes on Lillem's sleeve. "Shall we go?" Outside, she linked arms with the taller pair and drew them into the air. They swept over tents, flashed through the choking smoke ringing the camp, and joined the line of soldiers and wizards disappearing into the forest. Bethniel glanced back at the moat, where most of the dead from the last battle, human and Kragnashian, had been interred. "We buried so many in fire. I'm glad Thabean is taking Dealn back to the trees."

"There are no cerrenils here," Lillem muttered.

"But there is life. Elesendar will know the intent."

At the head of the procession, a shrouded figure bobbed behind Samovael as he walked to a glade split by a slow-running brook. Thabean and Fainend came next, followed by Saelbeneth, Grunnaire, their stewards, and Thabean's command staff and aides.

Birds called in the canopy, and a gust of wind showered blossoms over the gathering as Thabean stepped forward. "Dealn loved a good fight and fought for a good love more times than I can count."

"That he did," Samovael declared.

"He cherished duty," Thabean continued, "and he died

369

defending this Council. He died defending me. We've buried too many of our defenders in the weeks since the last attack—in the months since this war began in earnest."

Gazes swung to Vic. Shoulders back and chin up, she touched her chest and extended her palm toward the men and women under Dealn's command. The soldiers nodded solemnly, some returning the gesture.

"Dealn was my older brother—my 'big' brother in every sense. He was a hero to me when we were young." An aide handed Thabean a steel-tipped spade. "He remains so now, and though I do not share his faith, I will honor it as best I can." The blade crunched into the soil between the folded roots of a massive geilmor. The steel rang as pebbles rattled onto the grass. Thabean jammed the spade into the earth again, grunting as it struck and again as he heaved the second load aside. He worked with his hands, not the Woern, as the gathering watched. At Sashal's funeral, Bethniel and Elekia had dug his grave with help from Timny, Cimba, and Vic. Family buried family, unless there were none to do it. Then the task fell to those closest to the dead. Vic had dug plenty of graves in the Kiareinoll.

When the trench was knee deep, Thabean laid his brother within. The mourners took turns dropping flowers on the body, but Thabean shoveled earth over the shroud alone. When it was done, Saelbeneth stepped forward. "In the Kiareinoll, we sing our departed back to the trees." Her contralto dipped into an off-key dirge, and everyone joined her after she finished the first verse.

While the others sang, Bethniel's gaze fixed on Thabean. He stared at his brother's grave, his hand locked round the spade handle. The princess leaned toward him, her eyes glimmering in the dappled sunlight. Vic laced her fingers into Bethniel's, pulling her backward and softly clearing her throat. Her foster sister cast her eyes down, and they listened to the song flooding the glade.

Branches cracked a scant warning as Kragnashians erupted from the forest. Shouts and screams followed, and wizards shot upward, retainers in tow. Vic snagged Bethniel and Lillem and half Thabean's troops; he and Samovael scooped up the rest and hurtled back to camp.

On the grass margin lining the moat, Vic tore the robe's hem away. "Get Bethniel to safety, Sergeant," she ordered Lillem. Grabbing a pike, she flew up and churned the lava below, firing it to life as the Kragnashians emerged from the trees. They launched themselves across the molten rock. Wings buzzing, the creatures tumbled into the glowing earth, screaming as they flamed and sank. But more swarmed after, and the carcasses of the dead made a ford.

Alarms sounded, and troopers poured from the aisles between the tents, jammed their pikes into the turf and braced for the onslaught. Grunnaire flew up beside Vic, helped her stir the earth beneath the Kragnashians scrambling over their burning brethren. Gouts of fire and steam exploded, flinging Kragnashians back into the forest and into camp. But the creatures bridged the moat and plowed into the defenders. Vic gripped her pike, wrapped Woern-wrought armor round her belly, reinforced her ankle splints, and dove in among the soldiers, falling into the rhythm of killing. Dive, strike, roll, rise, dive, strike, roll, rise. More troops flooded to the line, and she glimpsed Thabean to her right, Samovael to her left, drenched in green ooze. The moat exploded again, and Kragnashian bodies sailed into the lines, crushing troopers and their fellows. Gritting her teeth, Vic dove under another carapace and rammed her pike upward. Grass-scented goo gushed over her.

She wrenched the pike free and spun, but the Kragnashian ranks ebbed toward the moat. The assault force scuttled across smoldering carcasses and disappeared into the trees, leaving wizards and troopers agape.

Grunnaire alighted next to Vic. The spinning wizard's mouth was sour; the gemstones usually whirring beneath her ears were missing. Nelchior landed, shook out a handkerchief, and wiped sweat and soot from his face. Thabean and Samovael handed their pikes to aides and joined them.

"I did not see Meylnara among them," Nelchior said. "An unfocused attack, without a mind to form it."

Vic kept her lips straight, resisting the urge to return his sneer. "It was odd, and costly, to them." She surveyed the chitinous corpses piled around them. Few human bodies lay among the arthropods. "Meylnara didn't show during the last battle either." Her doubts resurfaced—there were far too many Kragnashians in the area to live in the small enclave of Meylnara's Lair.

"Odd indeed," Saelbeneth said. "Although they breached our defenses, the moat kept their numbers down. Well done, Victoria. Thabean, do you need assistance with the remains?"

He grimaced at the carnage but shook his head. "We'll manage, madam."

Nodding, the Council leader shot into the air, followed by Grunnaire and Nelchior.

Samovael clapped a hand on Thabean's shoulder. "More to mourn, my friend."

"It is war, sir."

"It is. Let's get these beasts off your lawn." The painting wizard heaved a Kragnashian into the moat. Face red, he expelled a heavy breath and hauled up another.

Woern thrumming, Vic pried open a pair of mandibles and extracted a human corpse. Blood drained from the woman's nose and mouth as she laid her aside. She tossed the Kragnashian into the lava. Thabean dropped in a pair of warriors.

Samovael grunted as another fell into the burning earth. "Damn heavy, these things."

Vic laid another trooper beside the first, this one with a crushed skull. "Look at the ratio of their dead to ours."

"The troops have trained hard, learned well," Thabean said.

"That, or the Kragnashians weren't really trying to kill us." She picked up a chitin-clad trio and pitched them away.

"How do you do that so easily?" Samovael marveled.

"Victoria is very strong." Thabean groaned as he lifted another pair and sent them into the moat. "She is like a bull, however. No finesse."

She chuckled. "Samovael, you paint gloriously detailed pictures with the Woern. I cannot write my own name." She paused and looked at the sweat beading their foreheads. "Don't overtax yourselves, sirs. I'll help the pallbearers, if you wish to rest."

Samovael dropped another carcass in the moat. "Come with me, Thabean, and we'll honor your brother the way he'd honor you."

Thabean's mouth tilted. "Not quite—we must stay lucid." He frowned at the human limbs tangled in the chitinous ones. "Victoria, help the men clear the field, but do not do their work for them. You must not overtax yourself either."

The wizards left, and the pallbearers hooked grapplers round Kragnashians' heads and tails and dragged them out of the pile. Yanked free of its deceased fellows, a creature rolled to its feet, snagged a man with its mandibles, and flung him toward the moat. The man screamed; Vic caught him as a pair of soldiers charged the creature and rammed their pikes deep into its thorax.

"Madam!" A soldier sprinted out from the tents. "Your retainer is hurt."

"Lillem?" she asked, and the solider beckoned her to follow. They dashed past the barracks, canvas walls shredded or crushed under fallen Kragnashians. By the third row, there was no sign of the assault, and the tents stood crisp and taut. A tall, dark figure lay prone on the ground. "Sergeant!" Vic shot forward, eyes wild for Bethniel. "Is the princess safe?"

Lillem cupped the back of his head and levered up on an elbow. He blinked woozily. "Where is she?"

"Where is she? I told you to get her to safety!"

Groaning, he climbed to his knees. "Someone hit me."

"Someone, or something?"

He sucked in a deep breath and shook himself. "Some—I'm not sure." He looked around. "We didn't see any Kragnashians."

"Shrinejump! Go to her tent; I'll check mine. Find her!"

Nodding, he staggered into a run. *Elesendar, let her be safe*, she prayed as she sped toward her tent.

"I wish we could share it with him," Samovael said, draining the bottle into Thabean's cup before raising his own. "To Dealn's love of good wine."

Thabean swallowed and chortled softly. "Good wine to Dealn was any that was wet."

"That was the last of my store," Samovael said. "Stocks are low, my friend."

No supplies had arrived from the coast since they'd begun work on the moat. "Meylnara is blockading us."

"No doubt. Saelbeneth asked me to take a thousand troops and clear the path to the coast."

Thabean scowled. "She should send Nelchior with you."

His friend chuckled. "Nelchior's bad company for a mission, and worse after, as he'd claim all credit but no fault. I was hoping you'd come along."

"I can't leave," he blurted, Bethniel's face in his thoughts.

"Why not?"

"Sirs, I beg your pardon," said one of Samovael's guards. Victoria entered on his heels. Her eyes anxious, her hair flew about her face, half of it loosed from its braid. "Madam Victoria wished to speak to Sir Thabean."

"Is there a problem?"

"There is." Her shoulders drew back and she stood at attention, quivering like a taut bowstring.

"Could you excuse us?" he asked Samovael.

The other wizard downed his cup. "I hate to waste good wine."

Thabean chuckled. "So did he. Thank you, my friend."

When they were outside, Victoria grabbed his arm and drew him into the air. Her eyes were like emeralds. "Beth is missing. She isn't anywhere in the camps. Not in her tent or mine, studying with Fainend, or the hospital."

A vortex opened, an emptiness that spun wider and faster, shredding Thabean's insides the way cyclones would churn across the Relman plains.

"I fear—" Victoria choked, shook herself. "Earlier today,

Nelchior contrived to touch her, and she thinks he *knows*."

Molten fury poured into the rifts carved by shock and doubled grief, but he held his features still. "Why do you think it was he who took her?"

"Lillem was escorting her to safety, and someone hit him on the back of the head. He didn't see who took her. I didn't see Nelchior on the field until after the Kragnashians retreated—did you?"

How often had Nelchior followed Bethniel with hungry eyes? "No, I did not. Come."

As they flew, the sky glimmered like a bloodied sword as the sun sank into the canopy. The white stripes on Nelchior's pavilion gleamed just as red. As Thabean landed, he bit his tongue, quivering with the desire to crush the guards, tear the pavilion to shreds, and burn Nelchior down to his skeleton. Yet that was an old hunger, fed by every sneer in open Council and whisper in Saelbeneth's ear, dampened by Thabean's position as Saelbeneth's second. He knew she played him and Nelchior against each other— knew it, understood the reason for it, even admired how she kept them spitting at each other like cats. Because he knew she stoked his fury and resentment, he controlled it, because of her and to spite Nelchior. *And I'll yet control it, until I know Bethniel is safe*, he promised himself. To the guards, he said, "Announce me."

Gulping, one ducked inside. The other trembled as she held her spear across the door. A few moments later, Nelchior's aide appeared and invited them inside.

He'd never been within Nelchior's abode before. Damask draperies served as walls. Intricate tapestries carpeted the floor and covered furnishings of the finest cerrenil and drerwood, polished to a mirrored gloss. Absurd luxuries, while outside the fiend's troops lived in dilapidated barracks. A disproportionate share of the hospital's jungle rot came from Nelchior's camp.

The aide led them into a den where his rival lounged on a chaise, a tumbler of wine in his hand. The commodore rose from a camp chair and bowed; the pirate from Victoria's retinue followed suit.

"Thabean. Victoria," Nelchior said, sipping. "What a pleasant surprise. To what do I owe this honor?"

"Do you know where Lady Bethniel is?"

Nelchior's lips split wide. "Have you lost her?"

"I have not seen her Highness here," Gustave replied ahead of the wizard. Victoria's eyes narrowed, and the seaman returned a gap-toothed smile. "Do you believe she came here for . . . refuge during the battle?"

"Naturally, if she did," Nelchior sneered, "I would send her back to you as soon as safety permitted, Thabean."

"If you harm her, I'll kill you," Victoria said.

Nelchior chuckled. "There is no need for that, madam. Your woman is not in my camp."

"She is my *sister.*" Victoria stepped forward, her eyes hard. "Tell us where she is."

"If only I could! I am truly distressed to learn that someone under my dear Thabean's protection is missing. What can I do to help?"

Cheeks blooming red, Victoria grabbed Nelchior in a vise of power and flipped him upside down. Nelchior bent his fingers, and lightning crackled round her. Face contorted, she roared, and Nelchior sputtered and choked as blue flames enveloped him.

The commodore and Gustave scrambled to Thabean's side. "The princess is truly not here," Gustave cried.

"How do you know?" Thabean barked.

"Because when we arrived, Nelchior was receiving Saelbeneth's aid!" The pirate waved at the dueling wizards. "Can't you stop them? Victoria cannot die here."

Nelchior's lightning flickered around Victoria, but neither her hair nor garments were even singed. He felt a tick of pride that she employed the shields so well. Beneath Nelchior, the carpet smoked, and the room stank of scorched wool. His rival's face was a rictus as he tried to maintain his own shields. Victoria would not lose this duel, but the Council would take her life if she won it. Wielding a vacuum layer like a knife, Thabean sliced through the energy beams stretching between the fighting wizards.

Victoria stumbled, and he hauled her out of the pavilion and into the air above camp. "Madam, what were you doing?"

"Keeping him from harming her! Why did you stop me?"

He took a deep breath and unclenched his teeth. "Did you hear what the pirate said? Nelchior does not have your sister."

She shuddered, her fists balled. "Then where is she?"

They scanned graying tents, dim alleys, pavilions alight with the wizards' globes. The moat circled the camp with a lurid red glow, but roiling flames made grotesque shadow play on the forest. His gaze passed over the Kragnashians' makeshift ford, and her hand grabbed his arm.

"The Kragnashians!"

"Meylnara." The fury he'd held in check bubbled over, and he rocketed toward the Lair.

Shouting his name, Victoria sped past him and pulled up in front, her hand on his chest, a lasso of power preventing forward motion. "Wait! Not Meylnara."

He strained against her hold. "You said, the Kragnashians."

"Shrinejump, don't you see? They attacked this camp without Meylnara leading them, and they *retreated* after they touched Bethniel. They retreated! Then today, they sacrificed hundreds of warriors and killed only a few dozen of your men, and when they retreated again, Bethniel disappeared! I think a rival group of Kragnashians took her."

"Madam, your speculations are ludicrous. Meylnara commands the creatures; we must go to her Lair at once!"

"Why would she take her, when she already had her and let her go?"

"Clearly she changed her mind. Perhaps she needs a reservoir for herself."

"Think! If that were true, she would have kept her the first time. Bethniel told me Meylnara recognized what she was right away." She took a deep breath and loosened her grip. "You just stopped me from doing something stupid. Let me stop you from the same. Let's both stop and think, follow the Kragnashians' *trail*, and see where it leads."

† † †

"Did you find her?" Lillem pounced as Vic alighted outside her tent.

"Get your gear and meet me at the battle site, Sergeant. I think the Kragnashians took her."

He sprinted away and she hobbled inside. Ankle and head throbbed in an alternating drumbeat, and the baby had wedged himself against her bladder. Sighing, Vic sank onto the commode. "So much for staying off the foot," she muttered.

"Madam," Gustave panted from the doorway. "May I come in?"

"Wait outside while I change." She yanked the laces loose and shed the remains of the silk robe, donned a loose tunic and trousers, pulled on a single boot, and collapsed into a chair—she'd rest while she could.

Calling Gustave in, she asked what he was doing with Nelchior.

"The commodore was arguing your case to him."

"Did you run here?" His hair and shirt were plastered to his skin.

He slid a pack off his back and dropped it on the table. "First to my quarters, then here."

"Why? What do you care about the princess?"

Pink flesh poked through the gap in his teeth. "I am still under Etien's orders to assist you, and you will not regret my presence at your side. I speak Kragnashian."

Her stomach growled, hunger mixed with the stirrings of Woern-borne queasiness. "Any food in that pack?"

His hand dove under the flap and tossed a pome to her. "As you please."

Snatching it, she bit into the flesh. Sweet juices ran down her chin. "I suppose you'll be useful. Let's get to the moat."

At the perimeter, the air was hot as a furnace and stinking of tar and burnt hay. Flames climbed up columns of smoke that spun away into the night, slowly consuming the carcasses dumped onto the molten earth. The deceased troopers lay in neat rows, enveloped in canvas and waiting to be interred in the morning.

"More funerals," Thabean said, his boots striking the earth.

"I will find her, so you can stay for them. Gustave is here, and Lillem is coming."

His lips twitched toward a sneer, then sank into a frown. "Madam, as Nelchior said, your sister is under my protection. Also, if you should not return, the Council may withdraw the reprieve you've been given. Finally, if your ankle troubles you, you may need more assistance than can be given by a seaman and a soldier who despise one another."

Lillem strode up, wearing a pack and carrying a pike. "I will do my duty, *sir*, regardless of the company."

Vic peered through the flames at the towering black silhouettes of the trees. A new wave of fear washed over her as she thought of Bethniel in the vast forest, in the dark, alone. "I'll take Lillem over, if you can take Gustave, sir."

They veered around the smoke columns and landed on the opposite side of the ford. Light globes bobbing behind the wizards, torches flaring in the hands of the soldier and seaman, they scattered along the forest edge, hunting for signs. After the battle, the Kragnashians had disappeared here and there along the line of trees, yet no trace lingered. As they moved deeper into the woods, they called to one another:

"There's a riffling of the soil here—slight, but—no, it's snealaern tracks."

"A smear here, could be dew; it tastes . . . doesn't taste like them; it's sap."

"There's a break in the bracken. . . . It's undisturbed on the other side."

Thabean's light globes stopped moving. Vic wound through the undergrowth and found him kneeling, head bowed, a hand pressed into freshly turned earth. Grunting, he straightened. "Any sign of them?"

"None." She nodded at Dealn's grave. "He was an admirable soldier and was always fair and kind to me."

He chuckled. "He liked you; he thought you deserving of a place on the Council."

Her face warmed, and an unexpected tear slipped down her cheek. Swiping it away, she spotted a path diving into the forest. "Shrine."

Thabean's spine sprang erect. "That was not there."

"Perhaps the Kragnashians made it as they retreated," Gustave said as he and Lillem joined them.

Vic walked a few steps down a path swept clear of leaves and roots, clean as any trail made by Fembrosh. "The trees want us to go this way."

"The Kia." Lillem dropped to his knees, his gaze swinging from grave to path.

"A moment, madam!" Thabean backed away. "Do you mean to suggest this forest is enchanted?"

She blinked at him. "Enchanted? Aware, perhaps, like the Kiareinoll."

"Kiareinoll Fembrosh is an abomination!" Thabean looked around wildly, as if seeing the forest for the first time. "We have been in the midst of . . ."

"The Kiareinoll is home to the old mothers, sir," Lillem said. "You sang your brother to the trees today, and the forest is showing its gratitude."

"Dealn was not sacrificed to *trees*!"

Gustave rolled his eyes, and Vic resisted the urge to do the same. "This is not the place or time to debate religion," she said. "Bethniel is missing, and the only lead we have is this path."

Cheeks flushing, Thabean nodded. A knot coiled in her belly, she started down the path, wary of the tension behind her, wondering if her foster sister was better off away from these squabbling men.

The trail turned east, away from Meylnara's keep. Leagues passed as the route climbed steadily; boulder-strewn ravines sapped breath from lungs and strength from thighs and calves. Vic skimmed the ground until the pounding in her head drowned the throbbing in her ankle, then hobbled until the reverse had her using the Woern again. The path was rife with smears of Kragnashian blood, leg segments, filigreed wingscales, the swept look of the forest floor. Whether the forest laid the trail out so plainly to acknowledge Dealn's burial or for other inscrutable reasons, she didn't know or care, so long as it led them to Bethniel.

They rarely spoke, except to confer over signs. Gustave kept her fed with a steady supply of fruit and flatcakes, cheese and jerky. Lillem dashed forward and back to prove he could out-track the Blade. Thabean's face creased into something old. Vic kept her attention on the path, wedging her thoughts into the narrow focus of the Blade on a mission, knowing if she let her mind wander into the morass of emotion and motivation around her, she'd be paralyzed.

It rained. The track descended, broken by tree roots and stones, a staircase for giants, slippery with mud. Resting her Woern and fearful of turning her ankle, Vic often slid forward on her arse, dangled her legs over the edge of a rock, and swung down, clinging to a root or limb. She let Gustave lift her down the very large steps, while Thabean and Lillem pushed ahead, the soldier anxious to outpace the wizard, the wizard eager to show he didn't need the Woern to equal the soldier's endurance.

"Men behave stupidly when a woman waits for them," Gustave said, as the others argued over a fork in the path.

Gnawing on a hunk of cheese, Vic gave the pirate a sidelong glance. "Anyone waiting for you back home?"

His sneer melted. "Yes." His chest rose and fell, and he bowed his head. "Yes."

Sympathy washed over her disdain, and she clasped his shoulder. "I'm sorry."

His teeth glowed softly in the dim light, a faint whistle hissing through the gap. "How fares your ankle, madam?"

Her foot had become a throbbing hunk of lead. Prenlin would give her an earful. "It's still attached. Gentlemen," she said loudly, "I vote for the left fork."

In the last darkness before dawn, the trail abruptly ended at the edge of a cliff. Trembling with exhaustion, Vic eyed a stretch of moss as if it were a featherbed and gobbled down the dried pome Gustave handed her. Eyes sparkling, his lips played round the edge of a smile.

Thabean stared into the black chasm ahead of them, eyes hard. Clouds covered the stars, and they could see nothing, as if another wizard had created a black hole through space and time and bound it here. The trees rustled in the rain.

"Everyone," Vic said, "put out your lights." Her globes and Thabean's popped out; torches flared and sizzled as they were snuffed into damp soil. She walked to the cliff's edge and crouched, waiting for her night vision. Elesendar peeped above the forest behind them, rising between a hood of clouds and the land, the light lasting long enough to reveal a caldera, miles across, with a massive white dome in the center.

"Did you know that was here?" she asked.

"No," Thabean muttered.

"And you," she said to Gustave. "Did you know?"

The pirate chuckled softly, his voice oily in the dark. "The People are not one, madam. They never have been."

"Is there a Device there?"

"I don't know. Possibly."

That prospect quickened her heart. If they could leave . . . but who knew what the consequences would be if she left without killing Meylnara? A few of the fictions preserved in the Logs speculated about time travel and history, whether one could change it, and whenever it was changed, the outcome was always dreadful and full of paradox. The baby shifted; she did not care to risk unraveling the thread of his destiny to escape her own. Gazing at the Kragnashians' keep, Vic acknowledged her fate. Meylnara would die.

"Can we be sure this is where they took her?" Lillem asked.

"We must ask to find the answer," Gustave said.

"Victoria and I will investigate," Thabean said. "If she is there, we will bring her out and kill all who stand in our way."

"No," Vic replied. "Gustave speaks Kragnashian, and Lillem . . . is coming too."

"We can proceed much quicker without them," Thabean insisted. "Two foot soldiers will be a hindrance, not a help, in the battle ahead."

She felt the wizard's eyes on her, though she could not see his face in the dark. "I want to avoid a battle if we can. Lillem, you're with me." An arm around his waist, she rose into the air. "Enough scrambling; let's fly down."

Grumbling that it was almost dawn, Thabean took Gustave. "We could have her by now," the wizard muttered.

They descended into the abyss, the rain tapering off as they settled onto stiff grass at the base of the caldera. Above, lavender diluted the darkness, revealing a grassy plain between them and the dome. Vic peered at the structure, hoping Beth was there, hoping she was safe. "They went to a lot of trouble to get her. They won't have harmed her. The forest brought us here to talk to them, I think."

"You think! You speak of enchantments and miracles—you, an Oreseeker!" Thabean jabbed his finger at Elesendar, peeping out of thinning clouds, its light even brighter in the dawn. "That is a satellite, madam, not a god. It has no more influence over us than this rock." He kicked at a stone.

Air paling, the brush hugging the cliff's edge emerged out of shadows. Vic glanced at Gustave, wondering who he'd left behind in their own time. Thabean wanted to rush ahead and rescue Bethniel, as she'd once rushed to save Ashel. And failed. A wave of sadness surged, and tears streamed to her chin. Thabean stared at her, nostrils flaring with every breath. She would not abandon

Ashel, not again. "It doesn't matter whether that wandering star is god or spacecraft. We were brought here, Thabean. I will get my sister back, but I don't think a wizard's attack is the way to do it."

Still fuming, he paced the edge of the grass. It would be another hour before the sun crossed the cliff behind them, but already the sky blanched toward azure. "There is no way we can cross this expanse unseen. All chance of surprise is lost."

"I know." The grass ahead grew short, like the grass on the steppes and tundra of her homeland. "But I think they were expecting us anyway."

"So let us go forth," Thabean grumbled. Pirate and soldier three paces behind, they trudged across the grass, leaving footprints of crushed stems that slowly bent back toward the coming light. The dome grew larger, resolving into the familiar pattern of yellow-white hexagonal cells Vic remembered from Direiellene of the future. A Kragnashian crawled along the side of the structure, a larva held in its jaws. The party shrank to a crouch, but the creature ignored them and scuttled to a gray patch. Dropping the grub, it tore the gray material away, opening a black hole in the facade. They resumed walking. The Kragnashian finished its demolition, picked up the larva, and squeezed out a thick netting of silk, filling in the hole. The grub had to be Vic's size. Swallowing bile, she tried to convince herself it was no different from wearing leather boots.

Finishing, the Kragnashian disappeared round the other side of the structure, and they arrived at a ditch circling the dome, wide and deep and filled with obsidian-tipped spikes. Vic and Thabean nodded at each other, lifted the others into the air, and flew across.

"The entrance is probably on the other side of the building," Vic said.

They crunched along a gravel path that wound round the dome. The flesh of Vic's calf and foot swelled against the wrappings, the nerves numb and drowned in fluid. Thabean's jaw jutted forward, his eyes pinched, his face frozen into a furious mask. Today he would learn once and for all that the Kragnashians' intelligence matched humanity's, while their technology far outstripped anything humans possessed. For Bethniel's sake, she hoped he took it well.

A fiery orange lit the western rim of the caldera as they found the entrance. A ramp composed of glistening white fibers spilled out of a doorway high up in the dome's side, like a long white tongue lolling out of a gaping maw. Two Kragnashian sentries watched the party approach the incline.

Lillem stepped on it and slipped, nearly falling. "Damn thing's slick as ice."

Vic flew up and hovered above a level platform before the entrance; floating, Thabean joined her. Boots and socks tucked under an arm, Gustave climbed nimbly on bare feet. Lillem copied the pirate but still struggled, clawing the fibers with his hands and spewing curses under his breath.

The sentries' eyes glittered in the dawn. Antennae circled slowly.

Vic bowed to the creatures. "Gustave, ask about Bethniel."

Bowing, the pirate clapped and snapped, not bothering to translate for the rest of them. Thabean muttered about the show of nonsense. One of the sentries responded to Gustave's greeting; the other headed inside the dome.

"They're fetching the princess," Gustave said.

While the pirate and remaining Kragnashian conversed, Vic turned to Thabean. "It's time you acknowledge these are people, not dumb animals. They are very different from us, but they know us for what we are." She touched him, letting a tingle of the Woern pass to him. "And they gave me this, so they could send me here to do what I must. You have accepted that we come from the future—is the agency of these People so much harder to believe?"

His gaze bored into the black passage beyond the doorway. The clouds broke behind the dome, the sky aglow with yellow and a blue nearly white. The air dimmed as the emerging sun cast this side of the dome into a deep shadow.

Vic floated to Gustave's side. "Why did they take her?"

"It evades that question."

"He's made it all up," Thabean spat.

A Kragnashian, half a head taller than the others, wearing a stole woven from leaves and flowers, glided out of the doorway. Behind it, an attendant carried Bethniel. Eyes closed, she lay slack within its grasp. Thabean uttered a gurgling howl, and Vic grabbed him mid-leap. Pike raised, Lillem charged forward; Gustave tackled him, and Vic had to restrain him and the wizard until the pirate could wrest the pike away.

"Sit on him," she barked at Gustave. Holding Thabean still, she flew to Bethniel, found her drenched with slotaen. "She's just asleep." The Kragnashian laid the princess down, and Vic wiped orange goo out of her eyes and away from her nose.

As the salve evaporated, Bethniel's eyes fluttered, and Thabean's struggles eased. "Will you be calm?" Vic asked. He nodded, and she released him. Gustave stood and offered a hand to Lillem, who spat at him and struggled, slipping on the slick surface, to his feet.

Bethniel yelped and sat up, staring about her. "They got you too? All of you?"

With a guffaw, Vic handed her up. "We followed them here. Did they tell you anything?"

The princess shook her head, clawing her hands through her hair and shaking the gel off. "I'll be sticky for days." She sniffed her hands. "Smells good, at least."

"Good for the skin too."

The princess beamed, and for a hint of a moment, they were giggling girls again. But only a moment. Sobering, Beth turned and clapped at the Kragnashians.

Dipping its head, the one with the stole clicked a response. "It welcomes us," Bethniel translated.

"You can understand them now?"

"It's speaking slowly, and the language is more formal, more familiar. It says it is the Center of this Hive, the eldest of this lineage. It has been expecting us to come and wondered why we had not. It brought me here to show you the way."

An invitation, at such cost? A nauseating cold pushed the breath out of Vic's lungs. Hundreds of its people had died.

"A price worth it, Victoria of Ourtown."

Her gaze jerked to Gustave, and she suddenly wanted to shove his pink tongue back down his throat. "What do you know about this?"

"We are approaching a Concordance, in which all choices we make—each of us, any of us—will together determine the path of history. There are many paths. The Archipelago would like to ensure the path we know is the one chosen now."

"You are all here," the Kragnashian clicked again, Bethniel translating. "The One, the Fulcrum, and the Sacrifice. The lineages must come together now and choose the path." The Center loomed over Bethniel, antennae waving over her head, the tips lightly grazing then settling on her face. "You are the Fulcrum about which events will turn. Welcome." Bethniel blinked, her expression rapt as it released her and came toward Vic. Antennae drummed lightly on her forehead. Vic felt the Woern respond, her skin aflame and a fog of pleasure behind her eyes. "You are the One who kills." The pleasure vanished into searing pain. Reeling, she watched the Center move toward Thabean.

The wizard stared, disbelief and horror crinkling his forehead. "Let it touch you," Bethniel urged, her voice thick with rapture. "Let it touch you." Vic blinked at her, the fire of the Center's touch gone but the memory of it sharp. Obviously the contact had had a very different effect on the princess. As the Center approached, Thabean's mouth went flat and he loosened his shoulders and knees, settling himself into a warrior's relaxed spring, but he let the Center's antennae twitch across his eyebrows and cheeks.

"And you are the Sacrifice," Bethniel announced, gasping as the Center continued to click and snap.

Gustave finished the translation. "You will die to protect the mind of the forest."

Thabean stood frozen, the whites showing round his irises as the creature bowed to him.

"Which forest?" Bethniel clapped.

Snapping its wing covers, the Center waved its antennae at the woods surrounding the caldera. "The Mind of Direiellene lives now and will in future. It has been ordained."

"But not in our future," Vic protested. Thabean had died in the War of the Council, but so did all the rainforest around them. She thought back to every encounter with the Kia she had ever had and wondered whether Fembrosh had known this destiny for her. Had it pushed her toward it or away when she had found Lornk's trail? Had it protected her during the war so she could be *here*, and if so, did Fembrosh want her to save Direiellene or destroy it?

"Gustave, this Concordance you mentioned—the forest alive is not the path we know . . ." She faltered as she realized that regardless of the answers to these questions, regardless of the needs or desires of Fembrosh, the Kragnashians, or themselves, their fates were driven but *not* predetermined. A yawning chasm of infinite possibility opened up before her, and her determination that she would see Ashel again and that the world would be the same when she returned dissolved in doubt. She felt the aching cold of the sun's blaze, the searing chafe of bindings as she lay staked out on a beach in a distant and ugly future. A nightmare, but perhaps also a vision of a world ruled by the Kragnashians. Could that dream have been real? Bethniel stared at Thabean, blinking fast, her chest heaving, while the wizard stared back, goggle-eyed. Wondering which future would be determined by the choice she now made, Vic longed to watch, hear, and feel Ashel croon a lullaby to their son. She desired this outcome all the more keenly because of its uncertainty.

"Translate for me," she ordered Gustave. "What is it you want each of us to do? We will hear you, and then we will tell you our price."

"That isn't what she said," Bethniel protested as Gustave clapped. "He left out the price."

"I would advise against that language," Gustave warned, but Bethniel was already clapping and snapping her fingers.

The Center reared back, antennae waving while the sentries rolled forward, clacking angrily. A curious reaction from a people Vic knew as traders, and the vision of them as masters reared in her mind. "What are they saying?"

"They are insulted," Gustave said.

"They are incensed," Beth replied with surprise, then clapped back to them. "You wish us to simply accede?"

"Always with humans it is bargains," Gustave translated. "You will do what must be done."

"And what is the benefit to us?" Vic asked, Bethniel continuing to translate. "What will we gain doing your bidding? The future you say must be is not the future we know; can you guarantee it is one we would want?" She looked askance at Gustave again, trying to remember if he was among the smirking pirates in her dream. She took a chance. "I have seen another future for humanity in which we are your slaves, as you try to command us now."

Keening, the guards rushed at Bethniel. Thabean snatched the princess; Vic grabbed Lillem and Gustave and shot up as a sentry launched a wad of yellow acid. The Center seized the guard and flung it down. With a crunch, the guard deflated into a fresh-smelling lump.

Gustave called for peace, and Bethniel begged them all to stand down. "It doesn't want to fight. It's safe to go back and talk."

Thabean slowly descended, and Vic settled toward the platform. Gustave stepped down as if stepping off a gunwale, but Lillem slipped and fell, muttering more oaths.

"You talk to it, Beth," Vic said. "You're the diplomat."

Bethniel nodded, but her expression was far from soft. "What is it you want each of us to do?" she repeated Vic's first question.

"What you are destined to do."

"You did not bring us here to tell us riddles. We have agreed to nothing. You cannot force us to anything."

"The forest must survive."

"And what will be the cost of that?"

"The Sacrifice is here."

Bethniel's lips compressed, but she kept her eyes on the Center. "In our time, Thabean died, but so did the forest." Thabean's head whipped between them. Vic shrugged an apology. Tears ran down Bethniel's cheeks, but she held her shoulders straight and continued, "What is he to do?"

"He must give his life to the trees."

"I will not!"

"What is my role?" Bethniel asked.

"You are the Fulcrum."

"And what will turn about me?"

"The future."

"But what am I to do?"

"A Fulcrum does nothing but exist."

"There's an epitaph," Bethniel muttered, then resumed clapping. "How is the forest to be saved?"

"In the final battle, you will not destroy it."

"And why would we destroy it?"

"The Child has joined with the Mind. She has tied her essence to it."

Thabean gasped, his mouth twisted in disgust and awe.

"The One," the Center's antennae waved toward Vic, "will kill the forest to kill the Child. She must not. The Child must die, but the Mind must not. The Sacrifice must take its place."

"Meylnara has committed an abomination," Thabean said, his voice rough with horror. "For this—there is no just punishment."

The Center hissed, but Gustave stepped forward, snapping and clapping in a blur of words he did not translate. Vic clasped Bethniel's shoulder, and the princess fell into her embrace. Thabean scowled, his eyes on his boots, perhaps still stunned by the death sentence. Perhaps stunned that they already knew he would die in this war and hadn't told him. Vic gazed between princess and wizard, uncertain what to say. If it were Fembrosh they spoke of, she knew what she would do. But this Mind of the forest wasn't Fembrosh, for all it had led them here today.

Thabean raised Bethniel's fingers to his lips. "I will not be a sacrifice to save an abomination. But for you—"

"No," Bethniel moaned, and he wrapped his arms around her.

The wizard caught Vic's gaze. "The Council is now more justified than ever in its cause, madam. Meylnara . . ." He swallowed. "Long ago, wizards enchanted the Kiareinoll in this manner, and now it lives, and now it kills. We cannot allow Meylnara's act to go unpunished."

"Will the Council want to destroy Direiellene?"

He nodded, and his voice shook with abhorrence. "Saelbeneth reveres the Kia and will not wish to kill it here, but in this matter, she may not hold sway."

Lillem stood, his arms out for balance, but his face set. "Marshal, the Kia is here. It led us to this place. You *cannot* kill it."

"What is my alternative? Thabean, what has Meylnara actually done?"

He thought a moment. "It's difficult to understand—none of us have the skill to replicate this act. But from what the old texts say, I believe she has taken the life of the forest into herself and put herself into the forest. It will be nearly impossible to kill her without killing the trees, unless her life can be transferred from the forest to another."

"And can that be done against her will?"

"Anything can be done, madam, but I would not know how to begin." He turned to Gustave. "So, these creatures want me to be that other?"

"They do," Gustave said. "And they await your answer."

Across the caldera, the rising sun painted the forest in vibrant greens and blues, bright and dream-like. Closing her eyes, Vic recalled endless barren sands that covered this land in her time. Her mind reached out to the forest, Elesendar, the future, anything that would respond. But no guidance came from wood or god, ship or time, and the world shrank around her, one small pregnant woman who wanted nothing more than to put her family back together. "Beth, I want you to translate this." She waited for her sister to step away from Thabean, wipe her eyes, square her shoulders. Vic faced the Center. "Translate exactly what I say: we will help you defeat Meylnara, but you must help us in return."

LOVE'S LOSSES

As Saelbeneth's steward ushered them into her parlor, Bethniel hung back, waiting for the wizards to sit first. Vic plunked into an armchair and thanked the steward for the footrest he slid under her splinted ankle. Thabean hesitated, his eyes darting at Bethniel, then took a seat on the other side of the low table, his lips stretched flat. Heat flared across Bethniel's cheeks, and she wished she could erase the tearful embrace they'd shared in the caldera. The fate the Kragnashians had laid out was too awful to contemplate, but so were the consequences of feelings expressed by the brush of soft lips and the clasp of strong arms. Gaze fixed on her shoes, she sat beside Vic while servants poured wine and left the room.

"I'm afraid that was my last bottle," Saelbeneth said.

"I wasn't very thirsty," Vic said, eying the finger-depth of wine.

"You should be cutting that anyway," Bethniel chided, topping off the glass with water.

"Nelchior will be displeased that I'm sharing any wine with you, Victoria. He told me you tried to murder him two days ago."

"There was a minor incident which ended without permanent harm to Nelchior," Thabean said. "There is no need to dwell on it. I requested this meeting to share news of grave importance."

Bethniel had nothing to add to Vic and Thabean's tale of search and discovery. She remembered little of her abduction, just a looming shadow and a wet, cloying darkness that melted into oblivion. The slotaen had soaked into her nasal passages, wiping away fear before it induced sleep. Yet since waking, she'd felt nothing but terror. Her heart thrummed with it as Thabean told Saelbeneth about Meylnara joining with the forest and how the Kragnashians named him *the Sacrifice*.

"I believe their desire is that I should take the place of this Mind of the forest and become a vessel for Meylnara's essence that is more easily killed," Thabean finished, his voice remarkably calm.

"That will not happen," Vic said.

"But you accept what these creatures said as truth?" Saelbeneth asked. "You accept that they are capable of reason and communicating their desires to you?"

Thabean paled. "I do, madam. They have touched me twice, and both times I felt a vast intelligence which frightens me more than this news of Meylnara or even of my own doom. What we thought were merely beasts enslaved to her will are actually formidable foes in their own right."

"They are formidable, and the Kragnashians from the caldera have offered an invaluable alliance," Vic said. "We just have to figure out how to keep it without killing Thabean. First, I need to understand: what did Meylnara actually do?"

"She made herself nearly invulnerable," Saelbeneth replied. "Once in legend a wizard did this thing with his guard. He slept and ate and drank and fornicated while they all remained slaves to his mind. His enemies sent assassins, but every wound healed while the guards died instead. The wizard's rivals tried various opiates and soporifics to break his hold, but his soldiers remained a life-giving source under his complete control. In the end, his enemies had to kill every last one of his guards to kill him."

"How is that even possible? How could someone connect their essence, their lifeforce, whatever you call it, to another living thing?"

"Maybe it's like Ashel and Geram," Bethniel said.

Vic shot her a glare and a silent hiss about betrayed secrets only Bethniel was likely to Hear, but aloud she asked, "How? Meylnara has bonded with trees and shrubs."

"My brother Ashel and another man became psychically

connected during an ordeal they endured while imprisoned together," Bethniel explained to the others. "They are able to talk to each other over vast distances, and they share memories and feelings now. The Kragnashians called the forest *the Mind*, which I take to mean the Kia is here as well as in Fembrosh. From this story of the wizard and his guards, and what the Kragnashians said about Meylnara, it sounds like she has joined with the forest the way Ashel and Geram joined by accident."

"That is ridiculous. Humans and whatever sapience is in the trees are too distinct to be able to join together through telepathy."

"How do you know, Vic? Maybe mindspeech is exactly the answer. Meylnara has none; she's easy to Listen to. If I can get close enough to her, I might be able to Hear what she's done."

"Close enough? Beth, the only time she leaves her compound is to attack this camp with thousands of Kragnashians."

"When I came through the Device, at first she was friendly because she thought I'd come to help her. I could go back to her, say I'd come round to her side—"

"No!" Vic and Thabean shouted.

"You will not endanger yourself," he said.

"You're no spy." Vic's forehead crinkled over fierce eyebrows. "And the idea that Meylnara bonded with the bloody trees using mindspeech is idiotic. The biological differences are simply too vast."

"We *are* the trees, Vic! Elesendar joined with the old mothers to make—"

"Oh, Beth, not now. Meylnara must be exchanging subatomic energy with the woods somehow."

"Subatomic? Do you know what that means, or are you just spouting words you memorized in the Logs?"

"What I know, Beth, is that religious drivel isn't going to help us kill Meylnara and keep the forest alive so we can go home. Saelbeneth, is there any documentation of that other wizard?"

Blood roared up Bethniel's neck, whipping her fear into fury. She stood. "Madam, if you'll excuse me, I have duties in the hospital."

"Beth, I'm sorry, but—"

"Of course, my lady," Saelbeneth said. "Victoria and I will confer on this matter. Thabean, Samovael left this morning; I want you to go after him and help him restore the supply train. Then proceed to the coast and send a Caleisbahn frigate to retrieve my library. There may be something helpful there."

"Of course, madam."

Bethniel stalked out into a soaking mist, her ears twitching at Thabean's footsteps. His scent furled through the rain droplets, and her wrath shifted from Vic to ugly, vicious fate. Tears brimming, she recalled the warmth of his cheek against hers, the salty musk of his skin, the tingle as his Woern pulled toward her, and she sped her retreat past the rain-soaked tents in Saelbeneth's camp.

"My lady." Thabean caught her elbow. "Please hold a moment."

She kept her eyes down. "What can I do for you, sir?"

His fingers entangled hers. "I . . ." He cleared his throat. "Do not be angry with your sister. Dealn said to me once, each day we have together is too precious to let anger divide us."

The heat drained from her face as her lips flirted with a smile. "Did Dealn say it like that?"

"No. He said . . ." He laughed softly. "His language was coarse and unseemly. Victoria often reminds me of him."

A sigh huffed out. "Except you're the heretic and he was the faithful." She swiped at wet cheeks. "I believe if anyone can thread fate's needle and do what the Kragnashians want without sacrificing the forest or you, it's my sister. But I have also seen her collapse into herself and leave others in jeopardy because she tries to do everything alone. I don't blame her for failing, only for failing to take help when it's offered."

"That is not uncommon among wizards, my lady. We hold ourselves above others, and it makes us reluctant to rely on them."

"Except she was like that before she became a wizard."

"That is also not uncommon among us." His mouth curved into a grief-knitted smile. "I must go. Do not do anything rash;

your sister needs you more than she needs whatever information you might glean from Meylnara. Farewell."

She nodded and wished him a safe journey, her heart thudding with each step he took away from her. Though the mist was hot and cloying, her skin pebbled over with cold.

Rain drummed on canvas, a low thunder beneath the animal calls echoing through the canopy. Thabean clucked his mare forward while foot soldiers streamed past, searching the long line of wagons for survivors. The mare snorted, hooves dancing away from empty hitches. Traces were snapped, and bits of gore clung to harnesses, but the tarps covering each wagon were laced tight and secure. Mostly secure—a soldier poked at a loose corner, and a flurry of nightwings flapped into the understory, grain spilling in their wake.

"They took every last carter and horse," Samovael grumbled.

"The gruel will be thin by the time we get this load to camp." Thabean turned to an aide. "Send a party to inform the Council we've found the supplies and ask them to send draft animals. Samovael and I—"

His horse screamed; Samovael's shied backward into the circle of aides and officers.

Meylnara, astride a minion, emerged from the forest. "Give me the One and leave, or stay and starve."

Chewing her bit, eyes rolling, Thabean's mare spun. He flew out of the saddle and set a charge sizzling around Meylnara. Samovael launched a pike at her mount. The beast twisted aside, and the rogue wizard returned fire. Thabean dodged a glowing beam, wrenched a boulder out of the earth and flung it at the minion. The monster crumpled, but a dozen more swept out of the trees and Meylnara disappeared inside a writhing chitinous ball.

Soldiers fell upon the mass, jabbing pikes into clefts between mandibles and wing covers. Shafts snapped. Shrieking troopers were yanked into the knot; their mangled corpses spit out. The rolling congregation smashed into a cart. Thabean hurled spears, Samovael rocks. A fireball exploded against Thabean's shield; embers rained.

Fire, he thought and threw his waveform at a nearby tree, inciting its atoms to vibrate so violently it burst into flame. Meylnara shrieked, and lightning struck him, demolishing his shield and frying his nerves. He crashed into the underbrush, reeling. Samovael ripped open a tarp and hurled a load of obsidian at the Kragnashians. Keening, they broke apart, but Meylnara dodged the painting wizard's fireball and smacked him to the earth with a blue claw.

Shaking his head clear, Thabean marshaled his Woern and created a vacuum around the rogue. Her mouth stretched, the scream silent, but her creatures enveloped her and cut off his attack. One loomed over him and snapped its mandibles round his neck. Razor edges pierced sinews, and it took all his power to keep the pinchers from snapping together.

The creature was yanked back, and a Kragnashian smashed it to the ground as more of the creatures flooded over the ball surrounding Meylnara. The newcomer bent its head to Thabean, and he swallowed revulsion as antennae tapped his forehead. Gratitude and pride flooded him. He'd felt the same sensation from the creature that had killed Dealn and again from the Caldera tribe's leader. The first time, the feelings had frightened and baffled him. Now he understood what they wanted, and fury drove him to his feet. "I will not die for you!"

Screaming, Meylnara flew out of the shredded remains of her guard and hurtled away through the canopy. Samovael shot after her, and the Caldera tribe melted back into the woods.

"Should we follow them, sir?" a captain asked.

Blood wept from a gash on the man's shoulder; more troopers sprawled on the track or leaned, panting, on pikes. "No. We'll tend our wounded and bury our dead. Send that message back to camp, and tell them to hurry."

† † †

Fire crackling between them, Samovael rubbed the back of his neck. "Shrine, but I could do with a good fuck." On the canvas at his feet, black lines swirled into two figures fornicating.

Thabean's ale wet a smile. "Dealn always said that after a fight."

"Dealn always did that after a fight. Fuck, but I miss fucking. I miss saying 'fuck.' The Council is too bloody formal."

Thabean shrugged. "Most of us were trained as barristers and bureaucrats; you and Victoria are the only soldiers."

"You're warrior enough, my friend. And Victoria isn't on the Council, however fine we treat her. Why do we treat her so well? I like her, but she's an outlaw worse than Meylnara, with that whelp growing in her."

"Saelbeneth thinks she's the only one of us able to kill Meylnara. Some nonsense the Caleisbahnin have fed her."

"I gave it a good shot today; I'm sorry I lost her."

A log cracked, and embers settled as smoke swirled and drifted toward the stars. Samovael topped off Thabean's mug, then refilled his own. "What happened today?" His canvas displayed the Kragnashian tapping Thabean's forehead.

Thabean flicked a stone into the fire. "We were wrong about them; they are not dumb brutes, and they do not all belong to Meylnara. The attack after Dealn's funeral was a distraction so the creatures could kidnap Lady Bethniel. Victoria and I followed them to another lair where they released Bethniel and named themselves our allies." He waved at the supply train. "Today they demonstrated their allegiance. You and I would be dead but for them."

"And what price did they demand? I heard what you said."

A shudder seized his spine as he recalled the Kragnashian's appalling gratitude. When they had called him *the Sacrifice*, Bethniel's tears had rent his heart more than the news of his death.

Her face appeared on the canvas.

"Are you a Listener, sir?"

"I'm not, but I can see that you pine for this woman. I figured it's why you joined this mission."

Thabean scowled. "Saelbeneth ordered me here, but a separation is for the best."

Samovael swigged his ale. "What did the beasts want in return?"

He expelled a long breath. "My life." He told Samovael about Meylnara, the forest, and the Kragnashians' desire he take the trees' place.

"Elesendar, man! Why would you agree?"

He nodded at Bethniel's portrait. "So they would let her go. We must find a way to move Meylnara's lifeforce into another vessel so she can be killed."

"We can simply kill the trees!"

"Saelbeneth will not countenance that. She worships the Kia."

"And what about your lady love? Does she want you to step onto the pyre?"

He laughed bitterly. "No, she does not." She was his lady love, and he would die for her, but only to make her safe.

GAMBITS REVEALED

The air passed like a fevered breath through open doors and windows. By the calendar, autumn had begun, but sweat-darkened clothing and rank odors stuffed the crowded throne room. Geram used Drak's sight to watch as Senators, Ministers, and Guildleaders waved fans and flared nostrils.

For the Commissar's visit, the throne had been moved against the wall so the Device was in front rather than behind it and Parnden would materialize with Elekia facing him. Her fingers tapped the armrest of her throne. Timny stood to her right, damp curls plastering his forehead. Geram stood on her left. In Drak's vision, he maintained a stern composure, but as her scent entered and left his lungs, his hands ached for the weight of her braids and silk of her skin. He had not touched her since the night she met with the Center.

"Majesty," Silnauer bowed. "While we await the Commissar's arrival, I would like to address an ecclesiastical matter. Are you aware Prince Ashel has been delivering unsanctioned sermons in Betheljin?"

Elekia's gaze bored into the Harmony, and sweat dribbled down the sides of Silnauer's face. "That person has forsaken this nation and no longer holds the title *prince*. What he does outside this realm is not Our concern," Elekia said.

"He was never granted his Loremasters, Majesty, and his preachings are outside the canon."

"Then be glad he is far from here and unlikely to infect your flock with heresies."

"All humanity is my flock, Majesty. And did he not arrange this meeting? I think his actions are still relevant to Latha."

"This reception and my meeting with the Commissar have been arranged over many weeks of diplomatic negotiations, Harmony. Nearly our entire diplomatic corps, the Commissar's, and the Relman Council were involved in the arrangements."

Geram bit the inside of his cheek in anticipation of seeing Earnk. Ashel may have forgiven the new Relmlord, but his own hatred still burned hot and fierce.

Elekia's eyebrow arched as the air shimmered above the Device. "It seems our distinguished guests arrive at last."

Senators, Ministers, and Guildleaders mopped foreheads and brushed garments as two figures percolated into the room, coalescing into shapes three times a man's height. Shouts careened, and courtiers scrambled backward as a Kragnashian warrior spun toward the throne. Geram yanked Elekia up and shoved her away from the clacking mandibles, putting himself between her and Timny as the pair scurried from the dais.

"Get Ruler and Heir to safety," Olivet shouted.

"No, take Timnon and Cimba," Elekia ordered. Her arm twined through Geram's. "Lieutenant, stay with me and use my sight."

Steel-tipped spears lowered, Drak rushed forward with a dozen guards as a second pair of Kragnashian warriors appeared on the dais. Courtiers jammed the exterior door, some clambering out the open windows. Gaston hustled the royal cousins into the Manor. The inner doors slammed shut and the interior bar banged into place.

A stole-draped Kragnashian and another warrior flowed out of the depression surrounding the Device.

"What is the meaning of this?" Elekia clapped.

The stoled Kragnashian's antennae twitched, its chitinous features implacable. It was not the Center she had met in the eastern Kiareinoll. "The People assume control of this Device and all others in your world, as was ordained by the Treaty of the First."

"Protect the Ruler." Olivet thrust a pike into Geram's grasp.

They edged back as another pair of Kragnashians appeared, followed by Parnden wearing a vicious grin.

"Elekia, my dear, who'd have thought when we were students together that there'd come a day we would face each other as sovereigns?"

"Parnden, this is an inexcusable breach of protocol. Who are these Kragnashians, and where is the Relmlord?"

"Alas, your nephew has his own troubles to manage right now. I merely wanted to stop by—just for a moment—and express my joy at how often we'll see one another, now that Ashel has claimed his Betheljin birthright. I've already promised your son, and I'm formally advising you, that I will deliver Lornk Korng back into your hands, so you can put him under the Shrine, or whatever you like. I also wanted to personally inform you that I've made alliance with these good People. Goodbye, my dear."

Parnden stepped into the bowl and disappeared.

Trilling, Kragnashians charged, knocking aside the guards. Elekia dashed toward the exterior doors, Geram close behind and using her sight. A Kragnashian flowed across their path, mandibles snapping.

"Run!" Geram rammed his pike toward the chittering creature. The pike shuddered as the steel blade crunched into the thorax, the sound like a bug crushed underfoot. An acrid tang sliced the blooming spring scent, and Geram ducked. Something hissed past his ear. A splatter heralded a mortal scream behind him.

All that mattered was getting Elekia to safety. His feet wove through sound and scent, his vision swinging from one to another guard's like handlebars in the training yard. His pike jabbed and whirled, batting, slicing, plunging through armor and flesh, surrounded by thumps and grunts, clicks and burrs and shrieks.

"She's away!" Olivet cried. "Retreat. Geram, in front of you."

Geram ducked a whooshing mandible, leapt upon a sweeping tail and scrambled past slicing wing covers, climbed up the thorax and plunged his pike into a chitinous head. The creature collapsed, and he rolled across the floor toward the heat and shouts wafting through the garden doors.

"To the stables!"

Scrambling to his feet, Geram chased the gravel crunch of fleeing boots.

The last note of his hymn faded away, and Ashel settled cross-legged next to the cerrenil. Wineyll reclined on the grass, her fingers absently fingering the keys of her flute. Scanning the crowd, he sent another prayer to Elesendar for guidance. In the months since Demsch had confronted him at the theater, Citizens stopped him on street corners or cornered him at parties, expressing their outrage or sympathy, depending on whether they thought he was Parnden's ally or victim. Ashel kept his answers carefully neutral during these encounters, but here, next to the old mother, every word was heavy with multiple meanings.

And all for a man I despise.

He looked at the dirty faces and stained clothing of the Buzzards, who had claimed the places nearest him. The young prostitute who had shown him to Emily's was in the second row, lank hair hanging over closed eyes. Michael, Mary, and Fred came nearly every day, and so did Samson, though the inventor always sat apart from the other Oreseekers. They professed to be heretics, but the loss lining Samson's forehead mirrored Ashel's. *They're not here for scripture*, Ashel reminded himself, but rather for the coded messages embedded in his sermons. As the miners slowly infiltrated the city, as Ashel identified Citizens who would support Lornk against Parnden, they passed information back and forth, disguised as questions and answers about the Kia. He'd never worked so hard on his lectures.

"Welcome, friends," Ashel said. Eyes opened, and people folded legs into other postures. The Citizens, guildmasters, and merchants sitting behind the Buzzards brushed dirt from their tailored silks.

Ashel placed his palm on the cerrenil. "Soon the old mothers will shed their summer tresses. I'd like to talk about autumn and what it means as a transition between growth and quiescence."

"Soldiers!" someone shouted from the back. The crowd stirred at the edge of the copse, and a young Buzzard pushed her way through the crowd. "The Commissar's guards just came out the east gate and are headed this way."

People sprang to their feet, the wealthier ranks bubbling with questions. Ashel stood. "You'd all better go before they arrive."

The Buzzards streamed into the trees, and others rushed after them. Ellen and Alek forded the outrush. "Would you like to join us for morning tea?" Alek asked. "Our house has a private entrance to the parklands; if we're lucky, we can make it there before the guards."

Hurrying out of the copse, they paused at the edge of the greensward. The congregants had scattered, some strolling slowly as if their only purpose were to take the air, others dashing from bush to fountain as they fled. "The gate is just past that grove," Alek said, setting a steady pace across the grass.

"Why would they arrest you? Parnden already occupies your house," Wineyll whispered in mindspeech.

"I don't know."

In Narath, two Kragnashians appeared. Ashel stumbled as Geram hustled his mother off the dais.

Here in the park, the soldiers turned toward them.

"We'll make it," said Ellen. "It's just the other side of that rise."

Ashel stopped. "They've seen us. The Commissar is already suspicious of you, Alek, and there's no justice for Oreseekers, Ellen. You go on. I'll talk to Parnden's troops."

"As you wish," Alek said, and the couple hurried away.

"Your nephew has his own troubles to manage right now," Parnden said in Narath.

"What's happening in Latha?" Wineyll asked.

"Parnden just arrived with a force of Kragnashians. Earnk was supposed to be with him but isn't."

Her hand clapped over a cry.

"The People assume control of this Device and all others in your world."

Feeling Geram's blood surge with energy, Ashel fought quivering limbs as he made out Demsch leading the Commissar's soldiers.

He pasted on a smile as they drew close. "Major, always a pleasure."

"Come with us, Citizen."

"Where?"

"We've had word your father's rabble has been meeting near here. You'll be safer in your palazzo."

At the stables, Elekia ordered Geram to ride with her, while guards and servants streamed out of the paddock, two to a horse. Taking her hand, he swung up and wrapped an arm round her waist, suppressing a shiver of desire. Haunches bunched and sprang beneath his thighs, and the wind rushed over his face. Through Elekia's sight, he saw Kragnashians swarming the grounds and had to bite his tongue as the memory of blazing, crushing agony shuddered through him.

"They don't seem interested in following," Elekia said, squeezing his hand. "I think they wanted only to evict us, not kill us."

He nodded against her shoulder, breathing fast to master his terror and giving thanks it hadn't gripped his heart until they were away from the Manor.

In Traine, Demsch escorted Ashel back to the Korng palazzo. *Do you think Earnk betrayed you?* Geram asked.

No. Is it possible Fensin could have a scheme going with Parnden?

Shrine, I don't know. Another shudder rattled his spine, and Elekia cast a sympathetic look over her shoulder.

This could be the beginning of the Concordance, Ashel said. Walking amid Demsch's soldiers, the prince struggled to quell his ire at Geram's arms cinched around Elekia's waist. Ashel's irritation grew as Geram's anxiety ebbed into an unbidden joy that he had an excuse to hold her. The horse trotted down a narrow, switchbacking trail that ended at a back road to Narath. Once on the hard-packed gravel, Elekia kicked the horse to a gallop. Emerging from the forest, the animal barreled into a crowd bottlenecked at the city gate. Elekia hauled on the reins; the stallion reared, and Geram slid off its hindquarters. Elekia caught him in a net of power and resettled him behind her while she calmed the stallion.

It wasn't just the horses that needed calming. Fear choked the air. Narath had not been under siege for over two hundred years, and although the war with Relm had prepared them—the townspeople drilled, the oil stores maintained, the walls and gates reinforced—too many of those pressing through the gatehouse remembered how easily a single Kragnashian had breached the prison defenses and killed all the guards.

Elekia reached down, clasped hands and shoulders, and urged courage. People called out to her, and she paused. Head high, shoulders straight, she spoke aloud: "Latha has stood whole as a nation for four hundred years. Our enemies will not prevail because we are a united people, as sharp as crystal and solid as stone, and we will win back what is ours."

"The Ruler must reach the Senate," Olivet shouted. "Make way!"

The crowd folded back, and cries of "Make way for the Ruler! Make way for Queen Elekia!" heralded their surge past shops and houses, inns and Guildhouses. They reached the Senate just as Demsch led Ashel through the gate of the Korng palazzo. Dismounting, Geram used Elekia's sight to climb the Senate steps, then down to the siege chamber in the building's cellar.

Elekia paced while other officials filtered in, some with wide, terrified eyes; others whining or wailing; some stoic and silent as their Ruler. Soon Ministers, Senators, and Guildleaders sat round a heavy table shouting at each other while Elekia scowled. Timny sat beside her, staring at clasped hands. Cimba and Selcher huddled in a corner, arms round each other. Geram watched the other Listener through Drak's eyes. When she glanced up at him, they shared a nod of understanding.

"What does my housemarshal recommend?" Elekia finally cut off the arguments.

"Remove to Erin, immediately," said Olivet. "There is no Device there."

"That we know of!" Silnauer protested. "They could be swarming all over the Weavers by now."

The Senator from Erin pulled back his shoulders. "We know our own valley, Harmony, and there is no Device there. I agree—we move the capital there."

"Moving the capital is a wise plan," Fensin said, entering with Breon and another Caleisbahnin.

"Where have you been, sir?" Prime Minister Velbaor asked.

"Conferring with our allies." Fensin waved at Breon, who gave a shallow bow.

"The Archipelago is no ally of Latha," Velbaor said. "You are not welcome here, Ambassador."

"How can you say that when the Caleisbahnin supplied the Manor with steel?" Fensin replied. "Your Majesty, I'm so distressed to hear of the danger you faced today and how quickly your troops were overwhelmed despite the help of our friends."

Geram's ire swirled like sparks in the wind, igniting his fears and frustrations into a roaring fury. He lunged at Fensin, slammed him into the wall, his forearm pressed to his throat. "Did you know?"

"Know what?" Fensin choked.

"Did you know Parnden was in league with the Kragnashians, that they would invade today? Why weren't you at the reception?"

Fensin's breath, hot and sour, puffed feebly against Geram's chin. People shouted; hands grabbed his arms, but he leaned into the Senator. "Did you know?"

"Step back, Lieutenant," Elekia said sharply. Something solid wedged under his forearm and pushed him off Fensin's throat.

"Come on, cousin." Drak pulled him away.

Fensin coughed. "I assure you I had nothing to do with this incursion."

"It would not be the first time you conspired with our enemies," Elekia said.

"I have never taken any actions that were not in the interest of this nation, Your Majesty. I would ask if you could say the same."

Panting, Geram took Drak's sight again. Elekia glowered as Fensin coughed and mopped his face and neck.

"Everything I have ever done has been for Latha," she said.

"If that's true, you should speak with the ambassador. He has a proposal for you."

Elekia arched an eyebrow, her face otherwise impassive, but Geram Heard sorrow welling beneath the mask. "The Kragnashians claimed control over the Device and Latha based on a treaty with the First. What do you know of this, Ambassador?"

"I suggest we speak in private, Your Majesty."

She cast an eye round the room. "Very well. Velbaor, Fensin, attend me. Olivet, bring Lieutenant Geram as well."

They filed into a nearby chamber, where Elekia rounded on the Caleisbahnin. "What about this treaty, Ambassador? Answer me or I will send you to the Shrine—you and all your embassy."

"I know of no new agreements between the Archipelago and Kragnash, Majesty. Whatever they may be, however, I am here with an offer of help against this invasion if you answer a question for me."

"Captain, we cannot defy a treaty with the First," the ambassador's aide whispered in mindspeech, too quietly for anyone but Geram to Hear.

"I must know," Breon replied.

The pact, Ashel said as Demsch's guards and a Kragnashian positioned themselves in front of the palazzo gate. *They all swore fealty to Vic, just because she's a wizard.*

"Must know what?" Geram asked.

The aide's gaze flashed to him, but Breon turned to Velbaor.

"Sir, as Prime Minister, if it were to be revealed that the Ruler has broken one of your nation's laws, what would you do about it?"

"You dare come here with threats?" Velbaor said. "The Ruler will not hesitate to have you tried and executed for espionage."

"It is a question. If you do not know the answer, I suggest you leave the room."

Elekia glanced between the minister and the Caleisbahnin, her eyes falling last on Fensin. Shutting them, she expelled a long breath and sat at a desk. Dipping a quill into ink, she began to write. Geram took her sight, and his skin prickled with crippling cold as he watched the words stretch across the page. *Abdicate. Ruler-designate. Regent.* In Traine, Ashel breathed an oath.

Dripping hot wax onto the paper, Elekia pressed it with her seal. "Senator, you will get what you want, so long as you agree to these terms." She motioned Fensin and Velbaor forward.

Scanning the text, Fensin coughed into his handkerchief, and choked laughter emerged from the cloth. "You sent him to me, didn't you? Well played, Your Majesty." The Opposition stood straight. "As long as our young friend agrees to my guidance, I will not object."

"I object!" said Velbaor. "Majesty, with all due respect, your . . . forgive me, but your, your paramour is hardly fit as a regent. We need your leadership, not his or anyone else's!"

"I can serve Latha best in another capacity," Elekia said. "The Opposition is right, for once; this nation cannot afford a succession battle right now. Please call the Senate to order." The paper crinkled as Velbaor took it, and the door clicked shut behind the Prime Minister and the Opposition.

Elekia's gaze arrowed to Geram. He saw himself in an aura of golden light, standing like a hero with bright eyes. He cast her vision aside, feeling bent and crippled. Blind. She came toward him. Her perfume filled his lungs, stopping his heart. Ashel muttered his name over and over, and Geram's awareness of the other man faded, leaving his darkness total.

He reached for her. His hand clasped only air.

"I dare not," she whispered.

"Olivet knows; the Caleisbahnin don't care."

"If I held you now, I'd call them back and rip that paper up, all for a little more time with you."

"Why?" The question clawed out of all the questions, pleas, threats, and wishes crowding his thoughts.

She sniffed softly, and he imagined she wiped her eyes with her handkerchief, putting herself together for the pirates, for the world. "You will do well, my love."

He couldn't get a full breath. "I . . . I'm not suited, not trained. I don't know anything—I'm *blind*!"

Her fingers caressed his cheeks. "You are clever and wise and passionate about this nation, and you can Hear, Geram. I sent you to Fensin not just to spy on him but to learn from him and gain his admiration and respect, in anticipation of this day. I've known it might come to this since the moment my daughters disappeared and my son forsook me. But you have sense and sensibility, wit and insight. You will do well."

"I don't want this!" He wrapped his arms around her and pulled her close. Her scent was acidic yet sweet, like the late summer smell of ripening cerrenil fruit.

"Let me go," she whispered.

"I—" he stammered, "I can't." His mouth found hers, his tongue tasting the fresh, wet salt of her tears. Her lips parted for him, but her fists remained at her sides and her trembling grew more violent the longer he held her.

"You must stop." The whisper bathed his cheek in warmth, but her next words were cold and imperious. "Go and join the Senate."

He stumbled to the door, bumping into chairs and fumbling for the doorknob.

"She's going, then?" Selcher asked as soon as the door shut behind him. A pair of troopers stood at attention by the stairs, but they were otherwise alone in the hallway.

"She is," he mumbled around the thick knot of sorrow clogging his throat.

Selcher's hand curled around his wrist, and she spoke in a Listener's whisper. "She was broken a long time ago and has held herself together with nothing but rage and ambition. Don't hate her."

He blinked, a habit of confusion from sighted times. "Hate her? I love her!"

Selcher pinched his ear. "That was for Prince Ashel, dundlehead. *You* should have known better, Lieutenant, and stayed clear of her. How cruel and selfish are you?"

Geram shrugged out of her grip. "Will you go with her?"

"I will. What will you do?"

"Sir." A trooper clomped to the bottom of the stairs. "Velbaor asked me to bring you to the chamber."

"My duty." He stumbled to the staircase and felt for the balustrade, unwilling to use another's vision for this journey. "See that Elekia gets safely out of the city," he ordered the guards.

Did they wonder at his use of her name instead of title? The trooper said nothing as he led the way up two flights to the Senate chamber. Could they know what had just happened? His limbs like hardened clay, he gasped on the landing between flights—an old, wizened man. Kragnashians were in the Manor, in Traine, likely in Relm and Eldanion; the greatest threat to human history was upon them. He shrugged off the fatigue, shaking his head, and walked up the next flight without help.

Cries of fear and uncertainty spilled from the Senate chamber into the hallway, but when the door swung open and he stood on the threshold, the room fell silent. There was a creak of wood, then the squeak and thunder of dozens of chairs pushed back as people stood. The gavel struck three times, then three times more.

"Under the emergency powers of the Prime Minister, I declare a quorum in effect. Those assembled here represent the entirety of Latha." In fact, fewer than a third of the two hundred Senators were present, far less than the half needed for a quorum. But the Constitution dictated that as long as all Senators who were in town assembled, catastrophes could be legally addressed. One of the many bits of law Geram had learned since he'd become Fensin's unwitting pupil. "The Ruler of Latha has abdicated," Velbaor continued. "A candidate for regent has entered. What qualifications do you bring?"

Geram let the trooper lead him forward so they could not mistake his blindness. The darkness beyond his eyes yawned like the gulf inside. She was gone.

She's done what's right, what she must. Ashel's relief and pride washed over him. Geram set his jaw—he wasn't proud; he was devastated.

Knees weak, he expelled a breath and faced the direction of Velbaor's voice. "I bring the education of a tradesman and the honor of a soldier. I bring the wisdom of a Counselor and the discernment of a Listener. I bring the knowledge of an attaché to Elekia, the last Ruler of Latha."

"Do any object?" Velbaor intoned.

"I do!" Fensin's voice rang out. "Are we mad? Latha is under attack, and we're making this blind kitten regent?"

Startled, Geram took Velbaor's vision as the Prime Minister choked a surprised response: "I thought the Opposition would be pleased the queen chose an Alnan to steer the Republic."

"He attacked me not half an hour ago!" Fensin had the audacity to wink. "You asked him his qualifications, and he's offered nothing of substance beyond his intimate acquaintance with the queen."

Gasps echoed, and Geram's blood boiled. "I may be young and blind, Senator, but I assure you I am the fittest Alnan in this room."

"And I'm too old to get riled at insults, young man. However, I am willing to forgive your outburst and acknowledge it was motivated by patriotic passion." The Opposition steepled his fingertips at his chin. "So long as our young friend is willing to be guided by the senior members of this body, I accede."

Velbaor cleared his throat. "Geram of Alna, do you agree that Timnon of Narath should serve as Ruler-designate, and that you should serve as regent only until such time as the Senate deems him mature enough for the throne or selects another to rule instead?"

"I do."

"Do the assembled concur that Geram of Alna should be regent of Latha?"

The vote was unanimous, and Velbaor struck his gavel three times. "Your first proclamation, Eminence?"

His mind reeled, but one thought rose out of the vortex. "We are at war. The Senate should move to Erin, but the bulk of Lathan forces will stay here. Alert the outposts. We must retake the Manor."

As the door closed behind Geram, Elekia buried grief and remorse with rage. Kragnashians had invaded, and now she must reveal herself as an outlaw, little more than a year after her reign began. Lornk had been right—she hated that more than anything else.

"Olivet," she said, "you've always been loyal to the throne. You also must make a choice, now."

Her housemarshal leaned against the door, blocking entry or exit. "I have, madam."

The ambassador's gaze snapped to Elekia. She half-smiled, remembering that Olivet had been educated at the Academy. He would know how to address a wizard.

"What do you want?" she asked the pirates.

"We have a sacred pact. If you show your nature, our lives are yours."

"Is this true of your entire embassy?"

"Yes."

Eyes shut, she crushed wishes and regrets. Decades of hiding in plain sight would now end. Summoning the Woern, she yanked the feathers off their scabbards. Seabird plumage sailed twenty feet into her hand.

Breon dropped to a knee, head down. "Madam, in honor of what was, I pledge my life to yours. My sails and my sword are at your service." The aide knelt and repeated the pledge.

"Breon, meet me outside the city's east gate with your men," she said. "Olivet, we must reach the Academy before word of my abdication. There are some books there that I'll need."

Blood Brothers

"What shall we do, my lord?" Elsa asked. Housemaids and scullions wept together in a knot behind her. The grooms and gardener held back their tears but looked just as fearful. Wineyll clutched her flute case, murmuring a prayer while Kelmair paced, glowering at the Commissar's guards who stood shoulder to shoulder, penning them into a corner of the courtyard.

"For now, whatever they want," Ashel replied. Maids, scullions, and grooms mewled and clustered tighter, wild eyes darting at the guards.

"This is not Latha," Elsa hissed at Ashel.

Heat flashed up his neck. No, it wasn't. He pushed through the soldiers, ignoring muttered threats. "Major, a word, please."

She sauntered over.

"I'll ask you again: am I under arrest?"

"The Commissar will determine that when he returns."

"Will you ensure the safety of my staff? They have duties to attend without being hindered or harassed by your troops."

She frowned. "They'll be safe; on that, you have my word." She glared at the soldiers until each nodded. "But everyone must remain here until the Commissar is finished with you." A guard signaled from the door, and Demsch continued, "It looks as if he's returning now. Come inside, Citizen."

In the library, the table and chairs had been shoved aside to create a path wide enough for the Kragnashians, and the bookcase covering the secret passage stood open. Ashel followed Demsch

416

into the sloping corridor. Next to the Device stood two warriors, their antennae brushing the ceiling, abdomens curled in the confined space. It was difficult in the flickering light to distinguish the curves and points of the creatures' tattoos from ordinary shadows. As Ashel studied the markings, the air above the Device shimmered and resolved into Parnden, Earnk, and a Kragnashian, its mandibles pinched around his cousin's neck.

"Restrain Citizen Korng and bring them both up," Parnden clapped at a Kragnashian.

A warrior locked its mandibles around Ashel's neck, loose enough it did no harm but too tight to break free. It pushed; he staggered and caught himself, then walked with back straight, trying to maintain some dignity. As they passed into the library, the creature's wing covers rustled, knocking books off the shelves.

A guard set up two chairs, and the Kragnashians forced Ashel and Earnk to sit, pinning them as easily as Ashel might hold an infant.

Parnden sauntered forward and cupped Earnk's chin. "You were a fine youth, my lord. Do you remember the summer you clerked for me?"

"It was unforgettable," Earnk said, his face splotched red.

"What is the meaning of this?" Ashel asked. "What have you done?"

"And you, Citizen." Parnden rubbed the backs of his fingers against Ashel's cheek. "This beard *must* come off. Major, find a shaving kit."

A cold sweat beaded Ashel's skin, and he rubbed the empty knuckles, beset by visions of blades and blood and agony.

"Don't fret, Citizen," Parnden said. "You'll be in good hands. I believe I mentioned that I was born a barber's son? A wealthy barber, to be sure, one who owned several shops that catered to merchants and guildleaders, and who could afford to send me to the Academy. But a barber all the same." He rubbed his bald pate. "My own handiwork—keep up the skills, much like your music, I expect."

A guard rushed in with a sloshing basin and shaving implements, and Parnden asked the Kragnashian to adjust its grip, exposing more of Ashel's neck. The mandibles opened and pressed down on his shoulders, holding him tight against the chair back.

"I told you in Relm," Earnk said, "we don't know where my father is."

Parnden chuckled. "I'm sure that's true. Lornk wouldn't tell you, so you couldn't tell me. Nevertheless, the situation leaves me in a quandary: what to do with you both while Lornk Korng is at large." He snapped steel-bladed scissors. "I'll trim it first, Citizen."

"Remember what I said about Victoria being a frightful enemy," Ashel said.

"Oh, yes, I remember. Don't worry." Ashel forced himself to take even breaths while the Commissar snipped. There was too much at stake to unleash either his ego or his fear.

"Now the lather." Parnden stirred up a foam and brushed it onto Ashel's cheeks and neck. Exchanging brush for blade, he scraped a cheek. "As I was saying, there's a quandary. I doubt Lornk cares enough about either of you to trade his freedom for yours. And after expending the effort to reveal the lovely face under all this hair, I'd rather Citizen Korng decorate my parlor than my gibbet. And you, my lord—I'd much rather you remain on the Seat of Relm than stew in my dungeon. Lift your chin, Citizen."

Ashel's larynx bobbed on its own, his heart racing. The Kragnashian holding him crooned something, and he cleared his throat and forced his breath back into an even rhythm.

Parnden's blade scraped the cleft between the sinews in Ashel's neck. "So, the question I ask myself is, what guarantees from the Lord of Relm and Traine's newest Citizen would set my mind at ease?"

"I've given you shares in the copper," Earnk said.

Fiery pain lanced Ashel's chin, and a hot line trickled toward his collar. "Oh! I do apologize, Citizen." Parnden daubed the nick with a towel, then scraped the other side of Ashel's throat. His heart rampaging within his chest, he fought to keep still. "Shares that won't pay out until after this so-called Concordance has passed and your father's next coup attempt is over, one way or the other." He mopped the remaining lather from Ashel's face and stepped back. "That's what you've all been waiting for, isn't it?"

"What is a concordance?" Earnk asked.

Parnden smirked. "Did your father tell you to play the simpleton when you were my clerk, or was that your own invention? I've always wondered, especially when you refused the promotion I offered you. You were developing into such a fine lad, my lord. Now, Citizen. I haven't forgotten why you left your homeland and became involved in this charade. I've made inquiries about your wife and sister."

"And what did you find out?" he asked, bafflement, hope, and terror knotted together in his freshly shaven throat.

The Kragnashian's mandibles slid along his neck, bringing its head closer. It was humming so faintly he doubted anyone else could hear it. The tune off-key, it took several measures before Ashel recognized the song as "A Wizard's Last Embrace."

Parnden's grin shifted into a mummer's frown. "Alas, they were taken deep into Kragnashian territory, perhaps even to the southern continent, to be sacrificed in a ritual of grave importance to the Kragnashians. I fear there is no hope of their return." Lips curling maliciously, he made the Oreseeker condolence sign and pressed his palm to Ashel's chest. "I am so, so deeply sorry for your loss."

The words battered Ashel, stoking the doubt and fear that had plagued him nearly half a year. *Parnden is lying*, Geram said. *You know that—the Center confirmed they're in the past.*

Behind him, the Kragnashian's mouthparts gnashed softly as it whispered something to him. Its mandibles loosened, and antennae grazed his forehead. A strange sensation of hope bloomed, and his fear faded as if washed away by bliss.

"What assurances do you want?" Earnk asked, his voice shaking.

Chittering, the Kragnashians released them and twisted round, knocking more books off the shelves. With a chorus of burrs and clicks, the pair disappeared down the passageway.

Parnden smoothed a scowl into a sneer. "What assurances? A good question, my lord. I'm sure together you and your brother can conceive a satisfactory proposal. Major, henceforth the Lord of Relm and Citizen Korng shall be held here under house arrest." He stepped toward the hall, turned back. "Oh, I nearly forgot. Citizen, I believe you said you'd never seen *The Abolitionist*. I came across a copy and thought you might find it illuminating. I know Alek Storund is a friend to the Korngs, but don't fret. He'll be given the same choice I give all Citizens: he can escape the gibbet if he supplies someone to take his place." Handing the paper to Ashel, he left, followed by Demsch and her guards.

Breathing hard, Earnk hurried out. In Latha, Geram conferred with Senators and fieldmarshals as clerks rushed round, packing up the government's papers. Surprised and baffled by his own calm, Ashel peered down the passageway leading to the Device. A murmur drifted up, as if the Kragnashians were casually chatting. Sifting through the books scattered on the floor, he found the Kragnashian dictionary and slipped it in his pocket, then snagged the volume depicting the clan patterns and tucked Alek's pamphlet under the cover.

In the hallway, retching filtered from the privy chamber. Fetching a decanter and two glasses from the parlor, Ashel knocked on the privy door. Water ran, and the door slid into the wall. Earnk's face was white under damp hair.

"I think you need this." Ashel set the books down and poured him a drink.

"Thank you." The Relmlord drained the glass. Trembling, he sank to the floor and swiped at tears. "Father would not be pleased to find me here, blubbering."

Ashel refilled Earnk's glass and peered through cut crystal at his own amber liquor. "I've done my share of blubbering, here and other places."

Earnk rolled the glass between his palms and scowled. The

hall clock ticked. "The last time I watched Parnden wield a barber's blade, a good friend of mine died."

Ashel touched his heart and Earnk's chest. "I'm sorry for your loss."

"This morning, in Relm, his guards murdered mine in front of the staff. Then he left Kragnashians at the Device there, as here. Elesendar knows what the Council will do."

"Parnden brought Kragnashians to Narath as well. The Lathan government is removing to Erin. My mother abdicated, and Geram is now regent."

Earnk stared at him. "How—I thought I Heard Geram speaking to you. You can Hear him, even at this distance?"

Ashel guffawed softly. "Nearly all the time. He's aware of us right now."

Earnk sipped his drink and loosed a long, low whistle. "That must be hard."

"In Latha, they said they were assuming control of all the Devices in the world on the basis of a treaty with 'the First.' What did the Kragnashians say in Relm? If the Caleisbahnin have switched sides, Parnden's won."

Earnk sighed ruefully. "I never learned Kragnashian. But if Parnden and the First are allies now, he wouldn't still be looking for Father. He's on a frigate in the bay." He chortled grimly. "He gets terribly seasick, and he's likely been miserable for the last two months."

Ashel tapped the books. "I don't understand Kragnashian well either, but in the library just now, one tried to tell me something. We need to know which clan has taken over the Device." He grasped Earnk's shoulder. "Cousin or brother, we're in this together now."

Earnk returned the grip. "Blood or not, it's brother."

THE JOINING

Swollen belly encased in a shield of air, Vic floated through the clang of weapons and bellowed insults. She hovered among the drilling soldiers on the training ground, eyes closed, legs crossed, mind focused on staying clear of their blades.

"Feel them," Saelbeneth said, her mindvoice faint but clear. "The eddies of life that move around them. Shut out the sound. Shut out the smells and sights and feel only the eddies. Bring the Woern inside, pull the energy inside you, and you will feel yourself shift out of time, no longer able to hear and see that which surrounds you. Feel the eddies then."

"Madam!" a soldier screamed. Vic's eyes popped open; a spear hurtled toward her. She dodged, and someone crashed into her. Her hip and shoulder smacked into the mud. A soldier tripped, his boots flailing past her chin. Another charged, mouth contorted in a wild scream, a wicked axe blade hacking toward her head. Vic rolled clear and shot above the fray as the axe-wielder yanked the weapon loose and swung it wide. Another trooper hit him on the crown with her pike haft. With a gulp, the berserker staggered forward, shook his head clear, and stood at attention as a training sergeant screamed in his face.

Panting, Vic willed her heart to slow. The baby thrashed, and Saelbeneth whispered, "Did you feel the energy stretch between you and that soldier?"

"The one that just tried to kill me?"

Saelbeneth chuckled. "It's natural to repel an invasion, madam."

Vic took a breath and held it, released it slowly. "An invasion. I suppose that's what it is."

"Concentrate only on your breathing," Saelbeneth said.

In through the nose, out through the mouth. In, out. Below, troopers hollered. Weapons clashed. Breathing, Vic reinforced her shield and lowered herself into the sparring ground. She knew these sounds well, and were she fighting, she could easily tune them out and focus on herself and her opponent.

"Treat the eddies as your opponent, then," Saelbeneth advised.

Startled the wizard had Heard her, Vic refocused her attention on her breath. In, out. Cries and metal clashed in a familiar rhythm. Strike, parry, counterstrike. She latched onto the beats, let them drive the timing of her breath and heart. Strike, parry, counterstrike. In, out, in. Eyes closed, she felt the weapons move through space and smack flesh, the motion of air in and out of the soldiers' lungs, their blood surge and ebb through arteries and veins. It was excruciating and exhilarating, and she had the sensation of her mind opening, of possibility opening. Time and place opened to her. She could accomplish anything—all she had to do was choose. The baby stretched and settled as black joy blossomed, racing up her spine to her eyes—

A strange energy moved out of her. The troopers swooned and staggered, their weapons clattered on the ground.

"Victoria!" Saelbeneth's voice cracked, and a cramp twisted her womb. Gasping, knees buckling, she clutched at her belly as pain wracked her abdomen. Saelbeneth swooped down and held Vic's shoulders while the pain subsided and her breathing steadied.

Shaking off their stupor, the troopers backed away, and Saelbeneth pulled Vic to her feet. "Thank you," she said aloud to the soldiers, "for assisting us in this experiment. We have learned much today about how Meylnara might seek to harm us and how we may defend ourselves." An arm around Vic, she flew upward. "We must go."

"What did I do wrong?" Vic asked. "I felt the transcendence you described."

"I think you did everything right, Victoria, which is why I stopped you. Come with me."

They shot south to a granite outcrop that broke through the canopy. Settling there, Saelbeneth closed her eyes, breathed for three heartbeats, then looked at Vic. "If anyone else on the Council had witnessed that, they would have called immediately for your death."

A gasp twisted into a rueful laugh. "So I did it? We've been trying for a month, and I'm still not sure how . . ."

"I'm not certain either, but I believe this time you may well have succeeded in exchanging the energy inside those men with the energy within you."

"You attacked my child."

"It diverted your attention and permitted me to sever the connection before it was too late to reverse it. I couldn't let you gain control over those men."

"I'm glad to be free of them, but I can't let you hurt the baby again, Saelbeneth."

The Council leader inclined her head, and they sat in silence. Around them, blossoms dotted the foliage, reminding her of sunlit butterflies skimming the Kiareinoll's topmost leaves.

"I still haven't a clue how Meylnara could have merged with an entire forest or how to separate her from it."

Saelbeneth smiled sadly. "You must find a way, or we must destroy the trees. We cannot allow a haven for lawbreakers here. If Meylnara managed to steal your child or find some other way to make companions for herself, she could start a dynasty of wizards who would oppose us. Not now, perhaps, but in a generation or two or three. If we do not eliminate her, the numbers of rogue wizards will grow, and a Purge may be necessary in your own time. I would rather us kill one woman now, than force our descendants to commit a holocaust later."

"This forest brims with life—killing it is a holocaust too."

"It must be done, or more innocents without power will die, as they did so often before the Purge. The same is true for your time and your people, Victoria, especially because you're powerful and can blaze in and crush everything about you. It is easy to destroy. Making things is harder, but it's both more satisfying and more useful." She laid a hand on Vic's belly. "When you return to your time, you must find a way to bind yourself and your child and all your descendants to an oath against harm to others, or there will be a need for another Purge some time in your future."

Ducking out of the hospital, Bethniel mopped her brow, anxious for a bath. Nelchior emerged from the Council pavilion and hailed her, striding quickly across the yard. Biting her tongue, she pasted on a gracious smile and curtsied, keeping her hands clasped behind her back.

"Lady Bethniel, how fares your mistress?"

"She is well, sir."

"There was an incident in the training yard this morning."

Soldiers had flooded the hospital, all complaining of headaches. "The troops said Saelbeneth and Victoria were conducting an experiment."

"What type of experiment, do you suppose?"

"I wouldn't know; Victoria has put herself in Saelbeneth's hands for training."

An eyebrow cocked, Nelchior stepped closer. "You look tired, my lady. I shall let you retire." His fingers brushed her arm as he withdrew, and a sharp tingling flashed through her veins. One corner of his mouth curled upward; she kept her face still, never more thankful for her mother's teaching—her eyes did not widen, her cheeks remained cold. Courtier's smile still in place, she dipped her knees and hurried toward home.

As soon as she passed the first tents in Thabean's compound, her eyes and mouth tightened. She was damn close to crying, which was silly, as she had no reason, no immediate reason. Yet her blood seethed with revulsion at Nelchior's appraising leer. She had been the object of attention since her earliest memories, and it had never bothered her except from this man, who frightened as well as repulsed her. Tears built behind her eyes, an ache pulsed in her temples, and bile churned in her belly. *I'm not afraid*, she muttered silently. *I'm furious! He will not have my Woern!*

"My lady," Thabean called as she passed his pavilion.

She stopped, her heart in her throat. Thabean and Samovael had been gone more than a month. "Sir, you're back. Are the supply lines secure?"

Leaving Fainend and his other aides gathered round a table inside his tent, he took her arm. "They are secure, and Saelbeneth's books should be en route. May we speak?"

She dipped her head, and he led her to an alley between tents. "Close your eyes and cover your mouth, so you do not cry out."

"What do you—"

"Will you come with me?"

Gut clenched, she swallowed as his eyes rose to hers. An absurd wish that he was taller crossed her mind, and she immediately scolded herself. *It doesn't matter how short he is!* "Where are we going?"

A rare grin broke out and he wrapped an arm round her waist. "Swimming. Don't make a sound."

He pulled her close and rocketed up, leaving behind the squeal that escaped her lips. Wind tore at her hair, whipped her clothes as they flashed over the forest, then dove through the canopy, coming to rest in a fern-laced glade.

"Swimming?" she asked. "I haven't seen you for a month, and the first thing you do is ask me to go swimming?"

"Why are you angry?"

She blinked. "I'm not." She wasn't—perhaps a little, but she didn't blame him. She still felt awkward about the caldera and shivered, thinking of his arms around her. "I am . . . surprised. And I don't understand why you brought me here."

"There's a pool a short way off, filled with spring water, clear and still. Dealn would bring his . . ." He flushed. "I fear that sounds unseemly. I am sorry—I meant only to provide some relief from our troubles."

Charmed by his awkward formality, she teased, "Did you bring bathing costumes, sir? I can hardly swim in my hospital smock."

His eyes widened, and he laughed. "I didn't notice your garb." His humor melted into a smolder. "All I saw was you."

Heat gushed to her eyes, and breath froze in her lungs. Her fingers reached for his. Skin met skin, and he rose to her height, brushed his lips against hers. Her mouth parted, and his tongue courted hers with sweet flavors of fruit and ale. Her arms flew around his neck, fingers threading through hair luxurious and soft. He squeezed closer, and she met the pressure of his body with her own. He was hard and wiry, his arms solid and strong, and she wanted to stay in his embrace forever.

Pausing, he palmed her cheeks. "My dear, I violate the laws I hold sacred, but if I am to die, I should die with no regrets. Failing to love you would be a regret."

Joy churned with angst. "I . . . I want nothing more but to be with you, except to see you live. To love me is your death."

"My death is certain in any case. Let us love while we can." His eyes shimmered like still pools under a bright sky, and she tumbled into those depths, drowning happily.

Hand in hand, they stole down a narrow path. Bethniel froze as a giggle splashed through the trees. With a wicked smile, Thabean scooped her into the air and settled them on a tree branch high above a pool where a pair of teenage scullions frolicked in the water, their clothes laid out on nearby rocks. Signing for quiet, he pulled limbs and leaves together, weaving a bower, and they lay on their stomachs and watched the pair cavort. A splash and a squeal spun into laughter, then silence as the couple's lips met. Ripples expanded slowly around them.

Thabean's smile vanished as his eyes met hers.

She pressed his hand to her breast. "If the Council find us out, they'll kill you."

Mist steamed out of the forest. In the south, a storm wove

orange and pinks in bows of light. An avio flapped out of the sun's glare, sailed across the landscape of greens and blues and gold, and settled into the canopy.

"We all die, my lady." He touched her arm, and the electric longing of the symbionts razzed along her nerves. "Bethniel of Narath, will you have me?"

All the hairs on her arms stood on end. She nodded, and their mouths met across a gulf like a bridge. Black fire blinded her, drove her into his arms, sucking her into an abyss like the deepest corner of the sea, drowning her in flame and pressure. She pulled at his tunic, but it was too slow, too slow. She wished it gone, and it shredded away. Her own garments shrank to nothing. Pressed arm to arm, chest to chest, thigh to thigh, they floated in the bower, the heat engulfing them, soldering them into one.

Afterward, lying quietly together, Bethniel listened to his heartbeat and wondered whether it followed hers, or hers followed it. She was sorry it was over, happy it was done. Her belly warm, she sighed, thinking about marriage—that she was married now too.

He cleared his throat. "In Latha, they say the Weavers do not lie together without marriage, and that in lying together, they marry."

Grinning, she rested her chin on his chest. "It is the custom in all Latha now. I know we can't declare—that means, announce publicly that we've wed."

He kissed the crown of her head. "I declare to you, dear, that you are my wife . . . That's not a phrase I ever expected to hear myself say, even before I took the Elixir."

"Lucky for me you never met the right woman."

"Lucky for me I did. But you had never courted another?"

She shrugged. "Courted? Yes. Lain with, no. Half the young people of Narath have trysted without declaring, but I didn't want Elesendar to bring me back as some sort of promiscuous vermin, like a harrier."

He stroked her cheek. "Do you really believe that nonsense?"

Rising on an elbow, she mocked a scowl. "The husband of Latha's Heir cannot be a heretic! We shall have to convert you, sir."

A sardonic smile bloomed and melted as he traced a finger along her hairline. She shivered at the electric thrill, and he hugged her to his shoulder.

They lay in silence. Drowsy, she imbibed the moment, inhaling humus and blossoms, sweat and musk. His scent was a heady mixture of earth and herbs, and salt and sweet vinegar, warm and comforting. A breeze caressed her skin. Prickling leaves crinkled as she sank toward sleep, lulled by the lapping water below.

Orange clouds streaked a lavender sky. Bethniel sat up, peered through the bower at the empty pool, scanned the canopy. Where was he? Below, thickly tangled branches bore long, vicious thorns, followed by a long, empty drop to the ground. She wanted to call his name, but fear stopped her—of discovery or that he'd abandoned her, she wasn't sure. Casting about for her clothes, she remembered they had disappeared—literally evaporated. A laugh bubbled up and quashed the fear. She was naked at the top of a towering behemoth of a tree, with no way down. "They'll find my skeleton here," she mumbled, half-serious. "Bleached from the sun, and they'll wonder what in Shrine a woman was doing up here by herself."

Pleasure rippled along her skin as she remembered what she had been doing, and she giggled. He wouldn't leave her here. He had probably gone to get them clothes. He had certainly gone to get them clothes. She wondered how he would explain his own nudity when he got back to camp, or if he would be able to slip into his tent unnoticed. More than once she had found herself surprised by wizards appearing in rooms she thought were empty. Wineyll could spin illusions by altering what people believed they saw. Could wizards manipulate matter and light to make themselves invisible? *That* would be useful.

The air cooled while she waited, the threads of clouds thickening as the sky darkened. She hoped he'd return before it rained, wondered what could possibly be keeping him. How long could it take for a wizard to fly to camp, grab some clothing, and come back? Likely he was asked by Fainend to examine something or sought out Vic to assure her there was nothing to worry about. Likely both, or a Council meeting could have been called. Or the camp could have been attacked—and this might be the battle in which Thabean Graystone died.

Valiant Thabean

Right hand of Saelbeneth

Dead in honor

Mourned in glory

Forge on the Council.

"No, no, no," she whispered. "Not yet. Not yet." The Caldera tribe had said he was the Sacrifice. He would die to save the forest. He could not die without meaning, in some random battle. Surely the momentous events that would lead to his demise were not now occurring. She was the Fulcrum! She would need to be present for events to turn around her. Unless this was the act, the turning point, and she had fulfilled her destiny. Could this have been it? No—her blood churned with panic. No, of course not. He could not die now, without her near! She had to get back to camp. Heart thudding, she crawled to the edge of the bower and swung herself into the tangle of branches below. Tough round thorns dug into her feet and hands, scratched at her face and shoulders as she wormed her way through, but she thought only of reaching him before he was gone.

The gloaming deepened to full dark, and she could not see her way through the tangle. Branches snagged her, trapped her. She could not go down or up. Gritting her teeth, she wedged her arms through the thorns and found a gap. Spikes raked her breasts and flanks as she squeezed through, but fear blunted the fire of ripped flesh. She had to reach him. The bough began to taper and bend beneath her weight. Rain splattered into the canopy. Heavy drops struck her skin, and a deluge hammered through the leaves and branches. The air black, the bough creaked and snapped.

Her hands clawed through empty darkness, her yelp bouncing off hidden trunks. She crashed into a thicket of spindle ferns; the brush broke her fall, but she still landed hard. Groaning, she rolled onto hands and knees and sobbed. Where was he? How could he just leave her?

Anger burbled through worry, and she cursed him in one breath and prayed for him in the next. Shrine, she was alone, naked, and only the old mothers knew how far from camp. How would she get back without being seen, and how in Elesendar's name would she explain this to Vic?

A shadow parted from the underbrush. "Forgive me."

Air gushed from her lungs. "Where did you go?"

He held out a pack. "For clothing. I hoped to return before you woke. I'm sorry."

She looked up at the black tangle through which she'd fallen. "I thought there might have been a battle."

Wincing, he pressed the bag into her hands. "I'm sorry. You're hurt." A ball of light rolled out of the air, illuminating the forest like a tiny sun. "My dear," he touched a scratch on her face. "Why did you try to climb down?"

"You were gone so long, I thought you'd been killed." Tears gushed. He pulled her forehead to his, whispering more apologies. Submitting to relief, she wrapped her arms around him and kissed the crown of his head. His lips caressed the cuts and scrapes, and tiny electric bursts followed his touch, as if the Woern hungered for their kind in him. Everywhere his mouth touched, cuts knitted together and scrapes healed. Lifting her with the power, he turned her around, kissed her back, her thighs, her shins, and finally the bottoms of her feet. When he put her down, he took off his shirt. "Now, shall we at last have that swim?"

"In the rain?"

"Afraid of getting wet?" He slipped out of his trousers and ran toward the water. His skin was pale under the bobbing globe, but his buttocks and thighs were roped with muscle. Diving smoothly, he surfaced and beckoned her to join him.

Giggling, she scrambled to the shore and leapt, her body slicing into the tepid water. As she surfaced, she realized the aches from the fall were gone. "How did you do that? I feel wonderful! I thought all wizards did was manipulate matter and energy. How can you heal?"

Treading water, he grinned. "Are you not made of matter and energy?"

"Yes, I suppose."

"And power too, madam."

"What?"

His legs entwined with hers, but a poke in her belly made her titter and draw away. "That tickles."

Grip firm on her backside, he tugged her to him. His mouth crept along her throat, and blood and fire rushed to meet his lips. Embracing, they floated effortlessly, their legs braided together. "Who is keeping us from drowning now, madam?"

Every nerve tingling, she said, "What are you talking about?"

"I'm not using my Woern, and neither of us is exerting any physical effort to stay afloat."

"You're not suggesting . . ."

"I am, my love. All hail to Bethniel, last of the inherited wizards."

Back aching, Vic shifted a pillow and adjusted her weight against the chair. Her stomach growled, and she stuffed a piece of stew-soaked bread into her mouth. Hunger scratched and mewled like a wet cat down a well. "Damn, kid, you can eat," she muttered around another mouthful. The baby kicked and tossed, his elbow pressing on her spine. She patted her belly. "I suppose I can't keep calling you *kid*." What name would Ashel choose? Lathans and Oreseekers alike named their children for lost loved ones. Sashal? Vic had loved the warmhearted king who had welcomed her into his family and cared for her as his own, but Sashal's death had been gruesome and intimate, and she couldn't ask Ashel to cradle a son named for a father whose lifeblood had soaked his skin.

"Joseph," she said. "How about that name? It was my grandfather's."

Setting aside the empty stew bowl, she hoisted herself out of the chair. *Shrine, you're five months, not eight. Nowhere big enough to require hoisting.* But a year was two hundred and twenty-three days long, and babies were born in just over eight months. At five months, the kid—Joseph—was two-thirds of the way cooked, and cooked was how she felt. She was more tired than that time she'd chased a Relman patrol for three days straight, eating on the move, never sleeping, pausing only for the latrine, and hardly long enough for that.

She stumbled through her bedtime ablutions and extinguished the lights. The sun had set only a short time ago; it was too early for bed, but a massive yawn stretched her jaws. Perhaps nearly possessing a squadron of soldiers had taken its toll; she felt as if she could sleep a week, yet when she lay back, she tossed and turned. She was so weary she couldn't muster the energy for sleep.

Fabric shifted. Feet shuffled. "Vic?" Bethniel whispered in mindspeech, her silent voice eerie in the dark. "Are you awake?"

Groaning, Vic shaped a light globe. "Where have you been all day? I asked Fainend, and he said Thabean had sent you on an errand, but he wouldn't say where, and then I couldn't find Thabean . . ." Her mind leapt onto possibility, and she jerked up, her heart pounding hard, as if Meylnara stood in the doorway. "Shrine's bitch, you weren't together, were you?"

Bethniel edged closer. She wore a fine, bronze-colored silk that fell from her shoulders in soft waves, but her hair was a damp tangle, snarled with bits of leaves. Joy and consternation warred across her features—eyes alight, mouth tilting upward, eyebrows creased and forehead furrowed.

"Oh, Beth."

The princess collapsed and sobbed into the pillow. Foreboding and sorrow pressed on Vic's shoulders as she smoothed Bethniel's hair and listened to her recite a list of dire predictions. There was the doom the Kragnashians had demanded they fulfill, and the simpler, human consequences of broken laws and forbidden acts. "If the Council find out, they'll kill him."

Vic rubbed her shoulders. "We will find a way around this. The Kragnashians brought us here to change history—we'll save the trees, and we'll save him too."

Bethniel scrubbed her cheeks. "The Sacrifice will have to be made, one way or another." She chortled ruefully. "As if we didn't have enough problems, there's something else." Her hands clasped in her lap, she looked intently at the table. The spoon rose slowly out of Vic's bowl and wobbled toward them. Aghast, Vic let it fall into her palms.

Bethniel sighed. "Now there are two of us outside the Council's law."

Vic grabbed her foster sister's hand. A lively electricity met her grasp as living Woern raced toward each other. "How?"

"It triggered when Thabean and I . . . he said that's why the penalty for violating the vow of chastity is death."

"Holy Shrine, Beth." A laugh broke through Vic's shock. "Well, that ballad wasn't completely made up: Thabean did have a lover who was a wizard. I think he'll rather like being called 'your Majesty' when he's consort to the Ruler of Latha."

Bethniel shook her head. "I'll have to step aside as Heir and join you in Mora." Her mouth quirked. "I wonder if Thabean would like steed ranching."

"Ashel loves those things. We could all keep a herd together."

"Except Thabean's going to die," Beth said, tears brimming again.

Vic clasped her shoulders. "Not if I can help it. There has got to be a way to dispatch that woman without killing the trees or anyone else. I promise you, Beth, I will find it, and we will *all* go home."

The princess nodded, and they lay down together. Forehead to forehead, they whispered of the future long past the time for bed.

PART THREE

Personal Log, Captain Franklin T. J. Wong, United Mineral Mining Vessel, Registry LSNDR2237, January 5, 2154

Ornithology. Craig keeps talking about ornithology—the study of birds, not Charlie Parker. Ever since Craig drank that stuff the indigenous gave him, he's been acting strange. I'll catch him alone in a room, and he'll be looking like the cat that got the cream half the time, and the other half, he's sweating and throwing up in the trash bin. The last time I found him hanging over the bowl in the head, he asked me what I knew about ornithology. I told him biology was his department. He nodded and started talking about woodpeckers. They live in family groups with a dominant mating pair, and all the other woodpeckers in the group devote themselves to making sure the dominant pair's eggs survive. The subordinate birds might not ever breed themselves, but their genetic code was still getting passed on through the dominant siblings.

What the hell does this have to with us? I asked him.

He smiled. Sometimes, he said, an individual has to sacrifice himself for the good of the group. Then, water rained down from the ceiling, and he laughed like a maniac.

I ordered maintenance to check the pipes in the head—there must be a leak, or condensation, or something. But Craig . . . he needs to see the doc. The strain's getting to him.

437

TRICK OF FATE

Vic started awake.

"You'd better come." Prenlin's hand gripped her shoulder. The Healer's hair was awry, her eyes wet. "They've arrested Lady Bethniel. Sir Thabean can't be found."

Dawn glowed through the open tent flap; a week had passed since the night Bethniel came to her with news she was wedded and empowered. "What happened?"

"Saelbeneth's put her under arrest."

Vic scrambled out of bed, dressed, and rushed to Thabean's command tent, where Fainend stood surrounded by Samovael and half a dozen Council guards.

"Sir Thabean often patrols at dawn," Fainend told the others. His eyes flicked to Vic. "Good morning, madam."

"A grave crime has been committed," Samovael said. "Have you any idea how your sister obtained the Elixir?"

"What?"

Samovael's scowl deepened. "Lady Bethniel, madam. She has the Woern, just as you do."

"Where is she now?"

"In Grunnaire's custody."

Vic shoved down the fear clogging her throat. "Thabean's out patrolling?" she asked Fainend.

"He can be nowhere else, madam."

"What do you want with him, Samovael?"

"To inform him, of course."

"I'll find him. I'll tell him. I promise."

Outside, she hesitated between Grunnaire's camp and going straight to Thabean. *As long as she's not in Nelchior's hands, she'll be all right.* Hurtling skyward, she flew toward Meylnara's keep and the surveillance blind. A week since the marriage—a week of secret consummations and plans for a future together in . . . the future. They'd been so careful in their worry that someone might discover the affair, Vic wondered if they'd forgotten to hide Bethniel's newfound *power*.

Sensing Thabean's waveform, Vic beelined toward him, slowing as she approached the outcropping where she and Saelbeneth had talked. Thabean faced west, watching the sun rise and doing very little with the Woern. Only the color of his boots shifted from brown to black and back again.

He smiled, inclining his head toward the red globe. "A beautiful dawn, is it not?"

"What are you doing?"

"Resting, madam. Enjoying the time I have left."

Very gently, Vic laid her hand on his arm. "The Council has arrested Bethniel for illegally taking the Elixir. She's in Grunnaire's custody."

He flinched, then gave her a grave look. "The same crime for which you've been pardoned."

"Reprieved," Vic said. "Bethniel is not a soldier. She won't be useful to the Council. I think someone must have found out about your marriage—"

"How is it that you know, madam?"

Her grip on his arm tightened. They didn't have time for stupid questions. "She's my sister—did you think she wouldn't tell me? Nelchior has been stalking her. If he thought anything happened between you, he could have arranged this to bait you."

She had been prepared to restrain him, but he only laughed softly, bitterly. "It is exactly what Nelchior would do." He stood. "Shall we head back?"

"What will you do?"

"Do not be alarmed; I will not challenge him."

"Should we tell them the truth, that she's a natural wizard, or would that make it worse?"

Pursing his lips, he looked across the treetops. "Worse, I expect."

"Then we have to help her escape. She can stay with the Caldera tribe."

He nodded, his eyes on the forest. His expression became resolute. "Let us return, madam. I wish to see her."

The trees folded away beneath them, and Vic reminded herself again that Bethniel was in no immediate danger as long as Nelchior was kept away from her, but she was haunted by the sneering, leering looks the wizard cast her sister. The sun full over the horizon, they passed over the moat and settled next to Grunnaire's pavilion.

Her steward emerged and saluted. "The prisoner is inside."

Prisoner. Vic swallowed bile as they followed him through fabric hallways to a central chamber. Bethniel sat on a camp chair in an otherwise empty room. Grunnaire stared at her, arms crossed. "Do not disturb her," the wizard warned them, speaking silently.

Eyes closed, hands palm down on her thighs, the princess sat still as a statue. "What is she doing?" Vic whispered in mindspeech.

"Nothing," Thabean replied. "She is being held this way, but it is easy to break the spell. We wish to speak with her, Grunnaire."

"Saelbeneth forbade that she be disturbed."

"I will take responsibility. You may put her in my custody and rest yourself, if you wish."

"I may not."

Thabean's face remained impassive, as if Grunnaire's refusals meant nothing to him. He signaled Vic to follow. "We should see Saelbeneth."

In the air, Vic said, "I can get her out of there. I can do it right now, and we can take refuge with the Caldera tribe."

"No, madam. It is better you should wait until nightfall."

"Will we have that long?"

"Let us speak with Saelbeneth."

The Council leader received them in her parlor, where she breakfasted on tea and biscuits. At the sight of the food, Vic's stomach yawned. Head spinning, she sank into a chair.

"Victoria, you look likely to faint. Eat something."

Thanking her, Vic took a biscuit and stuffed it in her mouth. Thabean stared as if she'd gone mad. A hand on her belly, she swallowed—a warrior ate when she could, and when they left this tent, she would have no time for feeding.

"We wish to speak to Lady Bethniel," Thabean said.

"I cannot allow that until after she is tried."

"If she has power, she could help us," Vic said round another biscuit.

"She has power, but we have already set aside the law for you. If we do so again, for someone untrained in war, we open the door for every clerk, washerwoman, and soldier in this camp to take the Elixir. In a week's time we would be back to the chaos we knew before the days of the Purge."

"But you know she did not take the Elixir."

"I cannot say before open Council what I knew or did not know."

"But how can you allow me to live and not her?"

"You are still in custody, madam. Thabean is responsible for you."

"I would take responsibility for Bethniel as well."

Saelbeneth sighed, giving Thabean an appraising look. "Nelchior has also offered to supervise her parole."

The cords in Thabean's neck flexed and relaxed, but he showed no other reaction. Saelbeneth went on. "Which is why I've put her in Grunnaire's custody. Grunnaire cannot hold her quiescent for long, however. Her trial is set for noon today."

With a glance at Thabean, Vic stepped closer to Saelbeneth. "She is my sister. I will not let anything happen to her."

"Madam, your destiny—your task—precludes all else."

"Not to me. If you try to hurt her, we will leave you to end this war on your own."

The wizard's eyes hardened. "Do not threaten me, Victoria. Defy us, and we will rescind your reprieve and you will be executed on the spot. You must prepare yourself to accept the inevitable."

Vic stalked out, mind reeling through plans by which she could extract Bethniel and flee to the Caldera tribe.

Thabean grasped her elbow. "Your sister will not die today."

"No, she won't."

"Do not do anything rash, madam. There are certain legal actions we can take; I must speak with Fainend. In the meantime, I advise you to make arrangements with the Caldera tribe."

Vic nodded, throat tight. "So, we'll free her during the trial?"

Thabean nodded. "We will save her then."

In her tent, Vic devoured a pome while shoving fruit, biscuits, and a waterskin into a knapsack, then rushed to the Caleisbahn compound, a narrow wedge filled with well-tended domes. The structures were covered with dense erinsheen, tightly woven into elaborate geometric designs of red, green, and blue. In a central square, seamen lounged over breakfast and pipes. Shirtless and crosslegged, Gustave scraped a porcelain blade along a lathered cheek.

"Gustave, I need you."

The other Caleisbahnin jumped to their feet and bowed. Rinsing his blade, Gustave cracked his gap-toothed grin and scraped away another patch of lather. "Never disturb a man while he is shaving, madam."

"You can shave later. Get dressed and get armed. Now."

He rinsed and scraped the other side. "You cannot ask a man to go about half-shaven, madam, but I'll leave the rest for now. I was thinking of growing a goatee." Winking at his fellows, he sprang to his feet, wiped his face with a towel, and pulled a shirt over his head. Once he'd belted on his sword, she grabbed him and flew straight up.

"Where are we going?"

"Bethniel's been arrested, and I need to speak with the Caldera tribe."

"The princess's troubles are no concern of mine. I followed you here to see a task completed. I will not aid you in distractions from that task."

"I just need you to translate." The wind sheared past, and the forest ripped away beneath them as she sped toward the caldera. Legal actions, Thabean said. What could those be, which hadn't already been proposed for her own case? She might have to simply grab Bethniel and run straight from the Council chamber. She was stronger in the Woern than any one of them, but collectively? Thabean would certainly help her; perhaps he could hinder or slow the others without implicating himself. Once she and Beth were in the forest, they could stop using the Woern and hide. None of them had woodcraft to match hers, and the forest's Mind might shield them.

Might. Fembrosh always had its own reasons for helping or hindering. It could be unreliable, and the Mind might be equally fickle. There was also the possibility that this trial, or Bethniel's execution, might be the turning point the Kragnashians predicted. What if—no! Vic squashed the thought. She would not allow it. She would not lose Bethniel to fate; Ashel would never forgive her.

"You will never see the prince again if you fail to do what you were brought here to do."

"Do not Listen to me, Gustave, and do not dare threaten me." She felt as tight as a bowstring, her rage very close to erupting.

"No threat, madam. A simple fact. You will not have access to the Device until Meylnara is dead."

"Bethniel is as important to that as I am."

"A fulcrum is passive. Events this day turn about her; she is fulfilling her destiny now."

"Shrine's bitch." Anger boiling, she repressed the urge to twist the pirate in half. "If she dies, Gustave—"

"She will die. Or not. It does not change what you must do."

With a guttural growl, Vic let him go. His body crashed through the canopy; he grunted as branches struck him, but he did not scream. Catching him, she brought him the rest of the way down and dropped him hard on the ground. "If I didn't need you," she panted, "you'd be dead now."

Springing to his feet, Gustave drew his sword and pointed the blade at her heart. "You do need me, so do not threaten *me*, madam."

They stared at each other, the seaman and the wizard, both deadly. She could have squashed him like the Relman soldiers outside Re, but the awful, horrifying ease with which she could kill cooled her anger as fast as it had boiled. Shoulders slumping, she stepped back.

Lowering his blade, he did not sheath it. "Your task, madam."

"My task," she repeated bitterly. Melon-sized insects buzzed through the understory, and climbers called high up in the canopy. She sat on an outgrowth and dropped her head into her hands. She was the Blade! Getting in and out of guarded camps was her forte. Assassinating Meylnara in the midst of her thousands of Kragnashians, rescuing Beth in broad daylight from wizards and their thousands of soldiers—two years ago she would have called either impossible task a mere challenge. Two years ago, Ashel was safe, whole, and happy in Narath. Joseph stretched inside her, and she slung her pack off, dug out a pome, and bit off a chunk.

Gustave squatted and began sharpening his sword. "They call him Kinseller."

"Who?" The pome crackled as she took a second mouthful and looked through moss and leaves at the thin sky above. She felt as safe within this forest as in Fembrosh.

"You asked if anyone waited for me. The Oreseekers call him Kinseller, and the burden of regret weighs heavily upon him."

"What'd he do?" It wouldn't be difficult to elude the Council once they were out of camp.

Gustave eyed the edge of his blade, then turned his frown on her. "Sometimes what seems happenstance is preordained. We knew the Concordance was near, and we knew the One would come from the Oreseekers. We sent watchers, and the watchers sent word of the birth of Victoria of Ourtown."

Her attention snapped to him, and memories popped like sparks from a fire—a curt young man, a walk along a twilit beach, and a midsummer celebration that twisted into terror when slavers came. "Are you talking about Samson?"

"His mother was a watcher. When she died, she passed her mission to him. She told him it was a sacred duty, and he thought you would be honored in the Archipelago. He did not expect that you and the youth of Cairo would be sold as slaves."

Vic stared. "You're saying Samson betrayed me to the Caleisbahnin?"

He stood. "The Caleisbahnin betrayed him, Victoria, and so did you."

"Me? I never saw him again after the day we were herded like cattle into a warehouse. You're telling me he put us there?"

"No, he did not! My people did that, and it is a shameful betrayal of every principle of the Archipelago."

"I didn't know pirates and slavers had any principles."

He returned her glare, quivering. "Samson fulfilled his mother's charge to ensure you could fulfill your destiny as the One, and he is despised for it by Oreseekers and Caleisbahnin alike. Yet he believes in *you*. You are unworthy of that faith."

"I'm unworthy? He *is* a Shrinejumping kin-seller!"

"We stand here today, facing a choice between slavery and survival for all humanity, and you think only of your own self-interest. More than your sister's life is at stake: you hold the world in your hands, Victoria."

"And I want you to hand it to me, without reservation," Lornk had said. Seething, she stepped toward him, fists balled. "Is Lornk Korng behind all of this?"

"Lornk Korng would have prepared you for this fate, not set you careening aimlessly toward it as you now do. If you fail to preserve the Kia here and now, the ones we left behind in our own time will pay the price."

Doubts peppered her anger. Fate, destiny, luck had nothing to do with her circumstance, and what would happen to Bethniel this day was not to be determined by history or fate but by choice. "I will not let them harm Bethniel," she said. "We both know there is more than one possible outcome from this Concordance. If I lose her, I lose the future I want."

"You may lose your husband if you save her and change the course of history."

"And I *will* lose him if I fail to save her and yet preserve history."

He pointed at her belly. "You would have his child be a slave?"

"I've been a slave. Slaves rebel. They escape. A child alone . . . This argument is pointless. I want to talk to the Kragnashians, and I need you to help me do it."

Planting his feet, he raised his sword again and shook his head.

"Gustave, we're leagues from camp. Your fastest way back is to come with me, now. There's nothing you can do to stop me, but if you help me," she sighed, "I'll do what you want."

Long seconds stretched before he nodded.

As they approached the caldera, a keening crept into their ears. The wind carried bursts of fresh-cut grass. At the cliff's edge, Gustave's oath echoed hers. Kragnashians churned in a massive battle. Trills, keens, screeches, crunches echoed off the cliff face. The sweet, fresh perfume of their blood saturated the air.

Coughing, Gustave swiped watering eyes and pointed. A great roiling bulge of Kragnashians moved slowly through the warring creatures. Attackers tore defenders apart, leaving a trail of shredded corpses. A warrior broke through the outer shell, exposing a core of lighter, smaller nymphs carrying fat white larvae in their mandibles. The attackers pulled the young out of the bulge with doubled ferocity. Keens ripped over the field.

"Meylnara?" Vic asked, searching for a smaller bulge.

"There," Gustave said. A lump shifted slowly back and forth in the rear of the attacking forces.

A corner of Vic's mouth tilted upward as she eyed the pirate's sword. "Everyone thinks it takes a wizard to kill a wizard. Everyone worries about her essence or soul or life force—whatever you call it—being tied to the forest. But she is human. She could not live without a head."

Gustave grasped his hilt; his eyes glinted. Mouth quirked, he flourished a bow. "As I am a seaman, madam, my sails and my sword are yours."

Vic's grin broadened. "I thought I was unworthy."

"Perhaps Samson's faith in you is not entirely misplaced. Who is to say what happens now is not what needs to happen?"

Noon and Bethniel's trial were hours away. Time to do what could be done. She waved at the larger bulge, no doubt sheltering the Caldera Center. "We need them on our side."

Gustave indicated a clump of ferns where he would wait. She shot over the cliff edge, flying fast toward the larger defensive mass. She wanted to draw Meylnara out of the safety of the Kragnashians, so she did nothing to mask her waveform. Kragnashian blood soaked the air in spring, but her throat bore it, and she flew directly above the Caldera bulge, reached down with the Woern. Her power slipped around the creatures, but it lodged in the earth and air beneath them, and with that, she built a basket to scoop them off the caldera floor. A thousand thousand eye facets looked up as she tugged the basket toward the caldera edge. Black and brown bodies pursued in a churning flood.

A trilling scream shattered the smaller bulge, and Meylnara burst forth. Lightning crackled across the caldera. Vic raised an ion shield, deflecting the blast, and sped toward the caldera's wall, the great writhing mass of Kragnashians in tow. They reached the plateau, and the knot melted into the trees. Nymphs bearing larvae darted into the undergrowth. Warriors guarded the cliff edge while others hustled the stoled Center into the woods.

A fiery nimbus crackled around Vic's shield, and she dove

into the trees, pulling the flames with her. The canopy ablaze, she zigzagged among rocks and trunks and ferns, around the rim of the caldera, luring Meylnara toward Gustave. Howling, the other wizard flew after her, shooting blasts of energy from above the canopy.

Shrinejump, Vic cursed. She needed Meylnara on the ground, not high above it. She sailed out of the woods, and fireballs burst around her, scorching past her shield and setting her clothing afire. Snuffing the flames, Vic launched a lightning bolt, and Meylnara tumbled toward the caldera floor.

Fucking Shrinejump! Vic darted after, but Meylnara caught herself and charged, her face awry with fury. Diving and swooping, Vic dodged fireballs and lightning bolts and shot toward their trap. Landing on the far side of the clearing, she planted her feet and waited. The other woman sprang out of the air, landing near Gustave's hiding place. Vic sent a quick prayer to the abandoned ship orbiting the planet, grateful for this particular quirk of fate, destiny, or luck—whatever it was that put Meylnara so close to the pirate.

"The People told me to kill you, and I didn't," Meylnara spat. Her hair singed, her shoulder bubbled with black welts.

"You won't have my child or one of your own," Vic shouted.

"I would have sent you home."

Her hand on her belly, Vic shook her head. "I wouldn't have gone without him." The ferns rustled, and she grabbed Meylnara in a fist of air. Gustave's sword flashed. Meylnara squealed, and the pirate crumpled, his sword and a scream tumbling across the grass. Meylnara shattered Vic's hold, blasting her into the bush, and shot across the caldera, after her People and their enemies.

Shaking, Vic stumbled to Gustave. Hunched over his arm, he breathed in short, wheezing gasps. "Let me see," she said. From elbow to fingers, his arm was bloated and limp, like a bag of fluid. The skin was intact, but she guessed the bones had been pulverized.

"A clever trick," Gustave grated, tears leaking. "She has unmanned me."

Gently, Vic immobilized the limb in a cast of air and bound it to his chest. The last Kragnashians were climbing over the opposite rim. No help for Bethniel here, and Gustave, whatever his role in her destiny, could no longer help either. She sighed, a wave of fatigue rising. The task always had to be done alone.

WAR COUNCIL

Outside the command tent, hooves clomped and wagons clattered, signaling the arrival of another company. Geram held up his hand, asking Velbaor to pause in his reading. Thirteen divisions so far, less than a quarter the troopers Fieldmarshal Henrik wanted for an assault, and it had been a week. Word could spread only so fast, and armies traveled slower than that. Two months ago, there were still enough discharged soldiers hanging around Narath that they could have gathered the necessary force, but now there was nothing to do but wait for the regiments to assemble.

Scouts estimated three hundred Kragnashians occupied the Manor. At least they hadn't left it, come down Manor Hill, and overwhelmed the city. An army of Kragnashians falling upon Narath was the stuff of nightmares.

"Go on," he said as the racket outside quieted.

Velbaor cast his eyes across the list of supplies, restudying the list of weapons at Geram's request. When the Prime Minister reached the end of the page, Geram put his head in his hands. How many Lathans would die retaking the Manor, and could they block the Device once they'd won it back? If they won it?

"You are meeting with Elekia later?" the minister asked.

"What makes you ask that?"

"The head of state must sometimes act in ways the Prime Minister cannot," Velbaor responded, "but he must be careful in his dealings with outlaws."

"I'll bear that in mind."

Late that afternoon, a chill breeze gusted through the messernils as Geram climbed a steep slope, flanked by Drak and Fieldmarshal Henrik, a squad of twenty-four troopers surrounding them. They entered the ruins of an old fortress, once said to belong to a wizard, but now just a few piles of dressed stone atop a hill where Elekia and Olivet waited with half a dozen Caleisbahnin. The pirates' feathers jerked and strained in the wind. Geram released Drak's sight. He did not want to see her.

"Men?" Henrik asked, his mindvoice crisp in the darkness.

"Fifty-two seamen, all armed with steel," Olivet replied formally. "And you have fewer than a thousand."

"It takes time to gather troops," Elekia said, "but I do not believe we can wait any longer."

"Will any seamen be helping them?" Henrik asked.

Geram Heard Breon's reply before the ambassador voiced it. "No. The entire embassy is sworn to the wizard."

"Did you know about this 'Treaty of the First' beforehand?" Geram asked.

"We received no orders from the Archipelago, but even if we had, we are under Elekia's command."

"Tomorrow night, then," Geram said.

"Tomorrow night," Elekia responded, "in the dark of Elesendar."

They fell silent, but calculations were loud in Geram's mind. In a battle among humans, three to one would reckon them winners, but three thousand human troops to assail three hundred Desert People might not be enough.

"The Device." Henrik broke the silence. "Can it be blocked?"

"The master Device is in Direiellene. It can only be stopped from that location."

"Then we must destroy it," Henrik replied grimly. "I'm sorry, Eminence, but the required amount of sulfa will bring down the Manor."

Geram nodded. "Houses can be rebuilt."

"Sulfa will have little effect, Fieldmarshal," Elekia said. "People have tried before to destroy Devices and failed. We have no choice but to go to Direiellene."

"That's suicide!"

"Perhaps. But from the markings on the warriors who captured the Manor, I do not think the Center is behind this. I think the Center will help."

"Madam," Breon said, "if this is true, this rival faction has possession of the master Device or they would not be here."

"They could easily have come using another Device," Geram replied. "Vic learned there is more than one in Kragnash. I agree with Elekia. She and I have to go to Direiellene."

"Eminence!" Henrik cried. "You cannot participate in this attack, much less go to Direiellene. We cannot risk it."

"I'm a regent, Fieldmarshal, and a lot easier to replace than a Ruler or an Heir. As head of state, I have the authority to bargain with the Center." He faced in Elekia's direction. "Isn't that correct?"

"Yes, Eminence. It is."

"Then I will go. Tomorrow night, we attack."

THE COST OF LOVE

Rain pounded the canvas; the ceiling sagged, seepage dripping onto the carpet. Wash water dribbled off Vic's chin. The mirror showed bright green eyes rimmed red, the surrounding skin bruised and worn. Her thighs, back, and neck ached as if she had a fever; her head pounded, and the contents of her stomach churned like the lava moat. She hadn't realized how accustomed she'd become to Bethniel's ministrations until she'd used the Woern for hours without them.

Prenlin handed her a towel and an arm, helping her to a chair. She twisted Vic's hair into a column atop her head, her mouth set in a deep frown. When she finished, Vic gritted her teeth and stepped into an embroidered silk gown. The fabric rasped against burned skin as Prenlin pulled it over her shoulders and tied it closed. When she was dressed, the Healer gripped her shoulders. "Save her."

Tears rose up, stuffing her nose. She clasped the Healer's hand. "I will."

She met Thabean, and they floated to the Council pavilion side by side, shielding themselves from the rain while the men around them blinked in the downpour. His skin pallid, Thabean kept his features smooth and betrayed no more emotion than he had when Dealn died. It seemed the right thing to do; if he betrayed his feelings, it would only make things worse for Bethniel.

"I had the sergeant at arms restrain Lillem until after the trial," he said. "His interference could cause disaster."

Vic grimaced. "That wasn't necessary. Lillem is a disciplined soldier, but what's the plan?"

"Do not worry, madam. You will know what to do as events unfold."

In the Council chamber, he took his place on Saelbeneth's right, Vic hers at the far end of the table, next to Csichren.

Dripping rainwater, Bethniel entered, escorted by Grunnaire.

Saelbeneth read the charges in a voice solemn and foreboding. "What say you?"

Bethniel pushed aside a wet mop of hair. "I did not take the Elixir."

"Yet you have Woern."

"Yes."

"Explain how this is so."

Bethniel looked at each wizard, wearing the same fierce expression with which she'd cowed the Relman Council while a woman's hand burned to the bone. If the princess weren't sopping wet, Vic would have thought Bethniel had put the Council on trial.

"Eighty-four years ago," Beth said, "Kara died, and with her all life on Karaduin. For this reason the Council formed in 1998 and established the Code of Wizardry the following year. Afterward, all wizards who were not members of the Council, whether wealthy or poor, powerful or humble, were killed. So was every latent the Council found."

"Lady Bethniel gives us a history lesson," Nelchior quipped.

"She has the floor," Saelbeneth said. "Let her speak."

"You have said the Purge was a horror, but a necessary one."

Vic glanced around the table, expecting nods or eyebrows raised in assent, but the Council remained still. Even Csichren and Darien gazed at Bethniel, unmoved.

"Yet the choices of our ancestors need not—I argue should not—bear upon our decisions now. I review this history only to ask, what if any with the Woern were missed? The histories tell us the Council's enforcers roved across Knownearth and into the Unknown, going to every town, hamlet, and hermitage, testing everyone they found, from the youngest baby to the eldest grandparent, for the Woern. Everyone they *found*. But Victoria's people have no records of these visits, so we know the Oreseekers were not tested. Among the Caleisbahnin, the First ordered every household to present for testing, but there is no way to know whether they all indeed went. And what of those who hid from the Council? Can you be sure not a single latent escaped the kill squads? Among the mountain folk in the Elgrion, the Relman nomads, the Semena herders, could there not have been some small band, or even one individual, who escaped notice? Perhaps some prospector in the Elgrion who, unaware she possessed latent Woern, would not even have known to fear the Council and would have gone about her business, unaware of the search, much less the danger. I ask you to consider this as a possibility."

She straightened to her full height. Water evaporated from her hair and clothes, surrounding her in mist. Her tresses shrank into glossy curls, revealing her face. Vic's heart thudded as a golden nimbus surrounded the princess. The Council remained impassive, except for a soft curve to Thabean's lips and the greed in Nelchior's eyes.

"I did not steal the Elixir, but I have the Woern," Bethniel said.

"It is not uncommon for the Woern to take months to manifest," Grunnaire said.

"I speak truth. I did not steal the Elixir. The Woern have always been within me."

"You're still an outlaw," Tirnor said.

"As is Victoria," Bethniel said. "And Meylnara."

"Meylnara has been condemned." Nelchior stood. "Victoria's trial was recessed and never resumed."

"Is it her reprieve you seek?" Saelbeneth asked.

"The Code of Wizardry bans wizards from passing the Woern to others. It bans wizards from conceiving or bearing children. It bans individuals without the Woern from obtaining it outside the sanction of the Council. The Code of Wizards does *not* condemn children born of wizards."

Samovael said, "The law is clear: none may obtain the Woern without the sanction of the Council. We came to this land to defend that sacred principle, for which so many died two generations ago."

"Being born with the Woern is the same as illegally obtaining the Elixir," echoed Grunnaire.

Bethniel looked to Saelbeneth for permission to speak. Vic had to admire how she kept her cool, followed protocol, even when her own life was at stake. But then, she held her composure perhaps *because* her own life was at stake. "I bring the Council's attention to Article Fourteen, Paragraph Eight: 'No one may take the Elixir without the knowledge and approval of the Council of Wizards.' The law uses the word 'take' but I was born with it; I did not take it."

"That is a frivolous loophole," Nelchior said. "One could argue you took it from your mother."

"We came here," Thabean said, "with the purpose of preventing Meylnara from establishing a haven for rogue wizards. That is our charter."

"Ah, but we also agreed that Meylnara possesses the Woern illegally," Nelchior purred. "That is the reason behind the purpose."

"I would say it is the other way round," interjected Murnoran. "We told ourselves that, so as to justify this war."

"Do not let us begin questioning our purpose now," Valdesh said. "I have always argued none should be tolerated who are not among the Council." He looked pointedly at Vic, then nodded firmly at Nelchior.

"I will accept Lady Bethniel's argument," Nelchior said. "She is correct that there were many latents when the Council formed, and it would have been a near impossibility that some did not escape the Purge. Yet Meylnara is the only rogue we have seen in the last forty years, besides, of course, our own Victoria. But the emergence of Bethniel's powers begs a question, one far more important to this Council: if she was indeed a latent, what triggered her Woern to become active?"

His words hung over the Council. As his colleagues frowned in consternation, Thabean maintained a cool half-smile, as if he had put on a mask before entering the room. Bethniel also betrayed no emotion at Nelchior's question. Yet the room seemed suddenly cold.

"How did you activate the Woern?" Saelbeneth asked.

Vic held her breath. The Council leaned forward.

"I am uncertain," Bethniel replied. "I fell out of a tree, and my Woern were active when I hit the ground."

The Council members leaned back, dropping disappointed sighs. Thabean stood.

"I too have recently reviewed the Code on this and related matters. Article Fourteen, Paragraph Nine, states the following: 'The Council shall consist of all living Wizards but at no time shall exceed the number Twelve.' We have two wizards here not of this Council."

Bethniel stared at him, cheeks flushed and eyes wide. A knot clogged Vic's throat. Around the table, eyebrows rose.

Saelbeneth looked her age—a dozen or more years older than the rest. "What is your proposal, Thabean?"

He looked at each of his colleagues, his eyes resting on Vic, and then Bethniel. To Vic, his face was all hard angles, but his cheeks softened when he gazed at the princess, and Vic realized what he intended.

"Thabean, no." She stood. "This is a time of war, and laws made to uphold peace are sometimes suspended. Meylnara and the Kragnashians would change history. They would establish a colony of wizards here, people who obtained the Woern without rule and without concern for the powerless. That would endanger you, your people, the world itself. But you have so far been unable to defeat her, even with all your soldiers and all your power put together. Then we came, and you allowed me to live so I might help you. Do not lose the advantage another wizard gives to your cause and of the unique knowledge of this world we hold," she added, looking straight at Saelbeneth. "When Meylnara is dead, we will cooperate in returning the Council to the way it was."

"At no time shall the number exceed Twelve," Thabean repeated. "I contend that Victoria and Bethniel both are meant to be here. Room on the Council should be made for them."

"And who would you suggest retire?" Nelchior asked, his voice like cold acid.

"Darien has no power; she should step aside and allow Victoria to assume her place. I will step down for Bethniel."

"What?" Saelbeneth cried. "Nonsense! Thabean, you are distracting this tribunal from its purpose. Bethniel is an unsanctioned wizard. There can be no doubt of that. The only question is how we shall deal with the matter."

Fists on the table, he bowed his head. "I triggered the emergence of her power."

Bethniel's mouth hung open, her eyes stricken.

"I cannot permit this," Saelbeneth whispered hoarsely.

The Council wizards exchanged glances grave, furious, disgusted. Samovael's brows sank low, his mouth bent down. Nelchior rose, his fingers spread across the table. "I believe this warrants a full confession."

Thabean glared at his rival, his expression more contrite as he faced the other wizards. "Bethniel had no idea of the consequences." He took a breath. "I seduced her."

"No!" Bethniel threw herself forward, eyes beseeching each of them. "I did know—I knew it was wrong, against your laws. I committed a crime as much as he. More than he—I . . . I knew I was a latent. It was my plan, and he was driven by the Woern, unable to stop himself. I wanted to bind him to me, I thought it would make Vic and myself safer, I—"

"Enough!" Saelbeneth's eyes flashed. "The Law is clear on this point too—a wizard shall resist desire, or die. Bethniel, you were not a wizard until *after* the triggering event. Therefore, the Law does not apply to you." The Council leader looked as if she wished it did. "Thabean Graystone, we have heard your confession and, as mandated by the Law, condemn you to death. Samovael and Grunnaire, execute the sentence."

"I bequeath Lady Bethniel my family name and my place on the Council," Thabean said as the two wizards escorted him to the center of the room. "Fainend has the papers."

Nelchior's glee evaporated. Saelbeneth signaled to Halbert, who took Bethniel's elbow. "Join us at table, madam."

"No, this can't be." Tears streaming, she beseeched Saelbeneth. "He is the best of you. You can't do this."

"We will. We must."

Thabean nodded at Saelbeneth and the pair flanking him. Grunnaire's lips curved into a sad smile. Samovael's jaw was stretched in agony, his hands bent into claws. "I'm sorry it must be you, my friend," Thabean said.

"Fucking bastard," Samovael swore. "Fuck fucking fuck."

"Sir," Grunnaire admonished. "We have a duty." She gripped Thabean's arm.

Growling, Samovael seized the other arm. The trio shook, Thabean's tremors elongating, stretching into a violent thrumming until he shredded away to nothing.

Bethniel swallowed a scream. Vic stared at the empty air where Thabean had stood a moment before. No hero's death like in the songs, awash in Kragnashian blood and glory. No great sacrifice to save the Kia. Just . . . gone. "That's it?" she asked hollowly.

Grunnaire nodded and resumed her seat. Samovael stormed to his.

"This tribunal is over," Saelbeneth announced. "Victoria, Bethniel, come with me."

"Before we adjourn, I demand justice," Samovael said through gritted teeth. "Victoria is a rogue and will also bear a child with the Woern. Thabean *was* the best of us. We cannot execute him and leave this woman alive."

"Indeed," echoed Nelchior.

Saelbeneth's expression was thunderous. "Victoria is still under a reprieve. She will face the consequences of her actions in good time."

"We no longer need her, madam, as you know."

Not a breath sounded.

"What do I know?"

Vic's eyes met Bethniel's, and her sister's anguish rent her heart. The Sacrifice was dead, and the Mind remained at risk.

Samovael replied, "You know that Meylnara has placed her essence into the forest, and to kill her, all we have to do is kill the trees."

Gasps descended from the gallery.

"The old mothers," Halbert exclaimed. "We cannot kill the forest!"

"There are no cerrenils here," spat Nelchior.

"I am shocked, sir," Halbert said. "You know well the Kia, and know it does not live in cerrenils alone. There are messernil and geilmors here; why could not the Kia be within them?"

Samovael recoiled. "Sir! This Council condemned the soul of the forest in 2023. Do not put yourself in contempt of that decree."

"Ludicrous fearmongering!" Halbert turned to Saelbeneth. "You revere the forest, as I do, madam. We cannot kill the trees."

The Council leader glared at every face round the table. "These forests which surround us cover vastly more territory than the Kiareinoll. Do you not think destroying them might have some consequences to the entire world?"

"But it is the only way, madam!" Nelchior said. "We are all agreed Meylnara must be destroyed, and we all know the story of the wizard who put his soul into his guard." A smug gleam entered his eyes as he looked at Vic. "We all know what had to be done to destroy him."

"You can't!" Bethniel said. "All of us return to the trees someday, and to kill them is to take the lives of those you love."

Nelchior's gaze stayed fixed on Vic. "We can continue as we have, laying siege to the Lair, spending thousands in treasure and lives, or we can initiate a single, final campaign and be done with this place in a matter of days. But first, we must eliminate the rogue from our ranks."

All eyes landed on Vic, Samovael's gaze hot with hatred. Thabean had said she was stronger than them all. Now she would find out.

"Beth," she said in a flash of mindspeech, "tell Gustave to meet me where we made our sally this morning." Charging ions into a shield, she shot toward the chimney hole. Tentacles of power grabbed her, hauled her down, slipped off her shield, grabbed again. Inch by inch she edged upward through air viscous as mud, the sinews in her ankles, knees, and hips stretched. Leg bones spread apart, her spine separated into each vertebra. *You're stronger than any of us.* Shutting her eyes, she poured all that strength into her flight.

They did not attack, not with fire or lightning. Invisible blows glanced off her shield. She heard them gasp, groan, mewl. Someone shouted, and their grip vanished. She catapulted into the rain. Samovael and Grunnaire burst out of the roof, another two wizards following. Vic hurtled toward the clouds. Vapor closed around her. Her ion shield sparked, and lightning webbed through the sky. Thunder boomed as the energy rushed through her, and the Woern screamed with pleasure. Cursing, Vic moved higher through the bank, her body the epicenter of the electrical storm. When her pursuers entered the clouds, electricity crackled with a life of its own. The sky roiled with thunder; bright, blinding crooks of light stabbed into her. Screaming, she climbed higher, finally bursting out above the maelstrom. The sun blazed over surging gray, and she shot toward the caldera.

A blade of lightning blasted her. Shaking with pain, she wheeled and dodged a giant claw, wielded by Samovael. Vic knocked him down into the lightning-streaked charcoal and shot toward a trio of iron-colored anvils. Staccato spikes lit the inside of each tower; she fled inside one as Samovael emerged. Lightning shattered through her, and she felt it stretch from the stratosphere to the ground far below. The wind roared, spinning her around as the thunderhead suddenly collapsed, winding toward the ground, a cyclone dragging her down toward the churning forest and earth below. The howling gale yanked her limbs, pulling them out of their sockets, and it took all her power just to hold herself together. She couldn't breathe, couldn't tell up from down as she wheeled around the vortex. At last the tornado flung her away, and she sailed toward the thrashing canopy. Seizing control of her flight, she dodged through whipping branches and took shelter in the folded roots of a giant messernil.

Above, the storm raged, the thunder constant. Gasping, Vic huddled in a nest of ferns, thankful to be still, even in the slashing rain. If she used no power, they would not find her. She could make her way on foot to the caldera, find the Kragnashians, obtain refuge from them.

With a deep breath, she stood. The robe, soaked and heavy, clammed against her legs. Her stomach clenched. *Damn, you can eat,* she thought at her son.

A fist punched from the inside, shoving her onto her knees and ramming vomit up her throat. Gagging, she sent a pulse of energy to counter the spasms. Another cramp bore down, and matter surged past her cervix. "Elesendar," she gasped, splaying her hands across her belly. Pain ripped from her sternum to her groin. Her knees contracted toward her forehead, her abdomen twisting, wringing out the blood that gushed down her thighs. "Elesendar, please, no!" The abandoned spacecraft made no answer, and her tally of deaths grew by one.

HAVEN

Ashel's baritone beat like a heart. Wineyll's flute danced like the flickering light. She lost herself in the sound reverberating off the stone walls, reveled in the way it echoed up the passage to the library and came back louder, fuller, turning their duet into a symphony. Wing covers burred in time with the music, and Ashel laughed and patted a thorax when one of the creatures squealed, trying to copy Wineyll's melody. Its screeching hurt her ears, but she carried on through to the end, happy to see Ashel finding some joy in the exercise. The song ended, and the singing Kragnashian chittered at its fellow, who stood still and implacable.

Ashel bowed and clapped a thank you for the day's lesson.

"The Voice learns," the friendlier Kragnashian replied.

"Who is your ally?"

"The cup is full."

Thanking it again, Ashel angled his head up the passage. For a week, Wineyll had accompanied him while he traded songs for lessons. They'd spent most of each day immersed in Kragnashian vocabulary and syntax, but Wineyll felt her mastery equated to a toddler's.

"I wish I had some idea whether those People down there are Lornk's partners executing a ruse or truly Parnden's allies," Ashel said when they reached the stacks, "but all they ever say is, 'The cup is full.'"

"If wishes were horses," Wineyll sighed. "Everyone says Kragnashians never lie."

"Just because no one's ever caught them in a lie doesn't mean they don't. The Kragnashians were supposed to guide you all through the desert, and they let you get lost."

Earnk knocked on the doorframe. "The fishmonger brought word that Parnden will hang Alek tomorrow at sunset. Father's come ashore. Are you ready?"

Stomach twisting, Wineyll nodded and packed the flute into its case. Earnk clasped her hand, and they went down the hall together. *No*, she thought. *Just tell him no.* His father . . . wasn't she still tied to Lornk? *Not really*, she argued. Elekia was Lornk's wife by Lathan custom, even if they'd never declared. But what about the Penance? At Ashel's urging—or insistence—Earnk had promised to arrange a short sentence. A few weeks at most. But could she face the families of people who'd died because she failed? Or of Mane Thrushwind, the boy she'd killed herself? Surely only a madwoman would agree to that. Yet as the Concordance loomed, her fingers clung to Earnk's, and she did not have the strength to let go.

Kelmair met them in the kitchen, where Elsa handed them plain cloaks. Shouldering a rucksack, Ashel cracked open the courtyard door. "Two on the peddler door, four on the gate. No Kragnashians."

"I wish I had my sword," Kelmair grumbled.

Wineyll peered through the crack, studying Parnden's guards. One whittled, a pair leaned against the wall, the other three squatted round a game of dice. They seemed relaxed enough now, but whenever anyone entered the courtyard, the soldiers would spring up and watch with hard eyes, hands on hilts. Reaching into their minds, Wineyll placed an image of empty cobbles. "I'll go first."

She stepped into the crisp autumn morning. The dicing guards hooted over a throw; the whittling one glanced around and back at her carving. A wood shaving fell at her feet. Wineyll motioned the others forward. The door clicked shut, and the group walked casually across the courtyard. Wineyll's eyes darted for other witnesses, but no faces appeared in windows, no doors creaked open. Ashel edged past the guards beside the peddler's door and silently lifted the latch. The door swung open on well-oiled hinges, and they slipped past guards whose gazes never wavered from their game. A family strolled on the opposite sidewalk, mother and father swinging a little boy to and fro. The child hallooed as he sailed up, his parents laughing, and Wineyll filled their vision with a quiet street where the family walked alone.

They hurried down the block and had almost reached the corner when pain like a hard fist punched her below her navel. Her knees struck the pavement, and the flute case bounced away. The sidewalk smelled like fungus and earth. The air hot and clammy, sweat erupted, soaking her garments as another cramp seized her pelvis. "Elesendar," she breathed, palms splayed across her belly. Her knees contracted toward her forehead, her body encircling the pain.

Rain pours through limbs and leaves, making the ground a quagmire. Heavy silk, drenched with mud, clings to her legs, pulls her toward the earth.

Dimly, she Heard babbled concern. A hand pillowed her head, another shook her shoulder. The family rushed to help. Shooing them away, Kelmair hissed in mindspeech, "The guards!"

Arms slid under Wineyll's shoulders and knees. She bounced against a solid chest as feet ran down the block, dodging round one corner and another.

They skidded to a stop, and Wineyll felt herself set on sticky cobbles in a narrow alley. A cat hissed and sniffed round a bin. Kelmair danced from foot to foot, watching round the corner for pursuit. Ashel patted her hand; Earnk cradled her head.

Thunder booms, and tree roots shiver. Another cramp, another wail rolls through her.

"Kelmair and I will lead the guards away while you take Wineyll back," Ashel said to Earnk.

"No," Wineyll groaned, rotting midden and humus thick in her nose.

"They're coming," Kelmair said.

She is whimpering, begging Elesendar, but another contraction seizes her womb like a vise.

Wineyll thrust herself onto an elbow. "Be still," she whispered aloud, shoving aside Vic's sensations and Listening for the approaching guards. Her breath in short gasps, she projected a refuse-strewn alley, its only occupant a hungry cat. Two guards dashed past. Backing up, they reappeared in the alley entrance and peered into the shadows. One took a few steps toward them. Growling, the cat arched its back. Assuring each other it was clear, the guards rushed away.

Quivering, Wineyll fought to block Vic's pain. "I don't want to go back," she gasped. "But we can't stay here."

"What's wrong? Are you ill?" Ashel asked.

A fist ground into her gut. Earnk scooped her into his arms. *Tell Vic my heart aches for her,* he said so only she could Hear.

"We'll never make it if she's too sick to hide us," Kelmair said.

Earnk cradled her as her body clenched around the pain. "We can't go to the Storunds' now. It will be the first place Parnden's guards look for us."

Ashel clasped her shoulder. "Can you hide us until after they've searched? We could take refuge there after they've cleared it."

"I can." Wineyll gasped as another contraction tore at Vic. They all gave her looks full of doubt. "I swear, I can."

Nodding, Earnk climbed to his feet and headed out of the alley.

✝ ✝ ✝

A platoon of soldiers milled around the Storunds' block, coming and going through the palazzo gate. Ashel ushered everyone into another alley and prayed Wineyll could maintain her illusions through whatever strange illness had suddenly afflicted her.

A few passersby rushed past, eyes on their feet. Wineyll, red-faced, panted in Earnk's arms. Forehead pressed to hers, he rocked slowly, murmuring in an inaudible whisper, the words so quiet Ashel could neither hear nor Hear them. Two long hours passed before the soldiers finally filed out and marched away. When the street was clear, they scurried to the gate, and Ashel pulled on the bell rope.

The view portal slid back, revealing an aged eye. "They were just here looking for you," said the servant. "Tore the place apart."

"I know. We're sorry. Please tell Ellen—"

A side door opened, and a hand motioned them inside. Once they were through, Wineyll released a groan.

"She's sick," Ashel whispered.

A finger to her lips, Ellen led them inside the house. Servants rushed ahead, and they brought Wineyll to an elegantly furnished bedchamber. A maid righted overturned chairs while another scurried to put tumbled bedclothes in order. A third removed Wineyll's shoes, and Earnk laid her down. A heavy groan pulled her back into an arch. Her hand locked around Earnk's, she collapsed back on the bed, gasping.

"Go fetch Moralen," Ellen told a servant.

"I'll stay with her," Earnk said.

Ashel pulled the flute case out of his rucksack and left it on the dresser before he and Kelmair followed Ellen to a parlor, where she filled three glasses with harlolinde.

Studying the clear liquid, Ashel wondered at the malady that had taken Wineyll so suddenly. Her father had died of a wasting disease that left him in breathless agony, but her condition seemed different.

Their host had her own troubles; her face was mottled purple and yellow, striped with lacerations. "Did the soldiers hurt you?"

Ellen grimaced. "Not for the first time. They left me beaten and bloody the day they arrested Alek. The Commissar shut down the tavern too."

"I'm sorry you've been dragged into this."

"Oh, I've been in it since the day the pirates took us off Cairo's beach. The only reason Alek hasn't been executed yet is Parnden wanted me to pay the fine and find a substitute. He would have been delighted to see an Oreseeker child take Alek's place in the noose."

Ashel squeezed her hand. "I read the pamphlet. Democracy is a bold idea for Betheljin, one I doubt Lornk would embrace if he succeeds."

"The only thing your father and Alek disagree on, is how to organize elections across such a vast territory."

Ashel drained the glass, wondering if he'd get used to people calling Lornk his father. Everyone simply accepted it; he'd overheard the servants arguing who resembled Lornk more, Earnk or himself. "But Lornk still intends to call himself Commissar."

She smiled sadly. "One step at a time, Ashel. It will be easier to outlaw slavery when it can be done by fiat."

"Do you really trust he will help the Oreseekers?"

"Whatever Lornk's flaws, he is our best hope."

"Your confidence in me is always heartening, Ellen." Lornk entered and embraced the Oreseeker. "I promise you, Alek will not die upon that gibbet."

"How did you get in?" Ashel asked. "Parnden's troops must be swarming the neighborhood."

Lornk, clad in tattered culottes and a patched linen shirt, poured himself a glass of harlolinde. "This particular property has several secret passages and hidey-holes. I was already here when the guards came. What I'd like to know is why the troops are on the hunt—whose carelessness tipped them off?"

"It wasn't carelessness. Wineyll took ill suddenly, and we were seen."

"What's wrong with her?"

"We don't know."

"Moralen is coming," Ellen said.

"Do we strike tonight?" Kelmair asked.

Everyone turned to her in surprise. The Caleisbahn woman stood on flexed knees, as if ready to spring.

"I want to know about the Kragnashians in my house," Lornk said, turning to Ashel. A smirk pulled at his lips. "Forgive me. Your house, son."

Ashel's teeth clamped his tongue, and iron trickled down his throat while he opened the rucksack and pulled out the book on Kragnashian clans. "They aren't related to the Center. The markings looked like these." He pointed at the tattoos of a clan known to occupy the desert surrounding Direiellene. "Are those your partners?"

Lornk scowled. "You must be mistaken. There are subtleties—"

"This book says there are two main clans in the Kragnashian desert, and I've seen the Center myself. It's not that difficult to tell them apart."

"My allies would not betray me to Parnden."

"How can you be sure of that? Perhaps they want humanity too busy fighting each other to fight them? They said they were taking over all the Devices in the world based on a treaty with the First."

"And how do you know that?"

Ashel's pulse quickened as Geram's attention shifted to him. *This is the fate of humanity*, Geram said. *Like it or not, we must all stand together. Tell him.*

"Because that's what they said when they took over Latha. I Heard them through Geram."

Lornk studied him, lips twitching. He loosed a low chortle, then smoothed his features over. "I wish you'd told me sooner. This is a tactical advantage I should have known about."

"I've told you now that there's a tactical need for you to know."

"What else did the Kragnashians say?"

"Nothing specific, but when Parnden was showing off, a Kragnashian conveyed something to me." The memory of hope shivered down his spine. "It left me with a feeling that they do not necessarily support Parnden."

"A feeling?"

"A hunch. A suspicion. But one that flies in the face of the evidence that Parnden is in league with them. He called them his allies."

"I despise uncertainty, Ashel."

"So do I, Lornk, and it seems the only thing we can be certain of is that we cannot count on your so-called partners." He swallowed. "Maybe Vic has already failed and they've sought other alliances. Or maybe they have stepped in to prevent a partnership between Parnden and the Center. The Center told my mother it would bring Vic and Bethniel back if she pledged allegiance to them."

"Your mother. None of this would have happened if she hadn't meddled in my affairs."

"She had nothing to do with your failure to oust Parnden this summer."

"But she had everything to do with the debacle happening in Direiellene. You're right that this new alliance with Parnden suggests the War of the Council is not turning in our favor, which would not be the case had Victoria gone to Direiellene prepared!"

Ashel lunged up, fists clenched. "You call your depravities tactics in your grand scheme, but they're nothing but perverse indulgences."

"And when Elekia took your blind mind-companion to her bed, was that a perverse indulgence or a depraved tactic?"

Crystal jumped as Ashel's fist slammed the sideboard. Fury ran white hot through his blood, multiplied by Geram's outrage and shame and the anguish that had plagued him all summer. Muscles quivering, Ashel sucked in breath after breath until he'd corralled his rage. "I am counting on your desire to use a wizard to secure your place as Commissar, just as you are counting on me to be the tie that binds that wizard to you. I will stand beside you against Parnden because my love for her is greater than my hatred for you. But do not mistake alliance for allegiance."

Arms crossed, Lornk answered him with a menacing glare.

"When do we strike?" Kelmair asked again. "That is all that matters."

Ashel refilled his glass and poured the heat down his throat. "Lathan forces are gathering for an assault tomorrow night. My mother will use her powers to help retake the Manor. If we attack Parnden at the same time, it may tie down his Kragnashian allies here, giving them a better chance in Latha."

"Elekia has openly declared herself a wizard?"

Ashel growled the admission: "She has."

Lornk lips spread to reveal gleaming teeth. "In honor of my wife's sacrifice, I agree. We make our assault tomorrow night."

Across the Ages

The cool light of early morning breezed past sheer curtains. Wineyll rubbed at the grit on her cheeks. The horrible cramping was gone from her belly, but Vic's ached as she lay on ferns between the folded roots of a massive tree.

> *She holds him to her chest. Wrinkled skin, eyes shut tight, tiny, curled fingers. She wouldn't have guessed he'd have hair already, but it was there, black wisps. The size of a kitten, he looked as whole as a living child, but he had been stiff when he emerged from her womb. Her eyelids blink over dry eyes. Hope sheds tears. But not despair.*

Wineyll hugged a pillow, tears leaking into her hair as she poured sympathy into the emptiness of Vic's thoughts.

No, Vic cried. *Wineyll, don't.*

Vic felt no surprise that Wineyll had been with her all night. The dead child overwhelmed everything else. *Everything I've ever wanted . . . I've destroyed,* she said.

It was an accident—

It's all an accident! I do nothing with purpose! Nothing by choice.

You chose to love Ashel. And you're going to come home to him.

Vic groaned, clutching the tiny body under her chin, her fingers pressed deep into its flesh. Caught in the other woman's sorrow, Wineyll squeezed the pillow.

"How are you?" Slipping inside, Earnk shut the door and sat on the bed. "How is she?"

472

Wineyll crawled into the crook of his arm. In Direiellene, shock threaded through Vic's grief.

"Vic, I'm so sorry for your loss," Earnk said, squeezing Wineyll's shoulders. "I . . . I cannot imagine your pain. Please know we're doing all we can to bring you home."

Wineyll shuddered as Vic screamed through another paroxysm of grief.

Earnk let her go; a moment later he pressed the flute case into her hands. "Play something," he whispered, opening the latches.

She blinked at the softly gleaming pieces. "I dropped this yesterday."

"Would my brother leave that lying in the street? Play something."

Vic's grip on the baby loosened. *What brother? Does he mean Ashel?*

Assembling the flute, Wineyll blew softly over the mouthpiece, and a low C warmed the room. *Ashel is here with us,* she said. *We're all fighting for you.* The note a bit flat, she adjusted the headjoint and tried again. The sound true, she blew softly at first, then louder without changing pitch, listening carefully to the purity of that single tone as it fluctuated up and down in volume. Breathe. The same note again, only this time scaled up, then down an octave, back and forth, her spine straightening to support her breath. Breathe. Soft. Loud. High. Low. Same exercise, faster, slower, longer, shorter, with the tongue, without. The sound wrapped around her like a white cocoon, blinding and familiar. *I want to live in this sound,* she thought.

And never let anything in, Vic said. *Not all those deaths. Not—*

Wineyll swooped into "The Cerrenil's Joy," which people sang at wakes. In Direiellene, Vic's mouth stretched round a soundless rage. Wineyll closed her eyes, sunk into the melody, merged with it, feeling it as *forgiveness.*

When the last note died, Vic put the baby down. Wineyll opened her eyes, and Earnk threaded his fingers through hers. She nestled her head on his shoulder while Vic lay down beside the little body, breathing slowly and deeply. Her chest moving in like rhythm, Wineyll felt the steady beating of Earnk's heart.

"I wanted your father to meet you," Vic whispered, stroking the tiny head. "He would sing you to sleep if he were here."

"He should be here," Earnk said. "I'll get him."

Vic froze, and Wineyll could feel her protest—born of fear and grief and shame that she'd failed to protect this child.

"No, no, let him come," she murmured aloud.

Earnk paused at the door, blue eyes absorbing the sorrow that spilled from Vic into Wineyll, a tsunami that could drown them all. "Do not refuse him his chance to say goodbye," he said. "Do not deprive yourself of the comfort of those you love."

He left, carrying their grief away, and Wineyll knew the answer to his proposal.

Ashel fastened the last clasp on his vest, his gaze fixed on a narrow patio and garden and the city wall that loomed over it, the crenellations bright in the morning sun. His stomach growled with hunger, but he was anxious to know if Wineyll had recovered.

What was wrong with her? Geram asked.

Moralen wouldn't say.

You know how we affect one another.

Gut twisted with foreboding, Ashel resisted the insight dawning in Geram's mind. *What do you mean?*

In Olmlablaire, for a time, she was connected to Vic. I thought we severed that connection, but what if some thread of it remained?

An urgent knock rattled his door. When Ashel opened it, Earnk said, "Come to Wineyll's room. Now."

His heart stopped, and he felt Geram's lungs freeze. "Is Vic all right?"

"She needs you."

His feet as twisted and uncertain as a babe's, he stumbled after his brother. *He is my brother*, he thought, fixating on that notion, using it as an anchor to withstand the tempest swirling around him. Terror, regret, remorse, awe, incredulity, hope, and joy smashed at him like a violent sea.

"All that strength and courage you showed in Olmlablaire," Earnk said, gripping his arm. "She needs that now. She needs the best of you." He opened Wineyll's door.

"Oh, Ashel." Wineyll wrapped her arms round his waist.

The darkness that had smothered him in the Roost loomed around him, and he fell to his knees. "Is Vic alive?"

His Guild-sister dropped to the floor with him. "She lives. But . . . she lost the baby."

His breath trapped in his chest, he stared at brimming blue irises, replacing them in his mind's eye with green. Air stuttered into his lungs, and he cupped Wineyll's damp cheeks in his palms, knowing what Vic would feel. All the times Geram had kissed his mother, and he'd felt her lips on his mouth. Elesendar, all the time he'd spent drunk in taverns, in his bed, the night he'd lost himself to bliss, to Kelmair . . . he shoved it all aside. Vic needed him. Replacing Wineyll's dark thick hair with finespun amber, he kissed her forehead, spoke to the blue eyes that ought to be green: "My heart is yours. Always and forever yours. And your grief is mine. I share this burden of sadness with you, but when we see each other again, we'll trade heartache for joy. The Concordance is here, my love, and you're coming home."

"Shut your eyes," Wineyll murmured, "and you'll be with her."

The light dimmed into deep green shadows and rough brown bark. Vic lay upon the earth, hair ratted, face battered and streaked with dirt. One hand stroked black fuzz on a tiny head. The eyelids were folded shut over pouting lips, the skin translucent brown and delicate as porcelain.

He sucked in a shuddering breath, blew it out slowly, and pulled in another and another until his lungs worked as smoothly as a bellows. He'd missed his father's funeral. He would not miss his son's.

Over the mount,

There lies a place

Where love has lasting grace,

Where peace and joy go hand in hand,

Over the mountain, in that land.

His wife moaned and curled around the babe. Her shoulders shook as he sang verses he wrote for her to show a warrior the path toward peace. He opened his chest and tightened his diaphragm, singing with all his power, just as he had for the Center. He *would* bring his love home with a song, even if the only home they ever knew together was in this moment, a thousand years away from each other.

Vic's sobs quieted. She pushed herself onto shaky knees. A scoop of dirt rose from between folded tree roots and plopped into a small mound. "Joseph, your father's singing you to sleep." She laid the baby into the hollowed earth and caressed his cheek until the last note faded.

"I named him after my mother's father. He was mayor of Ourtown. He died before I knew him, but they say he was a good mayor."

"It's a good name," Ashel said.

"Goodbye, my love." She bent down and kissed the little forehead, then used her hands to push the dirt into the grave. As the earth settled, the roots seemed to bend around the mound like the protective arms of a parent. Vic pressed her hand to the tree and said softly and aloud, "Thank you." Sitting back against the trunk, she looked up at the canopy, far, far above. "I'm sorry I lost him."

"Oh, no," he murmured, pulling Wineyll into his arms, knowing Vic would feel the embrace. "It's not your fault." He rocked Wineyll, giving comfort to both the minstrel and his wife.

† † †

Vic wept in the ethereal arms that held her other self, a world and an age away. She wanted to rest in Ashel's embrace, but there wasn't time—she had to reach the caldera. She begged Wineyll to push him away, but the minstrel clung to him, stubbornly refusing to let him go.

Vic, you have to keep going, said Geram, cutting into their grief.

Leave her be, Ashel said.

We've all got a task, Geram replied, his voice like metal. *I grieve for you both, but every one of us has a battle to fight today.*

She shut her eyes tight and saw Ashel's careworn face, a ragged week-old beard, his eyes rimmed with shadows. He was not the beautiful, carefree fairytale prince she'd once pined for, but that had been an illusion, and the man she loved had never been so frivolous. *I just want to come home.*

You know you can't until this is finished.

With a howl, she drew her knees to her forehead. Her womb ached and bled. Her mouth was dry as sand, and her limbs shook with fatigue. She needed rest, water, food. She was in no shape to fight.

I know it hurts, Ashel said. *I wish I could come to you, hold you, give you all the strength and healing you need . . . but Geram's right.*

Startled and wounded, she stared at the trees. Rain dripped through foliage, splattering her hair. *You're not the one stuck here.*

This time tomorrow, it will be over, Ashel said. *Tonight, we're going to war to bring you home. But if you fail, history may change, and we won't be able to bring you back. Please, my love, you're the strongest person I know—*

You're the sharpest, Geram said. *You're the Blade. You're the one who never fails.*

Anguish flooded from Vic's eyes and tore from her mouth. *Fail? When haven't I failed?* She had no more tears for weeping, but the sobs poured forth. *All three of you suffered because I failed.*

So redeem yourself, Wineyll said, her voice hard and thin, no longer thick with sympathy. *We're not the only ones depending on you—it's all the peoples of Knownearth. You're the One, Vic. And you know it's possible for you to succeed because we're living in a world shaped by the success of the One. But failure is possible too. Only you can choose which it will be.*

Coughing, Vic flopped back against a log. *I don't know how to kill her. Everything Bethniel and I thought we knew about this time—it's completely different.*

You'll find a way, Ashel said.

You will and you must, Geram said. *I grieve for your child, but remember all the other children. Remember Victory. Maynon and Silla need you to do this for her.*

Victory. Hands clenched, she moaned, remembering the soft, fragile warmth of her friends' newborn daughter, named for her and for an ideal she couldn't live up to. She'd said she wouldn't let Thabean die, and she'd lost him. *Failure.*

Come home to me, Ashel said. *Bring my sister, and bring my wife. Bring my loves home.*

Bethniel. She'd sworn to protect her. *The job's not done.* Groaning, she climbed to her feet and threw her head back, mouth open, wetting her throat with raindrops. Her knees shook, and she swayed into a thickly folded tree root. If she didn't get more water, she'd collapse. Shutting her eyes, she pulled at the Woern. Pain shot through her skull, but she lifted herself into the air. The Woern were just as wounded as she was, but they would heal faster if she fed them, and they would, in return, give her strength. The Council might track her eddies, but Geram was right, there was no longer any time. She would bring her sister home if it killed her.

THE MARSHALING

Bethniel stumbled into the hospital. Soldiers and servants moaned in dense rows, victims of the cyclones that had ravaged the camp. Prenlin stepped over and around the wounded and bowed. "Are you ill, madam?"

"No," she sighed. "Just tired. I need to find Gustave of Sect Dameron."

"In the Caleisbahn ward. I'll get you something to restore your energy."

Thanking her, Bethniel picked her way to the far side of the pavilion. In the week since their wedding, Thabean had secretly trained her to use the Woern, but her first real lessons had come when she helped disperse the cyclones that raged through the night. As dawn broke, the thunderclouds had shredded into wisps across an azure sky, and Bethniel had finally been able to look for Gustave. The commodore had sent her here.

In a corner, the Caleisbahn physician slumped on a stool, surrounded by several dozen injured pirates. Gustave lay asleep, his right arm propped on a cushion. It ended at a thickly bandaged elbow.

Gently squeezing his shoulder, she whispered his name in mindspeech. He remained insensate, his breathing deep and steady. Cursing, she shook the Caleisbahn doctor awake.

"I must speak with Commander Gustave. Can you rouse him?"

The man's expression passed from groggy to scornful. "Be gone, woman! Master Healer," he said as Prenlin arrived, bearing a steaming cup, "advise your pan cleaner not to disturb my patients!"

"This will revive you, madam." Prenlin handed the cup to Bethniel and raised an eyebrow at the other healer. "This is Bethniel Graystone, doctor. She has assumed Thabean Graystone's place on the Council."

Eyes wide, he sprang to his feet and bowed. "Madam! My apologies. How may I serve you?"

"I need to speak to Gustave," she repeated and sipped the tincture. It was horribly bitter, but the nostril-flaring scent jolted through her blood, and the warmth eased her aches. The Caleisbahn physician held a potion under Gustave's nose until he gagged and his eyes fluttered open.

Bethniel shooed the healers away and knelt beside the pirate. "Gustave, Vic had to flee. She wanted you to meet her."

Head lolling, he mumbled the name "Samson."

"Gustave." She shook his shoulder. "Vic said you should meet her 'where you made your sally?' What does that mean?"

He sucked in a deep, noisy breath and roused himself. "We fought Meylnara at the caldera." His eyes fell on his missing forearm. Yelping, he twisted right and left, as if looking for it.

"Seaman!" the Caleisbahn healer barked. "Control yourself."

"Was he injured by the cyclones?" Bethniel asked.

"No. Victoria brought him in yesterday, before your . . . ascension, madam. All the bones beneath the elbow were pulverized. We had no choice but to take it."

"Why did Meylnara attack you?" she asked Gustave.

Gustave scrubbed his remaining hand over his cheeks. "She wanted to ask the Caldera tribe to harbor you. But Meylnara and her People had launched an assault on their stronghold. Victoria and I took the opportunity to try to kill her. We failed."

Bethniel stared at him, ears pumping with blood. What could Vic have been thinking, taking on Meylnara alone? And how could she have imagined Gustave would be capable of meeting her? Voice taut, she asked where to find the place.

Furious, she stalked to Vic's tent. Who did she think she was, the Blade still, going off alone to assassinate fieldmarshals? She had a child to think of! *She has me to think of.* In the pit of her stomach, a small voice wailed.

She stuffed clothes and supplies into a satchel, went to the mess and asked for cheese and flatcakes. Still clearing away debris, the cooks provided the food immediately and without a hint of surprise, as if wizards wandered in, demanding a week's rations all the time. Shoving the food into the satchel, she flew up and headed for the caldera.

Flying had come easily to her, as had much of what Thabean had taught her. Her chest tight, she pushed aside her grief and used her anger at Vic to speed to the caldera. Still fuming, she landed in the clearing Gustave described. *Elesendar, let her be all right.* She scanned the empty ground, the hollow spaces beneath trees and bushes. Samovael had seemed determined to murder Vic, but he and Grunnaire had staggered into the Council chamber at dawn and admitted they hadn't found her. Nelchior had insulted the returned wizards until the moment he vomited on the Council table.

Dropping the satchel in a gap between roots, Bethniel laid her palm on the trunk and prayed that Vic would find it. "She's all right," she said aloud. "She has to be. She still has a destiny to fulfill." But history had already changed. No records told of a 'Lady Bethniel,' a latent wizard who had been Thabean's lover and heir. History said he had died with honor and glory in battle, not that he was unceremoniously executed for violating the Code he held sacred. Even Meylnara was not the evil witch history painted her but a scared, lonely woman, sentenced to death because her mother committed the same crime as Thabean and Vic. Where was Vic? What if she'd been killed by the storm? *I might be alone now,* Bethniel thought, dread twisting.

Clicks blurred behind her. Two warriors stood in the clearing, their tattoos marking them as Caldera tribe. Antennae waving, they bent their heads toward her.

Her fear turned over once again to anger. "The Sacrifice is dead," she clapped.

The two spun round and vanished into the forest. Bethniel gazed at the screen of vegetation. "Thabean didn't die for the Kia, he died for me!" she shouted. "He shouldn't have died at all. None of this should be happening at all!"

Growling, she swiped at tears born more of fury than sorrow. Hunting a last time for Vic, she prayed to find her sister asleep under a bush.

The Caldera Center emerged from the forest and bowed. "We erred."

Her pulse beat in her throat. "How—" She wanted to ask how they could have erred so badly, but her father always said, casting blame does nothing to correct mistakes. "How did you err?"

"We did not anticipate that two would be one. The Concordance has begun. You are the Fulcrum; events shall turn about you. You must choose."

"You said the Fulcrum was passive."

"We erred," the Center repeated. "The Concordance is in your hands."

"What about Vic, the One?"

"The One will play a role. But you will choose the future of your people and ours. The lineage of the Child seeks dominance over all lineages and peoples. We follow the Treaty of the First and seek to coexist."

"And you will send us home when Meylnara is dead," Bethniel reminded them of the terms Vic had made.

"If the Sacrifice is made, those from history will be returned."

"But the Sacrifice is dead!" she shouted, clapping a moment later.

"The Child moves toward the camp of the Council. We will await the One." Like a ghost, it melted back into the forest.

The quiet heat inside her tent pressed into Bethniel's pores. She'd always lived in quiet, among people who used their voices only to express the most urgent or profound emotions. Because she'd always known it, she'd never associated silence with solitude, until now. In a day, she'd lost her husband and her sister. She'd inherited a title she didn't want to own, a people she didn't want to command, and a power she would have refused if given the choice. *"You must choose."* The words haunted her. *"If the Sacrifice is made."* She wondered why she wasn't curled up in a ball, weeping her eyes dry, but she had nothing to give over to weeping. She had nothing.

The tent flap rustled as Lillem came inside and stood at attention.

"Out," she commanded.

"What are you going to do?" he asked.

"Mourn!" she spat.

"There must still be a sacrifice."

She waved him off. "Fine, *Sergeant*. You're dismissed."

"Highness—"

"It's madam, now."

"Madam . . . Thabean is gone. Your sister is likely gone. *We* must do this thing."

"I don't know how," she said bitterly. Vic had been convinced her experience with the soldiers in the training yard was the key, but Bethniel had no idea what had happened there. Her only hope was to Listen to Meylnara and find a way to shift her connection to the forest through mindspeech.

Lillem knelt beside her. "There must still be a sacrifice."

Tears streamed at last. "I know." *Elesendar help me.*

"I will help you."

Wiping her nose, she rose. "The Caldera Center told me Meylnara is on her way here." She drew back her shoulders and raised her head. "I don't know how long it's going to take me to do it. I'll need you to guard my back and get Gustave from the hospital. If I . . . you'll need him to talk to the Kragnashians, so you can go home."

Lillem saluted. "Yes, Highness—madam."

"Tell Fainend I want to see him."

Lillem left, and Fainend arrived soon after. "Meylnara's on her way," Bethniel said. "I need to know what happens if I do not designate an heir to my seat on the Council?"

"If you died without a clear line of succession, the next Candidate for the Elixir would be chosen from the educated by lot. But in that case, Nelchior could claim the northern reaches for himself."

"No wonder he and Thabean were at odds."

"That was one reason, madam. For the others, one need only be acquainted with the wizard."

She snorted. "Before Thabean bequeathed everything to me, did he have a roster of candidates?"

"He did, madam."

"Come with me to Saelbeneth's, and tell me about them on the way."

Vic reached the caldera when the sun stood halfway to its zenith, heat beating out of a cloudless sky. It was as if the storm had dumped every bit of moisture from the air and the forest had sucked it all up, leaving nothing but brittle bark and sandy soil, ripe for fire. Panting, Vic landed in the clearing where they'd faced Meylnara. There was no sign of Gustave—she'd been a fool to think he'd be capable of standing, much less walking the fifteen leagues between here and the Council's camp. Defeated, she collapsed to her knees and spotted a leather strap near the forest edge. In a hollow at the base of a trunk was a satchel holding supplies. "Bless you, Bethniel," she breathed, opening a canteen. The water was hot but wet. She drank in sips, restoring moisture slowly, so she wouldn't vomit it all back up.

Soap and a comb folded into fresh clothing teased out a fleeting chuckle. "That's my sister." Yet as she scrubbed blood and dirt from her hands, her mouth twisted down. *Joseph.* Sucking in a breath, she pushed the sorrow away and changed into a tunic and trousers. The silken robe stank of iron and death. She rolled it up and stuffed it in the hollow. Joseph was a soldier in this war. She would mourn him when it was over.

She swallowed more water and bit into a pome, staunching her hunger. Some cheese sated the devouring emptiness in her belly. She ate slowly, chewed and swallowed carefully, gaining strength for the fight ahead. When she finished and was wrapping up the remaining food, the Caldera Center flowed into the clearing and clicked at her, tossing its head. Two warriors flanked it, their mandibles heavily tattooed, and added their clicks and whistles. Wishing she understood them, Vic held her hands before her and bowed.

Staccato chirps and long burrs flurried from the Center. Wing covers snapped open and shut, and the creature's mouthparts made a giant circle in the air. It lowered its head and thorax to a height Vic could mount.

All her life, she had railed and fought against fate. She'd followed it too—even chased it. But she had never surrendered to it, until now. The creature was incomprehensible, but she trusted it with that same certainty she had trusted Fembrosh a thousand times before. The Kia had steered her toward this moment, and the Kragnashians would see she met her destiny. Bowing again, she climbed onto the Center and settled between split wing covers.

They swept through the forest, gliding through brambles, glossing over logs, melting between trees. She huddled within the Center's carapace, safe from whipping branches and nettles while she fretted over the blood weeping from her womb, mucking her trousers and staining the silky gossamer wings beneath her. Her abdomen throbbed, and her body ached as if a fever were coming on. Fists clenched, she called upon the Woern and cooled the air round her skin. Do just enough. Aches receded, and she felt nerves and muscles come alive, preparing for the long day ahead.

CONCORDANCE

Cooled by the deluge, the lava was covered with a cracked, blackened shell, an easy ford for the People that swarmed across like a tsunami. Ranks of pikemen contracted before the onslaught, and the soldiers fell upon their larger foes like harriers on a lupear. The Kragnashians died like lupears too, each taking a dozen harriers with it. The air stank of offal and cut grass.

Bethniel hovered above the moat, waiting for Saelbeneth's signal. A whistle shrilled, and she sliced into the crust and dug out a lump of molten rock. She caused the molecules within to vibrate, and an explosion blasted Kragnashians into the air. All around the moat, the rest of the Council dug through the crust. Fire roared along the channel, and Kragnashians drowned in churning rock and flame.

Below, the infantry pressed the creatures back toward the lava. The Kragnashians' numbers thinned, and the troops fanned after them. Above, the Council stirred the molten earth, churning up the hotter masses from below. But the earth was stiff, as if the rains had cooled deep down into the magma. It felt like trying to stir molasses in the dead of winter. Bethniel's shoulders and eyes ached from the strain, but as the Woern coursed through her, they enlivened every corpuscle, and she felt alive. If she closed her eyes to the carnage, all she felt was joy.

"Meylnara!" Saelbeneth cried, and a flaming ball hurtled toward a dense clump of Kragnashians at the edge of the forest.

The fireball crashed into a giant messernil, and the tree burst into flame. The crust reformed over the moat, and Kragnashians streamed into camp.

Meylnara was the important one. Bethniel flew clear of the smoke, looking for a disturbance in the canopy that could be the rogue's Kragnashian escort. Other wizards left the moat, descending to fight with their troops or hunt their enemy. Bethniel zigzagged across the forest until she saw leaves seething near the edge of a clearing.

"If the Sacrifice is made." She froze, her skin prickling as a wave of terror spilled out of her eyes. "No," she whispered. Her heart beat wildly; there was a ringing in her ears, and her breath came in short gasps. She wanted to go home, complain about Heralds' gossip with her brother, play with her baby nephew. She wanted to assume the throne of Latha and be remembered as a Ruler under whom her nation prospered. She wanted to see her grandparents again and her cousins. And Mother. She longed for her mother's warmth and pride, like the day they'd arrived home from war.

> *Mother graces them with a rare smile. "I am glad—very, very glad—to see you all safe. Welcome home."*
>
> *Her arms are warm and tight. A tingling scatters over her skin like sunlight sparkling on dark sand. Bethniel gathers every moment of her mother's open affection, stowing it away to carry her through the long frigid time that will follow.*

A red streak singed her ear, dissipating in a shower of sparks. Leaves wriggled as the mass moved off. Bethniel wiped snot from her nose. *If the Sacrifice is made.* She wanted to fly the other way and hide until this was over. But if she failed, Ashel would be alone. He'd never again see the woman he loved, his wife. *My sister.* His son. *My nephew.* Heart thudding, Bethniel swooped toward the canopy. Ashel and Geram, Vic and Wineyll—it could be done. She was no Listener, but Meylnara had no mindspeech.

She was no Listener, but she'd been reared by Selcher, had lived with that strong Listener all her life. The trick would be how. And when.

As the Caldera tribe passed Dealn's grave, the warriors coalesced into a rolling knot. Vic hunkered under the Center's wing covers as it scuttled onto its warriors' backs. Others piled on top. Their heavy springtime scent choked her. Her skin crawled with the sensation of creeping insects, a feeling that stretched a thousand-fold as more creatures piled into the mass. Her ears shrank from the scrabbling of tarsi on chitin, her muscles cringed at the hundred hundred half-sheathed cat claws that tickled her spine, and she gulped one shriek after another.

Tendrils snaked beneath the Center's carapace, wrapped round her waist, and yanked her up into the dark, seething flow of chitin and silky, spiked legs. She screamed until they thrust her head and shoulders out of the crown. Coils slid round her legs and hips, holding her fast, but fresh air and light washed over her. Relief was short-lived. At the base of the knot, titans wrestled, mandibles crunching and slashing as Meylnara's warriors burrowed into the mass and were crushed and ejected by the Caldera defenders.

Vic drew on her Woern. The Kragnashians released her, and she rocketed clear of the canopy. In the distance, a pair of fireballs burst out of the green, just missing a lithe, dark figure floating above the treetops. Bethniel. In the air. Magnificent. Vic's heart rose into her throat, pride cutting through grief.

The princess dove into the forest. *What is she doing?* Vic surged after her, crying her name. Flames and smoke erupted from the forest, the columns thick and black. "Bethniel!" she yelled again.

There was no answer. Vic dropped into the understory, feeling for Meylnara's waveform, for a new pattern that would be Bethniel's. Leaves and branches blazed. Heat and smoke billowed in black, heavy clouds. The forest had been saturated only that morning, but now trees flared like dry tinder. Coughing, Vic sailed to the ground, her ears itching with the keening of the damned.

Bethniel heard Vic's call, glimpsed her flashing through smoke and fire. She lived! Thank Elesendar, she lived.

She shoved that joy aside—it would lead to wishes, and wishes would unravel her resolve. She'd ordered a massacre to save her brother; to save her sister, she would prevent one. First, she had to catch Meylnara's soul.

THE BLIND CHARGE

The Manor's main defense was the steep-sided hill upon which it sat. A cliff on the west flank, on the north and south grew dense woods thick with brambles, each with a single narrow track. Only the eastern slope, with its switchbacking road up from Narath, could accommodate a large host. So the builders had planned. Yet the army climbing sheer stone or scrambling through tangled underbrush had fought in the Kiareinoll for a generation, and they knew very well where the stockade surrounding the Manor could be breached.

Geram crouched next to a gap between the earth and the interlaced whole logs that formed the wall. The Kragnashians had remained within the grounds—a puzzle as well as a relief. Elekia had speculated the creatures waited for the Concordance, and Geram wondered how Vic fared in Direiellene. Could they succeed if she failed?

Ashel was with the Buzzards, marching on the square in Traine, but Geram fixed his mind on the dry soil under his fists, the scent of evergreen and sweat, the motion of the men and women bouncing on their heels beside him.

Passed from Listener to Listener, the all-clear signal flew fast as thought round the wall. "Ready," he whispered to Henrik. The fieldmarshal motioned they should advance, and Geram passed the order to every Listener in the host. Half a dozen troopers scuttled through the gap. Squirming on his belly, elbows digging into the earth, Geram followed the sound of knees scrubbing dirt, of soft curses and hissed orders. Inside the wall, he waited with Henrik and Drak while troops wormed through and fanned out along the perimeter. They would kill as many sentries as they could.

A whistle pierced the night. The Lathans broke for the Manor. Geram ran after the noise of boots on turf and gravel, his steel-bladed pike held like a javelin. At the gate, an explosion blotted the night, the flash bright enough to penetrate the murk of his vision. His squad hauled up, trying to blink the stars from their vision. "Move," Geram ordered, grabbing Drak's arm and dragging him toward the Manor. He knew these grounds, had memorized the feel of every path and flowerbed, and now the troopers relied on him to guide them.

"Shrine's bitch," Drak swore. "They're coming." Drak's vision, still stained with the afterglow of the explosion, fixed on the Kragnashians bearing down on them like frigates. Pike butts hit the earth, and troopers braced. The Kragnashians drove into them, mandibles swinging, knocking past the weapons and bowling over the troopers. A second rank rammed steel tips into oncoming thoraxes. Bodies twisted. Tails lashed. Mandibles bashed and snapped. Troopers dove and rolled, struck and dodged, and the dead lay heaped.

"We must reach the throne room," Geram panted. Pain spiked through his scarred thigh, and he breathed deeply to quell a racing heart.

Drak grabbed his wrist, and they skirted the melee and raced toward the Manor, troopers on their heels. Half a dozen Kragnashians defended the entrance. Mandibles sliced and crushed. Pike blades jabbed and scraped chitin. Kragnashians wrenched the shafts away, snapped them into sticks.

Elekia and Breon ran up, skidding on cobbles as they joined Geram's party. Trousers hugged her hips, and sleek curves stirred an uncanny need to hold and taste her. Drak's vision swung to the Kragnashians, and Geram blew the ill-timed desire from his lungs.

"Use the windows," Elekia said, and they ran round the corner. Sashes flew upward, and Geram boosted Drak to a windowsill.

His cousin disappeared inside; other soldiers launched each other through other windows. Thumps and rolls, a crash and shrieks poured out. His muscles quivered at every crunch and scream.

"Take my hand!" Drak shouted, and Geram jumped up and grabbed his cousin. The big man hauled him inside, hoisting Elekia and Breon next.

Kragnashians flowed toward them and jolted against an invisible barrier. "Now," Elekia said, and Drak drove his pike into a thorax. A massive body fell over.

A rush prickled against his neck, and Geram dove, rolled, and swung his pike up through empty air. Tarsi skittered near his ear. He spun the pike around, entangling it in the curtain-like legs, and yanked as a mandible plunged toward him. The creature tumbled forward; he scrambled away, breath short and heart fluttering like a trapped bird.

Their scent jabbed his fear, and it rose snorting and mad like a bull. His thigh quivered, the muscles jumping as if caught again in the vicious slicing grip while he lay buried under the dying creature. He'd fought in hundreds of battles, faced enemies armed with lethal blades and bows, watched the entire Dagger die around him, and he'd never known terror like this. He wanted to piss. He wanted to cry. He wanted to shrink into a ball with his hands over his head and lie still until it was over.

"Eminence," someone shouted, and a rolling pike thumped toward him. He snatched it as a mandible slammed his ribs. A crack and crunch shuddered through his chest as he pitched forward. Fire squeezed his lungs; his own wheezing layered over the clicking bearing down on him. His limbs froze as he recalled crushing agony and an icy cold that dragged him toward death.

Elekia yelled, a wordless battle cry. His heart surged, pumping a blazing energy to every muscle, stomping down his fear with the need to protect her. He flipped to his feet and swung the pike. It glanced off something hard, but he spun, following the momentum of the swing, bringing it back around with all his strength. The blade scored chitin, the shaft shuddering. A wet, pungent, grassy goop smacked his face as the Kragnashian squealed and crashed. He sprang back, and pain bit through his chest like teeth made of fire. But the creature was down, and he stood for a moment, trying to fill cramped lungs, not bothering to seek anyone's sight, knowing all he would see was chaos.

A swish and scrape behind him, he spun and dove, shoving his weapon upward. Fire stabbed inside him as the shaft juddered through chitin and squelched into tissue. Pulling it free, he stumbled against the dais.

"Geram." Elekia's hand clasped his elbow, her touch electric. He scrambled after her into the depression round the Device. His limbs leaden, his breath gurgled like a drowning man. "Here," she said, laying her hand across his ribs. They ground like stones against each other, the pain lancing through his chest but when he inhaled again, his lungs filled more easily.

"That's all I can manage," Elekia gasped.

"It's enough." He took her sight. Blood slicked the floor, pooling beneath dozens of prone troopers and a few massive, chitin-clad heaps. Leg segments and carapace shards littered the floor; one Kragnashian flopped in a corner, half its legs cut away. Troopers and seamen swarmed through the windows; some had barred the doors to keep any invaders still on the grounds from entering. Soldiers and seamen clustered around the armored warriors, jabbing and hacking, dancing away from slashing mouthparts. Drak fought alone, using his size and strength to drive his pike through their armor.

"We must go," she said.

He took her arm, and she grasped the knob and shoved it southwest.

REDEMPTION

The windows were shuttered on every guildhouse, the market stalls and cafe tables cleared away from Commissar's square. Gaslights brightened in the gloaming as the sun sank past the coastal range. Ashel walked amid the army of Oreseekers, miners, and Caleisbahn mercenaries, watching the multitude of heads and shoulders pour into the square. Every hand bore a cudgel or an axe, but the faces bore wildly varied emotions, some fierce and furious, some frightened, some shifting between the two. Few of the rebels were trained soldiers; there'd be no martial discipline to drive them tonight, only will and passion. Ashel hoped it would be enough. His belly tickled as if he were getting ready to go on stage— that energy will help you shine, he'd tell a nervous apprentice. But the dagger sheathed at his side, the heavy wooden shield bound to his right arm, were his instruments tonight. Death, not music. He breathed slowly and deeply, as did Geram, waiting outside the Manor walls. He hoped Geram's instincts would help him wield the unfamiliar weapons he'd been given, hoped the rebels' determined rage would carry them through the battle ahead, but the outcome was far from certain, and he was glad Wineyll had slipped down an alley and taken refuge in the Minstrels Guildhouse.

Across the square, ranked fifty deep, the Commissar's soldiers filled the proscenium. Behind them was a row of short-range catapults, armed and cranked. Strained timbers moaned, a harbinger of the deaths to come. A shiver gripped Ashel's spine as he recalled the massacre here only a few months ago.

Once in the square proper, he joined the Korngs within a cordon of Caleisbahnin, and they crossed the cobbles under a parley banner. Lamps glared from the gibbet posts, illuminating Alek. Dungeon filth and blood stained his clothes. Bruises and a broken nose disfigured kindly features. Arms bound, a rope already round his neck, his body trembled and swayed, as if exhaustion might pull him into the grip of the noose, sparing the executioner the effort.

Parnden and his guards, along with a foursome of Kragnashians, emerged from the Commissar's ranks and met them beside the gallows. "Poor Alek has been standing there since noon, waiting for you," said Parnden. Remaining behind Demsch, he flicked a sneer at the rebels. "It seems you've brought my pick of substitutes."

"No one is taking my place up here," croaked Alek.

"I'll give you a choice, Lornk," Parnden said. "Choose one of your sons to go up there, and the other will be my heir. I'd always intended that for Earnk, though you robbed me of my chance to groom him properly, just as your undeclared bride robbed you— twice, if I'm not mistaken. She kept your firstborn from you and stole your young mistress, so you couldn't train her up the way you wanted."

His anger coiling like a serpent, Ashel's knuckles whitened around the hilt of the dagger. Beside him, Kelmair bared an inch of steel.

"And what would you do with me?" Lornk asked glibly. "Let me retire quietly into your dungeons?"

"I've promised you to the Lathan authorities, actually. I believe they still have a place ready for you under the Shrine. So who shall swing at the end of that rope? The friend you urged onto the seditious path that put him in that noose, the son you claimed with a butcher's cleaver, or the one whose mother you drove insane?"

Lornk studied the Kragnashians flanking the Commissar. An eyebrow raised, he rested hot palms on Ashel's cheeks. "You were right about the markings."

Ashel shrugged him off, his breath short bursts around a surging heartbeat. "I won't do it," he said. "Not for you."

Snorting softly, Lornk patted his ear. "You will finish what I started, for her." He gripped Earnk's shoulder. "The Seat suits you. I expect you to rule Relm well." He turned to Parnden. "'Tis a far, far better thing I do now, than I have ever done," he said in the Ancient's tongue, pushed through the Caleisbahnin, and headed up the gibbet steps.

"What are you doing?" Parnden asked, his jaw slack.

Ashel closed his mouth and blinked at the gaping faces around him.

"I'd rather choke for a few minutes than languish for days under the Shrine," Lornk said.

Alek spluttered protests. Murmurs swept through the rebels and swelled into a roar. Kelmair tugged Ashel's arm, urging retreat into the screaming ranks, but his boots were glued to the pavement, his eyes on Lornk cutting the ropes round Alek's ankles and legs. Alek collapsed, still shouting objections. Lornk handed his weapons to the executioner and offered his wrists for binding.

"He is mad," Ashel breathed.

"There is no limit to what he'll do if it achieves his ends," Earnk said bitterly.

"Even his own death?"

"The only thing he cares about is his legacy."

Aggrieved loss opened a hole within Ashel. He would have felt nothing but satisfaction to see Lornk carted off to suffer a traitor's death beneath the Shrine, but to watch him hanged here, before the people he intended to save? He felt robbed, not only of the prospect of seeing justice levied against the sadistic fiend he knew in Olmlablaire's dungeons but also of the chance to understand the man who had so wholly committed himself to saving humanity.

"It's up to you both now," Lornk said as the executioner fitted the rope round his neck and cranked a winch. Clattering echoed, and the rope went taut. Lornk rose up on his toes and shouted, "For Victor—"

Another crank yanked him off his feet, and the Buzzards boiled forward. Demsch yelled orders, and the Commissar's guards hustled him back toward the palace.

Earnk cried Alek's name and sprang up the gibbet steps, Caleisbahnin right behind him. They lifted the older man and rushed him away, into the swirling horde. A Kragnashian swept to the bottom of the stairs, preventing any attempt to save Lornk, while the other three creatures charged into the mob. Eddies formed as rebels scurried clear of snapping mandibles.

Sword drawn, Kelmair cried Ashel's name, yanked on his arm as the surging Buzzards crashed into the soldiers. They sheltered beside the gibbet as the square boiled over with butchery. Cudgels smashed skulls, hatchets cleaved flesh and bone. Shrieks spread like a plague. Rue squeezed Ashel's chest as he recalled the screams of the Dagger as they died around him. Vic's patrol, all dead because of his selfish, mad desire for vengeance. Catapults whumped, and a limestone block smashed into the rebels and exploded. Pelted by shrapnel, Lornk's body jerked and twisted. Another catapult fired, raining flaming coals. Fear swamped regret, and he grabbed Kelmair and ducked under the platform.

There, they could hear the former Relmlord slowly choking to death. The noise crept through the smack, splat, and keens of battle, stirring the memory of Vic, vibrating with fury, strangling Lornk in a room clogged with dust. The same impulse he'd felt then, as a mountain fell around them, wedged through his rage and regret as a city tore itself apart. Then, he'd stopped Vic from killing Lornk because he'd wanted the Relmlord to face Lathan justice at the Shrine. Now, Lornk's death wouldn't satisfy Lathan justice, it would only strengthen Parnden's tyranny. Lornk had left the rebellion in Ashel's hands, but it might be years before he could communicate well enough with the Kragnashians to sway them from an alliance with Parnden. In that time, the Commissar would try to gain control of the copper supply, which meant war between Betheljin and Relm, with Latha caught between them. Who knew how Parnden might use the Kragnashians to terrorize and cow Knownearth into submission? And if Vic returned, Parnden would make her death his top priority. His lungs expelled a long breath. There was only one way out of this.

The Kragnashian guarding the stairs was the friendly one that had been teaching him its language in exchange for songs. "Is the cup full now?" he clapped. "Is this what you wanted?"

"The past slips."

"We can do nothing about the past! Do you want peace with humanity now? If you do, let me by."

Eye facets sparkled in the lamplight. Mouthparts clicked softly, and a long proboscis extruded then retracted. Antennae flicking rapidly, the creature shuffled aside.

Shield high against the raining stones, Ashel charged up the stairs. The executioner was gone—fled or dead, he didn't know. Kelmair released the winch, and Lornk's weight dropped onto Ashel's shoulders. Grunting, he lowered the other man to the platform, loosened the noose, and cut his hands free. Lornk lay slack.

"Is he breathing?" Kelmair put her fingers against his lips, her ear to his chest. Rising to her knees, she placed clasped fists over his breastbone and began pumping with stiff arms. "Tilt his head back," she ordered. "Open his throat."

"What are you doing?"

"It's an Ancient practice. If I can get his heart going, it might revive him."

Ashel tilted Lornk's head back, holding it while he wrestled with opposing hopes—that Lornk was dead and that he might yet live. There'd been no such hope when he held Sashal's prone body. That father's lifeblood had poured out irrevocably. This one's pulse was feeble at first but grew steadily stronger.

"To the prince, to the prince!" echoed from below, and Samson led a knot of Oreseekers up the steps. Mary, Fred, Mike, and half a dozen others made a wall and roof with their rough shields, providing meager shelter from the raining stones. Lornk's eyes fluttered open, and he sucked in a long, hoarse breath. Coughing, he turned watering eyes at Ashel. "I knew I could count on your sense of mercy, son."

Ashel let go, and Lornk's head smacked the platform. "Now you owe me twice for your life. Can you can convince the Kragnashians to change sides?"

Lornk took another ragged breath and rolled to his knees.

"Wineyll made contact with Victoria, correct?"

"Vic is alive, and she knows what she needs to do."

"I'll make sure they know."

The Kragnashian had entered the fray. Still wheezing, Lornk led them through the brawl toward it. Rebels flocked round them, stabbing and hacking at the soldiers screaming for their blood. A burly guard barreled through the cordon. Ashel rammed his shield into the man's breast. Samson stabbed him through the eye. The Kragnashian swept toward them, a pack of soldiers swarming after. Rebels and guards clashed; brutal weapons struck bone and flesh, and blood flew like sea spray. The square stank of iron and offal.

Mary fell in a bloody heap, and Major Demsch stepped over her, sword high. Ashel lunged, his shield blocking her swing, the long dagger darting for her ribs.

Panting, she spun out of reach. "I promised to kill you."

He swung the shield, bashed her shoulder, jabbing with his blade. He felt no anger toward Demsch; he only wanted to live and see Vic again. Demsch ducked and slashed. He didn't want to kill her; he just wanted her out of this fight and out of his way. Twisting, he rammed the shield at her; it caught her sword arm. She dropped the weapon, and he stomped on it just as she snatched it up. The metal snapped.

"Fucking Trainer smiths; can't make a decent blade." She sneered at him. "At least it'll hurt more when it guts you."

"I pray you'll keep missing me." He feinted with the shield, reversed the grip on his dagger and jabbed, but she dodged and struck with the broken sword and her own dagger, each in a fist. Steel rang, wood thumped and thunked as they parried, twisting, spinning, slipping across blood-slicked cobbles. A whiff of

Kragnashian—clean and fresh as the Kiareinoll—curled through the reek of charcoal and guts.

A blow smashed the rear of his knee. It buckled, and he fell. Rolling, he sheltered under the shield.

An oof lured his eyes over the rim. Demsch sailed over him, struck the cobbles, and lay still. Roaring, another soldier rushed forward, sword raised for murder, and the Kragnashian swept in front of Ashel and savaged her. A scream died in a squelch, and an oozing lump slapped the ground.

The Kragnashian clicked.

"It says, 'Greetings to the Voice,'" Samson panted, pulling Ashel to his feet. The Oreseeker was covered in gore. Mary lay on the ground, but Mike, Fred, and Kelmair still fought amid a thousand other Buzzards, seamen, miners, and dockworkers.

Bloodied mouthparts clicked and burred. "In honor of the First, we too fight for Victory. The world changes. You will come and bear witness."

"I won't abandon these people," Lornk said. Blood dripped from a sword in his hand. "I'll come when we've defeated the Commissar."

"So be it," Samson translated. The Kragnashian whistled, and the other Kragnashians turned on the Commissar's forces, sweeping through them like scythes through grain. Buzzards gathered in a circle around Ashel and Lornk, shields up and weapons pointed outward while the creatures swirled with brutal efficiency through the uniformed soldiers. Rebels followed in their wake, and the tide turned. The Commissar's forces broke, some fleeing the square, others on their knees, hands raised in surrender.

When it was over, the Kragnashians returned to them. "For what was," the leader said, swirling its antennae toward Ashel. They tapped across his brow, needle sharp, and he was overwhelmed with a sorrow deep and long, the grief of an entire People, for something precious that had been lost forever. A deep-throated wail rose from him and joined with a howl from Lornk. Their cries harmonized into a truer sound of misery than any song Ashel could have composed.

The Kragnashian backed away, and Ashel bent over, hands on knees, gasping to stave off a torrent of sobs. Lornk staggered away from the other Kragnashian. Head reeling, Ashel stepped over bleeding, broken bodies to reach the other man. From across the square, Earnk and Wineyll picked through the carnage to join them.

Swaying, Lornk rubbed his throat, dark red with blooming bruises. "What did you feel?" he croaked.

"Their despair. You?"

"Their hope."

Hurrying to him, Wineyll slid her arms around Ashel. His heart jumped into his throat at the pain etched across her face. "She's still alive."

"Let's put this day to rest." Lornk squared his shoulders. They strode through the gate and surveyed the palace. A steady stream of rebels rushed inside, but a Caleisbahn captain came out.

"The palace is secure."

"Have you found Parnden?"

"Not yet."

"Look in the dungeons. He might be hiding there, hoping to escape in a general amnesty. When you find him, keep him locked up. Where are the guards who surrendered?"

The captain gestured at a group corralled within a ring of cudgel-carrying Buzzards.

"Is Major Demsch still alive?" Lornk called as he approached.

"I am." Parnden's commander pushed through the captive guards. Blood seeped from a gash in her scalp.

"Do you acknowledge defeat?" Lornk asked.

Her eyes like steel, she nodded. "You have marshaled a successful coup."

"Will you swear to defend this palace with more vigor and loyalty to me than you did for Parnden?"

She bristled. "When it's earned, yes."

He stepped through the ring of Buzzards, drew his sword, and held the hilt to her. "I don't have time to earn loyalty, so I will buy it with trust. I need you, Major, immediately." He angled his head at the Kragnashians. "I am called away to witness an event of global importance, but I do not wish to lose this day. Will you defend the palace of Commissar Lornk Korng?"

Her mouth grim, she met his gaze evenly. "When your people bribed me, I took the money and turned them in."

He smiled. "I know that, Major. A genuine defender of the Chair, who would lead her Commissar's enemies into a trap. Let me ask once more: will you defend *my* palace with even greater vigor and constancy?"

Nodding, she took the sword. "Yes."

Lornk signaled to the Buzzards to let her free, then strode up the steps and raised his arms. "Defenders of Betheljin, I am your new Commissar. Help our Caleisbahn friends secure the grounds and the city wharves. I must go immediately and solidify agreements with the Center of Kragnash. I shall return before the sun sets again on Traine."

The Kragnashians carried them, traveling faster than any horse or steed, to the Korng palazzo. The gate stood open, the courtyard empty. Ashel slid off his bearer's carapace, the Korngs, Samson, and Wineyll dismounting from the others.

Lornk smiled as Elsa poked her head out the front door. "Cousin!"

"My lord!" she cried, running into his embrace.

"Where are the Commissar's troops?" Ashel asked.

"They were called down to the square this afternoon," Elsa said. "I suppose the Commissar thought he could come back and take over this house at his leisure."

The friendly Kragnashian beckoned, and they followed its hulking figure through the ground floor gallery to the library.

Ashel clasped Samson's arm. "Do you want to come with us?"

Eyes tight, trembling, the Oreseeker nodded.

"She's still alive," Wineyll said, her voice quavering. "She's still alive."

The Kragnashian squeezed through the library door and hunched into the passage. It chittered at its fellows, and they parted to make space around the Device.

Crouching with his left hand on the knob, Ashel held the maimed one to Wineyll. "Will you come through with me?"

"Yes." She threw her arms around Earnk, and they held each other for a long moment before she took Ashel's hand.

"For Victory," Kelmair said softly. The mantra echoed through the room, the voices rising as the world faded into an electric buzz.

THE HUNT

Bethniel squatted between folded roots and hunted for Meylnara's mind. It was like grasping at dust motes in the dark, her thoughts slipping into a void. She tried to remember everything Selcher had ever told her about Listening. It wasn't supposed to be something you could learn to do, or do at all if you weren't born with the ability. But Bethniel had to pry into Meylnara's mind and wrest away her connection to the forest. She must do it to save Vic and send her home. She had no choice.

The knot of Kragnashians protecting Meylnara passed, pushing through the trees. A conflagration roared in its wake.

Elesendar, the destruction of the forest was starting.

She stumbled after them, trying to stay out of sight and keep ahead of the blaze behind her. Sparks flew forward on the wind, igniting other trees and shrubs. Meylnara's mass rolled away, moving fast. Rising off the ground, Bethniel flew ahead of it and landed in a small hollow surrounded by messernil. The turf felt firm under her feet, and when she glanced behind her, she saw the hollow had lengthened. The blood drained from her head, and she swooned with vertigo. Grasping a trunk to steady herself, she Heard Meylnara.

She Heard the wizard's pain. The burning trees tore at the rogue like the sharp bite of an unscratchable itch.

She Heard the wizard's strategy. Meylnara herself was firing the forest. It was like digging after a splinter with a knife—it hurt yet had to be done. She would trap the Council within their own encampment. No more supply lines would get through, and they'd starve. When the drudges were gone, she would kill the wizards one by one until she found the One who carried the child, and she would keep her until the babe was born. The fire tore at her—it sizzled on her skin and hair—but it had to be done.

Slowly, afraid she would lose the connection, Bethniel removed her hand from the tree. Meylnara was still there, jabbering about her plans, talking to her People. Bethniel could not see the protective knot through the trees, but she knew where it was. Facing that direction, she stepped backward, her foot finding smooth turf. Another step. Another. Five steps more, and she bumped into a tree trunk. Glancing quickly over her shoulder, she saw the path veer left. She adjusted her course and Listened again, trying to find a way to pry Meylnara's essence from the trees.

The forest made a path for her, leading her on a course that kept her in front of Meylnara's People. She walked and Listened and learned. Meylnara desperately wished she was Kragnashian. She despised her own reeking species, which stole lands that had once belonged to the People. Small and weak, humans bred and spread like vermin. They had been invited guests on this world, but within three generations they had dug deep roots into the land, and within five they'd forgotten they'd even come from somewhere else. Deep in Meylnara's thoughts, Bethniel felt the rage as if it were her own.

Yet the forest burned. It cried, a thrumming that vibrated through her soles, up her calves and into her thighs. The fiery itch drove Meylnara mad, and she screeched and scratched her neck, her arms, her scalp, scoring bloody trails with her nails. Within the mass, the People massaged her with their tendrilled legs, but it did not assuage the pain. And yet, Listening, Bethniel realized Meylnara had no idea the forest was aware of what she had done and that it was determined to destroy her.

Fresh tears spun down Bethniel's cheeks. Meylnara couldn't be killed without a Sacrifice. A protest blubbered out of her nose, and she swiped at long, ugly ropes of mucus. Why did she have to do this?

To save the ones you love.

She sucked in a shuddering breath and shoved mortal terror into the box. She would do this. For her brother and her sister. For her mother and all the people of Latha. Of Knownearth. She had to. It's what Father would have done. *It's what Thabean did for me.*

The day stretched like a yellow ribbon as Bethniel sought a way to take Meylnara's soul. Each time the Caldera tribe attacked, Meylnara emerged from her protective knot until her People repelled the assault. Each time, brush thickened around Bethniel, driving her into the protective folds of a massive tree trunk. The forest echoed with screeches and trills, chitinous scrapes, thumps, and thuds as huge bodies collided and fell. Meylnara sent fallen trunks barreling into her Caldera enemies, exchanged lightning and fireballs with the Council wizards. When each sortie ended, the rogue sank within the protection of her People, the forest path would open, and Bethniel would move again.

As the afternoon wore on, Bethniel glimpsed Council wizards zigzagging overhead, spraying fireballs into the canopy. Embers rained, and Meylnara grew increasingly distraught, her People harried by the Caldera tribe, her body flayed by the burning trees.

The sun sank toward evening. Bethniel's throat was dry as paper, her limbs shook, her head spun. Her vision blurred; one tree became two, two rocks four, but she kept on, rifling through Meylnara's thoughts, looking for the key that would let her insert herself where the souls of the trees belonged.

Beneath the canopy, green-tinged light melted into black shadows. A soft exhalation pricked her ears.

"Highness, the Kia led us to you," Lillem said, carrying a pike dripping Kragnashian blood. Pallid and beaded with sweat, Gustave stumbled behind him. The bandage over the pirate's stump was an ugly brown, but the sword in his left hand was coated in green slime.

Her breath caught, and she thumbed the steel-tipped blade of Lillem's pike. The wizards had more metal than she knew existed in Knownearth. Hissing, she shook blood onto the grass and sucked the sliced thumb. "It's very sharp."

Lillem's eyebrows pinched together, but his mouth softened. "It hurts less when it's sharp."

"Is this how you'll help me end it?"

"It is, Highness."

"I still don't know how to do it. I need more time," she said.

"You will have it."

The Fulcrum, the Sacrifice, and the One

The trees had no voice, but they screamed. Vic felt it, a loosening of her sinews and a sizzle over her skin, as if traveling through the Device. Around her, burning limbs tumbled down, snapping, cracking, lighting underbrush on fire. Smoke billowed in dark, choking columns. Flames licked through the understory and canopy, fire and smoke wiping the forest away. Meylnara had burned a large circle around the Council's camp, ringing it with fire. Preventing escape, Vic thought grimly. The rogue was willing to sacrifice some of the forest that contained her essence so her People could hem in the Council and destroy them at will. The Council responded by spreading out and setting fire to massive quadrants of trees, beginning the destruction of the forest that would lead to Meylnara's death. Vic snuffed out the fires as she could, but extinguishing the entire conflagration was hopeless. Despite the deluge the previous day, the soil underfoot was dry as sand, the air parched. The trees screamed, and their dying exhalations were a painful reminder of promises made to the Caldera tribe. The One. The Fulcrum. The Sacrifice.

She stood in a dell. The grass was char. Nettles smoked like incense. Blackened crisps coated a smoldering log, the remains of lichen. A pair of geilmors twisted out of the earth, their trunks scarred, their whirling needles black crisps. Yet high above, green spikes on the uppermost branches reached for the sun. Vic laid her hand on one of the trees and shut her eyes, thinking of Joseph's small body curled in the dirt. Of Bethniel floating above the canopy. Of Ashel, waiting for her. *Bring my sister, and bring my wife. Bring my loves home.*

Sashal. Thabean. Joseph. Three beloveds dead because she'd failed. Wasn't that enough?

Just do the job.

The necessity of a sacrifice was nonsense—there had to be a way to simply put Meylnara back into herself and then kill her. She and Thabean had debated how to do it, and she thought she'd have time to figure it out. But there was no more time.

Just do the job.

She floated into the upper canopy, staying hidden there, and opened her senses, feeling for Meylnara's waveform. The Caldera tribe harried Meylnara's People; monstrous shadows swept through the smoke and green of the understory. When the titans met, they tore each other apart, and the scent of cut grass mingled with woodsmoke and ash. The Council wizards were everywhere, and picking out Meylnara's waveform from the soup of energy was like finding the single thread that would unravel the weave of an entire tapestry. All those months of seeking Thabean in the woods came to this—finding Meylnara in chaos.

A catapult's throw away, Samovael hurtled out of the forest, firing energy bolts into thrashing greenery. A fireball bloomed, and he veered off and down under the leaves. Treetops settled and became smooth again, disturbed only by columns of smoke. The setting sun behind her, Vic flew to the site and hunted for the roiling ball protecting Meylnara. Branches whipped and swirled, and she got ahead of the disturbance and plunged into the trees. Landing, she hid behind the folded trunk of a giant messernil. Flames crackled. Smoke wafted through the fading light. Vic pushed both palms against the bark. "I will do the job."

The tree quivered, and a cramp seized her womb, aching for Joseph. Tears welling, she focused her concentration on the subaudible thrumming coming through the bark, a whisper of air stealing in and out of her lungs, her heartbeat slowing to the sluggish rhythm of water and sap moving through channels in the wood. A child of the steppes and tundra, she'd never seen a tree until she was sold into slavery, never seen a forest until she came as a refugee to Latha. There, the old mothers had been her guardians and guides. They weren't divine, but they were conscious, and so was this tree, this forest. Her hand pressed to bark, she felt twigs shiver with the breath of the wind. She felt the achingly slow movement of each leaf, turning its face toward the dimming light. She felt the cells absorb that light and convert its warmth into life, just as her cells converted the food she'd consumed that morning. Her mind opened, possibility opened, time and place opened. Her blood seethed with the life of the forest, vibrant, varied, violent in its own slow, inexorable way. And there it was: a filament of wrong, like the thin line of infection that travels up the arm toward the heart. It was there— she just had to tease it out of the weave, take hold of it and slowly extract it, trace it to its source, and restore it to its proper place. A blissful black tide rose, flooding her eyes. She reached for the filament, controlling the Woern, knowing this work would be delicate, like slitting a throat with skill and care, so the blood ran back into the body.

She grasped the thread, and it melted away, fading from the forest. The trees sighed. Water shot up the channels of every trunk, burst from the pores in every leaf, and dew saturated the air. Mist caressed skin of plant and animal, a balm to the scorched skin of the earth. Above, clouds caught the last rays of the sun and blazed orange and pink, but that fire heralded rain.

A bemused smile curved her lips, the trees' joy shining through her own grief. How? She had done nothing—did merely joining with the forest enable it to rid itself of Meylnara? Was her energy a catalyst that pushed the rogue wizard from the ecosystem?

She sobered. However the woman's essence had been expelled from the forest, she still needed to be killed.

Just do the job.

Foliage peeled back, limbs bent apart, soil bubbled over grass, forming a path that arrowed toward her. The path widened, brush laying flat and sinking into the ground, grass springing up to form a clearing.

Darkness dropped through the forest like a curtain, and three figures stumbled through the twilight. One eye swollen shut, blood covering half his face, Lillem gripped a pike with a wicked blade, tainted green from tip to butt. Half his jerkin was ripped off; what was left was stained black with his blood. Gustave dragged his feet, his head hung low. A bandaged stump was all that was left of the arm Meylnara had smashed, but his remaining hand held a sword slicked green.

Unscathed, Bethniel followed them, walking backward with sure steps, no hesitation but no speed either. The path closed after her.

"Madam." Gustave collapsed against the messernil. "You live."

She laughed softly, embracing a bit of humor on this dark day. "I live, Gustave, as do you."

"Marshal," Lillem saluted and handed his canteen to the pirate. Gustave slurped at a slurry redolent with spring, and his grimace melted.

Bethniel's hair awry, soot streaked her cheeks. Her eyes were sunk deep into dark hollows, her lips pressed together in concentration as she knelt beside them. "I knew the Kia would bring us to you," she whispered.

"Report, Lieutenant," Vic said.

"We've been staying ahead of Meylnara, trying to give Her Highness time."

"To do what?"

"To save the forest." Saluting again, he moved off and disappeared among the shadows between the trees.

Dread budding, Vic peered at Bethniel. Her sister's lips twitched toward a laugh; her eyes brimmed with tears. "What are you doing?" Vic asked.

"It's all right; I've got her. When it's done, you can go home."

Hot bile clawed up Vic's throat. No. She swallowed. Elesendar, no. The thread of wrong had vanished, but it was none of her doing. Shrine, no! She squeezed Bethniel's arm. "What did you do?"

Tears spilled over a beatific smile, a painful echo of Ashel's. "I was terrified that you'd have to finish it. But I managed to get her, and she hasn't realized it yet. She's distracted by the fires, so I can go out and meet her."

Coughing with dismay, Vic shook the princess. "I will not allow you to do this. It is my purpose here! Not yours."

Beth palmed Vic's cheeks, smoothed her hair. Waves of warmth coursed down her spine. "Victoria of Ourtown. I love you."

Vic stared at her, all the strength gone from her limbs, helpless as a kitten being washed by its mother. Bethniel kissed her cheek. "Take care of my brother, and try to love my mother." She placed a hand on Vic's belly, and her lips stretched downward. "Oh, Vic." Her arms flew around Vic's shoulders. "There will be others. There will be. I love you, sister."

Mandibles clacked. Rising a hundred feet off the ground, a roiling ball of carapaces and heads and legs emerged from the woods. Bethniel released Vic and stepped into the clearing, alone. A flimsy bolt of lightning touched the mass and died.

A voice in Vic's head screamed, *Get up, shield her!* But she watched, paralyzed by the kiss and last words.

I love you, sister.

The mass rolled closer, and Vic imagined herself unleashing all her power at that wall of chitin. The Kragnashians' puny resistance to wizardry would not stop her. She would burn them, freeze them, crush them to the size of a pome. She would burrow through the mass surrounding Meylnara until she found the wizard, and then she would rip her head off her body.

She should do any and all of those things, but Vic slumped behind the tree, overwhelmed by grief. Thabean. Joseph. Bethniel.

The princess sent another thin, bright fork of electricity; it glanced off the carapaces like a stone on a pool. The chitin wall split open, and Meylnara stepped onto the grass. Her guard melted into the surrounding trees.

"I remember you," the rogue said. "You were a latent; now you are a wizard. Are you Council or rogue?"

"Council."

Sneering, Meylnara hurled a fireball.

Vic's paralyzing despair evaporated in an explosion of desperate fury. Roaring, she launched a countering fireball and flung herself in front of Bethniel. Flaming orbs crashed together, raining sparks on dew-soaked green.

Lightning forked from above, striking Meylnara and wreathing Vic in a crackling nimbus that fried the nerves. She whipped up an ion shield and batted aside the electric surge. Ozone and singed hair jabbed her nose as Samovael dropped into the clearing and fired again. Smacking aside his attack, she flung him at a tree. "Keep him there," she yelled, and rocketed toward Meylnara, her rage propelling her. The wizard would not kill her sister. Not today. Not ever.

She slammed into Meylnara, and they tumbled over rotting logs and ferns. Scrambling atop the other woman, Vic pinned her between her knees. Woern surged through Vic's nerves and blood, and she called upon the wrath that had brought down a mountain. No matter what vessel contained Meylnara's essence, she *still* could not live without a head. Meylnara kicked and clawed the dirt, her face bent round a twisted screech. Power thrumming, Vic gripped the other woman's crown and jaw and twisted. Electricity blasted her. Her vision went white, her ears filled with crackling, and ribbons of searing pain raced along her bones and muscles. Shrieking, she pulled away, but her hands were glued to Meylnara's skin. They screamed together until something yanked Vic loose and flung her into the bracken.

A sea of black-striped rings, zigzagged circles filled her vision, blooming against a white background. Blinking fast, she shook her head like a wet cat. Her gut turned over, and vomit surged out, a hot, foul mess. The crackling in her ears slowly faded into clicks, scrapes, and keening all around them. And Bethniel, speaking aloud in a voice hard and clear as crystal: "Do you accept my challenge?"

"You cannot kill me," replied Meylnara in her stringy, ill-used voice.

Panting, Vic rubbed her eyes. Pocked with jagged rings, the forest resolved. Meylnara and Bethniel stood in the center of the clearing, each wreathed in blue-hot flame. Vic tried to stagger up, but to move felt like swimming through stone.

Saelbeneth was there, her hand on Samovael's arm, holding him back. "Do not interfere. This is what must be. The Treaty of the First must be upheld."

"What have the Caleisbahnin to do with this?" Samovael spat.

Saelbeneth didn't reply. Groaning, Vic pulled at the Woern. Searing fire pounded her skull, and her stomach heaved again onto the grass. Agony robbed her strength, leaving her nothing but a whimpering heap upon the ground.

Out the corner of her eye, Bethniel glimpses Vic crumple, but her attention is focused on Meylnara. A flood twists down her cheeks, as if all the rain in this forest poured from her eyes. Aside from this passing wonder, she ignores her tears. Blubbering never did anyone any good.

> She mounts the dais, lowers her head for Velbaor to place the Ruler's copper pendant round her neck. Mother, arm in arm with Papa and Nana, smiles proudly. Timny, a handsome youth, kneels so she can designate him Heir until her own children are born. Cimba nudges an elbow into her brother as he rises, and they share a grin. Ashel steps out of the crowd, wearing a Loremaster's robes, and sings an anthem for her reign, while Vic nuzzles the cheek of a burbling baby.
>
> Thabean, standing beside her, takes her hand.

Lightning bursts, singeing her hair, jarring her spine. She feels no pain, just deepening sadness that all her ambitions must shrink away in the face of this single, utmost duty. She fires a weak stab of energy. Meylnara parries it easily. Bethniel reflects it back at her.

> *Sunlight shafts through golden leaves. White bark gleams like silver. His fingers squeeze hers, and his lips curve.*
> *"You buried your father here?"*
> *"My mother and I and Vic, with our own hands, like you did for Dealn."*
> *"I'm sorry I could not meet him."*
> *She lays a palm on the trunk. "His life is in her now." A wicked thought pulls a corner of her mouth up. "Remember when you wove that bower for us?"*
> *His eyes pop. "Here? At your father's grave?"*
> *She laughs. "He won't mind, and neither will the cerrenil."*

A vise grips her throat. She gulps for air, straining against the hold, and mirrors it around Meylnara's neck. She can't let the other woman feel herself weakening from her own attacks. Elesendar, why doesn't she do something sudden and final? But she suspects the Woern don't work that way, not in a wizard's duel. They would keep at this, lightning and fire, choking, battering until one of them dropped from exhaustion. Then it would be done.

She breaks Meylnara's hold and sucks air into her lungs.

> *Her chair creaks, the rails squeaking softly against the floorboards. In the corral, the grandchildren take the ponies through their paces, walking, trotting, cantering, in circles.*
> *Thabean clasps her hand. His hair is white. Wrinkles spread over his cheeks and brow. They share a smile, their chairs rocking together, in time.*

White fire punches through her. A spear haft juts from her abdomen. Her blood drips from the steel-tipped head. A wild chorus of keening rises, and the ground shakes as Kragnashians melt out of the forest into the clearing, their heads back, antennae waving wildly. Her eyelids droop, and she shakes her head. She wants to speak but has no breath. Meylnara stares at her, eyes stretched, mouth wide around a silent cry of surprise or fear. Bethniel drops to her knees. Meylnara stumbles and falls limp.

Kragnashians emerge from the woods. Moaning, they lift the rogue, holding her gently in their mandibles, and raise her over their heads.

This is the last thing Bethniel sees.

Beth crumpled.

Howling, Vic scrambled toward her. Lillem pulled his spear through and dropped to his knees, moaning. Charging full tilt, Vic rammed him down onto the grass. She pulled at the Woern to smash him into the sodden earth, but it was like sucking on an empty flask. Head pounding, heart lurching, she rolled off the lieutenant and scooped the princess into her arms.

Keening chorused from the trees, a bleak echo of the wail ripping open her jaws.

"Shield them," Gustave croaked, his sword pointed at the Kragnashians flooding from the forest. Lillem staggered up, braced the spear haft as Meylnara's People lifted her. The body hung as slack in their grasp as Bethniel lay in Vic's. A Caldera warrior leapt forward and snatched Meylnara's legs. Another grabbed her shoulders, and the pair wrenched away from each other, tearing the woman apart; gore sprayed the clearing.

Vic rubbed the hem of her tunic across Bethniel's brow, smudging blood and soot. "She can't look like this." Desperately, she worked some spit into her mouth, wetted the cloth, and rubbed again. She looked between Gustave and Lillem. "Do you have any water? She hates being dirty."

A force wrapped around her, freezing her in place. Eyes

bulging, the seaman and soldier groaned and strained, but none of them could move.

"Now we'll deal with this rogue," Samovael said.

"Let her go," Saelbeneth ordered. "Victoria shall not trouble us again. Feel her."

The wizard grabbed Vic's wrist and flung it aside. "She still deserves to die."

"She will," Saelbeneth said. "Leave her, Samovael. You know what will happen."

Growling, the painting wizard shot into the night.

Vic stared at the Council leader. "What happened?"

"I'm afraid your Woern are dead, Victoria. You should never have grappled with Meylnara. Didn't Thabean teach you?"

"He did," she whispered. She hunched over Bethniel, a sob stuck in her throat. Lillem mumbled a tuneless dirge, and desolation pooled in Vic's limbs. Rain pattered on the leaves above, drumming down through the understory and plinking on Bethniel's face.

Saelbeneth sighed. "You have done well, Victoria. The forest will survive this day. May you find your way home. Farewell."

The sob tore its way out, and Vic clutched Bethniel to her chest. *You have done well.* She did nothing! Saelbeneth's parting words stung like Bethniel's. *I love you.* It was her task, not Beth's— the task of a killer—not a princess. Not a *sister.* Failure heaped on failure.

"Madam." Gustave knelt, his good arm around her shoulders. "In honor of what was, my life and my sword remain yours. Now and always."

The Caldera Center clicked from the edge of the clearing and flowed forward. "The One has fulfilled her promise," Gustave translated. "Events have turned about the Fulcrum, and the Sacrifice has been made."

"I did nothing," Vic said aloud, half-whimper, half-curse. She did not mean him to, but Gustave translated for the Kragnashians, slapping his remaining hand against his thigh.

"The Child is dead. The Fulcrum, the Sacrifice, and the One

are one. The promise is fulfilled." Gustave squeezed Vic's shoulder. His skin ashen, his eyes gleamed with fever—or hope. "It says it will send us home now."

Lillem's dirge trailed into silence, and he placed his hand on Bethniel's head. Vic jerked her body away from him.

"She died like a queen, Marshal."

"You killed her!" Vic spat.

Lillem winced. "She fulfilled the mission as she and I planned it; it was the only way."

Gustave nodded, and Vic moaned. She was a soldier—she understood, but it made no difference. Her sister was dead. She pressed her face against Beth's, growling with frustration and impotence, then threw back her head and howled. "I did nothing!"

The men waited until her sobs faded and shoulders stilled.

"Marshal," Lillem said softly. "I'll carry her home, if you'll let me."

Taking a deep breath, Vic sat back, laying Beth back on the ground. "Gustave, ask the Kragnashians if they can make a litter for her." The rain had washed blood and soot from Beth's face. Vic combed fingers through her hair, taming frizz into curls. Kissing her brow, she finally said words she'd never said to this woman who had been her friend and sister: "I love you."

FULFILLMENT

Softly glowing globes staggered across the walls like pearls on a fine dress. The air was cool as a cellar. Startled, Elekia looked up from a flat platform in a strange room at a console studded with many hundreds of knobs and gems and levers. White walls bent around them in irregular curves instead of perfect hexagons. The dais, the ramp leading to the doorway, the Kragnashian who guarded the Device in Direiellene were . . . missing. The fear that had fired her blood during the battle turned to cold dread.

"You've never been here before," Geram said.

"No." She helped him to his feet. He grimaced and expelled a long, slow breath, working to relax the muscles of his face. His next inhalation stuttered, but his grip was strong as they stepped off the platform, hand in hand.

On tiptoes, she peered over the top of the console. Dozens of blue and green gems shone in the pale light, knobs and levers pulled this way and that. She should have realized there could be more than one master Device—why should the only one be in Direiellene? The consequences of this mistake—bile clambered up her throat. Eyes tearing, she said, "If I can make some sense out of this, we can go back."

"Wait. I think . . ." He cocked his head. "Ashel is coming. I think he's coming here." He drew her away from the console. "The Kragnashians in Traine turned on Parnden and helped Lornk win."

Her throat closed on gall. "That does not put my mind at ease."

519

"They said they 'fight for Victory.' They . . ." He shivered. "They touched Ashel. It was . . . disconcerting, but he trusts them." His grip tightened. "Elesendar, a lot happened while we were . . . in between. I don't know how long we were there."

A panel opened in the wall beyond the console, and a Kragnashian wearing a stole of copper fiber ducked inside. "Dealmaker. Slayer. Welcome. We considered keeping you away, but in honor of the One, we will permit you to witness the changing of the world."

Elekia stared at the creature, dread pebbling her skin. Squaring her shoulders, she replied with staccato claps. "We will not submit to you."

Eyes whirling red and green, it loomed closer, antennae twitching. "You would have doomed your species." The antennae came to rest on her forehead, conveying fierce, blood-boiling resentment. Jerking away, she clapped defiance. "You should never have supported Meylnara in her time."

The Kragnashian reared, eyes turning a fiery yellow. "The Center in Direiellene would have saved the Oppressor. My lineage honors the Treaty of the First!"

Elekia's heart stuttered. "If that is so, why would the Center in Direiellene have given Vic the power to destroy Meylnara?"

The rival Kragnashian's antennae revolved in slow circles. "Our lineage discovered the One and the Fulcrum in the desert. Our lineage brought them to Direiellene so the Center could not refuse to deliver the Waters of the Dead to the One. The Direiellene lineage would have left the One and Fulcrum lost in the desert. They would have let them die."

Elekia shook her head. "No. No—you're lying." The Direiellene Center had promised to bring her daughters home . . . if she submitted to it. "Where is the Direiellene Center?"

"Dead. The world changes, Dealmaker. The Voice and the Traveler arrive to bear witness."

Trembling, she shrank back as two hazy forms took shape and solidified. Ashel stepped off the dais, drawing a young woman with him. Elekia remembered her as the Listener whom Bethniel had taken to Olmlablaire.

"Hello, Mother." Dried blood speckled Ashel's face. The black stubble covering his chin was threaded with gray. Deep beneath her fear, she felt a terrible sadness for all he'd suffered. More than anything, she wanted to hold and comfort him as she had the night Sashal was murdered, but the pain in his eyes held her at bay. Swallowing, she crossed her arms as two more shapes shimmered on the dais. One was a ragged young stranger. The other was Lornk.

"Well, this is a pleasant surprise for me, although I suspect less so for you, Elekia." His clothes were spattered with blood, and an angry red weal encircled his neck. Yet clean-shaven, with his eyes like ocean depths, he reminded her acutely of the young man she'd loved long ago, not the filthy wretch she had taunted in prison. Cheeks burning, she dug her fingernails into her fists.

Lornk offered a short bow to Geram. "Eminence."

"Commissar." His shoulders perfectly squared toward Lornk, Geram returned the bow, making his a hairsbreadth deeper, as a regent ought to a head of state. In all the chaos of her feelings, Elekia felt a flash of pride.

Lornk gestured at the Kragnashian. "May I introduce the Center of the Free Peoples and the descendant of the lineage who will be sending your daughter and Victoria home, if all goes well with history."

"The world changes," the Center said. "When the forest of Direiellene was destroyed, the lineages fought over whether we should reclaim the lands given to the humans. Our lineage prevailed, and we destroyed those who would break the promise made to the First. We killed their nymphs and larvae and their egg layers and drones. We made the warriors and workers our slaves, and when they died, we sold their skins and their blood to the humans. That was how much we valued the word given to the First."

Elekia exchanged bewildered looks with the others.

"It isn't talking about the Caleisbahn First," said Geram, voicing their doubts.

"It means Craig Nash," said the stranger. "He made first contact with the Kragnashians and negotiated landing rights with them."

"Time passed, and my lineage took up habitation along the borders of this land, and we grew numerous and wealthy through trade with your people. Yet the lineage of the Oppressor remained in the heart of the land, recovering their numbers more slowly, rebuilding the city of Direiellene, and keeping alive the memory of magic by giving the Waters of the Dead to any human who came to them. That was how they honored the bargain of the First. Yet when your people outlawed magic, when the numbers of wizards dwindled to none, the Oppressor's People began to believe humans could not be trusted to honor their contracts.

"This they did not say openly, for our own lineage still outnumbered them. Yet as the City was rebuilt, and crops were sown inside the domes, and warm-blooded animals were husbanded, the Oppressor's lineage multiplied and sought to dominate our own. The Concordance is here. The world changes. We must wait to see the outcome."

The Center ushered them into an antechamber furnished with white cushions, molded out of their larvae's excretions. One hand pressed to his ribs, Geram sat down, and the Listener settled beside him, mumbling, "She lives, she lives."

"Craig Nash," Ashel said, a hand on the stranger's shoulder. "I should have thought of that."

"I suspect he must have been the first wizard," said Lornk. "The Logs say he went mad before he died a withering death. Wineyll, what is Victoria doing?"

"She lives." The young woman drew in a sharp breath. "She knows what to do! She's going to save the trees."

Elekia winced. She had no idea what was happening. Her chin high, her eyebrows arched, she projected calm, but inside she quailed with terror. She had made agreements with the *wrong* Center. How could she not know there was more than one?

Wineyll moaned, and Ashel knelt beside her and clasped her hands. While they conferred in whispers, Elekia looked everywhere but at Lornk.

Screaming, the Listener bolted to her feet, eyes and mouth wide, then collapsed.

The Kragnashian threw back its head, trilling with victory. "The Oppressor is dead! The world changes. Come and behold the changing of the world!"

It flowed out of the room. Leaving the men clustered around the swooning woman, Elekia followed the Kragnashian. A few steps up a sloping passageway, she heard Lornk behind her. His scent stirring old sensations, she did not dare look at him.

The air grew warmer, drier, as they strode uphill, and a hot wind slapped her face when they walked onto a platform jutting out over steeply sloped sands. All across the face of the dune, Kragnashians stood silhouetted at other openings, softly trilling.

Stars flooded the sky. The wind died, and trilling filled the silence, growing louder as clouds spread like ink. Lightning sharp, rain plunged in sheets. A dark smudge appeared, growing larger with each flash, spreading toward the bunker at frightening speed. Puzzled, Elekia stared at the oncoming shadow. "What is it?"

"Our salvation," replied the Center, its antennae pointing straight up.

"The future," Lornk added, his voice thick.

Elekia's eyes darted to his face and away, his passion reminding her acutely, painfully of the boy she'd loved. Rolling closer, the black shape resolved into the ragged shapes of trees. Massive trunks and shrubs climbed out of the soil, growing more distinct through the shearing rain. A low rumble built toward thunder. Alarm spurring her heart, Elekia nudged the Center. "Bring your People inside the bunker," she clapped as shrubs and trees clawed toward them.

The Center uttered a long, piercing whistle and pressed a panel, closing a fibrous door on the horrible advance of the trees. Elekia backed down the passageway, wondering what the return of the rainforest could mean. Around them, walls trembled as the woods reached the exterior of the bunker.

"Our bargain is sealed?" Lornk clapped at the Kragnashian.

"It is sealed. Deliveries will be made to the seamen and the nomads." The Center swept away toward the antechamber.

Elekia grabbed Lornk's arm. "What have you done?"

His teeth gleamed. "Saved humanity—and ensured my place in history. And I have you to thank, my wife."

A violent chill shook her spine. "Do not call me that."

Grin melting, Lornk put his hand over hers. Her pulse throbbed, even as she wanted to squirm away from him. *Fool*, she swore at herself.

He released her with a shake of his head. "This gulf between us. Has too much happened to bridge it?"

The pressure behind her eyes melted, and her lips twitched toward a smile. "I was going to have you executed."

He chuckled. "No harm done, my wife."

The sad warmth of loss bloomed in her chest. What if they *had* declared that spring day so long ago? What triumphs and heartaches would she have known? The Kragnashian said the world had changed. Yet she remembered being seventeen, preparing for Fembrosh, being desperately in love with a handsome boy from Traine but knowing too that marrying him, she would never realize her own worth to the world. "I could never have been your wife."

"And now you're an outlaw."

"And you are Commissar of Betheljin."

A mischievous grin tilted his lips. "Wizardry is not illegal in Betheljin."

"You're not asking me now, are you?" She laughed and sauntered down the passage, contemplating the repercussions of this day. The Kragnashian said Meylnara was dead, and yet the forest was back. The world changed. Direiellene dry sand, an unending desert—she seemed to remember it that way, yet that memory was like a dream. The forest had always been there, hadn't it? She thought of the history of the Council, how they had gone to war against a rogue wizard. After months of stalemate, the Wizard Thabean was executed for breaking the Code, and his heir was chosen to represent the Council in a final duel with the rogue. Thabean's heir. The Heir.

A scream ripped out of her. She pitched forward onto hands and knees, wailed as her forehead met the floor. Her heart stuttered in her chest. Her lungs struggled for breath. Hands gripped her shoulders, a voice nagged her ear, but the words could not reach her. "My daughter," she moaned. "My child." The final payment for Sashal's throne had been made.

† † †

Wineyll screamed, eyes wide, and crumpled. Ashel slid an arm round her, shook her gently. Her head hung loosely between her shoulders. "Can you do anything?" he asked Geram.

The Center announced that Meylnara was dead, and his mother and Lornk followed it out. Geram laid his hand on Wineyll's head, and her eyes fluttered open. Woozily, she sat up.

"What happened?" Ashel asked.

She looked at him, at Geram, her eyes wet. "They're coming home," she said aloud, her voice thick.

"Vic?" he asked, voice cracking.

She shook her head and spoke aloud. "I'm so sorry. Bethniel's gone."

Ashel stared at her, certain he'd heard wrong. This was a mistake—Bethniel? Wineyll murmured condolences, and Ashel tried to understand. Geram believed her. Samson touched his heart and spread his fingers toward Ashel. He blinked at all of them. Bethniel? Geram's certainty grew, not just a faith in Wineyll's word, but in his own understanding of history. Ashel's mouth and brows twisted as he resisted a shifting of memory and knowledge. There was no record of a Wizard Bethniel, was there?

The room rumbled and silt sifted through the ceiling. He stood, took a step toward the doorway after his mother, aching to say something but finding no words. The Center returned and went into the room housing the Device. Ashel gestured at it, turned back to the others, reached out with his hands and dropped them. Bethniel?

His mother's wail drew him. In the passageway, she curled on the floor, Lornk's hands on her shoulders, his mouth next to her ear.

"Let her go," Ashel said. He cupped her cheek. "Mother?"

"No," she moaned, lifting a tear-streaked face. "This isn't what I wanted."

"I know." He pulled her into his arms, holding her with the same fierce affection they'd shared when Sashal died. Bethniel . . . he couldn't understand why he was surprised. All the histories had spoken of a young wizard by that name, killing Meylnara in a duel, and dying in the effort. When they learned Vic and his sister were in Direiellene of the past, why hadn't they expected this would happen?

Death always comes as a shock, Geram said.

Arms tight round his mother, Ashel led her to the antechamber. Her feet dragged. Each breath was a coughing wail. His sister was gone. He couldn't fathom it. It was what was supposed to happen, but it made no sense.

They sat. Mother's weeping slowly quieted, and he felt Geram's longing to comfort her. Kissing her forehead, he stood, and Mother curled into the other man's arms.

Thank you, Geram said.

Be with her while you can.

Mother grabbed his hand. Her eyes were swollen and streaked with red, her face mottled. "I am so sorry," she whispered aloud. "This is my doing—your sister, your wife. It's my fault."

Each beat of his heart was an ache in his chest, but it was sorrow, not anger. Whatever she had done . . . it didn't matter. "It is history, Mother. It's no one's fault."

She crumpled against Geram, and Ashel turned to Wineyll. "Where is Vic?"

Her face was pinched with sadness. "On her way to the Device, in that time. It won't be long now. They're nearly there."

In the room with the Device, the Center stood over the controls, touching knobs and levers with its antennae and forelegs. Beneath its stole, its wings fluttered, shining silver filaments peeking in and out from under its carapace.

"It says the world has changed. But it feels no different," Lornk said.

Ashel looked down at his hands, turning them from palm to back again. On his right hand, the skin was folded over his knuckles, a stump with a thumb only. He clearly remembered Sashal's assassination, the war, the time he'd spent in Olmlablaire, and everything Lornk had done to him in an effort to control Vic. None of these memories seemed odd or new to him. Why was he surprised about Bethniel?

Lornk's eyes rested on the maimed hand. "I regret being unable to forgive your mother and father. I regret that my vengeance fell on you."

Ashel loosed a bitter guffaw.

"The palazzo, the mines, they are all still yours."

"Vic would never live in Traine."

An eyebrow went up. "Perhaps after you explain how things have changed . . . you never know."

"*Do not mistake alliance for allegiance,*" he'd said. Ashel glanced at Samson, thought of all the Oreseekers and outcasts who had fought in Vic's name. Their enemies' blood stained his clothes, crusted his face. Did he or Vic owe them any more? He was banished and Vic outlawed from a life in Latha, but a home on the Semena side of Mora was still possible.

"There is work to be done in Betheljin," Lornk pressed. "I plan to build a new society, one that will regain the knowledge and skills our people have lost since Landing. We will need people like you and your wife. People who *remember.*"

What Ashel *remembered* was another offer: denounce his parents and acknowledge Lornk as his father, and Lornk's torturer would stop burning the flesh off his hands. Refusing Lornk, in the midst of that agony, had been the hardest thing he had ever done. He wouldn't have succeeded without Geram's help, nor would he have succeeded in resisting Lornk again, months later, when Lornk had chopped off his fingers. *Remember,* he told himself, turning his gaze toward the Device, *Lornk did that, not Vic. Not Vic.* His wife was on her way home. Tears spilled, a gush of hope. *Not Vic.* At last, he forgave her.

"She's coming." Wineyll ducked a shoulder under Elekia's arm, helped Geram support her as they moved toward the Device. His mother walked like a woman twice her age, her steps small and tottering. Geram bore her weight despite the broken ribs grinding into the walls of his chest. Ashel felt a sharp echo of that pain, but his heart ached more for sight of his wife.

A mist coalesced into shapes; shapes became forms; forms became people. A man—the cavalier who had disappeared with Bethniel—cradled her body. Mother sprang forward and held her cheeks, moaning.

Gustave stumbled off the platform, a bandaged stump dripping. Samson caught him, and a gap-toothed smile lit the pirate's face.

The last swirl of mist became Vic. She stood on the dais, still as a statue, eyes wide and frightened of the world, just as he'd first seen her, in the square in Traine. Mud and blood tangled into her hair, her face was ruddy, eyes bruised. They fell on him, and her lips quivered around the borders of a smile. Ashel felt what she felt—grief, but relief and joy too. She was here. They drew closer. The rank smell of her was perfume to him, the rough fibers of her clothing the finest satin, and her ratted hair, that sunlight that had warmed his memories, was silk in his fingers. She was here. She was in his arms, and he was whole again.

APPENDIX

Timekeeping in Knownearth

1 day = 40 hours (approximate Earth equivalent)
1 week = 5 days
1 month = 4 weeks +/- a few days (average: 19 days)
1 year = 223 days
1 year = 4 seasons of 3 months each = 12 months
Gestation = ~160 days or ~8.5 months

For a full explanation, see:
https://amjusticeauthor.blog/2018/07/26/timekeeping-in-knownearth/

The Wizard's Council

Saelbeneth—Council Leader. Rules lands surrounding Narath. Ancestor of Elekia of Reinoll Parish.

Thabean—Council Second. Rules northern and eastern Relm.

Nelchior—Council Third. Rules southern Latha, bordering on Thabean's lands.

Grunnaire—Council Fourth. Rules lands in Eldanion.

Samovael—Council Fifth. Rules southern Relm.

Murnoran—Council Sixth. Rules Traine.

Halbert—Council Seventh. Rules eastern Latha, including large portion of the Kiareinoll.

Tirnor—Council Eighth. Rules Alna and northwestern Latha.

Valdesh—Council Ninth. Rules Aglor Duin.

Shirian—Council Tenth. Rules northern Eldanion, southern Betheljin.

Csichren—Council Eleventh. Rules western Latha.

Darien—Council Twelfth. Rules (in name only) northeastern Latha and Seneminieu.

Acknowledgments

Writing is a solitary exercise, but by the time a book is ready to be published—or out of the kiln—a lot of people have stuck their thumbs into the clay and made an imprint.

First and foremost are the beta readers who volunteered their time to critique what I thought was a final draft, but which turned out to be only an intermediate step toward the finished manuscript: Steve Howarth, C. C. Aune, and Devin Madson. Your feedback and guidance helped clarify the shapes in the clay. I also could not have polished the prose without the incredible advice and suggestions from Kimberly Wilbanks, Edward Buatois, Charlotte Hegg, Ashley Underwood, and Jesse Teller, and I thank Frank Dorrian, Luke Hindmarsh, and Jesse (again) for providing critical insights and information for the fight scenes in this book. It's always nice to have a few strong lads around to help one out of a jam. Finally, I want to thank the Refugees for having my back—I know I can always count on you.

I owe the final product to the tireless efforts of my editor, Amanda Rutter, who helped me shape and refine the tangled threads of this crazy tapestry into a thing that made sense (yes, I have just switched metaphors). Designer Steven Meyer-Rassow and model Michelle Duckett once again created a stunning cover that captures Vic's essence, and Steve's maps and interior design fill me with pride. Last but not least, I am ever grateful to the team at Wise Ink, including Alyssa Bluhm, Patrick Maloney, and Amy Quale for their help and support throughout the entire process.

The audiobook narrator, Leah Casey, deserves a shout-out for her outstanding vocal performances, which make the characters live and breathe in the ear.

Finally, I couldn't have put in the time and survived the aggravation and angst that came from this work without the unflagging support of my husband and daughter. However, any typos that remain I blame on the cats.

THE WOERN SAGA

"Kill Squad"

"The Weight of Bliss"

A Wizard's Forge

BIOGRAPHY

A. M. Justice is an award-winning author of science fiction and fantasy; a freelance science writer; and an amateur astronomer, scuba diver, and once and future tango dancer. She currently lives in Brooklyn with a husband, a daughter, and two cats. She knows her characters live only in her head, but they're real, and she puts them through hell.

www.amjusticeauthor.com

https://twitter.com/AMJusticeWrites

https://www.facebook.com/AMJusticeauthor/

http://www.goodreads.com/author/show/6903962.A_M_Justice